Mystic's
THE ANGELINI RUN

JORY STRONG

ELLORA'S CAVE
ROMANTICA PUBLISHING

What the critics are saying...

An Ellora's Cave Romantica Publication

www.ellorascave.com

Mystic's Run

ISBN 9781419958427
ALL RIGHTS RESERVED.
Mystic's Run Copyright © 2007 Jory Strong
Edited by Sue-Ellen Gower.
Cover art by Syneca.

This book printed in the U.S.A. by Jasmine–Jade Enterprises, LLC.

Electronic book Publication August 2007
Trade paperback Publication December 2008

MYSTIC'S RUN

စာ

Dedication

❧

Jennifer Kiziah
cheerleader, nag, proofreader, fan and friend —
This one's for you!

Trademarks Acknowledgement

❧

The author acknowledges the trademarked status and trademark owners of the following wordmarks mentioned in this work of fiction:

Barbie: Mattel, Inc.

Harley: Harley-Davidson Motor Company

Jeep: DaimlerChrysler

Milk-Bone: Del Monte Foods

Chapter One

✆

Mystic Renaldi's heart pounded so hard she couldn't believe the wolves left to guard them hadn't appeared on the scene. She couldn't believe she was doing this, but at the same time, short of being caught, there was no way she was going to turn back now.

The thought of an adventure was exhilarating. That it was with Gabrielle Zevanti and her twin brother, Gabriel, only made it that much sweeter.

"Almost there, Milk-Bone," Gabe teased as he helped her over a low stone wall.

"Don't call me that," Mystic said automatically as Gabrielle giggled and tripped, then hastily clamped a hand over her mouth, forcing Mystic to concentrate on containing her own laughter. For a werewolf, Gabby had a big problem with being stealthy.

Gabe snickered and whispered, "Why don't you just yell, 'Here doggies, come and get the escapees', Gabby? Then we could be back in the game room watching the action on TV instead of getting a piece of it ourselves."

Gabrielle rolled her eyes. "Funny, wolfboy. Where'd you hide the Jeep?"

"It's just up ahead."

"And you remembered to put the clothes in it, right?" Gabby asked.

It was Gabe's turn to roll his eyes. "Yeah, though it's not like they don't have stores in Vegas, or—" He moved his eyebrows up and down. "We could just hang out at a strip club." He grinned at Mystic. "One of us already has a great

9

stage name. I can hear the announcer now. 'Gentlemen, get out your wallets and prepare to pay tribute to the sultry Mystic, a woman who requires two men in order to satisfy her needs.'"

Mystic laughed despite herself. She'd probably be the only virgin in the club, much less on the stage!

There *were* disadvantages to being the only child produced in a bond with two vampire fathers and an Angelini mother. It didn't exactly provide a lot of opportunity for exploring sex.

Invite a human male over to meet the folks and they immediately got trapped in one of her fathers' gazes. *Try something with our daughter and you die.*

Mortifying.

Okay, no. Hardly that since the humans didn't know what had happened.

But all the same… How many times had she reminded her fathers they were in the twenty-first century now and they needed to get with the times! Yeah. It was a major problem having vampire fathers who were centuries old and grew up believing a woman should go to her husband's bed a virgin.

Invite a vampire over to meet the folks—well, not likely. She'd already met *plenty* of them. Her fathers saw to that. But the men they paraded past her were all cut from the same *ancient* cloth as they were. No thanks!

And the wolves… Mystic shook her head. She didn't even want to go there.

Gabrielle snickered. "Get real. Mystic is not going to go on stage and flash herself in front of a bunch of drooling *humans*."

"Hey, there are bars that cater to our type, you know. They don't call Vegas Sin City for nothing," Gabe said before shooting Mystic a look. "Maybe the Milk-Bone can even find Mr. Perfect, or two, and get married by Elvis. Not that her kind or our kind care about human vows, and besides, I think bigamy is still illegal in Nevada, but why not add to the adventure? Maybe even get some photographs to show her parents when they get back from Europe. There are plenty of Elvis impersonators. It would be easy for Mystic to do two separate ceremonies, one with each mate. No one would be any wiser and getting hitched would put a real dampener on the Super Studs' plans for their little Milk-Bone."

"That is a terrible nickname for Mystic," Gabrielle said, but she was laughing.

"Fitting though," Gabe said. "One look at Mystic and Hawk and Jagger were fantasizing about getting their teeth on her and their cocks in her."

Gabe put on an affronted look. "Hawk even cornered me and warned me off with threats of ripping the most precious parts of my anatomy from my body if I dared to touch what was going to belong to him!"

"Please, don't mention them," Mystic begged, not wanting to think about the two werewolves who'd been pursuing her for the last week.

It wasn't that they were terrible, they just weren't what she wanted in her mates. Of course, they had the dominant part down, and like most lupine they were attractive...but...she wanted something more than to be the link that bound two packs together into one. She wanted to be loved for herself, not because of what she was—or worse yet, because she could produce little werewolves and little Angelini vampire hunters.

"I'm not going to mention them by name," Gabby said. "But you have to admit they are drool-worthy. And your grandparents would be thrilled beyond measure if you ended up mated to two Weres."

Mystic grimaced. "I know. They've never really forgiven Estelle for mating with Falcone and Yorick. *As if* she had a choice. The Angelini magic *chose* them even though almost every Renaldi Angelini in the history of the Renaldi line has taken shapeshifters for mates, and almost always werewolves." Mystic nibbled on her lip. "It doesn't help that I'm it. I'm all there is—not that my parents are bummed out about it. I mean, Estelle is not exactly motherly. She doesn't even think of herself that way!"

Gabrielle laughed. "She's more like an older sister. And believe me, you are so lucky! Grow up in a pack and you've not only got your own mother, but every other adult female playing alpha, ordering you around and watching what you do!"

Mystic smiled, knowing Gabby wasn't exaggerating. Though the Weres had integrated into human society—somewhat—they still packed, taking over an apartment building or a neighborhood, working together during the day in businesses owned by the pack and then returning home where they were surrounded by pack members.

Estelle was an anomaly, not only for her non-maternal instincts but for her taking of two vampire mates, the end result being only one offspring. All of Mystic's Renaldi aunts had produced a lot of female children with their mates. And as it always did, Mystic's heart sank a little when she added, "Then there's the fact that I don't seem to have much wolf blood in me while my cousins can shift form."

Both Gabe and Gabby moved closer, brushing against her in a gesture of support and comfort, affection and acceptance. She smiled and let their warmth chase away the feelings that always arose when she thought of her Renaldi relatives and her own failings to live up to their expectations.

It hurt not to measure up when compared to the other Angelinis, but she had no desire to be anyone but herself. She intended to be happy with who she was, even if she wasn't like the rest of the Renaldi females.

Mystic's heart rate sped up as the Jeep finally came in sight. When they got to it, Gabe opened the door with a flourish and said, "Let the adventure begin."

* * * * *

Hawk Konstantin prowled through the Zevanti compound, fear and rage swirling through him in equal measure. They were gone. *She* was gone.

He should never have relied on others to keep what was his safe, guarded, contained until the moment when her mind would recognize him for what he was to her. A mate.

He knew it in every cell of his body. Felt it in every pulse of his cock.

Out of respect for her grandparents, and in the hope of lessening her parents' anger when they came home to find Mystic mated to a Were, he hadn't cornered her, hadn't trapped her in a bedroom so she would stop avoiding the truth her body already knew.

The sweet scent of her had just about driven him into a mating frenzy as it wrapped around him, invading all of his senses and urging him to act. Even the musk of the female Weres hadn't tempted him to mount them. Not as it had done to Jagger.

Hawk growled at the memory of seeing Jagger shift and take the small gray female, humping away on her with a silly smile on his face, his tongue hanging out and making him look like an adolescent whose cock had just entered its first channel.

So be it. If his friend, the one he'd hoped to share a mate and form a pack with, could so easily rut on another female, then he was not the one for Mystic.

Mystic. This time the growl came from the depths of Hawk's soul.

When he caught her, he would claim her. He would mount her repeatedly. He would revel in the scent and feel of her underneath him. He would savor the moment when the Angelini magic rose and Mystic locked his cock deep in her body and claimed him in the manner of her kind.

Outwardly she seemed unaware of the wolf lurking deep inside her. There were whispers that because of her vampire blood she was not as desirable a mate as another might be. But

Hawk thought differently. He *knew* differently. The wolf inside her was slumbering. He'd felt it and he would be the one to call it forward. He would be the one to claim both it and her as his mate.

He stripped his clothing off and shifted forms, turning into a huge solid black wolf with amber-colored eyes. They didn't have much of a head start on him. Their scent was fresh. Strong.

He left the Zevanti compound. His thoughts became more primitive, more focused with each stride. The anticipation of catching his prey grew as he felt himself gaining on them. He would mount her in the woods just as his ancestors had claimed their mates.

Hawk was almost shivering with need by the time he got to the place where their scent ended abruptly, permanently engulfed by the smell of steel and rubber. A car.

He lifted his head and howled in frustration as the edgy need to mate slowly gave way to the fierce resolve to follow Mystic. He shifted form so his thoughts would be less primitive, so he could better guess their destination.

Unwanted admiration moved in along with his more human thoughts. So they'd planned to escape all along. They'd known the elder pack members would set the wolves to guarding the cars so Mystic couldn't leave.

Even though there were whispers and worries, Mystic was a female Angelini, a Renaldi. Their line almost always produced females, and of all the Angelini, theirs was the only line whose females could often shift, making them as prized as a pure Were female. Beyond the obligation of keeping her safe on behalf of her Angelini relatives, the elders knew there were more than a few males who'd hoped to mate with her during the Howl.

Hawk's low continuous growl filled the air. Mystic's companions knew there would be pack members sent to bring them back. In her soul, *she* knew he would come for her.

He shifted back into his wolf form so he could return to the compound and search for clues as to their destination. The growl was a constant vibration in his chest, a steady rumble as he raced through the woods. Unless she'd found her other mate, then he would rip any man apart who tried to touch what was his. Her channel would know only two cocks. And his would be one of them.

* * * * *

Las Vegas. The thought of it sent a thrill through Mystic along with a shiver of fear. Her body felt too small for her, as though anticipation and excitement were combined in a balloon filling her to bursting. If she'd been alone she would have rubbed her hands over her breasts and down her abdomen. She would have cupped her mound and tried to ease the tension that had slowly been building over the last week.

Mystic bit her lip. She worried that so much of her time these days seemed to be consumed by thoughts of the Angelini mate bond. Then again, it was probably a natural reaction—not just an Angelini or wolf reaction but one even a human would experience. For the last week she'd been surrounded by stunning masculine specimens not only in the Zevanti pack, but in the visiting packs as well. And there was Hawk.

She shivered thinking about the dark-skinned man with the hungry light brown eyes. He wore his hair in a hundred small beaded braids, making her think of the hood a captive bird of prey would wear. But there was nothing tame about Hawk. Nothing.

She hadn't seen him in his wolf form but she could imagine luxurious black fur and golden eyes. He'd be like Gabby and Gabe in their fur coats, and yet very different.

Hawk was an alpha. He didn't yet have his own pack but his size would dwarf that of her friends.

15

Mystic shivered again and forced her mind away from the werewolf who'd been pursuing her relentlessly for the last week. He wasn't the reason for the heat in her body. He couldn't be. He was not the mate she wanted.

Strike that. She didn't want any mate. She wasn't ready for a mate. Period.

The reason for her body's restlessness had nothing to do with Hawk's presence and everything to do with all the testosterone present in the Zevanti compound. Well, the testosterone plus the hunger of the female Weres on the prowl for a mate. For the last week she'd felt like she was moving around in a thick haze of lust. Was it such a surprise her body reacted to it?

The heady and constant undertone of desire was part of the reason she'd jumped at the chance for this adventure. But it wasn't the only reason. The time was nearing when Estelle, Falcone and Yorick would have to witness her first hunt so she could gain the tattoo of an Angelini hunter.

Mystic dreaded it.

Already most of her cousins bore winged tattoos on their necks signifying they had joined the ranks of the other Angelini and stood ready to fulfill the purpose for which the Angelini had been created—to protect the humans by serving justice on the rogue vampires, though over time the role had been expanded to include hunting any supernatural who broke the laws they all had agreed upon. Mystic felt ill-prepared for the task, ill-suited for it. And her parents had been in no hurry to press it on her.

In truth, her parents acted more like human newlyweds on a honeymoon that had lasted for decades. Estelle often slept deep into the day so she could spend her nights in bed with her two vampire mates. And when they did venture out, they usually wanted to play, treating Mystic like a much-loved younger sibling, except when it came to the opposite sex, and taking her everywhere with them. Even when she was a small child they'd smuggled her into human bars and dance clubs.

They'd used vampire thrall to command the humans to ignore her underage status as she was growing up.

And unlike many of the Renaldi Angelini, who relished the chance to hunt down a rogue vampire, Estelle found it distasteful though she would do her duty when called. Instead, she and Falcone and Yorick had seen to it that Mystic could easily hostess a party or maneuver around a nightclub full of supernatural beings. It was a small measure of revenge directed at Estelle's parents—parents who obeyed the laws and enforced them with honor, though deep inside they believed the only good vampire was a dead one and the only useful human was the one served for dinner.

Mystic forced thoughts of the future away. Las Vegas awaited and as Gabe had so aptly said, *Let the adventure begin.*

* * * * *

It took Hawk longer than he'd intended in order to learn their destination. His muscles rippled with impatience. His temper was short and dangerous but the delay had been worth it.

He knew where they would find lodging. He knew what clubs and casinos interested them.

Too much was at stake to either set out blindly or to fumble around tracking them through huge crowds and monstrous buildings. He couldn't afford to be wrong and have Mystic slip from his grasp.

His cock pulsed against his abdomen. Hard. Hungry. As anxious as he was to claim Mystic for his mate.

He growled as he turned from Gabrielle's computer. His entire being was filled with savage need and relentless determination.

Time was running out. Mystic's body was awakening and Las Vegas drew supernaturals and mortals alike with its glittering promise and dark delights. He had to get to her. He had to mount her before she took others as her mates.

* * * * *

Syndelle Coronado settled more comfortably on a throw cushion in the middle of the most casual room of her house. Around her was drawn a partial circle, a segment left open so the being once known as Korak could enter. Near, but outside the open circle, her human mate began cursing, his fingers frantically working at a video game controller.

It was enough to stop Brann, her vampire mate, from pacing around the room—at least long enough to scowl at the other man and say, "Why is it that I am the only one concerned with what Syndelle intends to do?"

Rafe groaned and dropped the controller to his lap. His smile was mocking as he said, "Why am *I* the only one of Syndelle's mates who is smart enough to realize there is no point in fighting her when she thinks a risk is worth taking?"

The scowl on Brann's face darkened. His lip lifted to reveal a deadly fang. "I have shown you my memories of Roman as he was once, in the days when he went by the name of Korak, before he became a man and a vampire. I have shown you my memories of the one who created Korak, of Brallin. He was a powerful mage, the enemy of all vampires, fledgling and ancient alike. Without him the power of the other supernaturals combined wouldn't have been enough to banish us to the darkness. There is no way to be certain whether or not any of his magic resides in his creation. Roman is a vampire now. But once he was something else. He was a deadly predator without any thought but to hunt and kill on behalf of his master. If Syndelle is wrong, if Roman is still controlled, even in part, by the magic he was created from, as soon as he recognizes her for what she is then he will destroy her. We will be forced to watch helplessly from outside the circle while he rips her apart and soaks the carpet with her blood."

True anguish resonated in Brann's words. It forced Syndelle and Rafael to their feet and to his side. Bodies pressed together. Lips and hands stroked, soothed, gave way to the pulsing beat of lust and the need to join and be one physically.

"There's time before he gets here," Syndelle tempted, her hands gliding over their erections, her vulva swelling and scenting the air with arousal.

"You are our world, Syndelle," Brann said. Their mouths were so close together his words whispered across Rafe and Syndelle's lips. "Nothing can be allowed to happen to you."

"Nothing will. Trust me. Believe in me."

"Always," Rafe said, his fingers moving to the front of her shirt.

"Always," Brann echoed. His hands settled at the top of her jeans as his senses flared outward, making sure his wards were at full strength around the estate.

Because Syndelle willed it, he would allow the vampire now known as Roman into the compound. But if Roman threatened Syndelle in any way, then nothing would prevent Brann from destroying him. Nothing.

He'd waited centuries for Syndelle. She was vampire myth made into reality. She was a prize beyond all measure and she was his.

Not just yours, she teased—a familiar refrain as she cupped his balls and sent heat searing through his cock. *I also belong to Rafael. Or more correctly, you both belong to me since I am the Angelini and you are both* my *mates.*

"And you and Rafael are both my companions," Brann growled, his hands going to the ancient coins hanging from necklaces around both Rafe's and Syndelle's necks. His touch sent a jolt through them, making them cry out as the teasing faded quickly into the heated need for flesh to touch flesh, for the bonds that held them together to be strengthened through sex and blood.

Chapter Two

ဩ

Roman could feel Brann's powerful wards as he stopped the expensive sports car at the gate and waited for the heavy wrought iron to swing open or remain closed, either granting or denying him access to Syndelle. He didn't doubt Brann had argued they remain closed. Once, centuries ago, he and Brann would have been mortal enemies. They would have killed each other on sight. But time and magic and death had changed them both just as it had changed the world they lived in. Now they were neither friends nor enemies. They were merely wary of each other, unsure of the true extent of the other's powers.

He'd lived too long to be surprised anymore by the strange twisting path the magic governing the lives of the supernaturals took. That Syndelle, Sabin's daughter, was now mated to Brann was yet another twist in a road leading to a destination that could never be determined.

Roman laughed softly. Perhaps that was why he surrounded himself with his lushly figured human sheep. Their bodies offered a simple pleasure and their minds were easy to control though he rarely bothered.

Against his skin the wards changed in the instant before the gates swung open. He drove forward, moving along the sweeping, curved driveway of Brann's most heavily guarded estate, wondering idly if Brann intended to settle in Las Vegas now that he'd taken a companion and become an Angelini's mate.

Roman parked the car and got out. He wasn't surprised when the front door opened and only Brann was present. For a long moment they stared at one another, their power brushing like two large, dangerous predators sizing each other up.

"Enter," Brann said, the word almost a growl.

Roman nodded his head and stepped through the doorway. His heart pounded with anticipation while his body prayed Syndelle held the answer, as her father had told him she might.

Once he'd been a beast, created to kill and guard. Deep inside him that beast still lived though it had been centuries since he could take its shape. Now the beast wanted a mate. It demanded a mate.

Roman wasn't sure whether any still lived who would satisfy the beast. He feared the beast's rage at being denied not only a form but a mate might drive him to cross the line and break the rules governing the supernaturals. If that happened then he would become one of those hunted by the Angelini.

I see you are well, small princess, he said, using the link he shared with Syndelle's father, along with Sabin's nickname for her, as he greeted her.

She laughed and moved toward him. But before she reached him Roman's heart beat with sudden alarm. His body tightened with the need to fight even as his mind struggled to understand what was different about her, why her presence struck at his core when it hadn't the last time he saw her. Syndelle's gentle smile and soft eyes helped him fight the beast's instinctive urge to back away from her, to prepare itself against attack and retribution.

He drew a sharp breath as between one heartbeat and the next he knew her for what she was. He knew why the beast was reacting so violently to her.

She was filled with the old magic, with the ancient power from which all vampires once drew life during a long ago time when they roamed both the day and the night. It was a magic from the time before Brallin and the other supernaturals banded together and weakened it, banished it—when they'd hunted down and killed the most powerful of the vampires before turning the rest into creatures who could no longer bear the touch of the sun's rays.

Roman could feel the ancient magic swelling around her, tasting him, recognizing who and what he was, what he had been. Korak. Brallin's creation. Brallin's beast—until the mage's death changed the magic, and the blood Roman had consumed over the centuries as a killer of vampires had turned him into the very thing he'd once hunted.

Syndelle's touch on his hand drew his eyes to hers. And he, who had never been trapped by another's gaze, could not look away from the sky-blue eyes. They were Sabin's eyes and yet the cold, eternal flame of a vampire didn't flicker in their depths as it did in her father's. Instead Roman saw a black abyss, vast and filled with a silence so complete it was everything and nothing, a beginning and an ending.

The wild creation magic of the vampire roared through Syndelle. It pulsed through her veins so quickly her heart raced to catch up. The wolf that lived inside her without form stirred from its slumber, alert, wary, cautious—as was Syndelle in the presence of the ancient power and this vampire who had been created from a beast, not a man.

Brann's memories of what Roman had once been were tempered by Syndelle's vampire father's memories. Ancient memories of Rome and the day when Sabin had been drawn by the smell of blood to find a battleground littered with the carnage of war. Like him, other vampires had been drawn to the area, feasting on the blood as though they'd been invited to a banquet.

But it was Sabin who'd found the man known then by the name of Gaius Cicero, had felt the presence of vampire magic around him and not knowing who he was, had pulled the sword from Roman's chest, saving him from the screaming, agonizing death that would have greeted him with the dawn. It was Sabin who'd cemented their friendship for all eternity by standing with Roman against the other vampires when they would have vented their hatred and destroyed him.

It was upon those feelings of trust and friendship that Syndelle called, riding the wild magic and bringing it under control. The wolf joined with her, strengthened her will with its own, reinforcing her resolve that there would be no return to the old days, the old ways, when earth was both a playground and a battleground for the supernaturals, and humans were nothing but amusing toys and plentiful prey.

"I thought it would be safer if we did this in a circle," Syndelle said, turning her head and releasing Roman from the probing, ancient forces.

He smiled slightly, looking down at where her fingers still rested on his, soft and gentle, calming. The beast deep inside him was still wary and cautious, and yet even it could feel Sabin's stamp on this daughter. And like him, it could feel the courage and honor at her core, her heritage as one of the Coronado Angelini.

"I put my life in your hands, small princess," he said, laughing when she ducked her head in a gesture that both acknowledged the truth of his statement and conveyed she did not seek dominion over him.

She stepped away from him and he could see the heavily warded still-open circle, the golden threads of the symbols visible to his inner eye. And despite his resolve, his trust, Roman's heart jumped at the sight of them and the beast tensed at the idea of willingly touching the ancient magic again.

Syndelle moved to her mates. She sensed their uneasiness, their desire to be in the circle with her instead of trapped outside, helpless to aid her. *It will be okay*, she said yet again, kissing Rafe first and then Brann. *And when Roman leaves, we can go out to the garden and make love.*

She returned to the circle, entering it first. A blush washed over her cheeks as she said, "It might be wise if you left your clothes on the couch."

"Syndelle," Brann growled.

Roman laughed and teased, "I see why you created the circle now. Perhaps it would have been wiser to close it around us before asking me to strip."

Still, he quickly shed his clothing, and Syndelle's eyes lingered over him in feminine appreciation. His blond hair was as richly colored as Rafe's though Roman wore it short. His blue eyes were beautiful. They danced with amusement and masculine pride, along with the knowledge that he recognized her approval of his tanned, muscled body. He was every bit as gorgeous and well endowed as her own mates.

"Syndelle," Brann growled again as Rafe snickered, flopping in feigned casualness on a chair.

Roman stepped into the circle and took a position on the cushions Syndelle had placed on the floor for him. The sight of them reminded him of his life in Rome, of the days when Caesar still lived and Rome's armies destroyed anything in their path.

With graceful movements Syndelle traced symbols in the air and the circle closed to form a cage for both of them. Roman's heart raced, this time with anticipation.

The beast inside him paced with eagerness. It believed fully that if any could help it find a mate, it was this Angelini.

The being that was vampire hoped for something else entirely from this woman who was vampire myth made into reality. She was the Masada, the foundation on which the old magic would return and build. She was the one whose body was a chalice, whose blood was the elixir that could allow a vampire to walk in the sunlight.

Syndelle took Roman's hand. She turned it so the palm faced upward, contemplating it as she centered herself before allowing any of the magic to be set free, to ripple across the future and change the shape of it forever.

Her mind touched Roman's along the pathway he shared with her father. The wolf pressed against her skin, reaching for the beast that lived inside Roman, recoiling at the sight of it even as it was fascinated by the eagle's head and wings attached to a massive lion's body. Gryphon.

The wolf's thoughts melded with Syndelle's. Such a creature belonged in ancient times, in myths. And as if sensing the judgment, the beast crouched, pressed against Roman's skin as if gathering itself to fight to the death.

Before it could attack Syndelle bit down on her lip sharply, bloodying it. Then she pressed her mouth to Roman's in a kiss that would give even as it took away.

The rush of power was unlike anything Roman had known. It roared through him and savagely altered his form. Bone and muscle yielded to free a shape he had not taken for centuries. The gryphon shimmered into existence for one precious second before the old magic banished it forever in a roar of anguish and victory.

A huge male lion stood where Roman had been. Its tawny coat gleamed for an instant. Its long canines glistened as it crouched.

Then fur changed to feathers. Body mass compressed to leave a golden eagle perched on the pillows. It flapped its wings and lifted into the air, sharp talons and beak gleaming as its scream of victorious release filled the room.

For long moments it hovered. The wind generated by its wings made Syndelle's hair whirl and dance around her head until finally the eagle dropped back to the floor and relinquished its form to that of a man.

Syndelle rose to her feet. She was drained from wielding the old magic, from controlling the form it would take and limiting it to what she believed was the correct path.

Roman rose with her. His eyes shone with tears. *Small princess...*

She touched her hand to his once again. *If you are truly ready to give up your human sheep, then you will find your mate among the Renaldi Angelini. From the very beginning they have taken shapeshifters as mates. Though most have been wolves, their line also has traces of both lion and eagle.* A small frown formed between her eyebrows. *Unlike the Coronado, the Renaldi have not looked favorably on the taking of vampires as mates. But there is at least one among them not like the others. Estelle. Both of her mates are vampires and one of them, Falcone, was sired by my sister's mate, Gian. There is only one child from Estelle's mating, a daughter named Mystic. Perhaps she is the one who will prove to be your mate.*

* * * * *

It was nearing dawn when Gabe pulled the car over on a barren stretch of road at the edge of a forest. "Are we almost there yet?" Gabby teased as she climbed out of the Jeep and stretched.

Mystic followed her from the car, her hand automatically going to her friend's arm as the hairs on the back of her neck and along her spine rose in alarm. "Listen."

Far in the distance was the unmistakable sound of werewolves howling and yipping with urgency and frustration. The sounds grew more frenzied, more angry, and then abruptly stopped when the sun reached the horizon. As its rays pierced the darkness of open space and forest alike, the air filled with the agonized, horrifying screams of a human.

Even as the screams faded Gabriel was handing the car keys to Mystic and stripping out of his clothing, preparing to shift form. Next to him, Gabby also stripped, removing her jewelry and handing it to Mystic as well. Their dark bodies shone, powerful and beautiful in the early-morning light. The pack brands burned into the flesh above their pubic hair both a savage reminder of what they were and a way to identify them should they die wearing their fur.

Mystic felt the gathering magic against her skin, and then it was done. One minute her best friends were human. The next they were two sleek, black wolves.

She hurriedly retrieved an empty knapsack and crammed their clothing into it. Gabe and Gabby yipped and danced around her as she locked the car and secured the backpack.

"Go," Mystic said, steeling herself for pain, forcing her mind to seek a place deep inside herself so she could keep up with them even if she couldn't change form as they did.

Miles passed in a blur, the day coming more fully awake with each one. Mystic could feel the empty space left by the death of magic long before they found the hollow, sunken corpse of what had once been a vampire, and before that, a human man.

Next to her the wolves growled. Their hackles rose and teeth flashed. Bones popped and crunched as bodies reformed, going from beings that walk on four feet to beings that walk on two.

Gabby and Gabe stood naked. Neither asked for their clothing and she didn't offer it.

"Fledgling," Mystic said. The truth of it was in the bones that extended strong and white from beneath clothing that showed no sign of age or abuse other than a single slash where a blade had once been lodged in the vampire's heart.

His body looked as though it had lain in the woods for months and had been picked clean by the insects nature designed for such a task. But it was his screams that were the true measure of his age. The older the vampire the longer it took for the sunlight to kill them.

"I don't know of any law that allows us to hunt vampires this way," Gabe finally said.

Mystic knelt next to the corpse. "There are none. Only a human who's committed a horrible crime against a pack or pack member can be hunted like this. All others are judged by council or the Angelini. It's been that way for centuries in order to prevent the supernaturals from fighting with one another the way they used to do."

She steeled herself to touch the corpse, to roll it over so she could check for identification. The outline of a wallet pressed against the back pocket. She pulled it out and found a driver's license. Todd Moore, whose license claimed he was twenty-eight and lived in Las Vegas.

Mystic stood. She surveyed the area around them. Her senses reached out for the feel of magic and brushed against only Gabe and Gabby. She kicked at the ground with her foot and Gabe groaned. "You want us to bury him, don't you?"

For a long moment she said nothing, and then she nodded. Out of respect for her vampire fathers she would see this done.

With a sigh, Gabe changed into a wolf. Gabby followed. The woods remained quiet except for the sound of their powerful paws digging into the ground.

Chapter Three

ഇ

Mystic eased out of the hotel room close to sunset. The wallet from the dead vampire was a grim reminder that tattooed or not, she was still an Angelini with duties and responsibilities.

She cast a quick look at her sleeping friends before quietly closing the door and padding down the hallway. Between the run and changing form so many times, Gabe and Gabby were almost comatose by the time they arrived in Vegas.

The same could be said about her. She'd been exhausted by the escape from the Zevanti compound as well as the long run in the woods and the car trip to Las Vegas. She'd fallen asleep almost as soon as she crawled onto the hotel bed.

But now her body hummed with both excitement and something else, something that sent a wave of fear through her. She felt hunted, as if her days of freedom were nearing an end.

Mystic shivered as the image of Hawk rose in her mind. She hoped Gabby and Gabe had covered their tracks. She didn't think Jagger would try to follow them. His interest had been just as intense as Hawk's but it hadn't felt as focused and dangerous.

Hawk would follow them if he could. He'd drag them back to the Howl whether they were willing or not.

Mystic rebelled at the idea of it. She rebelled at the idea that she would somehow end up tied to a pack, restrained by pack hierarchy and politics. She was too much like her mother to be able to tolerate it. Estelle loved the city life. She loved to mingle with humans and vampires and shapeshifters alike.

In the very beginning, Angelini mates were always powerful humans. Witches, warlocks, sorcerers, shamans, but then humans had believed in magic and the existence of supernatural beings in those days. Now very few Angelini took human mates. Most were mated to vampires and shifters.

She could guess why that was so. What better way to protect the humans than to live among the predators who might threaten them?

Mystic worried her bottom lip as she climbed into a cab and gave the driver directions to Fangs. She prayed it wasn't a mistake to try to find Falcone's sire but she wanted to rid herself of the wallet and she couldn't think of anyone else to go to.

The Angelini and their mates were gathered elsewhere, in a meeting she was not allowed to attend since she didn't yet have the mark of a hunter. Or at least that's what her grandmother had told her as justification for sending her to the Howl.

If her parents hadn't been abroad then she would have gone with them to the Angelini gathering. They would have insisted. But she hadn't bothered to argue with her grandmother.

The cab pulled to a stop in front of Fangs. Mystic laughed out loud when she saw the humans dressed in black and pierced with silver. They were lined up, anxiously awaiting the chance to become a vampire's dinner.

Amazing. And yet not so. The pleasure of a vampire's bite was beyond compare—or so Estelle had said and Mystic believed her. The sounds of ecstasy that often filled their house during the night were impossible to ignore.

Mystic got out of the cab and went directly to the front of the line, secure in the knowledge that no one would challenge her. She'd been created to hunt among the humans, to attract and bespell them, to use them even as it was her birth duty to guard the border between their world and hers.

Flesh of her mother.

Blood of her vampire fathers.

Bound together by Angelini magic to create a child who would continue the Renaldi legacy.

Mystic grimaced. Continue the legacy—with a twist. As far as she could tell she was very different from the rest of the Renaldi Angelini. Even Estelle could shift to a wolf.

Three humans, two girls and a boy, joined Mystic at the door. They were younger than she was, barely legal. She wondered why they were granted preferential treatment. There was no hint of a vampire's claim on them.

The boy flashed his fangs then fell almost immediately into Mystic's gaze when she smiled at him. She looked away quickly in order to release him.

One of the girls slipped her arm possessively through the boy's. She glared at Mystic. "I haven't seen you here before."

"I only just got to Vegas." Then because she was curious, Mystic added, "I'm here to find Giovanni Banderali. Do you know him?"

The second girl's eyes widened then narrowed. Her shoulders stiffened. "He's married to a friend of ours. What do you want with him?"

Surprise hit Mystic. Apparently she had learned something her mother and fathers didn't yet know. She doubted a human wedding ceremony had been performed, but if Gian was introducing a woman as his wife then she was no doubt his companion. Both Falcone and Yorick claimed Estelle as their companion and she wore an elaborately crafted companion necklace signifying who she belonged to.

"What's his wife's name?" Mystic asked.

"Skye Delano," the girl answered. "No. It's Coronado now."

This time it was shock that rippled through Mystic. "Coronado?"

Like the Renaldis, the Coronado line of Angelini traced all the way to the very beginning. They were the first to take vampire mates. And like every Angelini child, Mystic had memorized the heritage and bloodline of each family line with the same thoroughness as she'd learned numbers and the alphabet.

"Skye told us she was found in a ghetto of LA when she was a kid," the boy said. "She didn't know what her real name was until her sister, Syndelle, showed up." He flashed his fangs again. "I'm Mike. This is my girlfriend Dawn. That's my sister Candy."

"So what do you want with Gian?" Candy asked.

"I'm a relative of his."

A cheer went up as the door opened. A human bound to a vampire stepped outside. He glanced at Mystic with curiosity but didn't question her as she slipped into the club.

* * * * *

The eagle screamed before it dropped to the ground next to a silver sports car. For a moment the bird stood, stretching its wings full length before shimmering and changing into a lion and then a man as the last of the sun's rays faded away.

Joy raced through Roman. Exaltation. Though the forms were both alike and different than his original one, he rejoiced in once again walking the earth as other than a man. He savored the feeling of sunlight and the rush that came from filling his stomach with the flesh of his prey as well as their blood.

It had been centuries since he'd greeted the dawn and lingered to meet the sunset. He hadn't been able to resist the temptation to leave the city and find a deserted area so he could hunt as he had once hunted. But now he needed to return to Las Vegas.

He might be both vampire and shapeshifter, but his need for a mate had not lessened. In this, the beast he once was still ruled.

Roman removed the car key from its hiding place and retrieved his clothes. As he dressed his thoughts traveled to Fangs. Tonight he would locate Gian and learn more about Mystic Renaldi.

Mystic. The name moved through Roman like a powerful chant as the beast that now had two forms allied itself with ancient vampire magic, and all were in agreement. He needed to find Mystic and claim her, even if he also had to share her.

* * * * *

Gian was more serious, more intense than Mystic anticipated. Her father's sire wasn't a man she could imagine lounging around a Victorian parlor all day, enjoying frivolous pursuits and reading poetry to the ladies he intended to seduce—not that Falcone had dared contemplate seducing anyone other than Estelle since being bound by Angelini magic.

Skye Coronado's other mate was a surprise as well. He was human, and a policeman.

Mystic placed the dead vampire's wallet on the table then described what she and Gabe and Gabby had heard and discovered on their way to Vegas. When she was finished, Rico turned to Gian and said, "My vote is we call Augustino. Let him investigate this until the rest of Skye's family gets here. He's Were and he's a cop. That makes him equipped to deal with this until Skye's family shows up."

"In this I agree with Rico," Gian said, brushing his lips against Skye's knuckles. "Let Augustino investigate. If the wolves can handle it among themselves, or if it can be brought before the Angelini, it would be better for all of us. There are plenty of vampires who have no liking for Weres, and vice versa. We don't know enough to act and we can't afford to let this become public knowledge. Were, human or vampire, there are too many who flock here looking for fun and are not adverse to trouble."

Gian glanced down at the driver's license, then back at Mystic. "You will guide Augustino to the spot where the body rests."

Mystic nodded. She was more than willing to take the unknown detective to where they'd buried the body if it would mean the matter was turned over to others and she could rejoin her friends.

Rico excused himself from the private table near the nightclub's bar in order to call the other policeman. Gian also left.

Mystic's gaze strayed to Skye's neck. It was free of the hunter's tattoo. "You're Jovina," she said. "You're the daughter of Richelle and her mates, Sabin and Riesen. Your name is among the ones I learned but no one knew what happened to you." Mystic cocked her head. "Just as few have ever seen your sister Syndelle."

Skye removed a cell phone from the pocket of her Harley jacket and opened it, using a built-in camera to take a picture of the driver's license before putting the phone away. "I was kidnapped when I was young though I can't remember the details of it." She looked around at the Goth crowd and the vampires drawn to Fangs. "I had no clue about any of this until recently."

"In these times it rarely happens that a child is separated from parents," Mystic said, wondering if the Angelini magic had chosen Rico for Skye because he belonged to the world of her childhood. "It would have been impossible to separate me from my parents. They give new meaning to the term overprotective. But it's an ancient custom of the Angelini to keep children safe by making them forget their origins so they blend in with the humans if they're lost for an extended period of time."

Mystic shook her head. "I'm not sure I'll embrace the custom if I have children. The old ways are not always the best ways." She grinned, thinking about how often she told her fathers that they needed to get with the times, and yet, among the Renaldis, Estelle and her two mates were hardly the norm.

It was Skye's turn to give Mystic a curious look. "Most of what I know about the Angelini comes from what Syndelle has shared with me. I can't believe your family is letting you roam around Vegas even if you're here with two Were friends."

"My parents are in Europe and the rest of my family is at the same gathering your parents and brothers are attending. My grandparents sent me to the Zevanti compound so I could attend a Howl with them. They're hoping I find Were mates."

"What's a Howl like?"

"I didn't officially make it to this one. The Howl itself takes place on sanctuary land owned by the Were council. Think rustic resort with hot tubs for those remaining human, kennels to house anyone who can't control themselves in wolf form, and game-filled woods to hunt in when wearing fur and you'll get the picture. The first several days are for negotiations and addressing grievances among the packs as well as for deciding larger issues. Gabe and Gabby and I stayed in the Zevanti compound while the others were dealing with pack business. This particular Howl is a large one, with lots of packs in attendance.

"The sanctuary is surrounded by several different pack territories. Weres come and go between the council lands and their own, or their hosts'. Most packs host Weres from outside of the area for various reasons, but usually it has something to do with alliances formed or alliances they want to form. The Zevantis had at least fifty Weres from outside packs in their compound and that doesn't include the ones they still consider "family". So lets just say the testosterone levels were high even before the actual entertainment started, and the lust permeating the air was almost suffocating."

Skye grinned. "So everyone was in an extreme state of horniness."

"Yes. That's why my grandparents were so sure I'd end up with mates there."

"I don't blame you for making a run for it. As much as I love my mates…" Skye laughed as Gian returned to the table, eyebrows lifted.

"As much as you love your mates…?" he questioned.

Skye rose partway out of her chair and brushed her lips against his before answering, "As much as I love my mates they do sometimes cramp my style."

Gian laughed. "I think you are speaking of your human mate who prefers that his wife follow the laws he's charged with enforcing."

"True."

Gian's attention shifted to a point behind Mystic. "Ah, good," he said, his voice silky. "We can turn this matter over to the wolves and then go play."

The scent of the werewolf reached Mystic first. Her body tightened as her breath grew suddenly short and her heart raced in her chest. She didn't want to stand. She didn't want to see the man whose heat rubbed against her like thick fur. She didn't want to acknowledge—either to him or to herself—that the trap of Angelini magic had sprung closed on her. But there was no denying the need to couple unfurling inside her, turning her body into her enemy and screaming she was in the presence of one of her mates.

Skye's eyes widened slightly, then narrowed. Her head cocked as though she was in a silent conversation. Gian frowned in response. His gaze traveled from Mystic to the man who was behind her, the man whose gaze felt as though it was boring through her.

Mystic clenched her fists and rose from her seat. Reluctantly she turned so she could meet the detective. Her body pulsed with lust when she saw his strong masculine features and hard body. A shiver of erotic fear slid through her when she glimpsed the feral wolf that lived inside him, that shimmered beneath the surface and looked at her through deep brown eyes.

Outcast or outsider. She felt it more than anything else. He had no obvious tattoo or piece of jewelry identifying him as a member of a pack, though the lack of either didn't rule out that he belonged to one. It was a fad among younger werewolves to wear dog tags, and many of the female Weres liked to wear pierced earrings with their pack symbol appearing somewhere in the design.

Mystic's eyes drifted lower. Desire roared through her at the evidence of his desire, at the sight of the large bulge at the front of his jeans. She wouldn't find a pack brand above the line of his pubic hair or on his inner thigh—and it didn't matter to her. She didn't intend to let him claim her.

Gian placed his hands on Mystic's shoulders, startling her. His amusement raced through her, a reminder of their shared blood link. "This is Mystic Renaldi, a daughter of my line. Though she does not bear the mark of an Angelini hunter, she is one. I have commanded that she, and she alone, take you to the place where the murdered vampire was found. Christian Augustino, do you accept full responsibility for this member of my family?"

Augustino's eyes narrowed and his nostrils flared. Mystic's heart jerked in her chest in protest. A small sound of denial escaped but it was too late to avoid Gian's formal, binding question—an amusement for her father's sire but a life-sentence for her.

She didn't want a mate! At least not right now.

But even as her mind screamed it, the Angelini magic was rising from her core and bringing wave after wave of heady, inescapable lust with it. The detective's jaw clenched and she prayed he'd refuse, or ask that Gabe and Gabby go with them to the burial site. He did neither. Instead, he nodded and said, "I accept responsibility for her."

Mystic's body shivered. It rejoiced even as her mind scrambled for some argument she could raise, some claim she could make that would put distance between her and the detective. Desperately she turned and looked to Skye. Hope flared inside her at the way Skye was frowning at Gian in displeasure. But before the hope could fully blossom it was pinched off, a bud not even given a chance to bloom.

Christian Augustino moved in before she could utter a word. His arm went around her, holding her in place as his free hand brushed her hair away from her neck. His lips touched her skin and his teeth clamped down in a stinging, claiming bite that whipped through her and made her whimper.

Mystic lowered her head. Her body overrode her mind. It melted and yielded in a show of submission.

Christian growled against her skin and the low sound stroked her pussy, flooding her panties with moisture and swelling her cunt lips further. She whimpered again. Resistance fled as her body went soft and pliant against his.

He released his grip on her neck. He bathed over the spot he'd marked with his tongue before dropping his arms and stepping away, his focus shifting to the driver's license of the dead vampire.

For a moment Mystic considered excusing herself. She imagined losing herself in the crowded club and then escaping back to the hotel room. But before she could take a step Christian's hand shackled her wrist and locked her to his side, telling her without words that she would not escape her destiny.

"Let's go," Christian said, his voice abrupt.

He pocketed the wallet and guided her out of the club, not releasing his grip on her arm until he had her buckled into his car.

Mystic shivered. Her skin was coated in a fine sheen of sweat. Every cell was on fire as wave after wave of Christian's potent pheromones washed over her, keeping her thoughts off balance and preventing her resolve to escape from firming.

"I need to leave a message for my friends," she finally managed.

She didn't want them to worry about her. More importantly, she didn't want Gabe to come looking for her. Mostly he was easygoing and fun-loving, but sometimes he could go all wolfie—in a dominating, overbearing, alpha kind of way.

The Zevanti pack had taken responsibility for her. Gabe might think he needed to take her back to the Howl—and force Christian to go along with him.

Anxiety for her friend coiled in Mystic's belly. She already sensed that the detective who would soon be her mate was not a man to be challenged lightly.

Christian couldn't stop himself from breathing in deeply and filling his lungs with Mystic's heady, lush scent. A mate! An exotically beautiful one made up of amber and earth tones, with skin as tanned as his and eyes showing a wolf's influence—light brown, the color echoed in the highlights of her thick mane of hair.

Every cell in his body quivered with anticipation. The urgency to mount and claim her was almost unbearable.

When Rico had called him he'd intended to swing by Fangs and get the license, then go to where the vampire was buried and work outward, trying to find the scent of the werewolves. That would have to wait. Nothing was as important as claiming his mate.

He reached for his cell phone. The wolf's primitive instinct to secure Mystic in its den and repeatedly mate with her warred with the man's intelligence. Reason prevailed. It would be better to avoid trouble and further complication by assuring her friends she was safe. "Use my phone," he said and a jolt went through his cock when her fingers brushed against his.

Gabby's voice was groggy when she answered the phone. "Where are you?"

Mystic bit her lip. "I went to Fangs."

Gabrielle instantly made the connection. "That's the club Falcone's sire co-owns?" There were sounds of movement. "You've got the dead vampire's wallet?"

"Not anymore. Gian, my father's sire, wanted the matter turned over to a Were."

A sigh of relief met her statement. "Good. Gabe's starting to twitch. He'll be awake soon, probably by the time I'm out of the shower—or sooner if I want to risk getting bitten by actually trying to hurry him along. We can get something to eat and then hit the casinos and clubs. How long 'til you get back?"

"I've met someone."

"Not a mate? Tell me you didn't find a mate!" There was panic and worry in Gabby's voice.

"Gian knows him. He's a policeman. I'll call you later, after… I'll call you later, when I can. I've got to take him back to where we found the vampire." Mystic wasn't sure whether or not she should give Christian's name to her friends.

Hawk's image rose in her mind. A touch of panic made her chest tighten. She decided against giving Gabby further details. Hawk would eventually find them in Vegas. "Don't worry about me," she said and hung up.

Heat rushed through her as Christian's hand covered hers. He closed the phone before taking it from her.

For one wild moment she considered bolting from the car the next time he stopped. But his hand returned to clamp down on hers as though he sensed what she was contemplating. Then all too soon they were pulling into a driveway, into a garage—the outer door closing and blocking any avenue of escape.

Chapter Four

ಌ

Christian loosened his grip on Mystic's hand though she could sense his reluctance to let go of her. His focus remained absolute as he slid from the car and immediately went around to her side.

When he opened the door and took her arm she muttered, "I'm not going to run."

He smiled, a wolf's feral show of teeth. "Good. It wouldn't be a very smart thing to do. I don't want you to look back on our first mating as a rape."

Mystic shivered. She heard the seriousness of his warning along with his firm resolve to couple with her. But she also sensed his desire to get off to a good start despite the wolf's urges and the potent Angelini magic.

She let him lead her into the house. She tried to focus on her surroundings but found it impossible to notice more than the huge TV, the couch and the bare walls.

"It's a rental," Christian growled. "I haven't been in Vegas long and I wasn't sure I was going to stay here."

He didn't release her arm until they were in his bedroom and the door was firmly closed behind her. Lust coursed through her but also a hint of nervousness. "Don't you think we should get to know each other a little better first? Maybe go out to eat and then hit the casinos for a while?"

Christian laughed though his face softened and his hand cupped her cheek. The roughness of his palm and the gentle way it rubbed against her skin were a startling contrast. "And start an orgy with the pheromones pouring off you?"

Her eyes widened. "Me! If someone could bottle you they'd make a fortune!"

He laughed again and used the hand cupping her cheek to pull her closer. His other hand went to her side, gliding up and down under her shirt.

Desire glittered in his eyes. Yet his gentleness told her he wanted their first time together to be more than a frenzied coupling.

Heat raced through Mystic, need. She'd thought he'd pounce on her as soon as he got her to his house. But now she could read his intent to try to slow things down, to respect her wishes to get to know one another a little bit better before fucking.

They wouldn't have much time before more primitive forces prevailed. The Angelini magic had ensured that her body craved his. Need already pooled in her belly, her breasts, her vulva. She'd been curious about sex for so long, anxious to try it—though without the complication of a permanent bond! But now it was his restraint that made the first inroad to her heart.

Her hands went to the front of his polo shirt. She pulled it from his pants and pushed it upward so she could touch his skin. Her fingers explored him, confirmed what she suspected. He didn't belong to a pack, or if he did, he wore the brand on his inner thigh instead of the more common place above his pubic hair.

The muscles of his rock-hard abdomen tightened even further at her touch. Feminine pride filled her when she looked up at his face and saw the struggle for control taking place there. A shiver of worry followed as the fear of disappointing him suddenly crowded in.

"Both of my fathers are vampires," she said, a blush rising to her cheeks. "Very, very old-fashioned ones." The blush deepened at the way her voice sounded squeaky and uncertain. "I know a lot, but I don't have much actual experience."

Christian's eyes widened slightly then slowly filled with masculine satisfaction and anticipation. He leaned down. His lips claimed hers in a soft, lingering kiss. "I'll take care of you, Mystic. Always."

His arms wrapped around her waist, pulling her tight against him as his mouth once again covered hers. But where his first kiss had been meant to convey reassurance, this one was meant to convey so much more.

Mystic moaned as his mouth devoured hers, as his tongue thrust against hers. The feel of his erection against her belly had her encircling his neck with her arms and standing on her toes so she could rub her pelvis against the hard ridge of his penis. There was nothing on her mind but the thought of getting naked so skin touched skin and they could explore each other's bodies.

Christian's lips moved to her neck, her ears. His fingers made short work of the buttons on her shirt, parting it and freeing her breasts at the same time. He pushed both shirt and bra off her shoulders, forcing her arms down and momentarily trapping her in the tangle of her own clothing.

Mystic arched into his mouth when he finally lowered his face and laved over her nipple then held it tightly between his teeth. The possessive grip sent a pulse of need right to her clit.

"Christian," she whispered. He bit down harder and she discovered that pain and pleasure were closer together than she'd ever thought possible. She arched, tried to entice him to start suckling even as she begged with words. "Please, Christian."

He growled, a low, possessive, dominant sound that caused something deep inside Mystic to stir. For a fleeting second it made her think of a wolf awakening and rejoicing in the sound of its mate. She shivered, and then began writhing as his mouth tortured her with pleasure. He ate and sucked at first one breast and then the other. With his lips and tongue and teeth he turned her into a creature of pure sensation.

She was panting, desperate for release when one of his legs forced hers open. His hands moved to her hips, holding her as she rode his thigh. His mouth only lifted from her breasts when she cried out in orgasm and became pliant.

Tenderness filled Christian as he looked at Mystic's face. It was flushed with pleasure and perhaps a hint of embarrassment at having humped his leg. He nuzzled her neck. He licked over her lips in a wolf's greeting before telling her once again, "I'll take care of you, Mystic. Always."

She didn't protest when he stripped her clothing off and gently placed her on the bed before removing his own and joining her. He straddled her on his hands and knees.

Pride filled him as her eyes roamed over his body, appreciative and unafraid. When she licked her lips, his cock pulsed and stretched against his abdomen. The tip glistened with arousal as his balls grew heavy with seed.

He growled with need and pleasure when her hands went to his chest and her palms glided over the tiny points of his nipples before moving downward. He stilled when she stroked his smooth abdomen. A hint of anxiety curled in his belly and he watched her face intently for an expression of disgust or distrust when she saw he had no brand, no pack affiliation. Bitter experience had taught him that among werewolves, to be without a pack was the same as being a leper in ancient times.

The anxiety uncoiled and faded when her face showed nothing except appreciation of her mate's body. His cock grew more engorged. His balls tightened. The tip of his penis beaded with arousal and his chest swelled in a wolf's proud display for its female.

Mystic laughed, a husky enticing sound that had him dropping his head, nuzzling her breasts, her neck, her ears, before capturing her lips. She met the thrusts of his tongue with hers. She stroked his buttocks, his thighs with her hands. She teased him just as he'd teased her earlier, by not touching the part of him that needed it the most.

Christian growled and lowered his body. He trapped her legs so they remained closed while his balls rolled against her mound and his cock smoothed over her soft belly. He reveled in the way she jerked and gasped underneath him, her nails clawing at his back.

Mystic had wanted to talk, to get to know him better. But she knew it was too late for that as soon as she felt the Angelini magic claim her. It made its own demands. It insisted that she yield to it, that she yield to her destiny and take this man, this Were, as one of her mates.

The magic clawed at her just as she clawed at Christian's back. It raked against her insides as she scratched his skin. It needed a certain amount of violence, a certain amount of blood. It required a show of dominance and submissiveness, of wild lust and caring so balance would be achieved.

As if sensing what was happening to her, Christian responded. He drove her higher and higher, adjusted their positions so he could ruthlessly strike her clit with his shaft and balls.

He plundered her mouth and claimed her cries. His tongue thrust aggressively in a promise of what his penis would soon do to her cunt.

Mystic writhed against him. She tried to get her legs open so his cock could plunge into her channel. Arousal coated the inside of her thighs.

Christian didn't yield. He held her in the position of his choosing. He told her without words that her pleasure was his to command, his to control.

Her movements became more frenzied. Her whimpers became more submissive.

Christian growled deep in his throat in approval. He lay more heavily on her. His hips shifted, changed the angle of his assault so she cried out in a release that went on and on as his cock glided back and forth over the unprotected head of her clit. When her shudders finally stopped, she lay limp beneath him, submissive though her cunt burned for him to take her, to claim her.

Satisfaction surged through Christian along with fierce possessiveness. He didn't know as much about the Angelini as someone who'd been raised among supernaturals, but he did know the balance would soon shift in her favor. Once she sheathed his cock in her hot channel, once she locked the head of his penis deep inside her—in a hidden place no human or Were female possessed—then he would forever crave her. He would need to mate with her often in order to find any semblance of sanity.

Once the bond between them was in place, she'd be able to touch his thoughts and he would be able to touch hers. There would never be any secrets between them.

It should terrify him but instead desire surged through him. His cock jerked with the need to finish what they'd started. But he fought the urge to spread her thighs and thrust. He wanted to linger, to bask in the moments before frenzied need and Angelini lust controlled them both.

A mate. He'd never thought to actually possess one. He'd never allowed himself to dream about being with a woman like Mystic. He was the son of a human female. His father an unknown, though probably like him, an outcast, a man without a pack.

Christian shuddered as he breathed deeply of Mystic's lush scent and wallowed in the feel of her hot skin. She was already a part of him. She called to his soul and welcomed it home. Her presence in his life was an invitation to live fully in the supernatural world he'd hovered around the edges of for most of his life.

A mate. A mate beyond compare. An Angelini female.

He covered her lips with his and the magic rose and flowed between them. He thrilled in how she opened for him, submitted to him, welcomed and accepted his demands.

An instinct not his own drew his mouth to her neck. His teeth clamped down, this time drawing blood.

He trailed hot, hungry kisses over her breast. A growl escaped as he recaptured her nipple. He bit. He suckled. His balls filled with more seed when images of Mystic one day nursing his children filled his mind.

She panted underneath him, writhed. A sheen of sweat coated her skin as she urged him to mate with her.

Ice-hot need spiked through his penis. His mouth found the place over her heart. He could feel its wild beat against his lips, and once again, driven by the magic governing Mystic, he bit her, marked her.

Christian moved lower. The scent of her arousal swamped him.

He couldn't resist the command of her body to bury his face between her thighs. He licked and sucked. He coated himself in her arousal as he rubbed against her wet pussy before plunging his tongue into her slit, relishing the way her inner muscles spasmed, grabbed at him and tried to hold him inside her.

His growls were constant. His cock was soaked, the foreskin pulled back, the tip engorged, leaking, anxious to pierce her. But he couldn't leave her cunt until he heard her scream in release one more time.

He attacked her clit, her swollen cunt lips, her channel. He used his tongue and his teeth and the suction of his mouth while he held her wrists to the bed and made her accept all he had to offer.

She fought to get away from him. She fought to take more of him. She screamed and pleaded. She cried and shrieked until finally her body arched upward in release.

He ate it up. He ate her up. He would have stayed for hours with his face buried between her thighs except for the white-hot pain in his cock and the tightening in his balls that warned his seed would soon be wasted on the sheets.

Christian turned his head slightly. He bit her inner thigh, gave her the third mark required in an Angelini mating before rising above her and offering his neck. He groaned when she bit him, shuddered in pleasure as her lips trailed over his chest and her teeth settled on the place above his heart, marking him there too.

"Mystic," he growled when her mouth neared his cock. He buried his fingers in her hair in order to prevent her from doing anything more than leave her mark on his inner thigh.

When it was done he flipped her to her hands and knees. He wanted to howl at the way she immediately lowered her chest and spread her legs to present him with her swollen vulva. In deference to the wolf he rubbed his face against her slick folds. He licked her before covering her body with his and driving into her.

She was so tight, so small. Ecstasy rippled along his spine as he fought through the resistance of her virgin channel. His breath was shuddering in and out of his chest by the time he was all the way in. He moaned in delirious pleasure at the feel of being surrounded by the tight fist of her feminine flesh, at being buried to the hilt in his mate.

His mate.

The words rippled through Christian and his hips jerked. Lust and need and overwhelming emotion filled him.

He gave in to the urge to claim her completely. He pumped in and out of her, faster and faster, deeper and deeper, harder and harder. His violent thrusts and the weight of his body demanded that she open the part of her reserved only for the males who claimed her and were claimed by her.

Mystic answered his demand by spreading her thighs and canting her hips, by softening. But she did not fully yield until his teeth settled on her shoulder in a wolf's demand for the complete submission of its mate.

Christian felt the change in her immediately. He felt the magic rush through him as she softened further, offered more of herself and allowed him to plunge deeper, into a place reserved for mates. He growled as she trapped the tip of his cock inside her with a ring of muscles possessed only by Angelini females.

His hips jerked in response as instinctively he tried to escape the sweet trap. A wash of seed roared through his cock. She keened in release and her orgasm caused him to jerk again, to fill her with more seed.

The cycle of pleasure repeated itself again and again, until they collapsed on the passion-scented sheets. For long moments they remained joined together, weak, sated, his cock still deep in her channel though he was no longer trapped there, both of them content in a way neither had experienced before.

Christian nuzzled her neck and she nestled deeper into him. Tenderness filled him at the way her gesture communicated a trust that he would see to her safety. He couldn't stop himself from cupping her breast, from toying with her nipple. Once again he imagined what it would be like to see her nursing his son.

A frown formed along with a question. He'd assumed any male child of his would be able to shift form but she'd said both her fathers were vampires and he knew very little about Angelini reproduction.

"What are your mother's parents," he asked. It was too soon to think about breeding her but the wolf demanded an answer, it was more driven by the thought of offspring than the man.

She tensed against him, just enough to warn he needed to proceed with care. "My grandfathers are both wolves. My grandmother is the Angelini."

Christian smoothed kisses over her shoulder and neck until she relaxed against him. Then it was his turn to tense when she said, "You don't have a pack brand."

"No." He sensed he could drop the matter but he also knew it would come up again.

They hadn't spoken mind to mind. They hadn't intruded on each other's thoughts and memories, but he could feel the link forged by the mating and the sharing of blood, by the Angelini magic.

"My mother was a small-town cop. My father was a man she met when she went to Miami for some kind of law-enforcement conference. She was on the Pill. He used a rubber." Christian shrugged, smiling despite the pain thinking of his mother brought to him. "Hard to keep those Were genes down. I don't know whether he had a pack brand or not. By the time I knew there was such a thing it was too late to ask her."

He growled when Mystic pulled away and his cock slid free of her tight sheath. But he was mollified when she turned to face him and he glimpsed the caring in her expression. "She's gone?"

Christian closed his eyes. "When I was a kid I used to be scared every time she left for work that some burglar or some lunatic she pulled over for speeding would grab a weapon and kill her. But she died in the hospital under a surgeon's knife. From cancer."

Mystic nuzzled into him. Her hand stroked his back. "Did she know what you were?"

Christian rubbed his cheek against her soft hair. "No. I could never tell her."

The link between them opened and he shared some of his memories with Mystic. They were treasured images of his mother laughing and smiling, of approval and love shining in her eyes as she'd watched and teased and encouraged him as he grew up.

"We were close. It was just the two of us. Despite the fact she was a cop, she wasn't rigid in her thinking. She wasn't someone who only believed in the things she could see with her eyes."

Christian tensed and rolled to his back. He pulled Mystic on top of him, nudged her thighs apart and lodged his cock inside her. He needed to anchor himself with the hot feel of her, in the reality of having a mate, before he delved further into the past.

"There was a redneck who wouldn't leave my mother alone. A guy named Jimmy. He was total scum. One of those guys who thought anyone who wasn't one hundred percent white meat was fair game for whatever fun he had in mind. He harassed Mom every chance he got. He came close to stalking her but not close enough to get arrested for it. There were a couple of rapes in nearby towns — mixed-race women like my mother was. No one could pin them on him though I think plenty of people guessed it was him. A couple of times I found beer bottles and cigarettes in the woods near our house, like he'd been camped out there, watching us, watching her."

Christian's grip tightened on Mystic. She was afraid of what was coming but she didn't shy away from it. She didn't flinch. *If it's easier, you can show me rather than tell me.*

He laughed but it wasn't a happy sound. "The words are less terrible." He hugged her tightly, as if he wanted to pull her inside himself.

"I was thirteen when I changed the first time. Thirteen and completely clueless. Unprepared and scared shitless." He took a deep breath. "I was like a top with razor-sharp edges that someone wound up and then let go. If I'd been sixteen, even eighteen or twenty, like most mixes are when they change for the first time, maybe I could have…controlled the situation. Maybe I could have changed the outcome. I didn't stand a chance."

Christian's lips sought Mystic's. He needed to lose himself in her warmth and softness for a while before he could continue.

"Jimmy's scent was around our house. His piss and semen. Like he'd marked his territory and jerked off in the woods while he watched my mother. I hunted him down and ripped him to shreds. I don't remember doing it but I know I did. I woke up covered in his blood and vomiting out the parts of him I'd swallowed.

"I washed in a creek and went back to the house but not before I saw the dog prints and a few strands of long black hair, longer than I've ever had. I took the hair and made sure I didn't leave any human tracks. Somebody found him later that day. Nobody was particularly sorry about his death.

"For the next week hunters crashed through the woods, drinking and shooting at anything that moved. All of them were looking for either a wolf or a huge dog."

"My mother didn't say she was glad he was dead but she was relieved. I couldn't tell her what I'd done, why I'd done it, how I'd done it. And even if I had, even if she'd somehow managed to accept and adjust to what I was, she was still a cop who took her job seriously."

Mystic leaned down and kissed him. His confession widened the road his earlier actions had carved to her heart. The bond forged by the Angelini magic, the need to touch and mate, to be with one another was already strong. She could sense his desire—or the wolf's—to have children, to form a pack. But where earlier it would have terrified her and made her instinctively fight or flee, now it somehow felt...right, natural.

She hadn't wanted a Were mate. She had dreaded the possibility of being immersed in pack politics and a pack lifestyle which would be overwhelming and confining after the upbringing she'd had. Now, touching her mind to his, her heart to his, seeing his memories of his mother and knowing that his choice of work, being a cop, was because of her, Mystic could only agree with the mate thrust on her by the Angelini magic. He was acceptable to her. Very, very acceptable.

Christian laughed and rolled so Mystic was underneath him with his cock still in her channel. "And my mate is very, very acceptable to me," he said before his mouth covered hers and his tongue twined and rubbed against hers.

Mystic wrapped her legs around his waist in response. Her arms went around his neck. She held him tight as his thrusts became more urgent, more demanding, as his body imprinted itself fully on hers.

His scent and taste filled her, invaded her as thoroughly as his cock. She moaned as he claimed her as completely as she'd claimed him. Only this time their joining was driven by human emotion instead of Angelini magic or animal urges.

Chapter Five

ം

Gabrielle found a pad of hotel stationary and scribbled a note for her brother. She left out the details of *where* she was going but she *did* include the news about Mystic finding a mate—one who would also be hunting for the Weres who'd killed the vampire.

If she was really, really lucky, she'd be back before he woke up and realized she had the Jeep. But if he did wake up, she hoped he'd stay in the hotel room and wait for her to return with more information about Mystic, her new mate and the search for the rogue Weres.

She'd secretly hoped Hawk was one of Mystic's mates. She'd almost been sure he was. Of course, he might still be one of them since Angelinis always took two mates.

Gabrielle shivered as she thought about the repercussions of this adventure. A Were and a policeman, she didn't think that could be a good combination. Pack members almost always lived close together and worked in businesses owned by the pack. Rarely did they work for humans in a human-run organization.

Unless they were outcasts. Or loners. Or had been sired by a loner or outcast on a human female and hadn't yet joined a pack.

Gabe growled, making Gabrielle start. She turned to look at him but he rolled over, grumbling in his sleep.

It wouldn't be long now before he was awake. She probably had just enough time to get to Fangs and find out more about Mystic's mate.

Gabrielle cringed. She didn't blame Mystic for what had happened. They'd all been anxious to turn over the wallet to someone else. And who would have guessed Mystic would find a mate in Las Vegas?

Sure, Gabe had joked about Mystic finding mates and getting hitched in the chapel of Elvis. But if he'd had any idea his joke would become a reality, he would have turned the Jeep around and headed straight to the Howl.

The Zevantis were responsible for Mystic. They were linked to the Renaldis by blood-ties that went back for centuries.

If Mystic ended up with a Were mate who was truly a loner, an outcast, or a renegade, then the Zevantis would feel the sting of shame. And she and Gabe would pay for it—if they survived Hawk.

This time true fear rippled through Gabrielle. She didn't doubt for a minute Hawk was hunting them. He'd made it very, very clear. He intended to be one of Mystic's mates.

Gabrielle left the note for her brother and slipped from the room. It took only a few minutes to learn the address for Fangs and get directions. When she got there she had to park the Jeep several blocks away and walk.

She was surprised to see the long line of people still hoping to get inside the club. They snaked through the parking lot, drinking, laughing, some sitting on jackets as though they already guessed it would be a long time, if ever, before they joined the lucky ones who were inside. It made her laugh. Humans! Who else would wait in line and pay to serve as food and entertainment for vampires?

She and Mystic had cruised through several vampire chat rooms on the Net after Mystic's parents mentioned Fangs while discussing Falcone's sire. But even knowing what to expect, Gabby still found the sight in front of her amazing.

Every human was dressed in black. Some had gone so far as to paint their lips and nails in the same color.

Most sported silver jewelry. And more than a few had cosmetically extended then filed their canine teeth into sharp points.

Gabby ran her tongue over her own very humanlike canines. When she was in her fur, the teeth were essential and her muzzle accommodated them, but in her human skin… She shook her head, amused, amazed, enjoying the adventure—until she remembered the purpose of her visit. Then uneasiness returned with a jarring crash.

She needed to find Mystic. As much as she hated the thought of doing it, she knew she had to convince Mystic to take her new mate and return to the Howl before there was trouble.

Several of the humans whistled at Gabrielle as she passed them. She went directly to where a gorgeous human with long black hair guarded the entrance.

His eyes narrowed slightly when she stopped in front of him. His nostrils flared, taking in her scent—or more likely, feeling the brush of a supernatural's aura against his skin in the same way she felt his tie to a vampire along hers.

She didn't think he was a vampire slave or a companion. And for a moment, she was distracted by him. She'd never been interested in humans, but this one… Even with only one form he was as alpha as any wolf. It oozed from him. It rubbed over her body and stroked between her legs.

One corner of the human's mouth curled upward in an arrogant acknowledgement that he knew his effect on her. Gabrielle ground her teeth together. Her lips pulling back slightly in a silent warning even as her vulva continued to swell and grow slick.

Something moved through his eyes. It made her shiver and wonder if he was a vampire's companion after all. Involuntarily she glanced at his neck. When she didn't see a medallion her stomach tightened at the thought of him being a slave.

"What's your name?" Gabrielle asked, unable to stop herself.

"Altaer. And yours?"

"Gabrielle Zevanti."

"What brings you here? Your kind doesn't usually come to places like this one."

* * * * *

Gabe barely had enough time to shower, dress, find the note Gabby left and start wondering what he should do before all choice was taken from him. He opened the hotel door, intending to get some breakfast, only to find himself on the floor with Hawk's booted foot on his chest.

"Where is she?"

Gabe didn't pretend Hawk was looking for Gabby. He grimaced and the gesture pulled his lips back in a small show of teeth that was the wolf way of saying, *I know you're alpha and can kill me. Please don't.*

The weight on Gabe's chest grew heavier in silent threat. The expression on Hawk's face was equally full of menace. "Where is she?" he growled, impatience written on every line of his body.

"I don't know, but I can guess."

Gabe's eyes shifted to the bed where he'd left the note. He desperately hoped Hawk would take the hint and read the note for himself. He did *not* want to be the one who had to tell Hawk about Mystic finding a mate.

For a long minute the room remained deadly silent. Gabe didn't twitch. He tried not to breathe.

Finally Hawk took his foot from Gabe's chest and walked to the bed. Gabe stayed where he was. He figured it was safer that way.

He wasn't an alpha. Hell, he wasn't even close right now. And even if he had been, he'd have thought twice about taking

Hawk on—especially when it came to Mystic. He did not have a death wish, ergo, he intended to do nothing that might draw Hawk's attention back to him at this particular moment in time. And if he was very, very lucky, he might just live long enough to one day joke about this.

Hawk growled as he read the note. His fury and frustration raged alongside his sense of urgency and panic.

She'd found one of her mates!

The second would follow quickly. Rarely did much time elapse between the claiming of Angelini mates.

"Get up," he said, wanting to rip Gabe apart for his part in helping Mystic escape. "Take me to where the vampire died."

* * * * *

Roman parked in front of Fangs. His eyes went automatically to the human women still waiting in line. His cock stirred, more out of habit than true desire.

There would be no other for him until he found his mate. There wouldn't be any satisfaction in fucking anyone else, not now.

Mystic. He was sure she was the one he needed to find. Her name whispered through his veins along with the ancient vampire magic and the ghost wolf he'd gained from Syndelle's blood.

He was no friend of the Angelini, save for Sabin's Coronado wife, Richelle. He was no friend of the vampire, despite centuries of being one and despite the fact that only the truly ancient remembered what he had once been.

He'd once been nearly a god to the shapeshifters, not only because of his form, but because he'd been created to destroy vampires and he had done his job well. Back in those days of wild magic and grim survival, all the supernaturals had loathed and feared the vampire. Why wouldn't they? Given a choice between feasting on a mortal or a supernatural, no vampire would pass up the opportunity to gorge on magic-rich blood until nothing remained but an empty husk. The death of their victim was like an after-dinner drink of the best cognac.

Roman ignored the flirtatious looks of those who waited to get into Fangs. His footsteps slowed when he caught sight of the woman talking to Altaer. She was small and beautiful, dark and deadly. She was a lithe predator who was out of place here, as out of place as he would be if vampire magic didn't claim the part of him that took a human shape.

Altaer's question reached him, echoing his own. "What brings you here? Your kind doesn't usually come to places like this one."

The female Were hesitated before answering. Her reply was cautious with so many humans present. "I'm looking for a friend of mine. She has no tattoo but she is a Renaldi and Gian is the sire of her father, Falcone."

Mystic. There was only one child from Falcone's Angelini union.

Pure joy raced through Roman as he glided to a stop next to the female Were. The lion and eagle pressed against his skin. They wanted to acknowledge and be acknowledged by this shapeshifter, the first they could truly greet after centuries of having only the memory of a form, and even then, a combined one. But Roman held that part of himself back. The instinct for survival urged him to move cautiously, if not for his sake, then for Syndelle's.

Even knowing who he had once been, all would wonder how he could now be both shapeshifter and vampire. And there would some, ancient vampires, shapeshifters, and Angelini, who would consider that only the return of the old magic could make it possible.

"Has Mystic been here?" Roman asked, watching as the Were's eyes widened in surprise.

Altaer smiled slightly and stepped away from the door to allow Roman to pass. "Gian's inside."

Gabby felt reluctant to enter Fangs but she was honest enough with herself to admit the reason for her reluctance had everything to do with Altaer and nothing to do with being afraid of supplying some vampire with a meal. Her stomach tightened as she forced herself to move through the door. Her cunt clenched in protest as she forced herself to stop thinking about the human with a vampire blood-tie.

Since she didn't know what Gian looked like it was easier to let the blond vampire lead the way—and probably safer. Gabrielle shivered as she felt hungry eyes follow her. Belatedly she wondered if stepping into the club made her fair game, of a sort.

They skirted the dance floor then moved along the bar, toward a private area. Six people stood talking around a table. Four of them were human though three were young, barely legal. Two were supernatural, a vampire and an Angelini woman. Surprise hit Gabby when the Angelini turned toward them and she saw there was no tattoo.

The golden vampire glided to a stop. His eyes swept over the three young humans before meeting the other vampire's. Something passed between the two men before the dark vampire smiled and gently sent the young humans on their way.

Gabby focused her attention on the Angelini female. She felt a burst of shock when the introductions were made. The Coronado line was as old as the one Mystic came from.

Her attention shifted to Gian and her heart fluttered slightly. Maybe Mystic could ask Falcone's sire about... Gabby grimaced. *About a human with a blood-tie to a vampire?* Hah. Her pack would probably hunt *her* if she dared to mate with anyone other than a Were.

With few exceptions, the Renaldi Angelini being one of them, only couplings between full-blooded female Weres and males capable of changing form produced female Were offspring. So pure females were a prize not to be wasted—especially on a human.

Gabrielle shivered as she realized that once again her thoughts had drifted from her purpose in coming to Fangs. Her stomach tightened and she wondered if this was how it had been for Mystic when the Angelini magic presented her with a mate.

Gabby forced herself to meet Gian's gaze. "Mystic called and said she'd been here. She said she'd found a mate, a Were who is also a policeman, someone known to you."

"Augustino?" Roman said, his voice a soft, menacing growl.

It was Skye's human mate, Rico, who answered. "What's this got to do with you, Roman?"

The air around them vibrated with tension as Roman gathered his control at being confronted so soon with the fact he would have to share Mystic. His mind had known it but the deepest part of him, the part created gryphon railed violently against the idea of sharing its mate.

He closed his eyes and let the ancient vampire magic that was both Syndelle's gift and curse seep further into his soul. He let it invade a place he had always kept protected, secret.

The magic was icy hot. Its purpose and will spanned all eternity. But rather than rush in and try to overtake the part of him that was also ancient, it swirled around the gryphon's ghost like a dense fog. It whispered a dark promise that the future was vast, and better things awaited if this path was taken.

The beast shrieked in a piercing eagle's cry even as its chest vibrated with a lion's roar. But in the end it yielded and was seduced by what was to come. It accepted that it would share Mystic.

Roman opened his eyes. He offered his hand to Skye and dropped some of his mental barriers. His smile was genuine when she took his hand and gave a small gasp, recognizing her sister's blood and magic in him.

"I visited with Syndelle. Your sister thinks Mystic Renaldi might be my mate."

This time it was Gabrielle who couldn't suppress a gasp though hers was one of distress. Hawk's features rose in her mind. *Could it get any worse?*

As quickly as the question arose, she suppressed it for fear of bringing more trouble for Gabe and herself. Their great adventure had rapidly become a nightmare from which she wasn't positive she would ever emerge—much less survive.

Skye's human mate narrowed his eyes while her vampire mate grinned. Gian's eyes danced with amusement and anticipation. But it was Rico who spoke, his frown and tense features indicating where his loyalty was just as clearly as his words did. "If you want to find Augustino and Mystic, then have Gabrielle take you to where they found the dead vampire. Wait for them there."

Roman nodded. He accepted Rico's unspoken warning not to look for the Were and Mystic until after they'd finished mating. It would be foolish to barge into Augustino's territory.

Roman wrapped his hand around Gabrielle's arm. He felt her resistance to helping him but he didn't intend to let it stop him.

"Shall we go?" he asked in a soft purr, reminding himself that she was a friend of his future mate's and needed to be treated accordingly.

Gabby's stomach roiled as Roman led her to the door. Her spirits lifted slightly when Altaer momentarily blocked their way. But then he stepped aside as if he'd received a silent order to let them pass.

She couldn't stop herself from glancing at him once she was secured in Roman's car. The vampire's laugh made her blush and look away.

"Do you often court trouble, little wolf?"

His words made her curious. "What do you mean by that?"

Roman's teeth flashed as white as a wolf's. "Altaer is the scion of Sabatino Licata."

Gabrielle shuddered. Only ancient, old-world vampires used scions. The majority of vampires lost interest in their mortal descendents, especially after several generations had been born and died. The vampires they themselves created became their children, their family. Most had changed with the times and preferred to have companions or humans they could control through blood and money.

Disappointment crowded through her despite the fact she'd been trying to ignore her interest in Altaer all along. Now she knew without a doubt it would be insane to couple with him, even casually.

Altaer was the oldest still-human member of Sabatino's family. He was human now so he could see to whatever family business needed to be taken care of during the daylight hours. But eventually he would become a vampire himself, his destiny determined by a relative who'd been dead centuries upon centuries before Altaer's birth.

"Where to?" Roman asked, interrupting her thoughts.

"Do you have a cell phone?" Gabrielle countered, thinking of her brother.

Roman indicated the glove compartment. "In there."

Gabrielle retrieved the phone and punched in the hotel number only to find Gabe wasn't there. She grimaced. So much for their great plan to delay trouble by getting throwaway phones in Vegas and leaving theirs at home so they couldn't be contacted and ordered back by pack members. With a sigh Gabby left Gabe a message telling him where she was going, but leaving out the part about Roman—at least for now.

* * * * *

Mystic slid from Christian's car and stretched in the near-dawn light. A small feminine smile formed as her body reminded her just how thoroughly she'd been mated. The smile widened when Christian moved around to her side and pulled her against him.

He was aroused. Again.

It was good timing. So was she.

Mystic twined her arms around his neck and rubbed her pelvis against his erection. She stood on her tiptoes so she could tease his lips with her own.

His laugh was husky, satisfied, utterly masculine. It curled deep in her belly and made her womb flutter and her cunt clench.

His tongue licked along the seam of her lips. It teased hers to come out and play.

Mystic shivered. She could feel her labia swelling, parting in invitation. It wanted Christian's kiss just as much as her mouth did.

She sighed softly and pressed more tightly against him. He groaned and deepened the kiss.

His hands roamed over her and pulled at her shirt until he could touch her flesh. They didn't stop moving until his fingers found her tight, hard nipples.

When the need for air drove them apart, Mystic laughed. Her cheeks flushed as she said, "I guess I'm more like Estelle than I knew."

Christian's eyebrows rose in question.

"My mother," Mystic said and the color in her face deepened. "Let's just say she's gotta have it."

Christian laughed softly. His palms rubbed over her nipples. His mouth went to her neck and trailed kisses down to the spot where he'd marked her.

Mystic moaned when his teeth gripped her flesh and sent a jolt of searing heat straight to her clit. "I need you again," she whispered.

"Take off your clothes."

Lust moved through her at his confident command. There was a hint of dominance and dark anticipation in his tone. She shivered. She'd do what he told her to. She'd do so much more if it would entice him to mount her again.

Christian loosened his arms and she stepped back. There was little chance of another car coming down this remote road but she looked around anyway. For a minute her thoughts returned to the Zevanti compound and Hawk, to the Howl she would have been at tonight if she hadn't escaped with Gabe and Gabby.

Nervousness found a familiar spot in her stomach and settled in. Christian's lips once again trailed along her neck. His teeth nibbled at her skin until he found his mark and clamped down, tighter this time, a male's hold on his female. *I'll take care of you, Mystic. Always.*

She pressed against him, wrapped her arms around his waist and enjoyed his scent, his heat, his protectiveness—his underlying possessiveness. She let the newfound closeness with him chase away her worry.

When the last of her anxiety had faded her hands lingered for a minute. They smoothed over the hard muscles of his back before dropping to his jeans-covered ass, his hips, and around to his abdomen. Her fingers hooked in his waistband and wiggled against his rigid stomach muscles.

Christian growled, a playful sound that made her laugh and look up at his face from underneath her eyelashes. In that instant she wondered why she'd ever thought she wanted sex without a bond, why she'd ever thought she wanted to avoid taking a mate.

She wriggled her fingers again, dancing them teasingly against his flesh until she encountered his penis. It was full and hard and wet.

His cock jerked in greeting. It brushed itself against her fingers.

Mystic smiled when Christian growled again. Despite his earlier command to take off her clothes, she dared to unsnap his jeans and lower his zipper. Her own need to be mounted gave way temporarily to the desire to explore her mate as thoroughly as he'd explored her earlier.

Heat blossomed in her cunt at the sight of his erection. Desire spread like a wolf stretching.

Her breasts grew heavy and her nipples ached. She wanted to rub against his cock. She wanted to lick and suck and pleasure him with her mouth until he came.

Mystic looked up at him from underneath her lashes again. Feminine satisfaction filled her at the sight of his face and the need she saw there. It echoed her own. Amplified it.

She gave in to temptation, sank to her knees and nuzzled his cock. Her cheek brushed against his penis as her mouth sought the mating mark she'd left on his inner thigh. She knew from her own marks just how sensitive the area was, how sensitive it would be from now on. It was an erogenous zone created to enhance the bond and he shuddered when she licked over the bite, teased it with her tongue.

Christian's hands tangled in Mystic's hair. He fought the urge to force her mouth to his cock. He fought to keep from shaking with the desperate need whipping through him. She was burning him alive, making him almost crazed with lust.

A moan escaped and his breath came in panting gasps. "Mystic." It was more a rumble than a word, more a plea than a command.

He felt her smile against his skin. Then her teeth clamped down on his flesh in a reclaiming that made him cry out.

Fierce emotion surged through Mystic as Christian's penis pulsed violently against her cheek. She'd intended to explore his cock, to lick and tease, but now she wanted to eat him up. She wanted to claim him completely. The intensity of his desire and pleasure were flooding their link and ratcheting up her own need. She bit him harder then released the grip on his inner thigh and turned her head.

He bucked when she took as much of his penis into her mouth as she could. He shuddered as she used her hands to manipulate the shaft, to control the depth of his thrusts. He growled as she cupped his heavy testicles and kept him from orgasming while she laved, and sucked, and hungrily pleasured him.

The wildness inside her grew with each of his panting grasps for air, with each of his groans and growled commands. She fought him when he tried to wrench her away from his cock. She thrilled at how he fought himself, torn between the desire to lean her over the hood of the car and thrust into her sheath or to experience the exquisite pleasure of coming in her mouth.

Feminine power swelled inside her, ancient and primitive. In this wild, wicked dance she and Christian were equal partners though one could choose to lead and the other to follow. In that moment she chose to lead, to take him over the edge and hear his cries of release.

* * * * *

Gabe briefly considered delaying the impending confrontation by "getting lost" on one of the nameless, deserted roads that crisscrossed desert and wooded area alike. But loyalty to his pack and an unexpected sympathy for Hawk prevented him from doing it.

He grimaced. Like Hawk needed his sympathy.

If anyone needed sympathy it was Gabby and him. They were going to be in a shitload of trouble over this—even if Hawk succeeded in becoming Mystic's mate.

Gabe shifted uncomfortably in the passenger seat. The silence in the car was getting a little hard to take. He was used to Gabby's chatter and the teasing they directed at one another.

Hawk hadn't spoken more than a handful of words since they left the hotel room. But unfortunately everything Gabe could think of to talk about led back to Mystic and he was *not* going to speak her name out loud. He was already sweating bullets, *silver* ones.

What if the Angelini magic didn't choose Hawk? What if Mystic had already found a second mate? *Could it get any worse than that?*

As quickly as the question arose he suppressed it. He knew the answer to that one.

Oh yeah, it could get worse. Then he'd be lucky if his own pack didn't kill him and give his fur to Mystic's grandparents for use as a doormat.

Chapter Six

ဢ

Gabrielle didn't bother to hide her curiosity. She shifted position so she could openly study Roman's profile. The longer they were in the close confines of the sports car, the more obvious it became that he was unlike any vampire she'd ever met.

That was saying a lot. Because of her friendship with Mystic, she'd met more vampires than most Weres.

Gabrielle could sense Roman was ancient. She could tell his power was immense. But every time it brushed against her, it felt like a shapeshifter's aura. It made her think of a giant purring cat weaving around her, friendly at the moment but capable of ripping her into shreds without warning.

Uneasiness chased Gabrielle's curiosity away. Dread filled the place where it had been.

Her mind wandered through the conversations she'd had with Roman since he stuffed her into his sports car. They'd talked about the vampire in the woods to begin with, but in the end they'd talked about Mystic.

Gabby grimaced at her own inability to keep her mouth shut. He'd drained almost every drop of information from her and at the moment she was starting to feel as hollow as a human whose blood was the main course at a vampire's feast.

She was tempted to divert him down one of the unnamed barren roads. She considered delaying the inevitable, but she didn't. Strangely enough she'd come to like Roman and see him as worthy of Mystic.

That was a dilemma. This disastrous adventure had rapidly turned into a test of her loyalties to her pack and their alliance through blood to the Renaldis.

Hawk wouldn't have been invited to the Howl if the Zevantis hadn't wanted him as one of their allies. In fact, her own parents had made it very clear to her that *they* welcomed his interest in Mystic. And then there was the small matter that she'd also thought Hawk would make a good mate for Mystic. She still did.

Gabrielle sighed and the car filled with the sound of her uncertainty. Who could have guessed their trip to Vegas would turn out like this?

Roman laughed. The young wolf was well named. He'd never know a Were to talk so freely or so much! But during the course of their drive he'd become fond of her—not just for the information he'd gained about Mystic but because Gabrielle was without artifice, without any agenda other than that of a loyal friend.

True, she'd told him much about his future mate. But she'd done so with the idea of helping him to be the mate she thought Mystic deserved. She'd given him insight and gentled him without even knowing she was doing it.

Mystic. Roman's heart ached to find her. His body ached to claim her.

He'd assumed she'd be as fierce as Skye Coronado but now he knew she was no hunter, at least not yet. It surprised him how glad he was that her fathers were vampires and her parents had chosen to raise her outside of the pack. It would make the transition for all of them easier.

He'd lived too many years as a vampire to be completely welcomed by the Renaldi Angelini and their werewolf allies. And he was still a vampire—though one like no other thanks to Syndelle.

Feelings of love and loyalty for Syndelle swamped Roman. He didn't fight them as they moved through him, swelling and receding like the ocean's tide, the ancient magic whispering without words until Gabrielle's nervous fidgeting turned his attention to her. "We're close now?" he guessed, anticipation filling him when she nodded.

"It's just up ahead." She bit her lip and he almost laughed at how difficult it was for her to *not* speak what was on her mind.

"Something troubles you?"

"We're a long way from any buildings. The sun's going to come up soon. The woods aren't thick enough, or at least they weren't for the other vampire." Her eyebrows drew together. "You're really, really old. I can tell though I can't tell exactly how old you are. But I've always heard the older a vampire is, the longer they suffer if they get caught out in the sun. The longer it takes—" *to die.* "It was really horrible hearing him scream and Mystic said he was just a fledgling."

Roman was touched by the worry in her voice. He couldn't stop himself from taking her hand though Gabrielle jumped with nerves when he did it. "I appreciate your concern, little wolf, but I'll be fine."

"How can you be so sure?"

"Because I am not *only* a vampire." He brought her hand to his lips and pressed a chaste kiss to it. "You will see for yourself and I think your pack will overlook your stealing away with Mystic once they know I consider you a worthy friend."

Gabby frowned. His words held the weight of importance. A memory fluttered at the edge of her consciousness, tantalizing but illusive. She sighed again, frustrated with herself. Politics and pack history held zero interest for her—which made her an odd wolf. Almost all of the Weres she'd grown up with were far more serious students of the supernatural world than she was. In fact, the only one she could think of who was *less* interested was Gabe.

The thought of her brother focused her awareness on him. He was close and getting closer.

Her stomach lurched as she wondered whether or not he was alone. She prayed he was but feared he wasn't.

They weren't close enough for their thoughts to touch. By the time they were it would be too late if Hawk was with him.

Gabrielle shivered. Her mind scrambled to think of a way to avoid what she feared was coming—a fight to the death between Roman and Hawk.

She'd never heard of such a thing between prospective Angelini mates. But among wolves it happened though the pack elders did their best to prevent it.

"Mystic might not be the one for you," Gabby blurted out when the tension inside her grew beyond what she could contain. "Maybe it would be better to meet her for the first time at Fangs—give everyone a little breathing room. Plus Gian would be there, and Skye…"

Menace moved through Roman as he picked up on Gabby's growing uneasiness. A lion's rumbling growl escaped and the little wolf next to him jumped in her seat and edged closer to the door.

"I will not kill her other mate," Roman said, thinking perhaps that was the source of Gabby's anxiousness. But her body only tensed further, warning him there was something more, something she hadn't told him yet.

Roman slowed the car as he considered what he should do. In the past he would have thought nothing of simply pinning her down and trapping her in his gaze in order to take what he wanted from her mind.

She was young and no match for him. No shapeshifter was though the most alpha among them might need to be weakened first by the taking of their blood.

But Mystic would learn what he'd done to her friend and… A laugh escaped. Not even mated yet and already he wished to avoid the wrath of his Angelini mate!

"You're worried about something?" he said in a soft purr, though he was unable to keep the hint of compulsion from his voice.

Gabrielle closed her eyes and concentrated on keeping her mouth shut. Her fear had been justified. She didn't need to feel Gabe's presence or hear his words in her mind. She could see the car's headlights in the side view mirror and tell Hawk was with him.

In a few more miles they would all be at the spot where they'd parked the Jeep to take a break—only to have their worlds turned upside down by the howl of werewolves and the scream of a dying vampire.

What should we do? Gabrielle asked. Her heart thundered so loudly in her mind it was hard to hear Gabe's answer.

What can we do?

* * * * *

Mystic reluctantly put her shirt on, buttoning it over flesh still heated from the hard fuck her mate had given her as she leaned over the hood of the car. She smiled when Christian chuckled and pulled her against his naked body.

"I wouldn't mind seeing you run through the woods without clothing," he said as he nuzzled the side of her neck.

She wrapped her arms around him and pressed close. She was amazed at how quickly she'd come to need the feel of his skin against hers along with the sound of his voice and his touch. She held him for a moment, soaking in his warmth.

Christian's fingers stroked down her spine. They traced each vertebra and made her shiver. Her vulva grew swollen in anticipation of another sexual encounter.

"The sooner we hunt, the sooner we can devote ourselves to nonstop lovemaking," Christian said.

Old feelings of being less than what the other Renaldis were assailed Mystic and chased away the warm glow of heat. "Are you going to shift?"

"Curious to see how large I am in my other form?" he teased.

Mystic buried her face against Christian's shoulder. "I think you might need your wolf's nose to backtrack the path Gabby and Gabe and I took. I won't be able to find it."

Christian's heart exploded with warmth at her admission. He rubbed his knuckles against the smooth untattooed skin on her neck. "You haven't been trained as a hunter?"

She gave an embarrassed laugh. "I can dance, mix drinks, play hostess, manage the music and even sing along with a band—all the things necessary for a good party, but— No. My parents haven't had time to instruct me in other things, in the things most of the Renaldis know."

"I will teach you. I will take care of you—always." He lifted her face and lowered his, kissing her softly at first—an affirmation of his promise, then harder, more aggressively—an affirmation of his pledge.

Mystic settled into him. She felt loved and cared for in a way she'd never known before, in a way that made her want to cry and laugh at the same time. If she never took another mate, she would be content with this one. And yet even as she thought it, the Angelini magic stirred deep inside her and Christian tensed. He lifted his head, suddenly alert to danger.

She heard the approaching cars. They were out of sight, blocked from view by trees, but the sound of them carried well in the still, night air.

Mystic's thoughts merged instinctively with Christian's. His mind was already busy computing the odds and trying to determine what the best course of action was in order to keep her safe.

If she'd been a hunter or a wolf then the decision would be easy. They'd go into the woods. Since she was neither,

Christian was afraid it would make her harder to protect if the cars approaching held the Weres responsible for the vampire's death.

Before he decided which course of action to take, Mystic knew one of the cars contained something much more difficult to deal with. Her body tightened and her heart raced in her chest. The need to couple unfurled along with the awareness that her second mate was approaching.

Christian growled in reaction. It was an unhappy, threatening sound as he released her and pulled on his jeans.

Mystic's breath shortened with fear when he opened the car door and retrieved a gun holster. He fastened it over his naked chest, checked the gun before retrieving a second one from the locked glove compartment and slipping it into the waistband of his jeans. The smell of silver bullets burned Mystic's nostrils.

"Get in the car," Christian said, his words menacing and possessive, his wolf nature not ready to accept what his human mind already had—that he *would* share his mate with another.

"Christian…"

His feral gaze halted her words. She quailed under the force of his will until something shifted inside her, firming into a resolve she'd never had to use before.

She was no match for him if she threatened him directly. He was more wolf than man right now, his blood running hot, his mind raging with an alpha's claim to keep its mate for itself.

Instinctively Mystic dropped her eyes. She looked at him from underneath her eyelashes. Her body went soft and she moved into his personal space, filled it with her own heat and scent.

You promised to keep me safe but you can't protect me from this, Christian, not without hurting me in the process and perhaps destroying me. You can feel the Angelini magic as well as I can. There's no denying it.

His lip lifted in a silent snarl and his eyes flashed dangerously where only moments earlier they had been full of amusement and warmth. *Who is he?*

Mystic cocked her head. She listened as the two cars approached. She knew one contained Gabby and one contained Gabe. She had a blood bond with both, a pact forged long ago by cutting across their palms and clasping hands in a custom found even among human children.

It was enough of a link to tell when they were near or if they needed help, but it wasn't strong enough to exchange information without the spoken word. "I don't know," she said though the image of Hawk rose in her mind and Christian growled again, a deep, menacing sound that moved along her spine and filled her heart with dread.

In the distance the first car came into sight. Mystic's stomach roiled. Her thoughts spun backward to the previous day when she and Gabe and Gabby had been standing in this same spot as the sun rose, listening to the frustrated yips and howls of Weres followed by the scream of a hunted vampire.

She could feel the dawn on her skin now. The prickly awareness was something she'd gained from Falcone and Yorick. She realized a part of her had secretly hoped for at least one vampire mate. It somehow seemed traitorous to her parents to end up with two Were mates—just as her often disapproving and rigid grandparents had planned when they used her parents' absence and the Angelini gathering as an excuse to send her to the Howl.

The Angelini magic grew stronger, more compelling as the car neared. There was no denying it. In the long history of their race there had never been a choice as to what the Angelini were—hunters, guardians. There had never been a freedom to take any mate but the ones chosen by the magic.

The heat inside Mystic continued to build and pool in her vulva and breasts. There was no fighting it, no suppressing it.

There was no choice but to yield to the desire and accept the mates the magic called to the bond.

She closed her eyes and bowed her head. She concentrated on the link with Christian and willed him to feel what she felt, to accept what she had to accept.

For several long seconds Christian fought the magic flowing through his bond with Mystic. The wolf thrashed wildly against it. The man argued he was all she needed. But even as the car moving toward them pulled to a stop several yards behind his own car he knew he'd lost the fight.

The passenger door opened first. Gabby shot out of the sports car and distracted Mystic though she felt Christian's shock and recognition as the name *Roman* moved along their link.

Her attention swung back to the driver's side and her heart lurched when she saw the man who was already out of the sports car and moving toward her. *Vampire.* And yet the prickling along her skin argued he couldn't be. The sun's first rays were only moments away now.

Mystic couldn't look away from him as he closed in, moving with a vampire's gracefulness. His power hit her first. Ancient. Older than her own fathers', older than any vampire she'd ever met, save Brann, the vampire council's executioner, the sire of her father's sire, who she'd met only once, when she was a small child.

Awareness pulsed through Mystic along with heat and longing. She shivered and fought the urge to move toward Roman, to rub against him in greeting, to touch her mouth to his and taste him.

His gaze locked with hers. Fear burst through her when she saw the cold flame of a vampire's life force and will dancing deep within his pupils. "The sun," she gasped and felt his smile all the way to the depths of her soul.

Tenderness rushed through Roman along with the beginnings of love. Her first concern had been for his safety.

He stroked along her soft cheek. His body raged with the need to claim her. His mind knew these early moments of give-and-take, of accommodation were a necessity, a time well spent—especially between Detective Christian Augustino and himself.

"I'm not as other vampires are," Roman said. He already felt the hint of a link with Mystic, Syndelle's blood recognizing Gian's blood.

Reluctantly he shifted his attention to the armed Were. The scent of silver in one of the guns burned Roman's nostrils. He lifted an eyebrow and decided on humor though the beast would have been pleased to rip his opponent to shreds.

"Are you thinking to challenge me to a duel? Or do you favor a shootout like those of the Old West?"

Before Christian could answer, the small wolf grabbed Mystic's arm and pulled her away. It was a pointless exercise. Her whispered words were as loud as a shout. "Gabe's got Hawk with him."

Mystic's heart jerked with fear. Christian and Roman tensed automatically. They turned their attention to the approaching car. Their resolve to guard her was written on every line of their bodies.

She pushed through the fear and reached for Gabrielle's hand, squeezing it. Her grip was reassuring and pleading at the same time, silently conveying the message that it would be up to them, and Gabe, to keep this from turning into a bloodbath.

Gabby's fingers tightened on Mystic's in solidarity before Mystic moved back to Christian's side. Mystic curled her fingers around his arm then reached out to touch Roman for the first time.

Her palms burned where skin met skin. The fear in her chest was equaled only by the heat in her belly and the ache in her cunt—the Angelini need to claim a second mate.

Hawk emerged from the car almost as soon as it stopped. Mystic's fingers tightened on Christian and Roman. Shock and confusion nearly overwhelmed her when her body reacted to the sight of Hawk just as intensely as it reacted to Christian and Roman.

Gabe was close behind Hawk, his face strained, his eyes worried as they swept over Roman, Christian and Hawk, before meeting Mystic's gaze.

"Move away from them, Mystic," Hawk growled, his tone possessive and commanding, as if he were *already* her mate.

Something stirred deep inside Mystic. It uncurled along her spine and gave her the courage to let loose of Roman and Christian. Before they could stop her she stepped forward and put the palm of her hand on Hawk's chest.

She met Hawk's gaze boldly where before she'd found his presence overwhelming and his interest in her unnerving. His nostrils flared and his eyes darkened at the touch of her hand and the magic that whipped between them.

Mystic licked her lips, wetting them in a nervous gesture. "No fighting. It's not the Angelini way."

Hawk's face hardened. "Most think the Renaldis are more wolf than Angelini. Fighting for a mate *is* acceptable under our laws. I will be your second mate, Mystic. I would have been your first if you hadn't run away."

She bristled at his charge. "I didn't run away!"

"You knew I intended to claim you. My mistake was in giving you time to get used to the idea and accept what your body already did. If I'd mounted you when I had the chance you would already know you belong to me."

His words rang true but she didn't let them distract her from her purpose in confronting him. Her fingers tightened on his shirt. "I am not like most of the Renaldis. I can't even shift form. I can't even tell whether it's you or Roman who is supposed to be my second mate."

The vampire's power brushed against her like a giant, predatory cat. "If you are uncertain then I have no problem with fighting this Were for you. Let the victor claim you as his mate."

"No!" The thought of it horrified her. "I won't accept another mate under those conditions!"

Christian moved to her side then. He pulled her into his arms with her back pressed tightly to his front. The feel of his guns against her added to her anxiety.

I'll take care of you. We'll find a way to resolve this without bloodshed, he soothed along their link though she could feel what it cost him to say it. She could sense the pleasure the wolf inside him felt at the thought of both the other men being mortally wounded so there would be no second mate.

"No fighting," she repeated.

The first of the sun's rays hit them. It broke the tension as they automatically shifted their focus to Roman and watched in disbelief as he stood in the daylight.

He lifted his face toward the sky. His eyes closed as though he couldn't stop himself from offering up a prayer of thanksgiving.

"What the hell are you?" Gabe murmured, awed.

Gabby moved closer. She dared to touch Roman. "You don't feel like a vampire now. You feel like a shapeshifter."

Knowledge skittered along Mystic's nerve endings, just out of reach. It was chased by Christian's curiosity and suspicion.

"You weren't able to walk in the daylight before, Roman," her mate said.

At the sound of the name, Hawk stiffened. "Roman?"

The vampire opened his eyes. He met Hawk's gaze. Curiosity replaced the challenge that had been there only seconds before. "You've heard of me?"

"If you're the one once known as Gaius Cicero, and before that as Korak, then yes I have heard of you."

Gabby and Gabe both gasped. Even Mystic felt a jolt of awe, though almost immediately Christian's irritation and confusion at being ignorant seared down their link.

She rubbed against him in an offer of comfort. Then she swiftly sifted through her memories, the lessons in the classroom as well as the tales told by her grandparents, and shared them with her mate.

To hear my grandparents speak of him, until Korak met a fate almost worse than death—and became a vampire—he was beyond compare. He was a universal hero shared by all shapeshifters.

Consternation and incredulousness flowed back to her from Christian along with images of Roman as *he'd* seen him— commanding a table at Fangs and surrounded by blonde, interchangeable humans with long legs and large breasts.

Uncertainty filled Mystic at the sight of the women Roman had called to himself. They were nothing like her. The old, familiar dread resurfaced, of being wanted not for herself but because of what she was.

It will be okay, Christian said. A part of him found it hard to believe he'd been forced into this role, into soothing his mate and helping her accept another male. Yet to feel her insecurity and vulnerability was even worse.

I didn't grow up in your world, Mystic. But what I've observed from watching Gian with his Angelini mate, and Brann with his, the magic that draws the individuals into a bond does so for a purpose and the choices seem right for all involved. Isn't it that way for the Angelini you know?

Mystic's first thought was to wonder what purpose could possibly be served by mating Estelle with Yorick and Falcone. But somehow she couldn't picture her mother with any others but those two, and not just because she loved her fathers.

The same was true of her grandmothers and her aunts. Even *she* had found it true when it came to Christian. Few of the Angelini could claim to be *in love*, as humans so often professed to be, when they first joined, and yet it was more than just an animal instinct to couple that brought them together and kept them together.

The bond between mates, the shared thoughts and memories, the intensity of the physical union made it impossible *not* to feel deeply, not to feel emotions beyond what could easily be held in such a small word as love.

Mystic turned in Christian's arm. She was grateful for his presence and his shoring up of her confidence, especially when she knew he'd prefer there be no other mates at all.

She circled his neck with her arms and pulled his head down for a kiss. The others were entirely forgotten as soon as his lips covered hers and their tongues dueled. The heat and need between the two of them quickly filled the air with the scent of heady lust.

Mystic moaned in protest when the kiss ended and Christian lifted his mouth. Gabe snickered and said, "This is a first. I never thought I'd see the day when the Milk-Bone got munched on with an audience present."

"Don't call me Milk-Bone," Mystic said automatically, turning, her gaze traveling to Hawk and Roman. Kissing Christian had only intensified the need to claim a second mate. But the physical craving made no distinction between the other two men. She shivered as she realized there was no choice but to give them both the opportunity to be with her. She had to leave it up to the magic to choose between them, to lock one or the other of them into her body and claim him in the way of the Angelini.

Mystic licked her lips nervously. She let Christian read what was in her mind before she spoke it out loud. He tensed. He protested. But in the end he had no choice but to agree. In the end he locked his guns back in his car. He shifted into his wolf form then set off toward the vampire's burial spot with Gabe and Gabby.

Chapter Seven

଼ଇ

Nervousness made Mystic stumble as they moved into the woods seeking a place that would grant them some privacy. Hawk and Roman steadied her automatically. Their hands on her arms sent a shock of heated need through her. Their touch intensified the fullness between her legs as blood pooled in her labia. The rub of her jeans and panties against her swollen folds made each step part of an erotic journey.

Anxiousness filled her when they came to a spot that looked as if it had been made for what they intended. It was a place of deep shadow and thin rays of sun, a place that smelled of nature's own hidden magic.

Mystic's stomach tightened. She took a step backward though her cunt and the Angelini magic protested her sudden reservation and her worry that she'd made a mistake in suggesting this, that it might yet end in bloodshed and death, in a guilt she'd carry with her for the rest of her life.

Roman took his shirt off and spread it on the ground. Hawk did the same.

Her heart sped up at the sight of them standing side by side. Together they were like day and night, Roman's skin warmed and golden for a life begun under a shapeshifter's sun, Hawk's darkened for hunting in the light of the moon.

Mystic licked her lips in a nervous gesture that brought their sharp focus to her mouth. Part of her wanted to turn and run, to escape, but the other part wanted to be captured and mounted.

She took another step backward. She wasn't sure she could go through with letting them both have her.

Hawk fought his instincts to pounce and force his mate into submission, then fuck her until her whimpers turned into howls of ecstasy and her fear turned into searing, insatiable desire. Every cell in his body knew she was his. But the kiss she'd shared with the other Were, the cop, was burned into his memory. Witnessing it made him realize he *still* needed to proceed cautiously with Mystic.

He'd seen how she responded to Christian. The wolf inside had howled at the sight of her softening in her other mate's arms, soaking up his confidence and reassurance. The man had protested the knowledge Mystic and Christian were already deeply bonded.

He couldn't risk she'd find him too rough by comparison, too primitive. Yet deep inside the wolf dreamed of the day when Mystic would take her other form and he could rut on her in a way that had nothing to do with emotion and everything to do with creation.

Hawk's hand went to his jeans-covered cock. Mystic's gaze followed, sending a roar of blood to a penis already close to exploding. When she didn't look away he unzipped the fly before kicking off his shoes and stripping out of his remaining clothes.

He let her see what she did to him and thrilled in the way her nostrils flared and her eyes dilated. His cock bobbed in greeting when he took a step forward.

"Come to me," he ordered. The wolf was willing to keep chasing her as it had been doing since the first moment it saw her, but the man wanted her to admit she was attracted to him.

His cock head beaded with arousal when she licked her lips nervously and took another step backward. A low growl sounded deep in his chest as the rest of Roman's clothing fell to the ground and her attention shifted to the other man's cock.

Roman could barely think of anything but getting Mystic out of her clothes. He wanted to explore her body with his hands and mouth. He fantasized about pinning her wrists to the ground while his cock tunneled in and out of her. He could almost taste her cries of pleasure as she locked him deep inside her channel and orgasmed repeatedly.

For centuries he'd taken human women to his bed. He'd preferred them tall and blonde and well endowed, interchangeable, their conversation nonexistent or non-important. No more. None of them warranted even a footnote in the centuries-old text of his life. Against Mystic's dark, exotic looks, they were pale ghosts of what a woman should be.

Mystic. Her name prowled through his heart and soul. It coursed through his veins and commanded his cock.

The lion's growl answered Hawk's wolf challenge.

Both of their beasts were still willing to fight to the death in order to claim this Angelini female. But when Mystic retreated again, fear and worry in her eyes, it was the men who pushed past their animal instincts and stepped forward in silent truce. Without needing to speak they both knew there'd be no winner if they continued to allow the most primitive parts of themselves to rule.

"We'll be good from now on," Roman teased, his fingers settling lightly on Mystic's spine and stopping her from moving further away from them.

She shivered at Roman's double meaning. Her gaze went to Hawk's face when he took her hand and urged her forward, back to the spot where their shirts were spread out on the ground in a gentlemen's gesture.

"It will be okay, Mystic," Hawk whispered.

The husky sound of his voice curled in her womb and shredded her resistance. She didn't protest when the fingers of his free hand made quick work of unbuttoning her shirt.

A moan escaped when his palm slipped under the parted fabric to cover her hard, tight nipple. Her face flushed with heat and a little embarrassment at yielding so easily, but there was no fighting the need for their touch.

Roman's free hand stroked over her belly in a caress that made her clamp her legs together. He laughed, a wonderful, satisfied sound.

Mystic turned her head and met his eyes. He leaned in and covered her lips with his. His tongue stroked into her mouth, offering seduction instead of domination, the kiss so mesmerizing she barely noticed when Hawk stripped her of her clothing.

Hawk went to his knees and buried his face in Mystic's cunt. His hands went to her hips to hold her so she couldn't escape his mouth and tongue. At the first heady taste of her he knew he was lost.

The scent of the other Were was on her but even that didn't diminish Hawk's hunger. If anything, it fed it, made him more determined than ever to mate with her.

He'd accepted from the first moment he'd seen her that he'd have to share her. Even the wolf had come to terms with it, both of them knowing she could not deny her Angelini heritage.

In the beginning it had been about taking a mate and forming a pack. But as Hawk's tongue fucked into Mystic's channel, as her scent filled his lungs, she became the only thing that mattered.

His cock strained to reach her. It bumped against his belly and wet it with arousal. It demanded he pull her down to the ground and mount her, that he rut on her until his sac was empty of seed.

Hawk growled against her cunt. He wanted to swallow her down, to consume her.

Mystic clutched desperately at Roman as Hawk's tongue invaded her. She bucked when he sucked on her clit and sent fire streaking upward to her nipples.

Roman's tongue thrust against hers. She cried in his mouth and felt dazed by the dual assault, by the need coursing through her.

She didn't resist when Roman eased her down to the ground. She didn't protest when he pinned her wrists above her head with one hand and captured her breast with the other. He tweaked and tugged at the nipple until she was arching, desperate for the feel of his mouth suckling her in time to Hawk's assault on her cunt.

Blue fire. Eternal vampire flames burned in the centers of Roman's pupils when he lifted his face. "Please," Mystic whispered, lost, panting, her mind racing toward the erotic flickering deep in his eyes.

Her blood burned in recognition. Her body craved Roman's bite as desperately as her pussy tried to hold Hawk's tongue in its depths.

Mystic tilted her head back in an offering of her throat and Roman knew she did it freely, not because of vampire enthrallment or even because of the Angelini magic. She was reacting to their touches, their attention. She was responding to the feel of their lips and hands worshipping her and paying homage to the beauty they found.

"Mystic," he said, his mouth taking hers again.

He swallowed her moan and gave her one in return when his fangs descended and she stroked them with her tongue, explored them. She was careful to do nothing but caress them until her lower body began to thrash under Hawk's assault on her cunt. Then she grew careless and scraped her tongue over the sharp point of a fang, bled as she arched upward and sobbed, orgasm shimmering through her.

Roman had to take his cock in hand in order to keep from joining her in release as her pleasure flowed into him with her blood. Even if he'd wanted to, he wouldn't have been able to resist the intoxicating lure of Mystic.

He held her tongue prisoner until the sensual throb of her pulse became a siren song he couldn't ignore. With a groan he relinquished her mouth in order to claim her neck.

Vampire, man, beast, all of them roared in victory when he bit her. He marked her as both vampire and Angelini blood demanded, knowing even as he did it that Hawk's face had turned into her inner thigh. That the Were was also biting, claiming her, giving her the first mating mark.

The shadow wolf that was Syndelle's blood gift rose in Roman. It bristled for a moment at Hawk's mark, but then accepted the interloper, chose to see him as a pack mate who would be an equal instead of an adversary.

In centuries of existence Roman had never encountered an Angelini with more than two mates. But he didn't question the ancient vampire magic whispering to him as it had earlier, telling him the future lay in this direction.

He fed, not only on Mystic's blood but on her lust. He filled himself with it as his cock throbbed painfully against his palm.

Roman knew the instant Hawk left her thigh and kissed his way up to her breast. He felt the moment when Hawk began suckling, sending streaks of white-hot pleasure through Mystic's nipples. It was enough to make Roman sheathe his fangs and seal the bite so his mouth could capture her other nipple in a carnal competition to see who could give her the most pleasure, before working in cooperation to make her scream for them both.

There was no fear for the future in Mystic's thoughts. No guilt. No confusion. There was only exquisite sensation and breathless need as the rhythm of their sucking became synchronized and their hands worked in tandem between her thighs, fingers pressing into her weeping slit, fingers swirling over her engorged clit.

"Please," she begged, needing them to finish marking her so she could do the same to them, wanting them to plunge their cocks into her channel and fuck her. The Angelini magic crouched deep inside her like a wolf waiting for the right moment to spring.

Hawk felt the wolf inside her. It howled and writhed with the need to be covered by its mate. Its desire was a thick, erotic musk that swamped his senses.

He lifted his face from her breast. He wanted to see the wolf looking out through her eyes. But despite how intensely he felt its presence, it remained hidden in Mystic like a cub not yet ready to leave the den.

For the moment it didn't matter. Her wolf would come to his call in the future. It would uncurl and take form so they could run together, hunt together, bond in their second form.

Hawk took her nipple in his mouth again. He caressed it with his tongue before moving to the place over her heart and biting down, giving her the second mating mark.

Something had changed with the first bite. The wild desperation, the fear he would lose her to Roman as well as to the other Were had given way to confidence. Mystic would be his.

Hawk kissed his way up to her neck and covered the place where Roman's fangs had penetrated her. "Please," she whispered, tilting her head back.

He could feel how much Mystic's hidden wolf wanted a show of strength and dominance by its mate. He growled in response, allowed some of his weight to settle on her.

When she whimpered and shivered he wanted to close his eyes and cover her completely. He wanted to wallow in her softness and the heady scent of aroused submission.

The Angelini magic was like a hot breath across Roman's body. It was so close to the surface it threatened his control. It made even the shadow wolf press against his skin along with the eagle and lion. All of them wanted to bask in the power and bathe in the heat. All of them urged him to mount her, to fuck his cock in and out of her channel until she locked him in her sultry depths and made him come repeatedly.

"Finish it," Roman said, freeing her wrists and moving a short distance away, allowing Hawk sole possession, sole access to Mystic's body.

Hawk needed no further urging. The wolf howled in victory even as the man accepted the unspoken terms of Roman's concession—that he would soon have to relinquish Mystic and watch as another took her and tried to coax the Angelini magic into making him her mate.

When Mystic's fingers tangled in his braids and guided his mouth to hers, Hawk gladly took her lips. He shared the taste of her passion as well as her blood with her.

His tongue dueled with hers. Sliding. Twining. Conquering.

He shuddered and thrust against her mound and belly as he fought the desperate need to plunge into her wet slit. With a growl he ended the kiss and pressed his neck against her lips. He rubbed his pulse over her mouth.

"Bite me," he commanded, his voice deep, rough with anticipation.

Mystic bit him and with the first taste of his blood the Angelini magic rose like a fever inside her. A growl vibrated in her own throat and she would have joked as she always did, to hide the pain of having no wolf, but the fire streaking from her cunt to her nipples made it impossible.

When Hawk eased backward, moving into a crouch and guiding her to her knees, she went willingly though she didn't release her grip on his neck until his fingers speared through her hair and urged her mouth to his chest.

The magic roared in an unstoppable inferno when his heart beat against her lips. *Hers.* He would be hers, bound to her with unbreakable chains, first of passion and then of love. The sharing of their bodies and blood was only the prelude to a sharing more intimate, more complete than any other—the sharing of heart and mind and soul, and with it the absolute trust that came with knowing another thoroughly and being known in the same way.

"Mystic," Hawk growled and she bit him. She felt the wildness inside him, the wolf crouched there, ready to pounce.

Hawk lifted his face to a sky partially blocked by the canopy of trees. Every muscle in his body was taut. His balls were pulled tight and his cock strained, ached, wept.

He wanted to howl but feared he would be reduced to whimpering. His buttocks clenched and his lungs labored to gain enough air to sustain him.

A constant growl resonated in his chest. It grew deeper as her mouth traveled downward.

He could sense Roman's presence. It brushed against him like another wolf, not a subordinate but an equal.

It was impossible for Hawk to care. He couldn't focus on the other male as Mystic nibbled over his abdomen, as her tongue reached the tip of his penis only a second before her lips did.

Hawk jerked. Panted. He nearly curled over and lay along her back. The image of doing so, of nuzzling and caressing her smooth, dusky buttocks as he fucked her mouth was an unbearable temptation.

He might have done it if he hadn't caught Roman's movement at the corner of his eye. He spared a glance and saw the vampire's rigid features, the blue fire dancing in his pupils, flickering in time as Roman's fingers gripped and stroked and pumped at a cock darkened and flushed with need.

Hawk knew that whether he came in Mystic's mouth or her channel, as soon as the last of his seed escaped, Roman would no longer be content to wait. The vampire would strike. He would bite Mystic and be bitten. He would shove himself into Mystic with ruthless intention and if Hawk were foolish enough not to mount her first, then Roman would do it. But even knowing what was at stake, Hawk didn't force Mystic's mouth to his inner thigh.

He closed his eyes and allowed her to explore his shaft with her mouth. He shuddered under the exquisite lash of her tongue then cried out when she took him into her mouth, his hips dancing in shallow thrusts as she sucked him.

"Mystic," he groaned, not a command but a plea.

He felt her satisfaction, her feminine pleasure and pride through the link created by the mating marks they already shared. With a husky laugh she released his cock. She teased over the tip before turning her face into his inner thigh and biting him.

The sting of erotic pain was enough for Hawk to take control. He tumbled her to her hands and knees. His hips bucked when she willingly parted her thighs, the sight of her swollen labia and glistening slit nearly driving him into a frenzy.

He wanted to feast again. He wanted to bury his face against her wet flesh and spear his tongue into her sheath but the wolf inside him had reached the limit of its endurance.

Hawk mounted her. He shoved his cock all the way into her channel in a single hard thrust.

At the Zevanti compound he'd fantasized about taking her virginity, about having to fight her inner muscles and claim her inch by inch. But now, as the need to mate rolled over him and the flames of the Angelini magic seared him, he no longer cared that another had taken her before him or that another would take her after him. All that mattered was the exquisite sensation coursing through his penis and balls, up his spine and straight to his heart.

The tight, wet heat of her was enslaving. The knowledge he would never know another female's body, would never want to because everything he could ever desire would be found with his Angelini mate, filled him with contentment.

With the first stroke there was no room for further thought. There was only fierce desire and overwhelming need.

Hawk's hips pistoned. Hard and fast.

His breath came in pants. His moans formed a chorus with Mystic's cries.

He kissed her shoulder in the place where her other mate had already bitten as he took her. He licked over the spot, nuzzled it, gave her gentleness before giving in to instinct.

Hawk didn't fight the wolf or his own nature. He clamped down on the tender skin, held her in place and felt her yield completely, open for him in a way only an Angelini female could do.

She accepted him, claimed him for her own. The tight ring of muscles deep inside her channel locked the head of his penis in her depths and triggering orgasm after orgasm, milked him of his seed in one lava-hot rush of ecstasy after another until he was weak, sated. Hers.

It surprised Roman how much he wanted privacy for what was to come. He'd been alive for centuries. He'd lived in times when debauchery was an art form and there were few limits set on behavior, especially for one such as him. He'd shared women more times than he could remember. He'd eaten grapes fed to him by slave girls as women pleasured each other, along with the men who gathered for sexual entertainment.

Later, he promised himself. Later there'd be time for just Mystic and him. There'd be time to linger, to play, to slowly explore each other, to come together in an intimacy shared by only the two of them. For now he needed to finish what had been started. He needed to mark Mystic and be marked in return. He needed to claim her while there was a window of opportunity to do so, while the magic and her other mates were willing.

Roman wedged his hand between the Were's body and Mystic's. He ignored Hawk's growl and pulled Mystic to him, under him. His lips captured hers. His fingers tangled in her hair.

The blood link between them was enhanced by what he'd gained from Syndelle. It was already strong enough for his mind to touch Mystic's so he could share his desire to have her to himself, to pleasure her in a luxurious bed and become lovers before yielding to the Angelini magic and becoming mates.

Mystic's heart warmed with the words and images Roman whispered in her mind. With a thought she told him she understood the need to finish this now. She told him there would be time for romance later.

Despite having two mates already she wanted him as well. She felt the rightness of joining with Roman. She didn't doubt his cock would become locked in her body when he fucked her, that their lives would become inextricably joined.

She didn't understand how it was she could claim three males. But she had been taught from childhood to accept the Angelini magic and yield to its choice of mates.

A small laugh escaped. Was it only yesterday when she'd fled the Zevanti compound, intent on having an adventure as well as avoiding taking even a single mate?

Roman's chuckle rumbled down her backbone and curled in her pussy. *And now you find yourself saddled with not one mate, but three. The burden will be ours to convince you we're worth the loss of your freedom.*

She smiled against his lips. She nibbled at the bottom one, suddenly grateful to have a mate who was less intense than the Weres.

Not a mate yet, he reminded her.

You will be.

She felt his smile against her senses.

Only time will tell whether you consider me a less intense mate, he joked as he lifted his face so their eyes could meet.

The sight of the erotic, blue flames in the center of his pupils both aroused and comforted Mystic. Once he might have been a legend among the shapeshifters, but now he was also vampire.

Bite me again, she whispered in Roman's mind, wanting to experience again the ecstasy that came when he pierced her with his fangs and took her blood.

I will bite you for each time you bite me, he teased, brushing his mouth against hers before licking over the well-marked place on her neck.

He rolled to his back, taking her with him so she sprawled across him. The heat in her cunt spiraled outward. It pulsed through her belly and breasts.

Mystic's lips tingled and her gaze went to his smooth, unmarked neck. She couldn't tell if it was her heartbeat or his that thundered in her ears.

His cock jerked against her abdomen, marking her with arousal wherever it touched. *Do it*, Roman said, need replacing the humor in his voice.

Mystic leaned in and licked his tanned flesh. His skin tone was lighter than Christian's or hers, was almost pale against Hawk's darkness.

She nibbled at Roman's neck, feeling playful until Hawk growled and she became aware of his searing gaze. Her pussy clenched in reaction. No wonder her mother often wore a satisfied expression after spending time in bed with both her mates.

It was darkly erotic to touch one mate while the other watched, forbidden to join in. Not for the first time, Mystic wondered if perhaps she was more her mother's daughter than she'd thought.

She gripped Roman's neck in her teeth and felt his pleasure, his satisfaction, his craving for not just a mate, but for her. She also felt the extent of his need and how desperately he fought to remain in control of the beasts that lived within him.

The place where he'd already made inroads into her heart expanded when she felt how much it had cost him to allow Hawk to take her first, how hard Roman was fighting to give her memories that were more than just a rough claiming.

We've got a lifetime to make other memories, she said, wanting to free him from the cage he'd placed himself in as she gave him the first mating mark then kissed downward and gave him the second and third.

Nothing in the centuries of his existence had prepared Roman for the lust the Angelini magic inspired. Even before Mystic released his inner thigh, Roman's reality had narrowed to the wild roar of blood rushing through his cock and heart and soul. Each pounding beat called only one name, demanded only one thing. Mystic.

He bit her as she'd bitten him. He marked her as she'd marked him. But when she would have rolled to her hands and knees, the man he'd become prevailed over the beast he was.

"No," Roman growled, positioning her underneath him and piercing her with his cock.

In this he would be different.

Roman sealed her mouth with his and gave in to the siren song of Angelini magic. There was no resisting its call. There was no fighting the need to plunge in and out of Mystic's sheath until the deep, hidden place welcomed him, held the tip of his penis prisoner as each instinctive jerk to free himself sent lava-hot semen rushing through his cock instead.

He gave himself up to the pleasure, to the bond. She would become his vampire companion but that was a matter for another time. For the moment his heart soared and his soul felt complete. After centuries of being alone, he had a mate.

Chapter Eight

ɷ

The trail leading to the buried vampire was easy enough to follow, which was a good thing, because even in his wolf form, Christian found it hard to concentrate. Every instinct in his body screamed for him to turn around, to go back and rip the other two males apart in order to prevent them from mounting his mate.

Gabe and Gabby ran behind him, perhaps providing a barrier out of loyalty to Mystic, or more likely, not wanting to get in his way and feel his wrath. Regardless, their presence on his heels and the need to lead kept him moving forward.

He stopped only long enough to take a quick sniff of the buried corpse. At this point the driver's license Mystic and her friends had retrieved was more important than what Todd Moore smelled like.

Christian hoped Moore's license was valid. He hoped the identity was real. The last thing he wanted was to be forced to return and exhume the remains in order to take fingerprints and look for dental records.

He'd like to find out about the victim and how he'd ended up on the wrong end of a hunt without having to provide a body and open an official investigation. It would be better for all concerned if this matter could be handled among the supernaturals with minimum involvement of humans. There was no telling where Moore's vampire lifestyle would lead or who it would expose.

It troubled Christian that the wolves who'd hunted Moore hadn't bothered to look for his corpse. He wondered if it meant they'd been lazy and careless, perhaps overconfident, or if it meant they thought a vampire would disintegrate completely in the sunlight. The answer would have told him a lot about where to look for the Weres who were responsible.

There was no trace of any scent at the scene of death save the ones which belonged there and those of Mystic and her friends. Christian glanced at Gabe for an indication of which direction the howling had come from. The other wolf pointed his nose forty-five degrees to the right and wagged his tail slightly. Christian set off, loping easily through the woods, enjoying the run despite himself.

He'd been trapped in the city too often lately. He'd buried himself in his work. Now he realized why. He'd been lonely.

Vegas was a city of tourists, dreamers and losers. It was a city of glitz and false hope with a dark underbelly of despair and degeneration.

On the surface it had suited him. Easy women, casual hookups to scratch a need that came less and less, plenty of work to keep him from noticing the lack of a family other than the cops he worked with, the lack of mate, the lack of anything to tie him in one place and say *home*. Now the word home and mate and Mystic were interchangeable.

Images of her being mounted by other men once again drew his attention away from the trail he was following. Christian growled deep in his throat and forced his thoughts back onto the matter at hand.

The wolves had given up their chase of the vampire a long way from where the hunt ended with the rising of the sun. Christian stopped when he got to the place where three different scents mingled, two male, one female.

Gabe shifted form and said, "I smell three of them here."

Gabby followed suit. She stood and stretched in her human form. "It was over quickly but it sounded like there were at least four wolves hunting." She shrugged, extending the movement into a roll of her shoulders. "There might have been more. As soon as the screaming started they stopped yipping and howling."

Christian shifted form and gave the other two a cursory look. Both of Mystic's friends were lean and fit, completely comfortable with their nudity as a result of growing up in a pack.

He was older now, self-confident, but he'd only rarely run alongside other wolves. The part of him raised human always took a second to adjust, to shut down its learned modesty.

Even though they were still in a wooded area Christian could feel the ascent of the sun. "I can run a little longer before I have to head back. I've got to go to work. If the wolves set Moore free at dark and ran him until sunrise, it could take all day to find the start of their hunt."

Gabby frowned. "Do you think they started from a house? Or are you thinking they parked along some deserted road?"

"I'd guess they hauled their victim out here by car or truck. But at some point they were human. Those are the scents I'm most interested in."

"So you can start trolling through wolf haunts in Vegas?" Gabe asked.

"Yes, unless I find out the driver's license was old and Moore had moved on to another city. He might have been involved with werewolves somewhere else, or maybe pissed off some vampire with connections to these Weres."

"How likely is that?" Gabby asked.

Christian shrugged. "It's an angle that needs to be covered."

Gabe nodded. "So you're a cop?"

Christian looked at him and wondered where the conversation was heading. Any number of times he'd found it dicey dealing with a Were from a pack. He suspected Gabe's pack was an old, well-established one or they'd never have been entrusted with Mystic's care. His gaze dropped for an instant to the brand above Gabe's pubic hair but the symbols were meaningless to him. "Yeah, I'm a cop."

"Do you like it?"

"Yeah. I like it."

"Even working for the humans?"

"Is it so different than working for pack members?"

Gabby snickered. "It's probably better to work for humans. Unless you're alpha, working for the pack means you not only get ordered around all day long by those with higher status, but when you get together at night, you *still* get ordered around by them, along with their mates and sometimes even their adult children."

"So don't work for pack members," Christian said, knowing how impossible it was even as he said it. There was no separation of home life and work life when you were part of a pack.

A knot tightened in his stomach as his thoughts flashed to the two men who were fucking Mystic. Roman he could deal with. But what if Hawk turned out to be her second mate?

Christian shuffled through the memories Mystic had shared with him and saw the other man's brand. It was different than the one Gabe and Gabby wore.

"Tell me about Hawk," Christian growled and the tension ratcheted up when he saw Gabby's instant nervousness.

"Do we really have time for this?" she asked. "Shouldn't we be trying to find where the hunt began?"

Christian didn't want to let the subject of the other man drop. But Gabby was right. If they didn't keep going then the only thing to come of this trip would be the knowledge Mystic had fucked two other men and he'd lost his claim as her sole mate.

They shifted into wolves again and ran. A short distance away they encountered the scent of two additional males, then much further they found the place where the five wolves had joined up with two more, a male and a female.

Christian shed the wolf's body in order to study the ground with his human eyes. His wolf smelled blood and fear, traces of urine along with the unmistakable scent of sex.

Gabe and Gabby continued to sniff the area for several minutes. Then Gabby plopped down to wait while Gabe became human and walked over to stand next to Christian.

"Weird," Gabe said. "Neither female is in heat but the males fought about something then all of them fucked one of the females. Maybe that's why they didn't catch the vampire before sunrise, they got sidetracked."

Christian found himself smiling. It felt good to have a nonhuman to discuss the scene with, one with the same acute senses as he had. "That's one way to read the situation. Here's another. Five Weres raced ahead, two hung back. Maybe the two who hung back are weaker pack members and can't keep up. Maybe they're scared and don't want to have anything to do with actually killing a vampire. Either way, the five frontrunners are frustrated and pissed at losing their prey. They meet up, come back, and when they get to the two stragglers, the fur flies. The omega male gets rolled and bitten. The female gets mounted whether she wants it or not."

Gabe nodded. "Submissive pee. Blood. Sex. That'd cover the smells here. But taken all together, in this situation, it's way, way more human than wolf, even if everybody's in fur."

Christian had wondered as much but he couldn't fully interpret the scene. He had no frame of reference other than what he'd read about wolves in books. He had no experience with pack life or pack dynamics, and even then, since Weres were neither completely wolf nor completely human, he assumed their culture and behavior were a hybridization. "So you're saying something about the scenario is off for a Were pack?"

Gabe rubbed his brand in an unconscious gesture. "Yeah, here's the thing. Weres are as obsessed with lineage and history as the Angelini are. If you ask Mystic she would be able to tell you the name of every Renaldi ever born. She could also tell you in excruciating detail more history than you'd care to know and she's not even an *A* student." He grimaced. "Unfortunately, Gabby and I have been called *weak links* more than once by pack historians. We are more like *F* students."

In response to Gabe's statement, Gabby lifted her muzzle and howled, the final notes wobbling off as if she were snickering—or choking up. Gabe's laugh answered the question in Christian's mind though the other man's amusement quickly faded into a serious expression.

Gabe waved his hand over the ground where the Weres had fought and fucked. "The dynamic is all wrong. Having two Were females here and fucking one of them… This could be a lot worse than just a bunch of rogue wolves hunting a vampire for sport."

Christian wanted to howl himself. He didn't have a clue what Gabe was getting at but he guessed it must have something to do with pack lineage since Gabe had started the conversation off by mentioning it. "You want to translate that into something I can understand?"

Gabby shifted into human form. "What my brother is saying is there are no outcast female Weres. A pack would kill a female before she was allowed to leave and breed with either a human or a Were who wasn't acceptable. The packs are like the Angelini in the way they guard their females." Gabby grimaced. "Trust me on this. If I don't end up a skin on someone's wall when we get back to our compound then I'm going to end up under some bitch's thumb and never out of her sight until a wolfie mate comes along."

Surprise kept the usual burn of anger from settling in Christian's gut. With the Weres it always came down to pack. Whether it was by choice or birth or exile, a man without a pack was an object of contempt. It was one of the reasons Christian had little contact with Weres who wore pack brands.

"You're serious?" he asked Gabby. He wondered if it was because he was Mystic's mate that they were so open with him but he hoped it was something more, a camaraderie that would extend into friendship.

"Completely," Gabby said, "which brings us to the other part of what Gabe was getting at. There are two options here since all of them were wearing their fur. The first is they're young members of an established pack who came to Vegas for a wild night on the town."

"But there's a huge problem with that scenario," Gabe said. "The females would be under the protection of mates or male relatives. If you're right and the lead wolves came back pissed off and took it out on the two weaker wolves, then beating the male up, yeah, that's wolfie if he's Omega, but ganging on a female and sharing her..." Gabe shook his head. "I'm not saying it absolutely couldn't happen but we're not programmed that way, especially when we're in our wolf form and the female's not in heat. Even during a Howl when everyone is pretty much a horn-dog, only mated pairs go at it in their fur."

"Which leads to option two," Gabby said. "Some of the Weres, the females in particular, are made and not born. Maybe that'd explain why they smell...different...off somehow."

Gabe nodded. "Yeah, maybe. I thought I was imagining things. Figured if they actually ate the vampires they hunted it would account for the smell."

Christian's first reaction was, *Now they're shitting me.* It passed when he saw how both Gabe and Gabby were touching the brands above their pubic line as though they were instinctually seeking reassurance they didn't have to be afraid because they had pack to back them up.

"Are we talking *Werewolves in London* remade into *Werewolves in Vegas*?" Christian asked, keeping it light in case his gut was wrong and they were playing with him. He hadn't been around enough wolves to make a judgment about the smell of the ones they were tracking.

"Here's where hanging out with *A* students would do you a lot more good than hanging out with Gabby and me," Gabe said, cracking a small smile. "A better understanding of history and lore would come in handy right now. What I know is this, there was a time when humans were turned, or at least the ones who survived being mauled by pure Weres were. But it's been outlawed for centuries. The survival rate is low. And besides, it's not as easy to get rid of the bodies of the ones who don't make it as it was in the past."

Christian felt his gut tighten. Fuck. Being a cop in Vegas was tough enough with the down-on-their-luck players, the lowlifes and the human predators, now he had Were-Vampire shit on his plate.

He glanced at the height of the sun and wanted nothing more than to escape responsibility and take his new mate back to bed. "Let's see if we can find where this hunt started."

* * * * *

Mystic sat on the hood of Roman's sports car. She alternated between scanning the tree line and glancing at Hawk and Roman. They were leaning against Hawk's car, discussing history and giving her some space. Not that her body wanted distance between them. She ached to lean against them and soak in their warmth through her skin.

It was the thought of Christian that had driven her out of their arms and out of the woods. Rationally she knew he was going to have to see her naked between Hawk and Roman's bodies. Emotionally she wanted them all clothed when he returned to find out he had to share her with two other men, not just one.

No doubt her grandparents would be pleased, extremely pleased by Hawk and Roman. They might even be able to overlook her inability to shift to a wolf and the fact she'd managed to flout convention by taking a lone wolf as a mate. Mystic grimaced. Not likely. She knew better than to hope they'd see her as worthy of bearing the Renaldi name. She'd long ago given up trying to gain their approval.

Her eyes traveled down Hawk's body and up Roman's. Both men were looking at her, smiling in satisfaction.

Mystic's heart turned over in her chest. She had them. She had Christian. She had Gabe, Gabby and her parents. It was crazy to focus on grandparents she couldn't change when she had others in her life who accepted and cared about her.

Her gaze returned to the trees in the distance. She could feel Christian drawing near along with Gabby and Gabe. She slid from the hood of the car and landed on her feet just as the three wolves emerged from the woods in a lope. Happiness rushed through her at the sight of them. Seeing her friends running in their fur always made her smile but seeing them with her mate as though they were one pack made her heart expand with pleasure.

The wolves shifted form as soon as they reached the cars. Mystic went immediately into Christian's arm.

Home. As soon as Christian held Mystic against him he felt complete. Even the scent of Roman and Hawk and the unmistakable smell of sex didn't diminish the wild rush of joy and pleasure crashing through him.

He took her lips and never wanted to free them. He thrust his tongue against hers and desperately wanted to shove his cock between her lower lips.

For long moments Christian lost himself in his mate. She became his only reality until the need for breath finally ended the kiss.

He lifted his face and met her eyes. He could feel the wild tangle of her emotions as she clung to him. The bond between them was wide open and he knew with a thought he could see what had happened while he hunted with Gabe and Gabby. He didn't need to. He could feel her link with both Roman and Hawk.

The wolf had known even as it loped to where Mystic waited. Neither man had been touching her but both of them radiated possessiveness. Both of them stood with the confidence of the undefeated.

Christian wanted to rail against a fate that had given her to him then forced him to share her with two other men, but he couldn't. Her concern over his reaction, her worry over causing him pain left no room for anything in his heart but tenderness.

It's okay, he whispered along the bond. It had to be. There was no other choice.

"Did you find where the hunt started?" Mystic asked when she finally pulled from Christian's arms and reclaimed her seat on the hood of the sports car.

Roman and Hawk came to stand on either side of her. As Gabe, Gabby and Christian dressed, they described what they'd found.

Hawk's response was immediate. "Mystic needs to be returned to the Zevanti compound where she can be kept safe until we know what's happening here."

His words had a predictable effect. Roman and Christian stiffened while Gabby snorted a laugh and Gabe grimaced.

"No," Mystic said. Excitement and trepidation spun wildly in her chest, along with something else, a feeling of independence that made her almost lightheaded. She was no longer an unmated female subject to the protections and restrictions of Were, vampire and Angelini culture.

"No," Mystic repeated. She wrapped her legs around Christian's waist and her arms around his then pulled him backward so his buttocks leaned against the car and his body served as a shield. "I may not be trained as a hunter but I'm not going to be sent away, Hawk." Her chin lifted. "Gabe and Gabby and I could have stopped to stretch our legs a hundred other places. But we stopped here. I think there's a reason for it. I should already have a hunter's tattoo. This is meant to be my first hunt."

The responses from Hawk, Christian and Roman were entirely predictable and completely negative.

"No."

"No."

"No."

Mystic didn't bother to argue. She opened the mental link and let them feel the surety she'd felt as soon as the unplanned words left her mouth. The Angelini magic had brought them together for this very purpose.

All three men growled in protest. But all three accepted this was the price they had to pay for gaining the mate they'd each wanted.

"Are you going to try again to track the wolves back to the place they shifted form?" Mystic asked Christian.

"Not today. I've got to get to the station. I've got other cases going, important ones I'm close to wrapping up. Plus I want to find out what I can about the dead vampire." He glanced at the sky. "There's a chance it'll rain later. Most of the time it's not enough to destroy a trail but..."

Gabe said, "Gabby and I can come back. We need to get something to eat first and sleep for a while, but if we could find one of the roads we just crossed while we were tracking them and park there, we'd gain back some of the time by not having to start from here."

Hawk growled, a low frustrated sound. "I'll go with Gabe and Gabby. We can't risk that it'll rain and we'll lose the track. If we can find the place where the vampire was freed and catch the human scent of the wolves then it'll be easier to hunt them. They'll be frustrated by losing their chance to savage this vampire. My guess is they'll be prowling in Vegas, if that's where they're from, and looking for a new victim to amuse themselves with."

"I'll take Mystic to her hotel room," Roman said.

"No," Christian said. "I've got a house."

Chapter Nine

ઈ

Christian steeled himself. Both man and wolf felt uncomfortable leading Roman into the sparsely furnished rental house. The wolf paced because it was his private lair, his den. The man tensed because he could easily imagine the luxury someone as ancient as Roman surrounded himself with.

It couldn't be helped. In less than twenty-four hours both man and wolf had gained a mate only to lose parts of her to others. Christian couldn't endure the thought of losing physical possession as well.

Take a shower with me before you go to work, Mystic's gentle voice whispered in his mind, freeing some of the anxiety knitted tightly in his chest.

He glanced at Roman and waved in the direction of the large-screen TV, the one item of outrageous luxury—though Christian considered it an essential—in his house. "Make yourself comfortable. I've got to get ready for work."

"Take your time," Roman said. "No doubt I can entertain myself with a nature program while Mystic plays the role of wife and helps you."

Mystic's amusement surfaced. "Don't get all hot and bothered watching lions mate and hunt on the Serengeti," she said.

Roman flashed his fangs in response, and picked up the remote control. "Would you suggest I watch golf instead?"

Mystic snickered and both her mates caught her ribald thought about Roman's ability to sink a hole in one. Roman said, "I can see you weren't spanked nearly enough as a little girl." He patted his thigh. "When Christian is safely off to

109

work perhaps we'll remedy the situation. A few swats across your bare buttocks and you'll learn to respect your elders."

"At least you said elders and not betters. I'd have to stake you if you'd said that."

Roman laughed. "Stop playing with me or I will indeed grow hot and bothered before you're ready to deal with the consequences."

Christian pulled Mystic into the bedroom and closed the door. He glanced at the disheveled mess that was the bed. Images of what the two of them had done there before they left to hunt the wolves flickered across his thoughts and sent the blood pounding through his cock.

"How much time do you have?" Mystic asked. Her fingers pulled his shirt from his waistband then danced over his abdomen before slipping into his pants and grazing across the head of his penis.

Lust exploded in the center of Christian's body and shot outward. *Fuck*, he said and pre-cum escaped with the word.

Mystic's laughter was a breeze chasing away any thought of her other mates. *Fuck. That's what I had in mind when I suggested a shower*. She reached for his belt. *Do you have time for bed and a shower?*

His hands joined hers, helping with the belt, then the button, then the zipper until his cock was freed. "Mystic," he panted, his penis jerking as she wrapped it in the fingers of one hand while the fingers of the other found his heavy sac.

Christian speared his fingers through her luxurious hair and pulled her to him for a kiss. She opened her mouth and welcomed his tongue. She greeted it with the slide of hers, with teasing forays and retreats until he was hungrily eating at her mouth and moaning.

Mated less than a day and he was already completely ensnared and lost in his Angelini mate. He couldn't imagine life without her.

I hope you're never sorry you're one of my mates.

Christian ended the kiss so he could look into her eyes. *How could I ever be sorry? The best I ever hoped for was one day I'd be lucky enough to find a human who could see the wolf and not flee in terror. Instead I got you and now I belong in a way I've never belonged before.*

He stroked her cheek and let her feel exactly what she meant to him. He was completely humbled by how deeply she cared about his happiness and how much she feared he'd grow to hate their life together because she shared herself with Roman and Hawk.

It'll be okay, Christian said, once again finding it hard to believe he'd been forced into this role, into soothing his mate over the presence of other males in her bed. But he couldn't do anything else. The need to care for her was as urgent and essential as the need for air. "We'll make it work. Speaking of which..." He gently nipped her neck before setting her aside and stripping. "It's time to take a shower. Even the humans can smell sex and I'd like to keep my private life from being a topic of conversation."

Mystic kicked her own shoes off but wasn't fast enough when it came to the rest of her clothing. She yipped when Christian lunged for her, then laughed at her own canine sound as he growled against her skin and helped her get undressed.

She yipped again when he tossed her over his shoulder and swatted her naked buttock before cupping it in his hand. "Maybe Roman is on to something," Christian teased, trailing over the crevice between her ass cheeks before moving to her slit. "I think you need a good spanking."

"Try it and you'll be sorry." She wriggled but couldn't escape the press of his fingers between her thighs.

Christian set her on her feet next to the shower but his fingers remained buried in her channel. "You're aroused. I can smell it. I can feel it." He carried her hand back to his penis. "Do you want to know what that does to me?"

"I can feel it along the bond."

"I'll tell you anyway. I want to bury my face between your thighs and take you with my tongue. But my cock is so hard and the wolf is in such a frenzy to mate that it's all I can do to keep from forcing you onto your hands and knees and fucking you like a wild animal."

"Do it."

Christian shuddered in response to her words. He could feel her desire along their link as well as with the spasming of her cunt around his fingers.

She was like a drug and he was a hopeless addict. "I'm supposed to be getting ready for work," he said, "but all I can think of is your sweet cunt." He curled his fingers and found the most sensitive place inside her. He pressed and glided over it repeatedly until she was shaking, clinging to him and begging him to mount her.

"Do you really think I'll ever wish for another mate when the one I've got makes me crazed with lust?" he growled against her lips.

"No."

He smoothed over her clit with his thumb before turning her to face the bathroom mirror. His fingers remained in her slit as he repositioned her.

"Put your hands on the counter," he growled. "Watch what you do to me. Watch what we do to each other."

Mystic did as he ordered. She leaned over and grasped the edge of the counter, hardly recognizing herself in the sensuous creature she saw in the mirror. She blushed at how closely she resembled the female Weres who'd prowled the Zevanti compound in heat, their hair a wild mane hanging down to cover breasts crowned with taut nipples.

When she ducked her head Christian nipped her shoulder. "Watch," he growled.

She moaned in protest when his fingers left her channel but she shivered in ecstasy when they were replaced by the tip of his cock. His gaze captured and held hers in the mirror as he slid into her an inch at a time.

Mystic shuddered at the feel of him embedded deep inside her. Her body quivered with joy at the sight of him covering her.

We were meant to be together, he said as his hips began moving in slow thrusts. *Now watch as you make me late for work.*

Pure happiness flooded Mystic's heart at Christian's mix of dominant male and playful mate. She gave herself completely to him and watched as the images of their mating burned into her memory. She watched until the pleasure became unbearable and instinct forced her head down so he would bite her and make her cry out in release.

They showered afterward. It was a quick affair ending with the promise of a longer interlude the next time. Mystic tugged on one of Christian's shirts since her own were still at the hotel.

"You'll stay here for the rest of the day?" Christian asked Roman when they finally emerged from the bedroom.

Roman hit the TV remote and cleared the screen of a horse race. "For the moment I think it would be best if I was seen only after sunset."

Christian nodded and walked to the front door. He needed to get to the station and yet he hated to leave. "I've got to go," he said, pulling Mystic into his arms. "I have so many questions and I want to stay here with you, but I've got people counting on me and I'd like to find out what I can about the dead vampire."

She hugged him. "I'll be safe here with Roman."

For the first time Christian found himself considering the advantages of her having another mate. He was a man without a pack or even a human family to watch over her. It had never been important with a woman before because his relationships had been casual, but now, and in the future, when there were children—he could see why the Angelini always took more than one mate. There was safety in numbers.

He kissed Mystic then reluctantly pulled away. "I may still be working after the sun sets. Call if you leave the house."

"Okay." Her smile made his heart ache with love. "You be safe, too," she teased.

"I will be." He kissed her again then left.

Mystic moved to the window and watched him drive away. A small sliver of loneliness and loss pierced her as his car disappeared from sight.

She'd never considered before what it was like for human couples. The Weres worked and lived together. The vampires had their companions who most often slept when the vampire slept and were rarely out of sight when a vampire was awake. The Angelini had their mates and the link between them was so strong that even when they were physically apart, with a thought they could touch each other. None of them was ever truly alone.

Her mind reached out to Christian's and a blush rose to her cheeks when she encountered the image of herself in the mirror as they'd fucked. She turned away from the window and allowed the connection to fade.

Roman was sprawled across the couch. As she approached he tossed the TV remote onto the coffee table.

"Alone at last," he said when she sat on the edge of a cushion. His hand went to her hip and settled there as if he was content simply to be in her company.

Mystic could feel his desire for her body and her blood. When he didn't pounce, a tension she hadn't been aware of eased. She immediately knew its source and wondered if he'd guessed at her old fears of being wanted not for herself but because she was Angelini and the magic gave a male no choice.

His masculine chuckle sounded in her mind. *I am looking for an excuse to spank you. If you continue to doubt your own allure then you will feel my hand on your buttocks. With or without the Angelini bloodline you would draw men to you.*

Mystic melted with his words. She wanted to believe them so desperately.

He took her hand and brought her wrist to his lips. *Believe*, he whispered in her thoughts as he kissed over her pulse and sent a jolt of heat racing through her veins.

She leaned in and he freed her wrist in order to tangle his fingers in her hair and draw her closer. Vampire flames danced in his pupils and promised an erotic experience that could be found nowhere else.

Mystic touched her lips to his. She opened her mouth and welcomed the sensuous slide of his tongue against hers.

I have waited centuries for you, he whispered in her mind.

His other hand cupped her breast and heat burned through the fabric of her borrowed shirt. Her nipples ached and she shivered with the need to feel his skin touching hers.

He responded by flicking the buttons free one at a time until the shirt hung open, exposing her naked breasts and uncovered mound. *Please*, she begged and he stripped the shirt off her.

She moaned when his hand returned to her needy flesh and his fingers caressed her areola before gently tugging and squeezing.

Lie with me, he said, using his grip on her hair and on her nipple to guide her down so she was stretched out at his side on the couch. He threw his leg over hers in a possessive gesture. She shivered at the feel of his clothed body against her naked one.

"You make it difficult not to pounce," he teased, leaving her lips to kiss along her jaw and down to her throat.

Mystic's breath caught when he licked over her wildly beating pulse. His fangs grazed her skin and she pressed against his mouth.

I was under the impression you might want to talk instead of make love. Tell me I'm wrong, Mystic, and I'll gladly give you what you seem to be asking for.

I do, she said, though she doubted the reprieve from the lust-induced magic of the Angelini would last for long. The need for constant physical intimacy would smooth over time, ride beneath the surface of their skins, but initially, in the early stages, they'd be driven to have sex time and time again in order to solidify and deepen the bond.

She laughed silently. Not that she needed any magic at all to desire her mates. Each one of them could easily star in her fantasies, and together…incredible, amazing, she could go on for days listing words to describe them.

Roman lifted his mouth from her neck with a chuckle. "I'm glad you find us *all* suitable."

"Very suitable."

Curiosity made her ask, "Do you know my fathers?"

"No, though no doubt that will soon change."

Mystic laughed. "No doubt. Be prepared to meet the parents as soon as they get back from Europe." She leaned in and pressed a kiss to his lips. "I think they'll like you very, very much."

"I hope you're right."

There was a nearly undetectable wistfulness in his voice, one she might not have noticed at all except for the bond she shared with him. "You've lived for so long," she said. "So much longer than my fathers and they've been alive *forever*. How have you lasted?" *And stayed sane? Honorable?* Her lips quirked upward in a teasing curve. *Even lovable?*

His smile and the look in his eyes made the muscles around her heart tighten almost painfully. "There were decades at a time when I slept, preferring the nothingness of death to the gray monotony of day after day that was the same wasteland of emptiness."

Roman's mouth found hers, captured it in a kiss. *You are a gift, Mystic. A priceless one I will cherish always. With you my life became fresh and new, vital, exciting in a way it hasn't been in long centuries. And it will only get better as time goes on.*

Her hand smoothed up his arm and along his shoulder. Her fingers went unerringly to the chain he wore around his neck almost like a collar and then to the ancient scripted pendant, a gryphon hanging from its center. He hadn't been wearing it in the woods. But now he was and she could feel the pendant's enchantment and power.

Roman kissed down her neck. He stopped above her pulse, licked, sealed the place with his lips and sucked, making her feel as though her heart beat in his mouth. *Will you become my companion as well as my Angelini mate?*

Yes. There was no doubt in Mystic's mind that she would let him bind her to him in the vampire way. It would give him power over her, not as much as if she was purely human, but more than he might have over an Angelini who wore a hunter's tattoo. There were rules governing the relationship, laws that made her vulnerable when it came to vampire law but her mother was bound to her fathers and she would do no less.

Roman's pleasure surged through their link along with his intention to fully claim her while he had her to himself. His fangs pressed against her skin and her heart skipped and raced in anticipation of first his bite and then his blood.

But before he could pierce her skin her conscience forced her hand away from the companion necklace and down to his chest. She pushed in a silent gesture for him to stop.

For long moments he held her pulse hostage in his mouth. Mystic closed her eyes and knew she was no match for him if he decided to ignore her wishes.

A single touch, a small press of his will against hers and her conscience would retreat in favor of the ecstasy only he could give her. No being was immune to the pleasure that could be found in a vampire's bite but she suspected she found it even more enthralling because of her own vampire heritage.

I think maybe you are going to be a test to my patience, Roman said, releasing her from the threat of his bite but licking over the spot where her pulse jumped as if it was trying to return to him. He lifted his head and met her relieved gaze. *You wish to delay until your other mates are comfortable with the arrangement they find themselves in?*

"I think it would be best," Mystic whispered as she reached up to trail her fingers over his lips.

Her heart knew it was the right thing to do—for Christian who had steadied her and bolstered her confidence even though he would never have shared her with another if there had been a choice, and for Hawk, who had not cornered and trapped her when she'd been at the Zevanti compound though now she could admit what she'd denied then, deep down she'd recognized him as one of her mates.

"If you think it is best, then we will wait," Roman said, *but not indefinitely.*

She slid her other palm up his chest and lightly grasped the etched pendant again. Along their link she opened her thoughts and her heart so he knew she would welcome the day when she would wear the companion necklace.

"If you're not careful you'll bring me to my knees with your openness," he said.

"I think Estelle might have confided a time or two that the best place for a vampire mate was on his knees." Color flooded Mystic's face as she recalled her mother actually had quite a bit more to say on the topic, but all of it came under the heading of girl talk.

Roman's fangs flashed. He threw back his head and laughed. "Your secrets are *not* safe from me," he said, reminding her with his statement and his amusement of how thin the barrier between their minds was.

Mystic laughed along with him. It was impossible to resist though her face continued to flame.

"I suspect your fathers don't mind being driven to their knees by their Angelini mate. Nor would I mind if that's the service you require of me."

His seductive words curled in her breasts and womb. She released the pendant in favor of unbuttoning his shirt so she could explore his bare skin.

Roman rolled to one elbow. The lower part of his body pressed hers to the couch while his upper body hovered over hers, his open shirt teasing her sides. "Would you like me to bury my face between your thighs and pleasure you as your other mates have done?"

A wave of desire washed through Mystic and chased the residual humor away. Arousal flooded her channel and escaped to coat her swollen cunt lips and inner thighs.

His elegant masculine features tightened into a predatory mask that sent a thrill of feminine fear racing along her spine. "I can smell your answer," he said, "and it excites the part of me that doesn't crave your blood."

Roman lowered his head and took her lips. His tongue thrust into her mouth. The images in his mind told her it was a rehearsal for what he intended to do to her cunt. She moaned in reaction and he settled more of his weight on her.

Mystic felt the fierce animal need to dominate rage through him. He'd alluded to his beasts, but his easy manner and teasing quips reminded her of her vampire fathers and set her at ease. Now she wondered how she could ever have thought he was less intense than her wolves.

"I was created a beast and changed by death into an even deadlier predator. For centuries there was no gentleness in me at all, no reason to even pretend to be human."

"I don't believe I wished for a human mate," Mystic teased, sensing that underneath his words was a worry she wanted only the vampire he'd become and not the beast he'd been born. "I don't believe I've cowered in fear or cried in disappointment at finding myself mated to big bad wolves and a gryphon once known as Korak."

As quickly as the tension and aggression had risen in Roman, it flowed away. He lowered his head and took her lips again, this time in a gentle kiss. His amusement soaked in with his heat. *You tame me with your courage and your acceptance.*

She wriggled her hand between his open shirt and his side. *But do I tempt you? You're still wearing clothes while I've got none.*

We can remedy that.

Roman rose to shed his clothing. When he returned to the couch he straddled her hips and caressed her slowly with his eyes. "Now where were we?"

Mystic's nipples tightened under his perusal. Her abdomen quivered and her cunt lips parted further as his attention lingered between her thighs.

"You are exquisite," Roman murmured. His fierce erection and taut features were outward proof of the desire she felt along their bond and yet a small trickle of doubt and uncertainty played havoc with Mystic's heart as the images of Roman as Christian had often seen him at Fangs—surrounded by blonde humans with long legs and large breasts—cast doubt on her own beauty in his eyes.

Roman leaned down and put his hands on either side of her head. His eyes glittered with deadly vampire fire. *I will punish you if you continue that line of thought. They were nothing to me. You are everything.* "Touch your breasts. Offer them to me and see just how beautiful I find you."

She blushed at his carnal demand. The heat that suffused her was a curling mix of desire and shyness.

Now, he growled, and she heard the lion's rumble in her mind.

Mystic licked her lips and regained a small measure of her inherent confidence when his cock jerked in response and glistened with escaped arousal. She placed her hands on her bare stomach and slowly slid them upward. Her breath grew short just watching his face tighten with savage intensity.

Both of them inhaled sharply when her hands cupped her breasts. *Like this*? she asked, watching him through half-closed eyes as she teased her thumbs over hardened nipples.

Little minx, you're going to go too far.

I'm just obeying my mate.

A heady rush of power filled her when she felt Roman struggle to keep from pouncing. She promised herself she would never again doubt her own appeal and allure as she angled her face so she could lick over a dusky nipple. *Does this please you? Or should I beg for you to suck them?*

Roman's breath came out in a pant. He slid backward, angled his face so he could lick over her wet areola. She met his tongue with her own. Teased him further by letting him feel it glide over silky feminine skin and puckered flesh.

I warned you, he said, latching onto her nipple, his teeth and mouth sending hot spikes of fire to her cunt and clit.

Lust consumed Roman. It was a feral roar in his head and heart and cock. It was a wildness that had nothing to do with Angelini magic but everything to do with the passion he felt for his beautiful, brave mate. Centuries of existence seemed too short a period of time to spend with her, especially now, when his body burned and hungered and needed.

Roman fed at her breasts. He sucked and laved and bit and reveled in the way she writhed and pleaded.

The scent of her arousal filled his nostrils until even the heady pleasure he found at her breasts couldn't keep him from kissing downward and burying his face between her thighs as he'd offered to do earlier.

He moaned against her wet flesh. Inhaled her. Tasted her.

Her clit was a tiny erect presence he couldn't ignore. He sucked it into his mouth and swirled his tongue over it. He shared a fantasy with her while he was doing it, showed her images of the two of them pleasuring each other orally at the same time—him suffering the lash of her tongue on his cock head as she experienced the feel of his on her small, swollen knob.

Roman very nearly slid them off the couch and onto the floor when he felt her willingness to take him into her mouth and turn his fantasy into a reality. He very nearly spewed his seed when he left her clit and plunged his tongue into her slick channel.

He tongue-fucked her until she orgasmed, then did it a second time before lifting his face from between her thighs. "When I'm with you, I lose myself completely. You chase away all thought."

Mystic snickered as he crawled up her body. "Do you want me to share some of Estelle's pithy comments about a man's reasoning ability and whether his big head can outthink his little one?"

Roman laughed against her lips as his cock slid home. *Your mother has much to answer for. It's a good thing there is plenty of time to eradicate her influence and reeducate you so you'll have the proper respect for your mates.*

Mystic wrapped her legs around his waist and rubbed her tongue against his. *When it comes to my mates, I think you'll find I'm a very willing student.*

He groaned and began thrusting. His amusement faded with each ripple of her channel against his penis. It was replaced by a soul-searing desire to be one with her.

"Come with me," he whispered, flooding the link between them with his desperate need for release.

Mystic shuddered underneath him. She answered his carnal call by spasming around his cock and milking him of his seed as orgasm shimmered through her.

They remained on the couch in the aftermath of passion, their bodies touching, sated for the moment, content. "Do you have a house here?" she asked as her fingers explored the muscles on Roman's arm.

"There is no place I call home."

She moved so she could look at his face. "Do you mean that literally or do you mean you don't have a place in Vegas you call home?"

"I own properties all over the world but they're investments I visit only occasionally." He traced her eyebrows. "The gryphon was created not only to hunt vampires but to guard territory and possessions. Even though I became what was once my prey, early on I found if I lingered too long in a certain place or acquired things of value, both became a deadly trap my enemies could use against me." Roman smiled slightly. "Now I have a mate and I will settle wherever she chooses to settle."

Mystic worried her bottom lip and wondered what would happen if Roman became territorial and possessive. The last of the gryphons had faded into mythology well before her fathers were either men or vampire. And though both of them were ancient in her eyes, the past Roman spoke of was lost in a gray cloud of history even her parents considered irrelevant.

Roman laughed softly. *Am I destined to hear the words ancient and irrelevant hurled in my direction whenever you're displeased with me? Do not fear for the future, Mystic, or worry about your other mates. My tie to you makes them important to me and I am no longer purely gryphon.*

Mystic let her worry slide away. The magic that made her Angelini would not choose the wrong mates for her. They would all adjust and adapt and find a way to live together.

She trailed her finger over his collarbone and down to his tiny nipple. He covered her hand with his and she could feel what her touch did to him.

Blood rushed to his cock and his heart rate sped up, but it was so much more than physical desire. A deep-seated pleasure and contentedness filled him.

Despite all of the blonde Barbies who'd paraded through his life, it was this closeness and intimacy he craved. She snuggled against him more tightly and let her mind wander until she remembered Christian's comment about Roman not being able to walk in the sun previously. She thought about Roman's own acknowledgement that it would be better if he wasn't seen until after the sun set. "How can you be out during the day?"

Roman hesitated for only a moment before touching her mind with his and sharing what had transpired at Brann's estate when he went to see Syndelle.

Mystic watched the images unfold in a riot of emotion. She was thrilled by the prospect her fathers might one day walk underneath the sun again. But she was terrified at what having the ancient vampire creation magic return could mean for them all.

"Do you think this is why the Angelini have gathered?" she asked.

"I don't know. I think it's likely that some of the ancients have sensed something, or experienced premonitions." He rubbed his cheek against her hair. "Several times I thought I felt the magic of the dark mage brush against me. Each time I told myself I'd imagined it. But now I wonder. It is something I'll speak to Brann about." He smiled against her forehead. "I didn't do it when I saw Brann last because I was stunned by my encounter with Syndelle, then consumed with the need to locate you."

Roman cupped Mystic's chin and forced her gaze to his. "You are young and don't wear the tattoo of an Angelini hunter. You don't have the protections the tattoo and the ceremony to gain it bestows on one of your kind. Will you let me weave safeguards against others invading your mind and seeing my memories of what transpired with Syndelle?"

"Yes," Mystic said and let her awareness of anything else fade as she moved freely toward the blue flames that danced deep in his pupils and didn't go out until she was completely entrapped in his will.

Chapter Ten

ഇ

Skye Delano Coronado eased the Harley to a stop in front of the wrought iron gates of Brann's most heavily protected estate. Cameras were mounted on the walls, a recent addition though she wasn't sure exactly what purpose they served since Brann's wards would keep humans and supernaturals alike from entering without permission.

She leaned forward to press the intercom switch but her sister had already noted her arrival. The gates to the estate—to Syndelle's luxurious prison—swung open.

Skye drove in and parked the bike in front of the house. Syndelle greeted her at the door with a hug before ushering her down a hallway and past rooms full of priceless art and antiques.

They finally entered an entertainment room deep inside the house and designed for comfort. Syndelle's mate Rafael half sat, half lay in an oversized chair. As usual, he was completely focused on a game being played out on a large screen in front of him. His fingers and thumbs moved in a frenzy of activity on the game controllers.

Skye shook her head. "How can you stand it?" she asked, not for the first time.

Syndelle laughed. "By *it*, I assume you mean the game and not my very handsome mate."

Skye grinned and let her gaze roam over Rafe in mock assessment. She was deliriously happy with Gian and Rico but as she'd told them often enough, just because she took mates didn't mean she'd gone blind.

Rafe, with his muscle shirts and long blond hair, was serious eye candy. Of course the effect was sometimes ruined when he opened his mouth.

An opinion you share with Brann, Syndelle said along their family pathway, her amusement fading into sadness as she added, *I wish you hadn't been lost to us. Our brothers have been known to spend days positioned in front of the screen and battling each other.*

Skye gave Syndelle a quick hug. *Don't feel sorry for me. Otherwise I'll have to share my own sadness about you not having the same freedom as I do.* Out loud Skye said, "I'm glad Gian amuses himself by running Fangs and Rico sees enough as a cop. I might get violent if they played video games at home."

Rafe paused the game and tossed the controllers to a nearby beanbag chair then turned his attention to Skye. "As if you don't already have a reputation for violence. Are you here for a social visit or are you here to get Syndelle in trouble again?" He opened his arms to encompass the room. "As you can see, Brann isn't at home and hovering. So do your worst. Syndelle and I are both fully recovered from Brann's last little punishment."

"Rafael," Syndelle chided, her blush making Skye curious and then slightly embarrassed as brief images flickered into her thoughts before she firmly shored up the barrier between Syndelle and herself.

Skye hadn't known anything about her Angelini heritage or her family until recently. She hadn't even believed in the existence of supernatural beings though she'd known she wasn't like everyone else. Now she often relied on Syndelle to fill in the gaps in her knowledge. As a result, when they were together Syndelle tended to hold her mind open so Skye could search for answers. But the question of Brann's punishment was *not* one she needed to explore.

"Sorry," Skye mumbled.

Rafe laughed and rose from the chair. "And you accuse Syndelle of being sheltered." His eyes danced with mischief as he moved to stand next to Syndelle. "Maybe we should sneak out and explore some of the places where vampire companions are sent for training. Some of them have to be taught how to enjoy pain with their sex. And some vampires prefer to have it done by professionals."

"I hope he's kidding," Skye said. She couldn't always tell with Rafael. He'd spent years in the sex trade.

Syndelle slipped her arm around Rafael's waist and pulled him to her for a kiss. When it ended she said, "There are clubs favored by vampires and companions who like the BDSM lifestyle, but they aren't restricted to only our kind."

Rafael sighed and rubbed his nose against Syndelle's. "Fun spoiler."

"Troublemaker."

"Kids," Skye said, shaking her head but smiling at the same time. It made her happy to see Syndelle relaxed and almost childish. So much of the time her sister was left serious and somber by the weight of being the vampire Masada.

It was the desire to see Syndelle carefree that led to the trouble Rafael alluded to. She and Syndelle had managed to escape the compound while Rafe was there and then lose him as he tried to follow the Harley.

Skye hadn't been foolish enough to take Syndelle into a casino or a club. They'd toured the city on bike and raced through the desert. Then when Syndelle said she wanted to learn how to handle the Harley, they'd found an abandoned parking lot and hung out there until Syndelle got the hang of the hog. They'd capped their evening of freedom with triple scoops of ice cream and girl talk in a quiet park.

It had been an extremely tame evening, even compared to a night spent at Fangs where Gian and his vampire partners kept things in order. Unfortunately Brann didn't see it that way.

Skye snickered. Then again, based on the images she'd seen before shoring up the barrier, Syndelle savored the memory of that evening—both during their freedom run and afterward, when she faced the ancient vampire who would never allow her to leave his estate if he had a choice.

"If you're not afraid of getting into trouble..." Skye said and laughed at the expressions on both Syndelle and Rafe's faces. "I see you're not."

She pulled her cell phone from her pocket and flicked it open. Within seconds the driver's license she'd photographed before Christian Augustino's arrival was displayed on the screen. As Syndelle and Rafe studied Todd Moore's picture and information, Skye shared the sequence of events mentally—from Mystic's arrival to the detective's and finally to Roman's appearance at Fangs.

Rafael made a show of limbering his fingers. "So despite the part where your mates—who don't always see eye to eye— agreed this was a matter for Augustino to investigate, am I right in thinking you are here to suggest we join the hunt?"

"Brann's bragged numerous times that you have your uses," Skye said. "I thought maybe you'd prefer a real challenge over a video game."

Rafael smirked. "Come with me to my office, little girls," he said in his best parody of a horror film voice.

* * * * *

The rain Christian had worried about fell in a heavy, violent downpour then tapered off and ended almost as quickly as it had begun. It was more a squall than a storm and to the tourists on The Strip it was a laughing excuse to run for the nearest casino. For them it was merely another experience, one adding a different texture to their Las Vegas trip. For the three black wolves that experienced the storm before it moved on to hit the town, it was reason to howl in frustration. The scent of those they were hunting was lost.

They waited until they got back to Hawk's car before shifting form. None of them spoke until after they'd dressed and were heading to Vegas. It was Gabe who broke the silence. "If they stick together it might not be too difficult to find them in their human form. We can look for a pack of seven with five males, two females."

"That's assuming they're based in Vegas," Gabby said. "They may have just gone there to play, with hunting a vampire being their idea of fun. It still bothers me they left the body."

"Maybe this was their first hunt or the only time they haven't succeeded in killing their prey," Hawk said. "They might have assumed the vampire would turn into ash. Some of the truly ancient ones do."

Gabe nodded. "That's what Christian thought." He sighed in frustration. "If Gabby and I hadn't needed to eat and rest before shifting and running again maybe we could have found their human scents before it rained."

Hawk took a hand off the steering wheel and settled it on Gabe's shoulder. "You're both young and you're away from your Alpha and the strength that comes from being among pack. You did better than most would have done." His fingers curled and dug in to Gabe's muscles. "I believe things have worked the way the Angelini magic meant them to but if you ever help Mystic run from me again, I will challenge you in wolf form and tear you apart." He released his grip and returned his hand to the steering wheel.

Now that he'd issued his warning, Hawk could enjoy Gabe and Gabby's company and contemplate the future. He'd known who they were but until Mystic's stay at the Zevanti compound he'd had little interest in the two young wolves.

His cock filled just remembering that first glimpse of Mystic. She'd come into the house laughing at something one of the twins said and he'd known immediately he wanted her for his mate.

One of the elder Zevantis had noticed his interest and said, "She's a Renaldi Angelini. Her grandparents sent her to us in the hopes she'd find her mates among the wolves. Her fathers are both vampires."

"Does she shift?" Jagger asked.

"No," the elder Zevanti said. "But her sons would be wolves and a bond with her ensures an alliance with any number of packs that have ties to the Renaldi. They have always favored the wolves when it comes to mating."

Hawk growled as he remembered the next words out of Jagger's mouth. *I'd mount her even without the promise of a bond. She's gorgeous.* He should have known in that instant his friend wasn't destined to be Mystic's mate. Looking back on it, it had been a waste of time to involve Jagger. It would have been better to get to know Gabe and Gabby beyond simply observing and asking about them. Then again, maybe including Jagger had served a purpose.

Right from the start he'd accepted he'd share Mystic with another male. He'd imagined what it would be like when he and Jagger took her, both together and separately. As a result, he now found he could handle the thought of sharing her with Roman and Christian—not that he intended to do it when they got back to Vegas.

Christian was at work and Roman had been alone with Mystic for hours. Now it was his turn to have sole possession of their mate.

Hawk tried to find a comfortable position as his erection grew in anticipation. The image of Jagger humping away on the gray female with his tongue hanging out in ecstasy flashed through Hawk's mind and he could easily imagine the same expression on his own wolven face.

It was deeply satisfying to make love to Mystic as a man. And even though they'd only been mated for a short time, he knew each coupling, each shared thought or intimacy would strengthen their bond until eventually he would be able to wake the wolf sleeping inside her. She would become a true mate in every sense of the word. She would be his as both wolf and Angelini.

* * * * *

Mystic stirred in Roman's arms. Without conscious thought she reached for Christian and Hawk with her mind and assured herself they were okay.

Warmth pooled in her cunt and heart as she felt Christian's mood swing from frustration with work to delight at her wifely show of concern. *You're still at the house?* he asked.

Yes. Roman is here and Hawk is only a short distance away. Because of her vampire heritage she didn't need to open her eyes in order to know the sun was close to setting. *Did Hawk call you? Did they find any human scent?*

The rain washed it away. But Hawk also thought the wolves smelled "off" somehow. Christian's attention was jerked back to an interrogation taking place at the police station. The link snapped and Mystic allowed it to slide from her consciousness. Her eyebrows drew together. She didn't remember it raining. She opened her eyes and looked up into Roman's face.

It was only a quick squall. He pressed a kiss to her forehead. *You needed to sleep.*

Mystic wrapped her arms around his neck and rubbed her nose against his as her memories caught up with her. She should probably be mad he'd taken it upon himself to knock her out completely instead of simply weaving protections into her mind. But it was hard to be angry when she felt so relaxed. She'd appreciate the sleep even more once they started hunting through the clubs for the seven Weres.

I don't think you'll be doing any hunting tonight. It would hardly be fair to Hawk if you denied him a chance to be alone with you the way both Christian and I have been.

Mystic's mind found Hawk's. She delved into his thoughts and her nipples tightened in response to the lust and anticipation she found crouched inside him.

She shivered at the intensity of him. Hawk did nothing to mute or hide his intention to fuck her repeatedly when he got to her.

He was a strong alpha and even though she had no wolf, she responded to him on every level. She knew it would be nearly impossible to resist his will when it was focused solely on her—just as she knew she was no match for a vampire as ancient and powerful as Roman.

On the contrary, Roman whispered into her thoughts as he kissed down to the pulse thundering in her neck. *You are the perfect match for me.*

He sucked her pulse into his mouth and desire burned through her. His hand covered her breast possessively and she felt his intention to pierce her with both his fangs and his cock.

A thought flickered between them—of Hawk walking in with Gabe and Gabby. Mystic wasn't sure whether it was Roman's thought or hers but she stiffened in response. Though sex was a public and often indulged in activity among the wolves when they gathered for a Howl, it wasn't something either she or her friends had participated in.

Roman released her neck and kissed her before rising to his feet. "Hawk will be here in a matter of minutes. A quick shower might be in order before I'm kicked out on the street with nothing but the clothes on my back."

Mystic laughed. "As if anyone could really throw you out."

She cocked her head as a question suddenly occurred to her. "Could you hypnotize him if you wanted to?"

"That's a dangerous question."

"So if you answer it, you'll have to wipe my mind?"

Roman chuckled but he sat down next to Mystic and traced her lips with his forefinger. "I think you will find I have not tampered with any of your memories. I only placed protections around some of them."

He leaned down so his face was only inches above hers. His hand moved to stroke her cheek. "Yes, I am powerful enough to hypnotize Christian and Hawk, though your Angelini bond with them and the fact they are both alphas would make it more difficult and more dangerous—for all of us. They would fight, physically and mentally, and it would most likely take a great deal of blood loss before they would weaken to the point where my will would prevail. But I would prevail in the end." *It's not something I would contemplate doing unless your life was at stake, Mystic. And even then, I would do so accepting my own life would be forfeit should something go wrong and you end up dead.*

I believe you.

You humble me with your absolute trust. It is not something I have experienced very often.

You're my mate, Mystic said. It was as simple and as complex for her as that.

She might have fought against gaining mates in the first place, and she suspected she would soon agree wholeheartedly with Skye Coronado and conclude mates tended to cramp a girl's style, but she wouldn't engage in phantom battles over the issue of trust. To doubt the trustworthiness of her chosen mates was to doubt the very magic that created the Angelini.

Roman kissed her then stood and offered his hand. "Shower with me. I promise to behave."

"And what if I don't want you to behave?"

He chuckled. "If it's within my power, I'll give my mate anything she desires."

Mystic put her hand in his and allowed him to lead her to the bathroom. Much, much later they emerged to the smell of pizza and to find Gabe, Gabby and Hawk in the kitchen. One box of pizza had already been polished off and they were well into a second one.

"There's plenty here," Gabby said, waving a slice in the air.

Mystic joined the others at the table. Roman sat down next to her so she was positioned between him and Hawk.

Gabe said, "As soon as we finish here, Gabby and I are going to start hitting the clubs our kind favors. Christian called while you were in the shower. The dead vampire grew up in Vegas."

Mystic frowned and turned to look at Roman. "That's not right. He was a fledgling. He shouldn't be in a place where people who knew him when he was alive and human would recognize him."

Roman nodded. "I plan to visit Brann's estate and Fangs when I leave here. I'll take the matter up with Brann as well as Gian and his partners. A short while ago a witch was using dark magic to create vampire children. I was under the impression all of them had been found and dealt with. Perhaps not."

Gabby pulled a piece of paper from her pocket and unfolded it before handing it to Roman. Mystic recognized it as the printout of places they'd intended to check out during their Vegas escape.

"I've been thinking," Gabby said. "The wolves wouldn't have gone to a place like Fangs to find their prey. And I doubt they got lucky and just happened to find a lone vampire in a dark alley somewhere. I've never met a fledgling as young as Todd Moore, or as young as we think he might be, but I'm guessing he'd still be strong and fast and not easy to take down, especially with a single knife to the heart. None of his arm bones had cut marks on them. That probably means he didn't think he needed to defend himself. The only reason I can think of a vampire letting someone, especially a Were someone, close to his heart is if he's feeding—which means maybe the vampire went hunting for, or was lured by Were blood."

Gabrielle glanced at Mystic then back to Roman, and finally to Hawk. "Except under certain circumstances, the Zevanti pack forbids its members from being a vampire's food source. Most packs are the same, aren't they?"

Hawk nodded but Roman laughed and flashed his fangs. "This is Sin City, small wolf. What happens here is supposed to stay here if you believe the advertisements. It's a place for thrill seekers and rule breakers and gamblers alike. Still, your points are well thought out and excellent."

Roman looked down at the list of clubs and removed an elegant pen from his shirt pocket. "None of these are places a vampire would wander into alone." He wrote *Wolfsbane* along with a street name. "You'll find a more mixed crowd here. But I would suggest waiting until Christian is off duty or I've finished my tasks before going to his club. Three is safer than two." Roman's gaze flickered over Gabby. "Especially when the small wolf might be a temptation. Depending on the mix of customers, Wolfsbane can range from civilized to dangerous, all within the span of a single night."

He handed the list back to Gabby before leaning over and kissing Mystic's forehead. "I'll be back before sunrise or I'll call to let you know where I am."

Mystic's hand settled over Roman's heart for a moment as she studied him, memorized his features. Everything about him was urbane and polished—except for the mating mark she'd left on his neck. She grinned and didn't bother to suppress the satisfaction she felt at seeing her off-limits sign posted on him.

She could easily picture him gliding across a ballroom in old England or attending a salon where wealthy nobles pretended an interest in poetry so they could arrange sexual liaisons with each other's spouses. He was a chameleon, like most vampires. But where dancing was still a possibility for him, adultery wasn't—not for an Angelini or their mates.

"Don't let anything happen to you," she said, leaning forward to kiss him one last time before he left.

Gabby and Gabe finished their pizza and cleared the table of what dishes and debris they could. When they were finished they stood with their attention on Hawk as if they needed permission to leave.

It surprised Mystic, until she thought about it. Hawk was a strong alpha. Even in the Zevanti compound Gabe and Gabby would have deferred to him in any direct interaction that didn't conflict with their pack loyalty.

But when Gabe asked, "Do you want us to check in with you?" a flash of excitement shot through Mystic at the possibility this could lead to something more in the future. This could be the start of the pack she knew Hawk wanted.

It was inevitable that young Weres moved around. It was necessary if for no other reason than to keep from inbreeding.

Every supernatural body had its elders who governed though they generally concerned themselves with the framework of a society instead of the details. New packs had to be sanctioned and territories determined. Leaders needed to be true alphas with a web of alliances and the will to control pack members, ruthlessly if necessary.

Pride filled Mystic as she looked at Hawk. Warmth rubbed through her like a wolf's affection. He was a man she would trust with the future of her friends.

As if sensing her thoughts, Hawk reached over and stroked the back of her neck though his attention remained on Gabe and Gabby. "Call Mystic's cell phone and leave voice mail each time you hit a new location. Don't take any chances. If you get into trouble start trying to get a live person. Me. Christian. Roman. It doesn't matter. Tonight is for reconnaissance. It's about gathering information, not being noticed."

Gabby nodded in agreement. Gabe grinned and saluted. Mystic tensed but Hawk didn't react other than to slide his chair back from the table and say, "When you've had enough fun and decide to quit, crash in your hotel room." His teeth flashed. "We'll call you when it's safe to come over."

Both Gabe and Gabby laughed. Mystic's face heated up, which embarrassed her even further. "You'd think nothing would make me blush after living with Estelle, Falcone and Yorick plus visiting the wolves," she mumbled, completely disgruntled.

Hawk pulled her onto his lap as Gabe and Gabby left. "I like your blushes," he murmured against the mating mark on her neck. "And your modesty is refreshing." He bit down, remarking her neck. His aggression sent a sharp spike a need through her. Mystic's heart began racing when he eased her off his lap and onto her feet. "But now that we're alone, I want you naked. Strip."

Chapter Eleven

🔊

Mystic shivered in response to Hawk's command. Her cunt spasmed when he placed his hand on her thigh. Her nipples tightened.

She studied the contrast of his skin against hers. He was nightfall and she was the brown-gold of an autumn forest at dusk.

"Strip," Hawk repeated in a low growl, the order given to appease the wolf that crouched inside him and didn't like having Mystic covered with another male's shirt and scent.

He didn't follow up the command with a threat of punishment. He didn't need to. He knew she wouldn't deny him. He could smell her arousal. He could see it in the tight points of her nipples.

His hand slid up to where the fabric of Christian's shirt touched her skin and Mystic's breath caught. A small whimper followed as he stroked her flesh.

Hawk clenched his other hand into a fist in order to keep from reaching for the front of his jeans and freeing his cock. He'd do that soon enough, or he'd have her do it. At the moment he simply wanted to enjoy this first time of being alone with her. He wanted to savor the knowledge she wouldn't try to flee the room and his presence any longer.

He'd rarely succeeded in getting her to himself at the Zevanti compound. Her friends had run interference or she'd outwitted him.

Another male might have been angered by her continued evasions, or been driven to become more aggressive in his pursuit, but Hawk had seen it as confirmation that on some level Mystic recognized him as her mate. She wouldn't have felt so threatened by him otherwise.

Her eyelashes lowered to hide her expression as her hands went to the front of Christian's shirt. Hawk couldn't suppress a smile. She was beautiful, alluring, a potent mix of innocent and bold. His heart thundered in his chest and he had to concentrate in order to control his breathing as her fingers freed first one button and then another. A pant escaped despite the control he held over himself when the shirt parted and then fell to the ground. He wanted to lift his face and howl in joy and victory. He wanted to lean forward and press his face to her pussy and wallow in her scent and heat.

Hawk stood and scooped her up into his arms. There would be other days and other times for fucking her on the kitchen table or against the counter. For this first time alone with her, he wanted to be in a comfortable place.

He strode into Christian's bedroom. Though Christian had left for work hours before, the scent of sex was raw against Hawk's senses. It fed his natural need to dominate. It stirred the wolf into a frenzy even though the man knew he would need to get used to it.

Mystic would always smell of her other mates. Whatever place they eventually called home, he doubted any surface would remain virgin for long.

Hawk tumbled her onto the bed and stripped out of his clothing before joining her. He covered her with his body. There was no denying either the wolf's or his own need to touch as much of her as possible.

A moan escaped and he shuddered at the feel of her hot, smooth skin against his. He was no stranger to a woman's body and yet this woman made him revisit those adolescent moments when he'd feared he might spill his seed in a single stroke, or worse, before he could even get inside the fevered female flesh waiting for him.

As if to test him further, Mystic touched her lips to his and whispered, "I need you inside me."

Hawk grabbed her wrists and pinned them to the mattress before she could strip him of his control. The rush of blood to his cock and the fierce urge to impale her was almost unbearable. He took her offered lips and thrust his tongue against hers. He hoped to take the edge off his need to rut on her, but within seconds he knew he was lost.

The Angelini magic rose between them as it had in the woods. Its song was a primitive siren call that left them both helpless against it. There was no denying it, no fighting it.

"We'll go slower next time," Hawk promised before he got to his knees so she could roll to hers.

His cock strained and leaked. His wolf quivered in anticipation and reached out along the bond in an attempt to prod Mystic's hidden wolf into waking.

She positioned herself on her knees and elbows so her flushed rosy slit was exposed. Its open, wet folds were a temptation no male could resist.

It was impossible for Hawk not to explore the lush feminine mystery any time his face got close to her silken cunt. He licked her from her clit to the tempting pucker of her anus. He thrust his tongue in and out of her channel and hungrily swallowed her juices as the wolf moved closer to the surface of his human skin and reveled in the taste and scent and sensation.

Her moans fed both the wolf's hunger and the man's. His mouth remained against her slick folds until his cock pulsed in warning and he testicles tightened and burned in protest.

Hawk bit her inner thigh just as he'd done her neck, a hard aggressive remarking of his mate. He gave her a gentle nip on one ass check before pressing kisses up her spine until he got to her shoulder. A small lick and a low growl were all the warning she got before his cock plunged into her sheath and his teeth sank into muscle and flesh.

Ecstasy rushed through Mystic like hot lava. She cried out as she gripped the bed sheet and used it to anchor herself.

Hawk thrusts were hard and fast, fierce and primal, as if his wolf was looking for one inside of her to mate with. She felt the magic rise to meet the essence of Hawk's wolf as if it would substitute for what she didn't posses herself.

Mystic shivered at the sensation. It was exquisite agony and unbearable pleasure to be so full of magic, so full of cock. She pressed backward and thrust her buttocks against Hawk in an effort to drive him deeper.

With a low, dominant growl he went into a wild rutting fever. He pounded harder, faster, until the ring of muscles hidden inside her trapped his cock and locked him in place in the way of her kind, in a way that satisfied Hawk's wolf as well. He released his grip on her shoulder and they both cried out as the first rush of seed splashed into her womb, only to be followed by another, and another, and another until they collapsed on the bed in a weak heap of sweat-slick skin and tangled limbs.

Hawk closed his eyes and savored the feel of her against him. He buried his face in her luxurious hair and smiled in complete satisfaction. He'd felt her wolf rise to meet his own and mate with it. And though her unguarded thoughts told him she believed it was Angelini magic answering his wolf's call, he knew differently.

In the long hours he'd spent with the Zevanti twins he'd had a chance to question them about Mystic. At first they'd been cautious about sharing any information other than what he could have learned from the pack. But after they'd hunted and run together as wolves, he'd slowly become not just *an* alpha but *their* alpha. It was a subtle shift brought about by a shared purpose and their tie to Mystic, but it was enough for them to open up and confide in him.

Much of what he'd learned confirmed what he'd guessed, given her vampire fathers and nontraditional mother. From the day of her birth Mystic had been under intense scrutiny not only by her grandparents but by the other Renaldis and their wolf allies. From an early age there had been whispered rumors she would be unable to shift form because her blood was too diluted by her vampire heritage.

Whether it was fear of failure, or because her wolf slept too deeply inside her, or because the magic had decided it wasn't time for Mystic to embrace that part of herself, when she never took a wolf form her inferiority was confirmed in the eyes of her Renaldi relatives. Added to that disgrace was the way her parents had raised but failed to train her. No one expected her to become a gifted hunter. As a result, Mystic's value in the eyes of her grandparents rested in what alliances might be gained if she took Were mates.

Hawk growled in protest at the pain she'd suffered. She was more than anyone had given her credit for and one day she'd believe it as firmly as he did. But for the moment he could only reach for her wolf and continue coaxing it into wakefulness. When it had risen and accepted him as alpha, then he'd be able to guide Mystic through the change. Until then he would subtly stroke and prod because he was afraid if he told her he could feel the wolf's presence, it would hurt her and cause her to shield parts of herself from him in order to avoid more pain.

She'd long ago accepted she couldn't shift and so she'd come to think of the wolf's stirrings as belonging to the Angelini magic. She would think that's what he felt too. She'd cringe in the belief he was seeing what he desperately wanted to see—that she was as desirable a mate as a pure Were female—and she'd worry he would ultimately be as disappointed in her as her grandparents were.

It could never happen. But Hawk knew the subject of her wolf was too sensitive to discuss, to painful to be eradicated with words. He stroked Mystic's side and felt his heart swell with tenderness. He would never willingly cause her pain.

At the Zevanti compound he'd been driven to possess her. She'd been the cornerstone of his dream to form a pack.

But now she was so much more. She was his heart, his soul, his life.

He nuzzled aside her hair and nibbled on her neck. The frenzy he'd felt to mate and mate repeatedly had eased. He felt calm, content. A chuckle escaped. Or perhaps she'd just milked him of seed so thoroughly he had nothing more to give.

Mystic turned in his arms and gave him a quick affectionate kiss. *What's so funny?*

Hawk cupped her breast and lazily rubbed his thumb back and forth over her nipple. He mentally shared the source of his amusement with her and smiled when her eyes danced with mischief as she said, "The night's young. I think you're underestimating yourself."

He nearly purred when her hand encased his cock and she stroked him slowly, up and down, over and over again until his penis was rigid and pulsing against her palm. She tormented him until his buttocks clenched and his hips flexed in order to drive his hard flesh through the fist of her fingers.

Hawk growled in protest when she freed him, then moaned in pleasure as her fingers explored the sac containing his testicles. It felt so good to have her touching and caressing him.

There'd been days in the Zevanti compound when he'd had to ease himself more than once because he refused to couple with any other female but Mystic. Some of the fantasies he'd used as he'd brought himself to orgasm had been of rough matings with her, but others had been like this, with her hands and mouth willingly seeking him out and giving him pleasure.

Heat began to build, first in his balls and then in his cock. It moved up his spine and into this chest and threatened to steal his breath.

He jerked when Mystic's hand once again captured his cock. He panted and wondered how long it would be before he begged.

It took every ounce of control he had to let her be the aggressor. He wanted to spear his fingers in her hair and force her down to his straining cock. Instead he tangled his fingers in her hair and guided her mouth to his.

You're torturing me, he said as his tongue licked over her lips.

I thought you were tougher than this.

He laughed. *Not where you're concerned.*

Her lips parted and she met his tongue with her own. She pushed into his mouth only to retreat. *So you want me to stop?*

No.

She rewarded his answer by luring his tongue into her mouth and holding it hostage. She sucked in the same rhythm as her hand pumped his cock.

Hawk shuddered under the dual assault. His hands left her hair to trail down her sides and grasp her hips. His balls tightened with the need to come. *Mystic*, he growled. The wolf inside him couldn't stand the thought of his seed coating her mound and belly. The man promised himself one day he'd mark her like that.

Mystic released his tongue only to lean down and lick over a hardened male nipple then blow on the wet nub. Hawk grunted and felt every muscle in his body tighten with the urge to pounce.

"Put my cock inside you."

She looked up at him from underneath her lashes. Her smile was sultry as her thumb rubbed the exposed head of his penis in a not-so-subtle challenge to his authority.

Hawk's hands tightened on her hips in response. His nostrils flared to capture the scent of her arousal. Man and beast battled over how to respond to her disobedience but before either prevailed Mystic ducked her head and found his nipple with her tongue and teeth.

Lightning flashes of erotic fire whipped through Hawk as she licked and bit and sucked. His hips jerked and his chest rose and fell in fast pants as her hand caressed his cock and her thumb ruthlessly tormented the sensitive head. A continuous growl rumbled in his throat as she took him to the point of release over and over again.

He reveled in being the sole focus of her attention even as he fought the wolf's urge to force her to her elbows and knees in order to mount her. This time he wanted to see her face as they made love. He wanted to watch as ecstasy shimmered through her and she cried out in orgasm.

Hawk's hands left her hips and went to her hair. His fingers tangled in her luxurious locks and forced her mouth away from his chest.

He guided her face to his, took her lips in a hard, wet kiss, before saying, "Put me inside you, Mystic. Fuck your mate until he comes."

Delicious sensation slid through Mystic as she looked down at Hawk's face. His cock pulsed in her hand and her cunt clenched in reaction.

She guided him to her entrance and took just the very tip of him inside her. His face tightened, the muscles in his abdomen were hard and taut. She lifted off him then settled again, using her hand to keep him from sliding all the way in.

His lips pulled back in a snarl. The wolf was a shadowy presence in his eyes and she could clearly read what it wanted—to dominate completely.

"Mystic," Hawk growled. Tension vibrated from him but rather than intimidate her, it emboldened her.

"Play with my breasts while I take you," she whispered, arching her back in a provocative display.

Hawk's smile was a flash of feral confidence as he obeyed her command.

Her buttocks clenched when his palms rubbed and circled over her nipples. Heat curled and spasmed in her clit when he began tugging, squeezing areolas already made sensitive by the attention her mates had given them.

Mystic moaned and took all of his cock inside her. She felt his pleasure along their link and saw it in his face as she moved up and down on his shaft. She lingered. She savored. She drew their lovemaking out until neither of them could stand the torment any longer. And then she did has he'd commanded earlier, she fucked her mate until he came, until they both came.

A contented smile settled on Mystic's face. She trailed her fingers over Hawk's muscled abdomen until she got to the pack brand he wore near his right hip. He only had the one, a crescent moon with an intricate symbol in the bare space formed by the moon's curve.

An older wolf would often have two or three brands, each one connected by a lightning bolt in order to identify which was the pack of origin and which was the current pack. A banished or outcast wolf would have an ugly pucker where the brand had been burned away.

"Tell me about your pack," she said, tracing the symbol inside the moon's curve.

"My old pack." Hawk rolled to his elbow and covered her thighs with one of his. His braids hung down on either side of his face like dark beaded curtains. "Now that I have a mate I plan to petition the council for a pack. You'll support me?"

"Yes," she whispered, heart racing and nerves fluttering in her stomach. She'd known what his intentions were from the moment he'd appeared at the Zevanti compound. She'd feared them.

She'd thought he only wanted her because she was Angelini and could help him gain a pack. Now that they were bound together, she didn't question the rightness of it, but she was still afraid she'd let him down. She had no wolf form.

Even worse, without the tattoo of an Angelini hunter and the magic that came with it, she was weak, very nearly human.

Enough, Hawk said, lowering his head and growling against her throat before giving her a sharp nip. He'd intended to answer Mystic's question and tell her about himself, but when she became softly submissive underneath him the blood rushed to fill his cock.

Hawk growled again, this time against her mouth. *Open for me*, he said and she parted both her lips and her thighs.

He thrust his tongue into the wet heaven of her mouth as his cock forced its way into the clinging heated core of her. *I was willing to talk.*

Mystic's arms and legs wrapped around him. She smiled against his mouth. *We can talk later.*

Hawk began pumping, slowly at first, just as she'd done when he allowed her to mount him. Then faster as her moans drove all thought from his mind and the only thing left was fierce emotion and overwhelming sensation.

Afterward Hawk reached down and pulled the comforter over their bare bodies, not because it was cold, but because suddenly the idea of cuddling under the covers appealed to him. He smiled when her fingertips found the pack brand and she teased, "Being mated to you isn't nearly as bad as I thought it would be." Her leg slid over his and she pressed more tightly against him. "For one thing, you're very, very warm."

"Warm?" He trailed his fingers down her spine before his hand cupped a sleek buttock. "You're supposed to say I'm hot."

Her laughter made his heart sing. A curtain parted deep inside him and a lifetime of fierce determination gave way to feelings he was loath to put a name on.

"Point taken," she murmured, rubbing her lips on his collarbone before peeking up at him through dark lashes. "Not that you need to have your ego or anything else stroked. You sent more than one of the females at the Zevanti compound into heat just by walking into the room."

He flashed his teeth and growled softly. "I didn't realize you stayed in any room with me long enough to notice that kind of thing."

She pressed another kiss to his collarbone. "I had to run from you. The magic wanted me here because of Roman and Christian and because of the dead fledgling."

Hawk repositioned her so he could take her mouth with his. *Just don't run from me again, Mystic,* he said as his tongue thrust aggressively against hers.

I won't.

He gentled the kiss. She'd become his sole focus from the moment he'd first seen her but now she was so much more. Any time he touched her he felt the overwhelming need to meld every inch of himself to her.

This was what it meant to be an Angelini mate. On an intellectual level he'd known it would be like this. But nothing could have prepared him for the reality. When he was younger he probably would have railed against the loss of freedom that came with such a bond, but now, now he could only moan and shudder with pleasure as his heart swelled with intense satisfaction at having Mystic for a mate. She was everything to him. His life. His future. His dream. All in a body that made him constantly hard.

He took her again. Filled her sweet, wet channel with his cock as the mental barriers fell away and their souls danced and merged, two hot flames becoming one incandescent blaze in a timeless place of magic.

Chapter Twelve

ဢ

"This is worse than we thought," Syndelle said as she studied the information on Rafael's computer screen.

Rafe gave a low whistle. "Born in Vegas, grew up in Vegas, supposedly died and was buried in Vegas the first time, but lived as a vampire in Vegas. Could anything be more wrong with that picture?"

Skye leaned forward though she had to battle the beanbag chairs Rafe favored as furniture in order to do it. "Any way to find out how Todd Moore became a vampire?" She glanced at Syndelle. "If you handled the bones, would you be able to read anything from them?"

Rafe snickered and let out a mock werewolf howl which earned him a quick nip on his bare shoulder from his mate and a disgusted look from Skye. *How do you stand it?* Skye asked her sister — again.

Syndelle pressed a kiss to the fading mark on Rafe's shoulder. *Because as you've seen, he has his uses. And one of them is he makes me laugh.*

"I am sitting right here between the two of you," Rafe grumbled, though he struggled to keep the amusement out of his voice. He added for Syndelle alone, *Laughter isn't the only sound I can coax from you.*

Syndelle rubbed her cheek against his arm and fought against the need to crawl into his lap for greater physical contact. She said, "There has to be blood in order for me to know anything about the vampire. There wouldn't be a trace of it where Mystic and the others found him, not the way he died." She frowned for an instant then grew animated. "But if we found the blade used to stop his heart and make him

150

helpless so he could be moved to the hunt site, there might be enough blood to read his history."

"*We?*" They all jumped at the purring menace in Brann's unexpected voice.

"Shit!" Rafe said, shooting Syndelle a look of mock reproach.

Syndelle laughed and got to her feet. "That's the trouble with the truly ancient and extremely powerful vampires. They can be impossible to detect, though why one of them, a creature known far and wide as the council's executioner, would choose to skulk around in his own heavily warded estate and sneak up on his companions and their guest is a question I'd like to have answered." She got to Brann and wound her arms around his neck.

He bent his head and kissed her thoroughly before saying, "Perhaps this ancient has learned only too well that his companions can't be completely trusted to either obey his rules or stay out of danger. What trouble has my unanticipated arrival kept you and Rafe out of?"

Syndelle led him back to where they were gathered around Rafe's computer. Brann settled on the carpet with Syndelle on his lap though he leaned over and gave Rafael a kiss as thorough as the one he'd given her.

Because they all shared a mental pathway it was easy to transfer information to Brann. When he was in possession of the facts, he said, "Let me see the dead vampire's picture."

Rafe clicked a file where the image on the driver's license was stored, along with others gathered from a blog. With a thought Brann reached out to Gian and Skye grimaced with the realization it'd probably been too much to hope for that her mates wouldn't find out about this visit.

Brann's eyes flashed with both amusement and triumph. His arm tightened on Syndelle possessively.

Happiness poured into Skye that he was Syndelle's mate. If anyone could keep her sister safe, it was Brann.

Skye found herself smiling despite the flare of irritation she felt along the bond with Gian. Even without the tattoo of an Angelini hunter and the added magic that came with it, Skye was supremely confident in her abilities to fight and survive. She'd been tested by a horror-filled childhood. She had tested herself as an adult by becoming a finder of missing people and a hunter of dangerous criminals. Her life had prepared her for the violent deadly indoctrination into a supernatural world she'd never guessed existed.

She knew a lot more now than she had before Syndelle's arrival. She would know even more when their parents and brothers arrived in Vegas. Even so, Skye believed she could hold her own against almost all of the threats she was likely to encounter — except for Brann. Since entering the realm of the supernatural he was the only being she'd confronted who had the power to truly scare her.

Keep that thought in mind and perhaps you'll avoid bringing my sire's wrath down on us both, Gian said along their private link. *Only the fact Brann is not completely in control of his own Coronado Angelini has saved me from yet another of his lectures. We will discuss your visit to Syndelle when you get back home.* The last was a silky purr probably meant as a threat but underneath Gian's words Skye felt the potent need for sex.

Her smile widened. If he wanted to regain his sense of control by fucking her into submission, she was game. But first she wanted to make a little more progress in hunting down the origins of the dead vampire.

Skye turned her attention back to the others and forced her expression not to reveal anything as she asked, "So should we hit WyldFyres and see if anyone knows anything about our dead vamp?"

A small shiver rippled through Syndelle at the mention of the vampire club where she'd fought for her life. She knew her sister was joking, or at least she hoped Skye was.

WyldFyres was a place where vampires went to feed and fuck their slaves and companions while in the company of other vampires. It was a private club that catered to a variety of tastes in a never-ending celebration of the lusts and sins to be found in Las Vegas.

Brann hissed. His arms tightened around Syndelle.

"WyldFyres is out. For all of us," Syndelle said, interlacing her fingers with Brann's and sifting subtly so her buttocks rubbed against his erection in a move that was both distraction and supplication.

He bent his head to press a kiss against her neck before also letting her feel the touch of fangs. *You are not going anywhere, Syndelle.*

Have I said I was? This time her shiver was one of need. Across from her, Skye's eyebrows drew together. "Do vampires keep records like the Angelini do?"

Syndelle shook her head. "No. Blood calls to blood. Vampires can tell if they are near someone of their line, or to a lesser extent, someone their sire or dam is aligned with through the sharing of blood. One of the most sacred and powerful bonds, beside the companion bond, is the bond between a vampire and his or her 'created' children." She frowned. "Fledglings are dangerous to all of us. They are more like rabid animals at first, though some gain control of the hunger more quickly than others.

"One of the first rules is that a fledgling must avoid places where they would be recognized by humans who know they are dead. It also serves to keep them from being tempted to change their family and friends into vampires. Rafael is right. Todd Moore being in Vegas is wrong on many levels. A vampire can be sanctioned and destroyed for creating a fledgling and then not instructing and caring for it. And if the fledgling 'child' can't be controlled, then it's the responsibility of the parent to destroy it. If the parent fails, then it falls to the one who created him or her, not only to destroy the fledgling, but to pass judgment on the one they created. If not dealt with quickly, then it becomes a matter for the vampire council or the Angelini."

Rafael moved so he was partially sprawled across Syndelle's lap. She smiled and stroked his chest. Brann's hand followed hers though it settled on Rafe's belly, only inches away from where his erection pressed boldly against the front of his pants.

"Trust me on this," Rafael said, "even the craziest of the vampires don't want to draw the attention of either the council or the Angelini. Most of them would kill a centuries-old firstborn in a heartbeat if that's what it took to avoid being punished."

Skye's stomach twisted, remembering her own shocking introduction to the reality of vampires and to the witch who was creating fledglings from black magic—a magic that it had taken Brann and several other vampires to counter. "Do you think this guy might have been created by the witch? Is it possible we missed one of her fledglings?"

Brann's thumb stroked idly over Rafe's stomach. Rafael hesitated for only a few seconds before saying, "No. I traced every thread and weeded through hundreds of blogs and chat rooms. We got them all. You saw the coffins, Skye. You saw the bodies. The witch liked to keep her children close and the fledglings weren't strong enough to create others like them. We accounted for them all."

A chime sounded throughout the house. Rafe grunted and rolled to a sitting position. He grinned at Skye. "Is this one of your mates coming to collect you?"

Syndelle said, "It's Roman."

Skye felt it then, the humming in her veins, blood recognizing blood.

Rafe rose to his feet. "I'll meet him at the door." He quirked an eyebrow at Brann. "I assume you intend to let him through the wards. After all, there's no reason for him to strip in front of Syndelle again."

Skye choked back a laugh at Brann's expression. She couldn't stop herself from saying, "I wish I could have been here for that. Is Roman as gorgeous without clothes as he is in them?"

Syndelle's eyes danced with amusement. "He's worthy of starring in any number of fantasies."

Brann hissed in response and lowered his face. Syndelle jerked when his fangs sank into her neck. Her eyelids lowered and her body went soft.

Skye looked away from the intimacy. She was too new to the world of vampires and Angelini to feel completely comfortable with how quickly teasing or arguing or even simple conversation could be set aside for lovemaking. Sex between strangers she could watch without batting an eye, but this...

Rafael snorted and managed a parting shot before leaving the room. "Better get used to it."

* * * * *

The telephone next to the bed rang. Hawk growled low in his throat but he didn't intercept Mystic's hand when she reached for it.

It was Gabe. "Let me speak to Hawk."

Mystic was torn between aggravation and amusement. She shook her head and passed the phone. No doubt it was both a man-thing and a wolf-thing. Apparently years of being close friends didn't entitle her to hearing things firsthand, not when there was a take-charge alpha available.

"Stay there," Hawk said to Gabe. "If they leave, try for a license plate. Follow them if you can but don't split up and leave Gabrielle vulnerable. Mystic and I are on the way."

Hawk rose onto an elbow. He dropped the receiver back into its cradle before giving Mystic a quick, fierce kiss and rolling out of bed. "Let's go."

"Where?" Mystic asked, scrambling after him and wishing she had her suitcase and the fresh clothing it contained.

"A place called Bangers. It's a strip club. Gabe says a couple of Weres are there and they seem *off* to him. He's betting they're the ones we're hunting."

Mystic shimmied into her jeans and grimaced at the feel of fabric against her ass. She didn't know how guys could stand to go commando when the thought of catching her pubic hair in the zipper made her cringe.

Hawk's low growl stopped her when she reached for one of Christian's shirts. "Wear mine," he said.

She didn't argue though she did roll her eyes. She was definitely going to get her suitcase from the hotel room tonight before they came back here. Otherwise she'd end up walking around naked when one of her other mates got home and growled at her to take off Hawk's shirt.

They left the house a few minutes later. Mystic sighed in relief when she spotted her suitcase in the backseat of Hawk's car. She was tempted to rush back into the house and change clothes. She got in the car instead, though she couldn't hold back a laugh as she thought about her mother.

Was it really any wonder her mother didn't hurry to engage in a hunt? Estelle was a slave to fashion, or more accurately it was a slave to her. Human, vampire, even the occasional Were were all quick to copy whatever style her mother adopted.

Mystic grinned. At least she'd managed to suppress the urge to delay them by going in to change and put on makeup. This *was* an important hunt after all. This was *her* chance to prove herself.

Hawk chuckled. "I think I'll like your mother. But you have nothing to prove, Mystic. I believe I speak for all of your mates when I say we would be happy if you never wore the tattoo of a hunter. Between Christian, Roman and me, there is no need for you to bloody your hands. Your battles will fall to us."

"I need to be able to fight my own battles," she said, her heart rate speeding up as she looked out the window and put a thin shield between her mind and Hawk's.

He growled in acknowledgement of the barrier but didn't push against it. She placed her hand on his thigh, grateful he could accept her need for privacy.

For most of her life she'd been able to put aside thoughts of becoming a hunter. The few times when she'd mentioned her lack of training to her parents, they'd shrugged it aside and said there was still plenty of time to prepare her, and besides, there were plenty of hunters. Why rush to do something none of them was looking forward to doing?

She hadn't argued. She wasn't in any great hurry to kill. She was too much her parents' daughter. They liked parties and entertaining. They encouraged her interest in music and she found it far more pleasurable to spend hours on the piano bench than to learn how to sneak up on someone so she could drive a knife through their heart.

Her stomach turned as she remembered the last summer she'd spent completely in her grandparents' care as a child. At her grandmother's orders she'd been taken into the woods with her uncles, aunts and cousins. They'd spent some time in human form—enough of it anyway to give her orders, instructions, and then tell her what she was doing wrong at the end of each day—but most of their time had been spent furred. If she wanted to eat, then she had to forage for herself because by the time the pack finished with anything they killed, there wasn't even enough left to make stew out of, much less roast over a campfire.

It had been the longest, most agonizing summer of her life. She'd gotten so hungry that eventually she'd tried sneaking up on herd of deer with the intention of driving the blade she'd been given into one of them and killing it—which was the whole point of her grandmother's order to begin with, but she'd failed. Even now Mystic wasn't sure she could have done it.

She saw Hawk out of the corner of her eye and lifted her chin in resolve. *That was then, this is now.* The Angelini were hunters. It was their purpose and their destiny. She believed Hawk when he said he didn't care whether she had a hunter's tattoo or not, but the truth was that it would matter in the future. Her failure would reflect on their pack and on their children.

Among the Angelini there were plenty who couldn't shift form. But only the young or inexperienced were without the winged-tattoo signifying they had taken their rightful place in their world. For the Angelini, you became a hunter or you died trying. In fact, most were hunters before the magic rose inside them to claim mates.

Mystic frowned as that thought came to her. Her eyebrows drew together as she paged through all the names and family lines she'd memorized over the course of her life. Had the magic chosen mates for any of them before they'd proven themselves worthy? A couple of them maybe, early on, but not among those in her own generation or in her mother's generation.

The car stopped at a red light. Hawk covered her hand with his and the feel of his calloused palm distracted her from her thoughts. She had no idea what he did for a living. She had no idea what businesses his pack managed and where he stood in the hierarchy. She'd been so busy running from him and hiding from the truth of what he was to her that she hadn't learned any of the details of his life.

She turned so she could study him and his eyebrow lifted in silent query. Mystic laughed, suddenly feeling on familiar ground. People watching and making guesses about strangers was a favorite pastime when she went out to dinner with her parents.

They made a game of it, and of course, it was easy enough to settle who was right. Falcone could capture a human's mind from across the room. Yorick was almost as powerful. Estelle needed to be closer, but if it was a man, she rarely needed to use her ability to hypnotize. Most would regale her with their life story just to hear her voice or feel her eyes on them — not that either of her fathers allowed her to linger with any other male, human or not.

Mystic's nipples tightened when Hawk took her hand to his mouth and stroked his tongue over her knuckles. "I am trying to respect your privacy but you are making it difficult with your mysterious smiles."

She laughed. "I'm just trying to make an educated guess about you."

"Ask and I'll tell you anything you want to know."

"Maybe I'd rather pretend you're a box of chocolates and unwrap you slowly," she teased.

His nostrils flared and she felt her cunt swell as the barrier between their minds wavered and fell under the shared fantasy of her undressing him and then leisurely exploring him with her lips and tongue.

Hawk placed her hand on his jeans-covered erection. He pressed it firmly against the thick ridge and her fingers curled around his cock. Lust pulsed between them in a fierce, rapid beat.

The car behind them honked. Hawk snarled and Mystic jumped in her seat. Heat rushed to her cheeks at how quickly she'd forgotten where they were and what they were doing. Her earlier thought returned. She was very much her parents' daughter. After decades of being together, her parents were still like human newlyweds on a honeymoon, sometimes to her great embarrassment.

Hawk shifted the car into gear. Mystic guessed, "Your pack owns a construction company."

He glanced sideways. A grin flashed across his features. "True. I work as a foreman when I'm needed and when my uncle can spare me."

"So it's not your main job."

Hawk brought her hand to his lips again and for a second time explored her knuckles with his tongue. "There should be a penalty for a wrong guess and a reward for a correct one."

Mystic's womb fluttered. She had the feeling that whatever he had in mind, she'd enjoy paying the penalty or gaining the reward.

"When I play this game with my parents, the loser ends up doing some of the winner's house and yard chores," she teased.

Hawk's eyebrows lifted. "You don't have blood servants or hired help?"

"No blood servants. My parents don't want the responsibility. No blood slaves. My mother doesn't approve of it. My fathers don't care for the practice either. Plus all three of them value their privacy over the inconvenience of doing chores. And besides, they have me." She laughed. "They like to disguise the fact I'm often cook, housekeeper and yard person behind the convenient excuse they're training me to manage a home of my own."

Hawk growled in response to her comment. A scowl settled on his features as waves of outrage on her behalf washed down the bond.

Mystic squeezed his hand. "I wouldn't trade my parents for any others. If you'll check my memories, you'll see that while it might *feel* as though I am the one most often stuck with the chores, the truth is we have always worked together as a family."

Hawk placed her hand back on his thigh and left it covered with his own. Without warning he said, "It would be difficult for a newly sanctioned pack to carve a territory out near your parents' home."

Surprised rippled through Mystic, followed by the realization she should have known he'd consider what taking her as a mate might entail. Hawk had never made any secret of his intention to form a pack of his own rather than try to take over an existing one.

"From the first moment I saw you, I knew you belonged to me," he said. "I made discreet inquiries. The packs who claim the areas around and within an easy traveling distance from your parents are strong. Most of them are barely on speaking terms with the wolves the Renaldis consider allies. And beyond that, I'd rather start a pack from nothing than to gain one through challenge.

Mystic laughed and stroked his inner thigh with her fingertips. "It's not an accident my parents settled where they did. It's kept them free from the worst of pack politics since they screen their calls and most of my Were relatives are loath to ask for permission to enter what they consider *hostile* territory on the off chance they can involve Estelle in their power plays."

She leaned forward and nipped Hawk's neck then soothed the spot with her tongue. "I'm not ready to decide on a place to live yet. Let's finish this hunt first and get to know each other better. There are four of us to consider, not just two."

His lip curled and a small snarl escaped but Mystic could feel his willingness to put the discussion aside as Bangers came into sight.

Chapter Thirteen

ಬಿ

Bangers was a sleazy place in a bad area of town. Mystic wrinkled her nose as she climbed out of the car and the stench of alcohol, sex and unwashed human bodies assailed her. The smell came from the open doorway, from the cars around them. It even seemed to be baked into the asphalt.

"Looks promising," she said.

"Stay close to me," Hawk growled.

"I may stand right behind you so I can bury my nose in your shirt."

"I've smelled worse. At least there's no death here, not at the moment anyway."

Hawk moved around the car to place a proprietary hand on Mystic's hip. His wolf didn't like this. It paced and snarled and would have charged down the bond to bite Mystic's slumbering wolf until it woke if Hawk hadn't kept his beast caged in a place where she couldn't feel it.

The wolf wasn't at ease with the situation. It wouldn't be until others in its pack were present, and even then it hated having its mate locked in a human form.

If Hawk hadn't been worried about Mystic's safety himself, he would have been amused by the strange sensation of being slightly at odds with his beast. For most of his life they'd been one, a cohesive unit working and hunting together. But then, early on he'd had the power and control necessary to shift between forms without the added boost of an adult, an alpha, or the moon.

"Places like this can erupt into violence quickly," he told Mystic. "Stay alert."

"I will."

Both wolf and man were tested as soon as they got to the entrance. The bouncer's eyes roamed over Mystic. His hand went to his crotch and his tongue glided over thick parted lips. "You're a fine piece of ass, baby. There's no cover charge for you. Twenty-bucks for your friend but I'll let it go for a look at those tits."

Hawk's muscles bunched. He nearly launched himself at the other man when Mystic moved forward, crowding into the bouncer's personal space and forcing his gaze from her chest to her face. In the blink of an eye the bouncer's expression went slack. "You'll let us both in for free," she said.

A shiver of awareness slid up Hawk's spine. The hairs stood on his neck like a wolf's raised hackles. He was immune to the compulsion in her voice and yet he could hear it clearly. He hadn't expected her to have that ability.

The bouncer stepped back and gestured for them to pass. Hawk guided Mystic through the door and into the dark club.

Nice parlor trick, Hawk murmured along their bond.

She laughed silently. *It's one advantage of having two vampire fathers and very little wolf blood to dampen the effect, though I think I've also gained from Roman's blood. It took almost no effort at all to capture the bouncer with my eyes and compel him to let us in.*

Hawk only barely avoided growling a protest at her easy dismissal of her wolf. He knew they couldn't afford to be distracted by an argument over her true nature. His hand tightened on her waist in order to direct her attention to the right. *There's Gabe.*

They fought their way through the sweaty mass of drugged and drunk humans. Even with their bloodstreams polluted by intoxicants, the men reacted to Mystic's presence, crowding her, eating her with their eyes, fucking her in their fantasies.

Barely clad women writhed and gyrated against poles as others stripped on a stage. Cocktail waitresses wearing little more than thongs and tassels tolerated drunken groping and fingers sliding cash past the elastic of their panties.

"I should have handed you off to Roman instead of bringing you here," Hawk said when they reached the booth where Gabe and Gabby waited. A quick jerk of his head and Gabe slid out so Mystic could slide in and be against the wall.

"As if I would have let you," Mystic shot back, purposely twisting away from Hawk's hand and sitting next to Gabby, refusing to be forced against the wall of the booth.

"Mystic," Hawk growled.

"Oh man, trouble in paradise already?" Gabe said, deflecting Hawk's attention from Mystic and earning himself a dark look along with a snarl.

Mystic took advantage of the interruption. "So where are they?"

Gabby leaned forward. Her excitement made the air crackle. "When Gabe called you guys, there were two Weres who seemed *off* to us, a male and a female who both make me look like an uber-alpha-bitch—in a pack sense of course. But a little while ago another female joined them.

"The new one has been taking money from some of the human males and they've been disappearing into the private lap dance booths with the weaker female. Her body language says she's not happy about being pimped, but she's too scared of the alpha bitch to refuse."

Gabe risked a glance at Hawk before sliding onto the bench seat he'd just vacated. "It's got to be them. Or at least three of the seven we're hunting. The profile fits what the tracks in the woods told us. The apparent nonconsensual sex, plus a weak male and female who like to separate from the rest of their pack when they can but who are both completely dominated."

Hawk's gaze captured Mystic's. *Don't think I'll let your challenge to my authority go just because your friends ran interference and we have other business to attend to*, he growled into her thoughts.

I'm not a wolf nor are the four of us officially a pack. I am your mate. Your equal.

In some things but not in situations like this.

She looked away rather than to continue arguing with him. True, she wasn't trained, but she could certainly manage the humans and there was very little danger to be found in a booth!

That's what you think, Hawk said. He reached across and tangled his fingers in her hair in order to force her gaze back to his. *Take a deep breath. Smell beneath the sex and sweat. Go beyond the stench of unwashed clothes and dirty bodies. What do you find?*

Mystic grimaced. She'd been trying very hard *not* to inhale most of what was assaulting her nostrils. But she knew what he was getting at. *Okay, there are guns and knives, probably other weapons as well.*

Hawk released her hair and stroked downward until his fingers curled around her neck in a gesture that was possessive and protective as well as threatening. *Without the tattoo of a hunter you are nearly as vulnerable as a human. A stray bullet or misaimed knife could kill you as easily as it could kill one of them.*

I know.

Then obey me without question while we're hunting, Mystic. Your other mates will stand with me on this.

Okay, she said, knowing he was right.

One of the reasons the Angelini were such frightening hunters was because their children remained extremely vulnerable in the supernatural world they lived in until they'd finished their first hunt and gained the tattoo. Neither Angelini parent nor child easily forgot what it was like to live as a human and have human fears. They never forgot how fragile the beings they'd been created to protect were when it came to vampires and wolves.

Mystic lifted her lip in a silent snarl then laughed at herself for doing such a wolfie thing. She didn't doubt every one of her mates would be more than willing to keep her naked and in bed 24/7 if she'd let them or they could find an excuse to do it.

Hawk's chuckle slid down her spine and made her nipples tighten. *Credit us with a little more imagination than that. Naked, yes, but even within Christian's sparsely furnished house there are many, many places other than the bed where we would enjoy mating with you.*

Delicious images shivered through Mystic. She wanted to believe it was just the newness of sex that had her so easily craving more of it after she'd already had *so much* of it. But she suspected the men in her life were always going to have this power over her. She guessed it would always take very little on their part to make her forget what she was doing or thinking in the moments before they tempted her with the promise of pleasure.

It took more effort than she'd ever admit to in order to force the sensual scenes parading through her thoughts away. When she did she noticed the scene taking place in front of her and frowned.

A human male was standing next to the table with the three Weres. He was heavyset and greasy-haired, clad in leather with a chain tethering his wallet to his jeans. But it was his eyes that bothered Mystic the most. They were mean and small. Pig eyes.

His head jerked toward the weaker female and she cowered. The noise in the club drowned out any possibility of hearing the whimper of protest but Mystic knew one had come from the female's lips.

The alpha bitch said something. The human spat on the floor. The alpha shrugged and turned her face as if dismissing the human. He glowered at the weaker female then reached back and yanked his wallet out of his pocket. Several bills landed on the table.

Mystic stood when the weak female stood.

No, Hawk said, rising and grabbing Mystic's wrist before she could take a step toward the Weres. "This is not our fight." *Do you want to risk your friends among a drunk and heavily armed crowd? A crowd that will erupt into violence with little provocation? We cannot shift here and we are outnumbered.*

The human and the female Were approached the row of booths set aside for private lap dances. A bouncer leaning against a nearby exit pushed away from the wall and moved to intercept them.

More money changed hands.

Mystic's stomach turned. She knew Hawk was right. Gabby could hold her own in her fur but in human form she wasn't much better at fighting than she was at being stealthy.

I'm a lover, not a fighter. It was their shared motto, their shield against the failure others wanted to assign them.

The human and the female Were entered one of the booths and closed the door.

Everything inside Mystic screamed she should do something. Pack life could be brutal, especially for members of lesser standing, she knew and accepted that, but to abuse a female like this, to sell her...

"How long?" Hawk asked.

"Fifteen minutes," Gabe said. "If they're not out the bouncer will open the door and collect more money or tell them to leave."

Hawk squeezed Mystic's wrist. "Sit. You're starting to attract attention and unlike the alpha female, I won't tolerate a human male either touching or talking to you."

Mystic's eyebrows lifted. "Talking? Don't you think that's a bit extreme? I *am* part of this hunt and as you saw with the bouncer at the entrance, I *do* have certain abilities you do not."

Her chin went up slightly. It might be an overstatement but she *did* feel as though she'd gained from Roman's blood. "I bet it would take me only a few minutes of leaning against the bar and questioning the men who came to me for us to know a lot more about the Weres. Surely you don't intend for us to sit in the booth and do nothing other than wait for them to leave so we can follow them."

The muscle in Hawk's cheek spasmed.

"It's not a bad idea," Gabe volunteered.

Hawk shot him a lethal glare. Mystic tried to pull out of Hawk's grasp. His teeth flashed in warning but she didn't back down. "You can go to the bar with me," she said, "but I imagine we'll have better results if Gabe or Gabby go instead."

Her gaze flicked to the private room where the human male and the Were female were no doubt engaged in sexual acts. "I understand why we can't interfere now. But I can't sit and do nothing."

A frustrated growl vibrated in Hawk's chest and throat. He should have passed her off to Roman. Better yet, he should have found a way to convince her other mates to agree with him and send her back to the Zevanti compound where she'd be safe.

Her upbringing hadn't prepared her to deal with violence, with situations and places like this one. The stink of human anger and despair mixed with drugs and alcohol and hidden weapons was a combination guaranteed to erupt at some point.

"I don't like the idea of you making yourself available to the men here," Hawk said.

"I know." Mystic took a step so she was standing next to where he sat.

Her scent assailed him. Her heat curled around his cock. When she placed her hand on his forearm he knew he was going to lose the battle.

"I need to learn," she said, her eyes soft and pleading. "What better way to do it than with you and Gabe and Gabby here to watch over me?"

Instinct warred with reason. Wolf battled man. But in the end he nodded sharply and said, "Stay close to her, Gabe."

Mystic squeezed his arm. Reluctantly he let her pull her wrist from his grip.

It nearly killed him to watch her walk away from the booth. The sway of her hips, the sultry attraction of Mystic alone was enough to draw hungry male eyes to her. The erotic allure of the Angelini only served to make the humans moths to a compelling flame.

He partially rose from his seat when a man grabbed her arm. A ripple of anger and possessiveness streaked down his spine like raised hackles.

Gabby's hand on his wrist stopped him from following Mystic. Her urgent, "She'll be okay. Give her a chance," reined in Hawk's need to sever the human's hand from his arm for daring to touch Mystic.

"She should go back to the Zevanti compound. You both should."

"They'll all be at the Howl."

A muscle twitched in Hawk's cheek. Gabby was right. By now the heady fever to pair up and breed would be riding the pack members. The females would be in heat and the males eager to cover them. He didn't think the Angelini magic would rise again and demand Mystic claim a fourth mate, but in the midst of a fog of lust... His teeth snapped together with a frustrated growl. They would see to her safety here.

He settled into his seat. He watched as Mystic escaped the human and got to the bar. Immediately the bartender came to serve her. Even in the dark, smoky club, Hawk saw the instant when Mystic captured the man in her eyes.

Pride filled him. The wolf inside snarled but subsided. He relaxed enough to look away from Mystic in order to study the Weres.

The alpha female was dangerous. The lesser male was an unknown. But if they could separate the weak female from her companions they could probably gain enough information to capture them—or kill them. He was fairly certain these were the wolves who'd hunted the fledgling vampire.

Hawk preferred to capture them and hand them over to a jury of Weres and vampires. Either way, he would do what was necessary. He was an alpha strong enough to petition for a pack of his own, he would see this hunt to its conclusion.

His attention shifted to the private booth where the weak female was entertaining the human male. The easiest way to get the Were alone was to pay for her company.

According to the tracks they'd found in the woods, she and a weaker male had hung back as the others hunted. And given the way the alpha bitch was selling the weak female against her will, it was possible she would latch on to him as her savior.

His gaze flicked to the emergency exit. An alternative would be to intercept the female and hurry her outside and into one of the cars.

He looked at his watch. Five minutes remained before the bouncer would expect to be paid for additional room time. His eyes found Mystic. She was talking to a second bartender. Gabe was several stools away, nursing a beer and leaning casually against the bar.

Hawk smiled in approval. He was impressed with both of Mystic's friends.

His focus shifted to the alpha bitch and the male. He measured the distance from their table to the booth and then to the emergency exit guarded by the same bouncer selling time in the lap-dance booths. He considered the risks as he worked various scenarios out in his mind. His gaze lingered on the bouncer and his stomach tightened with thoughts of sending Mystic to see if he could be used to help them separate the weak female from her two pack members.

Hawk took in the crowd. It was almost exclusively human though several of them wore black and smiled with vampire-like fangs.

"Have there been any other Weres here?" he asked. He wondered if the rogues knew how to spot others like them. If they'd been created rather than born, they might not know, just as they might not have known the fledgling wouldn't disintegrate with the dawn.

"I felt something earlier," Gabby said.

"Did you and Gabe check all the way around the club?"

"Yes."

He nodded toward the emergency exit and the bouncer leaning against the wall. "Any idea what's on the other side of that door?"

"More parking. While we were back there a guy was screwing a hookup against the wall. Guess he was too cheap to pay for a booth and too high to care that one of the bartenders was having a smoke and watching the action."

"Where's your car?"

"On the other side."

Gabe and Mystic returned to the booth. "What'd you learn?" Gabby asked.

"There are seven of them, just like we thought," Mystic said. "Usually there are only two or three here at a time. They've been coming around for the last month." She leaned forward. "And get this, lately they've started asking about a woman named Marta, a guy named Hugh, and another guy — Todd."

"The fledgling," Gabby said. "He wasn't a random kill."

Mystic nodded. "That's what it looks like."

"Did you get a description of Marta and Hugh?" Hawk asked.

Mystic shook her head. "The bartenders only vaguely remembered the names. One of them thought he may have seen a picture. But they wouldn't have admitted to knowing anything at all if I hadn't compelled them."

Hawk stroked Mystic's cheek. He wanted to pull her into his arms and kiss her to demonstrate how pleased and proud he was, only he worried over whether to acknowledge her victory or not. She was Angelini. He would have easily accepted her as a hunter if she'd already been one, but the idea of her *becoming* one didn't fit comfortably with his need to protect her.

"You did well," he finally said and was glad he did it when he felt how much it meant to her.

They turned their attention back to the Weres. The bouncer checked his watch and pushed away from the wall. He opened the door to the private booth. The female emerged with the dead eyes of a habitual victim.

A muscle spasmed in Hawk's jaw. "I'm going to buy fifteen minutes with the female. If I can be alone with her in the booth I may be able to turn her with a promise of safety. But failing that, when our time is up, I'm going to steer her to the exit."

He glanced at Mystic. "Once I'm in the booth, I want you to go over to the bouncer. See if you can compel him to help us, or at least not to hinder us. Stay there while Gabe escorts Gabby to their Jeep."

His attention shifted to Gabby. "Position the car just outside the exit and be ready to open the back door. Gabe—"

Hawk cursed as he watched the Weres stand and slip on their jackets. Frustration rippled through him.

He opened his mouth to tell Gabe and Gabby to position themselves outside the front door but before he could get the words out a human approached the Were's table. His wallet was in his hand before he arrived.

Where the other man had been heavyset and bull-necked, this one was thin and lanky. The alpha bitch smiled a greeting and sank back into her seat. The male Were followed her example. The weak female remained standing as money changed hands.

Money changed hands again with the bouncer.

"We're in luck," Gabe murmured as this time the bouncer indicated the booth closest to the exit door.

"Walk Gabrielle out to the car then come back inside," Hawk said. "Gabby, make sure the car is where it needs to be in fifteen minutes. Leave the engine running. Once we come out, open the back door and then get back in the front seat. Be ready to drive."

Gabe and Gabby left after checking their watches. Mystic covered Hawk's hand with hers. "Thanks for not using me to talk to the bouncer then sending me to the car where you think it's safer."

He flipped his hand over and captured hers. "I'd like to send you to the car. Better yet, I wish you were somewhere else, with one of your other mates."

"Or the Howl?"

His nostrils flared. "Only if I was there to mount you."

A flash of heat spiked through Mystic's pussy. The Weres thought nothing of mating in the presence of others during the Howl, though it was an entertainment reserved for adults only.

Gabe returned a few minutes later. Mystic glanced at her watch. She was nervous but excited. What she'd told Hawk earlier was true. She *had* gained from Roman's blood. Not only had it been easy to draw the bartenders to her, but it had been easy to question them and guide them through the fog of their memories. She'd never been able to hold another's mind so long or probe so deeply into thoughts that weren't her own, especially in a stranger who had no blood link to her.

"I should go," she said, squeezing Hawk's hand but waiting for him to release her rather than pulling away from him.

"Go out ahead of Gabe. Get in the front seat and get your door closed. Gabe and I'll handle the Were. We'll come back for my car later."

"Okay."

He let her hand go despite his reluctance and his misgivings about her involvement. She slipped from the booth and headed for the bouncer.

A waitress blocked her path as she was passing close to the Were's table. Mystic frowned as their aura prickled uncomfortably against hers. Usually Weres felt warm and smooth, a continuous heated flow of energy her blood recognized. She resisted the urge to look at them when she felt their attention on her as she waited for the waitress to move out of the way.

The waitress wriggled and laughed as money was slipped beneath her g-string. She finally shifted her position, leaning over another patron so closely her breasts brushed against his hairy forearm.

Mystic hurried past her and toward the bouncer. His gaze was hungry and hard, locked to her as the front of his pants tented in reaction to her approach.

She captured his eyes as soon as she got close. "Will you help me?" she purred and heard Hawk's growl along their bond.

"Anything you want," the bouncer said.

Mystic licked her lips.

The bouncer's hand cupped his crotch and rubbed.

Don't press your luck, Hawk said in a voice that promised retribution if her actions resulted in the bouncer touching her.

How much time is left? she asked, not wanting to lose eye contact until the last moment.

A couple of minutes. Gabe and I are walking past the Weres' table. They're nervous. Tell the bouncer to open the door and pull the female out.

"My friend's in the last booth," Mystic said. "I need her out of there right now."

The bouncer didn't hesitate. In three steps he had the door yanked open. The Were was bare breasted and on her knees with a cock in her mouth. That didn't stop him from grabbing her arm and jerking her out of the booth.

Go! Hawk commanded, suddenly there, his hand circling the Were's arm, his mass pushing Mystic toward the exit.

Mystic had no time to recapture the bouncer's mind as she was herded out of the club and into the parking lot. And then there was no time to do anything but react as the two remaining Weres exploded through the door and attacked.

Hawk fended off the male with kicks and punches while trying to hold on to the prostituted, omega female. Gabby rushed forward to grab the female's other arm.

A knife flashed in the alpha bitch's hand, her attention wavering between Hawk and Gabe for an instant before settling on Gabe. She slashed with deadly precision, driving him away while at the same time maneuvering closer to Hawk's exposed back.

The prostituted female stumbled and fell, dragging Hawk and Gabby with her. The bitch saw her opportunity. She whirled, intent on plunging the knife into Hawk.

Gabe and Mystic both reacted. They launched themselves at the alpha female and took her to the ground.

She screamed in rage and stabbed wildly. Gabe grunted as the blade connected.

The bitch writhed and twisted, bucked and snarled as she fought. Mystic tried to pin her wrists, but Gabe's blood made the Were's arm slick.

With a savage lunge the bitch slammed her forehead against the edge of Mystic's eye socket. Mystic's concentration was lost in an explosion of pain as she fell away. The shock of a knife slashing her chest and stomach made her scream.

Hawk was there instantly. His fists connected with the sound of flesh striking flesh.

The bitch rolled away and scrambled to her feet cursing. She grabbed the omega female by the arm, then with an order to the male, the three of them ran, leaving her knife on the ground next to Mystic.

Gabby's breath was heaving in and out of her chest as she crawled over to Mystic. She took her shirt off without hesitation and pressed it to the deep cut across Mystic's belly, trying to stop the worst of the bleeding.

Hawk knelt down, wadding up his shirt and pressing it against the gash below Mystic's collarbones. Despite the pain radiating through her, she could feel his agony, his anger, his guilt. "I just need Roman," she whispered. "His blood will fix me right up."

"Where is he?"

Mystic didn't have to reach down the link to find him. Both Christian and Roman had known the moment she was hurt. Both of them were demanding answers.

Roman was already feeding her pictures of how to get to Brann's estate. She let the information pass through her mind and into Hawk's.

A sob escaped when Hawk lifted her and placed her on the backseat of the Jeep. Gabby remained with her, keeping the bloody shirt pressed tightly against the wounds.

Mystic was vaguely aware of Hawk talking with Gabe. Then the car was moving and great waves of pain were crashing down on her.

Chapter Fourteen

ဢ

Hawk paced the floor, unable to meet anyone else's eyes. The hot rage burning through him was the exact opposite of Roman's cold fury. Each time the vampire looked up from where Mystic lay across his lap, the icy flame of his anger licked over Hawk's flesh.

Guilt and horror chewed at Hawk's gut. The sight of the female Were being prostituted had gone against rules and customs so deeply ingrained in him, it had led him to make a foolish decision, one that could have ended in the death of his mate—in his own death. The promise of it was there in Roman's eyes and Hawk didn't blame him.

Mystic sighed and the sound brought a tiny bit of relief to Hawk. He blinked away the sudden moisture at the corner of his eyes before turning toward the couch.

Roman's wrist was pressed against her mouth. But instead of being unresponsive, her lips were sealed to his skin as he stroked her neck and encouraged her to swallow.

The bloody shirts had been discarded. The knife wounds dealt with so her skin was once again smooth and unblemished.

Hawk closed the distance and knelt next to the couch. He took her limp hand in his, twined his fingers through hers.

He wanted to bury his face in her stomach and cry in relief. He wanted to beg her forgiveness though he knew she'd insist he wasn't at fault.

You're not, she whispered in his mind and he could feel her weeping over the rawness of his emotion.

He glanced at her face. Her eyelids were closed, her forehead slightly wrinkled, as if she was fighting to return from the place where pain and loss of blood had forced her to retreat.

Never again, he said.

For long moments there was no response. There was only the sound of her drinking at Roman's wrist.

Hawk buried his face against her side. Her fingers tightened on his. The bond between them filled with erotic fire as her awareness returned on a blood-induced heat wave.

With a gasp Mystic licked across Roman's wrist then turned her face away. Her pussy throbbed with need and her nipples were hard tight points in a bra that did nothing to hide the state of her arousal.

When she would have struggled to a sitting position, Roman and Hawk held her down. Roman's eyes captured hers mercilessly and she could feel him moving through her mind, her body, ensuring himself she was fully healed. Only when he was satisfied did he allow her to sit up and escape from his lap, though he didn't allow her to go further than the cushion next to him. Hawk joined them on the couch.

Without a word Roman removed his shirt and handed it to her. As she put it on she took in the presence of the others sprawled and seated in the room. Skye, she'd already met. Lying near her, on another beanbag chair, was a gorgeous long-haired blond man wearing a muscle shirt. Syndelle Coronado was on a second couch and Mystic didn't need the hum of blood calling to blood to know the identity of the man next to her — Brann, the council's executioner, the sire of her father's sire.

She'd only met him once, when she was barely old enough to speak, and yet his image was burned into her mind. His power was unmistakable. He was one of the truly ancient. Mystic ducked her head in a quick acknowledgement of him.

Brann's mouth curved upward in a smile. His eyes slanted toward Syndelle. "Finally a female who gives me the respect I deserve," he purred.

Syndelle's hand curled around Brann's inner thigh, her knuckles brushed against the heavy, clothed outline of his erection. "If you want us to put you up on a pedestal, we can do that. But I've heard pedestals are cold lonely places."

Brann grabbed Syndelle's hand when she would have pulled it away and Mystic found herself a helpless voyeur when the blond on the beanbag chair took Syndelle's other hand and placed it against his lips. Heat flowed between them and scorched the air around them. They were a picture of love and lust solidified by an Angelini bond.

Mystic's eyes widened when she saw the vampire companion necklaces on both Mystic and—*Rafael*, Roman provided. It was rare for a vampire to take more than one companion, just as it was rare for an Angelini to claim more than two mates or to claim them without first wearing the tattoo of a proven hunter.

Her attention shifted to Syndelle's bare neck, to Skye's, to thoughts of her own and the knowledge Roman had locked deep in her mind about Syndelle. Uneasiness shivered through Mystic. She felt as if forces were at work, as if the old vampire magic was impacting all of their lives, paving the way for…what?

Perhaps to combat the dark mage magic Brallin once possessed and channeled, Roman said. *That is what Brann and I were discussing before you were hurt.*

Mystic realized Gabe and Gabby weren't there. She remembered the slickness of Gabe's blood on the alpha bitch. She knew Gabby had been in the backseat with her on the way to Brann's estate. "Is Gabe okay?"

"He followed us here in my car," Hawk said. "His wounds weren't bad enough to prevent him from shifting in order to heal. Rafe gave him some clothes to replace his bloody ones. I sent Gabe and Gabby back to their hotel with orders to rest."

A fresh wave of anger and recrimination buffed Mystic along the bond with Hawk. She rubbed her hand along his inner thigh and tried to lighten his spirits by saying, "Maybe we should spend an hour each day doing hand-to-hand combat drills. I think I could do better next time."

"There won't be a next time," Roman said.

Mystic turned her head. "You don't know that. This hunt isn't finished."

"Good point," Skye said. "And as terrible as your injury was, I suspect you'll say it was worth it. Now that you're fully recovered Syndelle can look at the knife left behind by the rogue Were. If the vampire fledgling's blood is on it, if any vampire blood is on it, Syndelle will be able to tell what line they came from."

Mystic leaned forward, glad for Skye's moral support. "You're right. Not that I want to get beat up or stabbed the next time out, but if we can learn something from the knife, then what happened at Bangers was worth suffering for. Did Hawk or one of the others tell you we think the Weres were hunting Todd Moore? They've also been asking around about two other people, Hugh and Marta."

"Hawk told us," Skye said. "And Roman told us it's possible the rogue Weres were made instead of being born as shifters. In exchange we told him what we'd found out. The fledgling was born in Vegas, died in Vegas the first time, and should have been nowhere near Vegas once he'd turned. That makes finding something with Todd Moore's blood on it critical."

Mystic squeezed Roman's hand. The ancient vampire magic and the dark mage's magic had been banished long before she was born. It was ancient history though she knew her fathers hoped the myth of the Masada was true and one day they would be able to walk in the sunlight again. Even the tales of Brallin, the dark mage who'd grown greedy for more and more power once the strongest of the vampires were destroyed and the rest had been banished to the night, had been relegated to a scary tale for campfires.

She shivered. She found it easy to believe both the ancient vampire magic and the dark mage magic had found vessels to contain them so they could pour out into the world again.

Hawk rose from the couch. "I'll get the knife."

No one spoke until he returned. But as soon as he entered the room Roman stiffened and Brann rose to his feet with the fluid ease of a vampire.

"It's tainted," Brann said. "I can feel the traces of dark magic from here."

"I can as well," Roman said.

Rafe rolled from his sprawl across the beanbag chair and stood. "Well, I can't feel anything despite the fact I'm supposed to one day grow up to be a warlock."

Skye laughed. "The operative words are *one day grow up* — as in, the distant future."

"Very funny," Rafe said as he offered Skye his hand and pulled her to her feet.

Mystic left the couch and joined the others as they gathered around Hawk. Like Rafe, she sensed nothing odd about the blade though the sight of the dried blood made her thoughts flash back to the fight and the pain.

Roman's arm went around her waist. He pulled her against him so her back pressed to his front then glanced at Brann. "It's not so much the blood as the remnants of a spell."

Brann nodded. "Dark magic mixed with vampire blood."

"Let me hold the knife," Syndelle said, reaching out only to have her wrist grabbed by Brann.

Rafe sighed. "You're only delaying the inevitable."

Brann sent him a look that would have made a vampire cower. Rafe rolled his eyes in response to the flash of fangs and the silent promise of retaliation Brann's glare promised.

"You know this is necessary," Syndelle said in a soft voice though she made no attempt to pull her wrist from Brann's grasp.

He hissed. Skye shook her head and lifted her eyebrows when her gaze met Mystic's. "*Mates.* You've got to love them otherwise it fucks with your mind. But they do cramp a girl's style."

Mystic couldn't contain her laughter. She'd been mated almost no time at all and she already agreed wholeheartedly with Skye's assessment.

The tension in the room eased with Skye's comment. Brann held out his hand for the knife.

Hawk laid it across his palm and Brann's lips moved in a silent chant. This time Mystic could feel the magic gathering, condensing, dissolving.

"Do not touch the edge of the blade," Brann growled as he released Syndelle's wrist.

Syndelle ducked her head quickly, but not before Mystic saw the smile she was attempting to hide over her mate's command.

Neither Rafe nor Skye made any attempt at subtlety. They both snickered and Mystic found herself grinning. For the first time since leaving the Zevanti compound she wondered about making a home in Las Vegas. She could see herself spending time with Syndelle and Skye, doing things with them that had nothing to do with the Angelini but everything to do with friendship. She could see them welcoming Gabby and being happy to include her as well.

The amusement faded as Syndelle's fingers settled on the blade's handle. Her face was a study of concentration, her pupils dilated into bottomless pits that should have held the cold flame of her vampire heritage but instead held something more frightening.

Syndelle followed the black of the handle to where the steel of the blade kissed it before disappearing inside. She ran her fingers back and forth at the tiny crevice there.

With sharp clarity Mystic imagined the alpha bitch driving the knife all the way in to the hilt as she pierced Todd Moore's heart and interrupted the flow of vampire magic animating him.

Syndelle turned the blade over. She stiffened and glanced up to meet Brann's eyes. Concentration gave way to puzzlement and worry.

"The fledgling was captured with this knife?" Roman asked.

Syndelle stopped touching the knife. Rafe moved in and pulled her against him.

"Yes," she said. "It seems likely." Her face remained troubled. "I can't tell who Todd Moore's sire was, but I can tell he is part of Dusan Juric's line."

Roman tensed. "That's a very old and powerful line. If Juric has been seduced by the dark magic…"

"Then he will die," Brann said, "as will any in his line who are also tainted."

Mystic shivered at the lethal resolve in Brann's voice. When he was interacting with Syndelle and Rafe it was easy to forget he was the vampire council's executioner.

"You'll seek out Juric tonight?" Roman asked.

Brann speared Rafe, then Skye with a glance. "Yes, otherwise I'll be reduced to serving as jailor in order to ensure neither Gian's companion nor my own get into trouble."

Syndelle laughed. She wound her arms around Brann's waist and pulled him into the embrace she shared with Rafael. "Please don't go alone."

Tenderness filled Brann's face. The intensity of it made Mystic slip her hand in Hawk's waistband so she could be touching both of her mates at the same time.

"This isn't a matter for humans or wolves or the Angelini," Brann murmured. "At the moment it's a matter for vampires only."

"Then take Roman," Syndelle pleaded.

Brann cupped her face with his hand. His thumb brushed across her bottom lip. "I have served as an executioner for centuries, Syndelle. If Juric is tainted I will know it as soon as I'm in his presence. Unless he attacks me first or I have reason to think he poses an immediate threat to the supernatural world then I won't act until I've spoken to the council. If he hasn't been touched by the dark powers then surely I can be trusted to conduct a simple interview in order to determine how the fledgling came to be of his line."

Syndelle turned her head to press a kiss in the middle of his palm. "I'll feel better if you don't go alone. Please."

Brann sighed heavily. "I have your promise you'll remain here?"

"Yes."

"Rafe?"

"Your wish is my command."

"If only that were the truth," Brann growled, but through the blood-link Mystic shared with him and the link Roman had with Syndelle, she could feel Brann's amusement.

Brann turned his head slightly so he could direct his question at Roman. "You'll accompany me?"

"Of course. It'll be interesting to find out what entertains Juric these days."

Mystic frowned as she glimpsed a scene of naked, writhing bodies before Roman cut her off from his memories. She turned in his arms so she could see his face. "Are you going to Wyldfyres?" she asked, finding the thought of him going there without her intolerable. She knew no one was admitted unless they were part of the entertainment. She had little doubt that human and vampire females alike would rush to serve Roman.

His eyebrows lifted. Amusement danced in his eyes. *Your assessment of my charms is gratifying.*

Before Mystic could prevent it, Christian's memory of Roman surrounded by blonde human sheep flashed into her thoughts. All traces of humor left Roman. *I am bound to you now. If you visit this meaningless scene from my past again I will punish you for it. I will strip it from your mind and replace it with memories that will make your cunt spasm with a hunger only I can appease.*

His hand cupped her neck. His mouth lowered to take possession of hers. *I have been gentle with you because we both find pleasure in it, but that doesn't mean I am incapable of being ruthless where you're concerned.*

Roman's tongue plunged into mouth, a testament to his words. There was nothing playful in the slide of his tongue against hers or in the way he held her tightly against him.

He was hard male and infinite power. He was beast and vampire, brute strength and ancient cunning.

Mystic didn't resist his onslaught. She melted against him and welcomed his dominating, possessive kiss.

Her pulse beat wildly against his palm. Her clit stiffened in reaction to his primal display as heat pooled in her cunt lips.

They were both breathing hard when he lifted his mouth and set her away from him. "Christian will be home soon?" he asked.

Mystic concentrated on her link with Christian. His anger over what happened at Bangers scorched her while his love and relief she was okay acted as a balm.

"He's going to stop by the apartment complex where the fledgling lived then he'll be home."

"Good. The dawn isn't too far away now. Unless there's trouble I won't see you again until after sunset since I don't want to be seen out in the sunlight. In the meantime, Christian and Hawk can keep you safe."

Relief settled in Mystic's chest when she touched Roman's thoughts and found he'd made his peace with Hawk's decisions when it came to hunting the rogue Weres.

They parted company a few minutes later. Roman and Brann left first, then Skye. Hawk and Mystic lingered so Rafe could show them his collection of files on Todd Moore.

"Maybe Christian will get lucky and find someone at the apartment who knows something," Mystic said, impressed by how much information Syndelle's mate had gathered.

Rafe grinned and wriggled his fingers over the keyboard. "Call if he does. It'll save me the trouble of hacking into the police files to see what he's up to."

Mystic laughed though she decided she'd better shield this particular conversation from Christian. He would not like hearing Rafe could access the police computer system.

Christian was the first Were she'd spent time around who wasn't affiliated with a pack. As a result she didn't know whether all lone wolves were like him, or if it was just Christian. But for him, what he did for a living, his being a cop was a large part of his identity where those born in a pack rarely defined themselves by their work. They defined themselves as Were first, pack second, their rank in the pack third, and beyond that, by bloodlines and mate-lines.

"I'll call you," Mystic said, feeling a connection with Rafe. In a lot of ways his irreverence reminded her of her fathers, especially Falcone.

The drive back to Christian's house was made in silence. Hawk's earlier anger at taking her to Bangers and allowing her to get hurt returned. It hovered like a dark cloud over their relationship as they stepped into the bedroom.

She opened her mouth to tell him to stop torturing himself, then thought of a better way to disrupt his brooding and hopefully derail Christian's anger. Without a word she went into the bathroom. She stripped out of Roman's shirt and dropped it in the clothes hamper. Her bloody jeans were probably a lost cause but they followed the shirt.

She could feel Hawk's torment. His desire to join her as she stepped into the shower was juxtaposed against the guilty belief he needed to do some type of penance.

Tenderness flooded her. She should have guessed there was a softer side to him when he pursued her so relentlessly at the Zevanti compound yet always allowed her to escape his attention.

Because she could touch his feelings and thoughts, she knew that beyond his horror at having her get hurt, his masculine pride had suffered a blow. He hated thinking her other mates would no longer trust him to keep her safe.

Mystic sighed and lifted her face to the welcoming spray of water. She longed to have this hunt behind them so they could settle into a comfortable relationship. She longed to kiss Hawk and make all his needless suffering go away.

Yes, what happened at Bangers had been scary and painful and dangerous. But she was alive and wiser for it. And they had learned more than they could have hoped for tonight.

She turned her attention to the liquid soap Christian kept in his shower. She blocked her thoughts as she concentrated on her plan to not only lure Hawk away from his dark mood but to greet Christian with a sight that would have him thinking with his cock.

Mystic filled her palms with soap. Out of the corner of her eye she saw Hawk stop prowling around the bedroom in order to watch her through the open door.

She bent over, subtly positioning herself so Hawk could see her slick woman's folds through the clear glass of the shower stall as she ran her hands over first one leg and then the other. She knew the exact instant his attention became riveted on her vulva.

The wolf rose in him and urged him to mate. She widened her stance and let him watch as her soapy fingers slipped between her thighs and lingered there, rubbing back and forth across her cunt lips and clit. A moan escaped despite her efforts to pretend she was doing nothing other than cleaning the fight with the Weres off her skin.

Hawk's lust closed the distance between them. It stroked her like a wolf's tongue but he continued to fight his beast and deny them both what they needed in order to put the violent part of the night behind them.

Mystic's hands went to her belly. She stretched, arched her back. Her hands moved higher, stopping when they reached her breasts.

Another moan escaped as she smoothed her palms over her nipples before taking the hard tips between her fingers. Hawk's growl told her he'd moved closer but she didn't need the sound. The heavy musk of an aroused male mixed with the steam of her shower.

He wrenched the door open and crowded her against the wall. The slash of his mouth told her he guessed what she was doing but he didn't have the strength to resist her.

His hands took possession of her breasts. His fingers gripped her nipples and tightened until she arched, offered her throat in a show of submission as her belly pressed to the rigid, hot flesh of his cock.

He leaned in. His mouth found the pulse racing in her neck. His teeth closed around it. Along their bond she could feel him fighting his wolf's demand to bend her over and mount her.

With the confidence of a female who'd finally discovered her sexuality and the power that came with it, Mystic knew she could tip the scales in the wolf's favor—and she wanted to.

But Christian was drawing near and finding her being fucked in the shower wouldn't result in the harmony they all needed.

She let Hawk resist the temptation she offered him. When he finally released her and stepped back she soaped her hands and ran them over the hard muscles of his chest and arms and legs.

She avoided his tiny nipples and engorged shaft until finally he gripped her hand and carried it to his cock. He forced her to stoke him. She voluntarily cupped and fondled his heavy testicles, satisfaction rushing through her when he groaned and threw his head back in surrender.

"Let's go to bed, Hawk," she said and brushed her thumb over the exposed head of his penis in order to further entice him.

They stepped from the shower and hastily dried off. His eyes darkened with lust when they reached the bed and she took his cock in her hand again.

"I want to put my mouth on you," Mystic whispered.

His penis pulsed in response and there was an echoing throb in the swollen lips of her cunt. She ached with the need to have one of her mates sheathe himself in her channel.

As if he guessed the exact position and place she wanted him, Hawk knelt on the bed, close to the edge but far enough away so she could position herself above his cock on her hands and knees. Her hair brushed his thighs and penis as she hovered over him, exploring the smooth foreskin and exposed head with her fingers.

Moisture escaped through the slit in his cock head. He growled when she massaged it into his hot flesh.

His fingers burrowed into her hair. His desire pressed down on her in a command every bit as compelling as a vampire's.

On the periphery of her senses she knew Christian was home. Slowly she lowered her head and took Hawk into her mouth.

Chapter Fifteen

ஒ

The wolf inside Christian wanted to surface and rip Hawk apart. It felt as savage as the man did.

He stripped his jacket off and tossed it on the coffee table. The harness and his gun followed. He was too angry to trust himself with a weapon.

Hawk's groan from the bedroom only set Christian's teeth on edge. A muscle spasmed in his cheek. For a second he contemplated turning around and leaving.

A low growl formed and escaped from the deepest recesses of his soul. This was his territory, his mate. He wouldn't be chased from it like a defeated and outcast wolf driven from the pack.

He stripped his shirt off because he could no longer tolerate it against his skin. His socks and shoes followed.

When his hands went to his belt, alarm bells rang in his mind. He realized he was subconsciously preparing to shapeshift and fight. And since the wolf was just as lethal as the gun, Christian forced his hands away from the buckle. The pants would slow him down. He hoped.

Another groan came from the bedroom and Christian's lip lifted in a silent snarl. He didn't question his behavior, his need to get to Mystic. The man was still running on emotion. The wolf was, too.

His thoughts were a chaotic mix. He had no plan of action as he stalked toward the bedroom door and once he got there he had nothing but pure instinct.

Mystic was kneeling on the bed, her hips raised and her thighs spread. He had a fleeting impression of Hawk with his head thrown back as Mystic's mouth worked his cock, but Christian couldn't focus on anything except the glistening, dusky folds of her cunt.

Lust roared through him. His penis pulsed and leaked and burned as if the blood engorging it was lava-hot.

On some level he knew she was manipulating him, purposely trying to distract him from his anger by presenting him with her swollen vulva and wet slit. He didn't care. His wolf didn't care. The sight of their mate slick and ready, positioned for fucking drove everything from his mind but the urgency to cover her.

He stripped out of his remaining clothes as he walked from the bedroom door to the bed. Only pride gave him the strength to shift his focus to Hawk and growl—though her other mate didn't react. He was already lost in the bliss of what Mystic was doing to him with her mouth and tongue.

Christian snarled again but the scent of her arousal drew his eyes back to her dewy lower lips. He crouched, unable to stop himself from pressing his mouth to her flesh in greeting.

She moaned and leaned into him. She may have positioned herself in order to divert his anger but her need for him was real. The truth of it howled down the bond along with her hunger.

He deepened his kiss, stroked into her hot channel with his tongue. She called his name mentally, begged him to shove his cock into her.

Christian resisted. His hands smoothed up her thighs, cupped her hips, palmed her silky buttocks.

He alternated between fucking her with his tongue and sucking on the swollen folds of her labia. The anger and fear over nearly losing her gave way to euphoria at having her safe—in his home, in his bed.

The wolf's internal growling became rumbling groans as Christian licked, kissed, coated his senses with Mystic. His cock throbbed in warning. It burned against his abdomen and wet his flesh with arousal. His balls drew up tight and hard, so full of seed his hips pumped subtly in an imitation of the mating act.

Please, Christian, please, she whispered in his mind, widening her thighs, letting him feel how much she needed him to mount her, how much she wanted the three of them to orgasm together.

When her inner muscles tightened and rippled against his tongue Christian couldn't hold out any longer. He crawled onto the bed behind her and sheathed himself in a single hard thrust.

With a moan he yielded to the rhythm defined by her mouth pleasuring another man's cock. He was helpless to do anything but pant and thrust as Mystic's bond with both her mates linked all three of them together and locked them in an erotic circle of ecstasy.

Fire streaked through Christian's testicles and penis. His hips bucked and jerked in perfect synch with Hawk's. Ice-hot shards of lust ripped along his spine and exploded in his skull, leaving him mindless to anything but the climb to orgasm. He hunched over to kiss Mystic's back and shoulders, to press more of his skin against hers, to bite her as the last of his control fell away and semen jetted from his cock.

They collapsed on the bed in a pile of tangled arms and legs. Christian nearly whimpered into Mystic's hair as aftershocks of sensation rippled through him. His hips jerked as her cunt continued to clench and unclench on his cock. He closed his eyes and shuddered with pleasure, content for the moment not to think about the rogue Weres and Bangers.

* * * * *

Time has changed very little, Roman thought as he and Brann followed a blood slave into a playroom designed for erotic pursuits.

The garish, velvet-cushioned throne sat on a raised dais at the far end of the room. Two smaller chairs were positioned beneath and to the left and right of it. Dusan Juric wasn't present at the moment but the room wasn't empty. A blindfolded male vampire was strapped onto a St. Andrews cross. A naked female vampire was on her back, spread-eagled and tethered to a piece of equipment while another was bent over and strapped for fucking or spanking.

"The master wishes to know if you want something to drink. There are humans here who haven't taken vampire blood."

Roman shook his head. "I've already fed."

"As have I," Brann said.

The slave indicated the two chairs below the throne. "If you'll make yourself comfortable, the master will be in momentarily."

It was stated as a request but the slave didn't leave until both Brann and Roman were sitting. Roman idly studied the naked vampires. It was impossible to ignore them given the strategic placement of mirrors around the room.

They weren't fledglings though all of Dusan Juric's vampire offspring started out as his bed partners. Few lingered there for long before the novelty wore off. Yet even after they matured to the point where they could exist without Juric's blood, he routinely called them home to demonstrate his dominance by fucking them.

Roman's attention shifted to the centuries-old male vampire on the cross. His penis was rigid, but whether his erection was due to sexual arousal at the prospect of regaining Juric's attention or because of the cock ring restricting the flow of blood, Roman couldn't tell.

The females were younger, a century, maybe less. Like the man, they were blonde, well endowed.

Roman grew aroused as the conversation with Mystic played itself out in his mind. Perhaps he'd deliberately let her see his memory of these particular blondes so she'd think about the human sheep in his past and give him an opportunity to make good on his threat to punish her.

He shifted subtly in order to adjust his cock then started to open the link to her but stopped before he could be swamped by lust and the images of her being fucked by her other mates. He'd have to make sure Hawk and Christian weren't around when he satisfied Mystic's curiosity about the enjoyment to be found in carnal punishments.

Wolves liked to chase and pounce. They liked rough shows of dominance, rolling and pinning, mounting and aggressively mating. But as a rule they didn't appreciate being tethered or spanked. Roman chuckled. Not that he intended to try either tethering or spanking with Mystic's two alpha Weres. Still, he worried Christian and Hawk's wolves might take charge and rush in if they saw their mate being restrained or punished.

Roman repositioned his penis. Thoughts of having Mystic at his mercy had him fully engorged, anxious for this night to end and the next one to begin.

Brann chuckled at his obvious discomfort. "It gets worse with time, not better."

"I can believe it." Roman turned his attention back to the male vampire. *I don't sense Brallin's taint*, he said, finding it mildly amusing that Syndelle's gift of blood had forged a link between him and the council's executioner. Then again, Brann was one of very few vampires who was also a sorcerer.

Roman's lip curled in a wry smile. Given his own beginnings as a mage-created gryphon, perhaps he was cursed to always have some type of connection to beings who liked to dabble in magic. Thankfully he wasn't mated to one.

There is nothing here but vampire magic, Brann confirmed.

They both leaned forward slightly as several blood slaves entered the room. A moment later Roman and Brann stood when Juric stepped through the doorway.

"Sit, sit," the vampire said, waving negligently. "Let me get my slaves started and I'll join you." He laughed. "I can only wonder what imagined transgressions bring the council's executioner and his most unusual sidekick to my dungeon."

Juric paused next to the female vampire who was bent and tethered into a splayed position. His hand smoothed over her buttocks with the casualness of a merchant testing the quality of a bolt of silk.

"Do you have children, Roman?" he asked.

"No."

Juric tsked. "I don't know whether to applaud you or pity you. They can be a great joy, but they can also be the source of such painful tribulation." His hand rose and came down on the female's buttocks with a sharp crack, followed by several more until he reached beneath the bench and retrieved a wooden paddle.

"You give them life after death, you feed them from your vein." Juric shook his head and handed the paddle to a male slave. "They mature and go out on their own then they forget who brought them into this world. Pretty, pretty children. It seems the more beautiful they are the more they need to be reminded where they came from and what behaviors you expect of them."

His hand soothed over the female's reddened buttocks. "Twenty spanks, Carlos. Then fuck her. When you're finished let Stefan do the same."

Juric moved to the female tied spread-eagled and blindfolded. "Do you have a preference, Brann?" With a flick of his wrist he indicted the waiting slaves. "You used to enjoy the show at Wyldfyres before you found yourself mated to an Angelini." His smile became sly. "Better you than me. I'd feel gelded."

Brann chuckled. "Yes, better me than you."

Juric's sly smile faded with a shrug. He positioned three male slaves at the female's breasts and cunt, instructed them to use their mouths to drive her to orgasm. With a bored wave he sent the remaining female slaves to the St. Andrews Cross with the freedom to do what they wanted to the vampire secured there.

Moans filled the room as Juric claimed the throne on the raised dais. He spared a brief glance around his playroom before turning his attention to Brann and Roman. "Why are you here?" he asked, all humor gone from his expression.

"A fledgling from your line is dead," Brann said.

Juric's eyes narrowed. "Who?"

"He was born and died as Todd Moore."

"His name is not familiar to me."

"His human life began and ended in Las Vegas. His second birth and new life began here, too."

"Impossible."

"Would you doubt the word of a Renaldi Angelini?"

A look of distaste settled on Juric's face. "No."

Brann's gaze flicked over the three vampires being attended to by slaves. "The children you keep close are all accounted for?"

Roman's attention shifted to the three men attending to the female vampire. She was fighting against the tethers, responding despite the fact slaves suckled at her breasts and feasted at her cunt at another's orders.

He doubted she wanted the pleasure forced on her along with the reminder she had a master who expected to be obeyed. Still, he found the sight of her writhing fueled his own fantasies of having Mystic tethered to the bed.

"None of my children would be so foolish as to create another of our kind without gaining my permission," Juric said, drawing Roman back to Brann's interrogation. "I have ended second lives for less. It is one of the rules I ensure they understand before they leave my home."

Brann tilted his head slightly in the direction of the restrained vampires. "And yet apparently your children do not always obey."

An unfriendly look passed through Juric's eyes at the reminder. "You have better luck with yours?"

Brann shrugged. "They are not the reason I am here. Are your children all accounted for?"

A muscle spasmed in Juric's cheek. His gaze settled on the female being paddled. "Harder, Carlos. She has displeased me greatly."

The other female screamed in orgasm. Juric said, "Make her come again. Do not stop until I tell you to stop."

His face darkened as he looked at the male vampire on the St. Andrews Cross. "I am missing a son. As a lesson I banished him to California, to Mendocino County. He disappeared almost immediately and I have not been able to find him."

Juric turned his head to meet Brann's eyes. "He was barely out of his coffin, barely strong enough to remain alive without feeding directly from my vein. He couldn't have created a fledgling."

Brann opened the narrow case he'd carried in with him. Juric stiffened at the sight of the knife lying on a bed of black satin edged with golden symbols. His nostrils flared and he licked his lips. "I smell werewolf and Angelini."

"And beneath those?" Brann asked, lifting the knife from its case and handing it to Juric.

Juric hissed. His eyes flashed red and his fangs elongated. He touched his tongue to the crevice Syndelle's fingers had explored. "My blood. My missing son's blood. The blood of a fledging I have no knowledge of."

* * * * *

The lassitude and contentment lasted less than fifteen minutes. Mystic sighed as she felt Christian's anger growling to life along their bond.

Please, she said, *let it go. Look how much we learned. It was worth it.*

Look what we nearly lost. Nothing is worth your life. He lifted up onto an elbow behind her and even though she couldn't see his face clearly, she could see Hawk's. She could feel their wolves bristling and snarling at one another.

Mystic sighed again, more dramatically this time, as some of the reasons why she hadn't wanted mates, especially werewolf mates, came back to her. She put a thin mental barrier between their minds and hers then wriggled out from between them and headed toward the bathroom.

Even with the mental separation she knew they were fiercely aware of her every move. Good. Sex wasn't the only weapon in her arsenal even if it was the most powerful one, even if was her *Plan A*.

She took a quick shower and put on Roman's shirt. She didn't think she'd get as far as the front door but she would stop at her suitcase and pull on a pair of pants for show.

They were arguing when she stepped out of the bathroom. She didn't bother listening to their words or picking the theme of their conversation from their minds.

"Is your car in the garage, Christian?" she asked. "I'd take Hawk's but I've never gotten the hang of a stick shift."

She didn't make it two steps before they'd both rolled out of bed and were stalking toward her. Her intention to put on a show for them left her mind completely. She forgot to keep walking because she couldn't take her eyes off their heavy testicles and rapidly filling cocks.

They were magnificent mates. Hard muscle and well endowed. Any woman would be happy to claim them, even if they were growling.

Mystic hid her smile. Her mother was fond of saying, "Passion is passion. Handled correctly, a man's anger can be turned into something else and put to a much better use."

Usually Estelle said that after she'd taken a solo run in the woods as a wolf. Based on what Mystic had seen—or not seen since her parents tended to disappear into their bedroom for days afterward—her mother knew what she was talking about.

"Where do you think you're going?" Christian asked, reaching her first and crowding into her personal space so she shivered with the need to rub against him and lick his lips in a gesture of appeasement.

"You can't go to Roman," Hawk said.

Mystic's frown in his direction was real. "I have other choices besides being with you, Christian or Roman."

"No you don't." Hawk's voice held the absolute authority of an alpha wolf.

Mystic bit her bottom lip to keep from starting a fight with him over the issue of her freedom. She didn't doubt it was a subject they'd do battle over, but at the moment what she really wanted was to lie in bed with mates who weren't snarling and snapping at each other.

She took a deep calming breath before meeting Christian's eyes. "I'm going to hit the casinos while you and Hawk sort things out." She let them both feel her resolve to leave the house.

"You're not going anywhere," Christian said. "You need to stay here, where it's safe." His eyes left hers long enough to glower at Hawk.

Mystic thought about making a run for it, but given how they were crowding so close they were nearly touching her, she didn't think she'd get far enough to make her point. So much for *Plan B*.

Plan C for dealing with her mates arrived with a wicked thrill. She made a silent promise to tell Estelle she was the best mother to ever grace the planet the next time she talked to her.

Mystic placed one hand on Christian's chest and the other on Hawk's. She stroked their warm flesh and watched as their cocks pulsed and bobbed. She made her body relax into a more submissive female pose. Their human minds were instantly wary but their wolves responded immediately, stretching inside them and radiating dominant intensity.

It was hard not to smile. She'd never imagined it would be fun to play with alpha wolves—not that what she intended to do was without risk.

"You'd both like for me to stay home while you hunt the rogues. You've made that perfectly clear. We could argue every time we have a new lead to follow or we could resolve this here and now in a way you'd both find very, very pleasurable."

She laughed softly as their wolves bristled with suspicion. She could feel Hawk and Christian rubbing against the mental barrier she'd erected.

"What do have in mind?" Hawk asked.

"We play a game." She looked at him from underneath her eyelashes. "If either you or Christian wins then I'll agree to obey you when it comes to the hunt. I'll stay in the house if that's what you want." Her fingernails scraped against Hawk's taut abdomen. "Though I don't promise not to misbehave with whichever mate is left to guard me."

The foreskin on Hawk's penis pulled back. Liquid arousal seeped out to glisten on the velvety head.

He grabbed her hand and forced it to his cock. Mystic wrapped her fingers around his erection.

"And if we lose, we'll have no say in what you do?" Christian said, taking her hand to his penis and making her heart swell with tenderness.

His hips jerked when she brushed her thumb over his engorged cock head. His hand tightened on hers.

Curiosity and lust flooded the bond along with utter masculine confidence and satisfaction. Both of her mates were positive they could win at any game she might propose. They were already envisioning her willing imprisonment.

Mystic licked her upper lip and felt a jolt of lust go through their shafts. "If I win then you two will stop objecting every time I want to participate in the hunt. Advice is okay. I don't want any of us to get hurt. I've had no training as a hunter so I'm willing to listen to what you say. But you'll let me be part of this and you won't snarl at each other if things don't go exactly as planned."

Both men growled in reaction but she could feel them examining her words, studying them for hidden traps. Hawk said, "Explain the game."

She rubbed her thumbs over their cock heads again. "It's simple. You and Christian will take turns fucking me. You'll trade off after a certain number of strokes. Each time you trade off, the number of strokes increases. Whoever comes *last* wins."

Christian's amused laugh was immediate. "Clever. The instant you lock our cocks inside you we'll lose."

Hawk tilted his head. His beaded braids and intent gaze made her think of a bird of prey getting ready to swoop. "If she loses control and ties one of us, then that person is the winner."

Christian's eyes narrowed for an instant before his face relaxed. "Agreed. Mystic?"

She could feel his absolute confidence that he could make the Angelini magic rise so her hidden muscles would tighten and hold his cock deep inside her. She could feel the same certainty in Hawk.

She nibbled on her bottom lip, not in worry but to hide the smile threatening to emerge and make them wary again. If they weren't so utterly convinced they were going to win she might feel guilty about what she intended to do in order to make them lose this sexual challenge.

"Okay," she said, letting herself sound just a little bit worried.

Chapter Sixteen

&

They led her back to the bed and she remained standing at the foot of it while they sprawled on their backs, leaving a space for her in the middle. With a sultry smile, Mystic made a show of slowly unbuttoning Roman's shirt and dropping it onto the floor. Satisfaction raged through her at how quickly heated, masculine glances of appreciation turned into focused expressions of predatory lust when she put her knees on the mattress and crawled provocatively toward them.

She stopped midway up their bodies and sat back on her heels. Her hand caressed the inside of Christian's thigh. "Pick a number."

"Five."

She circled his cock with her fingers, stroked up and down his velvety shaft five times. His hips lifted in tandem to each upstroke. His hands gripped the bed linen as if he was fighting the urge to pounce.

"We can start at five and go up by five each time the two of you switch places." She took Hawk's cock in her other hand. "Does that sound doable?" she asked provocatively.

His nostrils flared. In her mind she saw his wolf lick its lips in anticipation of the challenge. "Yes," he growled.

She rubbed her thumbs over the wet tips of their cocks. "We need to decide who goes first."

Mystic released them and went to her hands and knees again. She widened her thighs and lowered her upper body in a stance that was an invitation to play as well as to mate.

The Angelini magic rose inside her. For an instant she felt as if she possessed her own wolf and it was stretching out, pressing against her skin and enjoying this game with its mates.

Mystic licked her lips. She rocked back and forth, rubbed her nipples against the comforter and watched as their breaths grew short.

"We need to decide how to fuck, this way or with me on my back. Or maybe I'll decide for all of us." She tilted her head and kissed the mating mark on Christian's thigh. She sucked on it and his hips jerked violently. His hand went to his cock and she wanted to take him into her mouth, to suck him until he came. The game would be over with a normal human male, but not with a Were, not with an Angelini's mate. Christian would harden again. He'd hunger to plunge into her channel and spill his seed there, too.

Mystic gave in to temptation. She bit the mating mark and felt the icy-hot spike of lust go up Christian's spine. She took everything above his hand into her mouth and began sucking. It was primitive, darkly carnal to find the taste of her arousal on him.

In a heartbeat all playfulness left her. She was merciless, as savage in her pleasure as her mates were.

Next to her she heard Hawk's heavy breathing, his low growls. She felt his eyes on her, devouring her as hungrily as she was taking Christian.

He intended to pounce, to thrust inside her and fuck her until she screamed in release as soon as Christian came, the game she'd proposed only a shadow thought underneath the need to mate burning inside Hawk.

With a shout Christian thrashed, fighting against the need to come even as hot seed erupted. Mystic swallowed it down. She would have swallowed *him* down if she could.

The more she was with her mates the more she craved them, the more she wanted to merge so completely there was no separation between them. She released Christian's cock only when Hawk's hand curved around her waist and his low growl warned he'd waited long enough.

With barely restrained violence he pulled her down onto her back and covered her with his body. He thrust all the way into her in a single hard stroke.

Mystic had the presence of mind to say, "That's one."

He stilled. He snarled at the reminder of the game they'd agreed to play and the stakes involved. He sent a glower in Christian's direction.

Mystic felt Christian's wolf bristle. Competition flared between the two men.

She spared a glance at Christian. He was hard again, challenging Hawk with his glare to see who could make her come first.

Delicious, wicked satisfaction filled Mystic. They'd play this game again for fun, but this time she couldn't afford to lose.

She tangled her fingers in Hawk's braids and pulled his face down to hers. She captured his lips and plunged her tongue into his mouth, giving him the taste of her arousal as well as her other mate. He thrust hard and fast—two, three, four, five times in an instinctive effort to rid her of a rival's marking.

He rolled off her, growling, his face taut as Christian took possession. Mystic felt the Angelini magic starting to rise with Christian's first savage thrust. Her channel tightened on his cock. It gripped and clung to him.

The sweet bliss of joining with him made Mystic want to lock her arms and legs around him and tie him to her. He was her first mate, the one who'd cut the deepest roads into her heart.

She whimpered when he pulled away after ten stokes, then did the same when Hawk filled her. She arched. She wanted complete intimacy with this mate as well.

As Hawk's tongue twined with hers and his cock filled her she was tempted to forget about the game. It felt so good to have him inside her.

She moaned. Her hips rose to meet his thrusts.

She didn't think she'd ever get enough of them. She didn't think she'd ever want to leave the bed again.

The thought reminded her of what she stood to lose, and gain, if she came before they did. They'd hunt the Weres while she stayed home and fucked.

She couldn't afford to give in to the cries of her body for release. Too much was at stake to yield to the Angelini need to claim a mate in a way that reinforced the permanence and thoroughness of the bond.

Hawk rolled off her and Christian covered her again. Five strokes in and she was nearly mindless with the need to orgasm. If she made it through twenty she'd never make it through Hawk's twenty-five.

Panic made her ruthless. She opened the link between them. She let her pleasure flood down the bond. She let them feel what it was like for her to have Christian's thick cock tunnel in and out of her sheath.

He growled and fought against coming. He only barely managed it.

Hawk knew he was in trouble as soon as he covered Mystic. The wolf had been driven into a frenzy not only by having to pull out each time it had tried to tie with her, but with the sight of her other mate fucking her.

The sensation she'd shared, of another male's cock thrusting into the hot, tight place his wanted to be was the final straw. He'd lost what little control he still had over his beast.

By the second thrust Hawk was no longer able to count. All he cared about was mating.

His hands held Mystic's pinned to the sheets as he pounded into her. His breathing was harsh and ragged. His reality was the wet fist of her sheath.

His hips bucked. Sweat dripped off him. The muscles on his arms rippled and the bed shook under the force of his thrusts. He nearly passed out when white-hot shards of ecstasy ripped through him as he came.

It had taken all of Christian's strength to pull out of Mystic the last time. How she'd come up with such a devious game was a question for later. At the moment he was trying to hold on, to drive her over the edge before him.

With a savagery to match Hawk's, Christian fucked in and out of her slick channel. He kissed her ears, her mouth. His lips found the mating mark on her throat. He growled against it, clamped down on it with his teeth.

The Angelini magic burned hotter and he slipped into the hidden place deep inside Mystic's body. For an instant he knew triumph. He thought victory was his. But then she raked her nails down his back and over his buttocks. The sharp unexpected pain was all it took for him to lose control. His seed spilled out in a hot rush. Only then did she clamp down on his cock and lock him to her.

Mystic smiled in contentment between her two very warm Were mates. She snuggled her back against Hawk's front as she stroked Christian's chest.

"You went by Todd Moore's apartment," she said, daring to bring up the hunt for the fledgling vampire's killers.

Christian's hand covered hers. He guided it to the mating mark above his heart and held it there. "Former apartment. He moved out before he died the first time."

"Did you talk to the apartment manager?" Hawk asked.

"Yeah." Christian sighed. "I had to badge him to get his cooperation. Let's just say he wasn't happy about being dragged out of bed."

Mystic worried her bottom lip. "Will you get in trouble for doing it?"

Christian turned onto his side. "If he calls in a complaint I'll have to do some fast talking about why I'm asking around about a guy who has no traceable connection to any of my assigned cases." He shrugged. "I didn't learn much. There was no forwarding address and the apartment manager claims he can't even picture Todd much less remember anything about him. A neighbor was coming home as I was leaving. He said Todd hung out with another guy. He thought he heard Todd calling his friend Hugh and joking about going to a high-school football game. Beyond that he didn't have anything to offer."

"The rogue Weres are asking around about a guy named Hugh," Mystic said.

"Did you get a description of Todd Moore's friend?" Hawk asked.

"Dark hair. Maybe brown, maybe black. Maybe not dark at all. Could be purple. I think the neighbor was taking a guess."

Hawk grunted. Mystic levered herself up onto an elbow and reached across Christian for the phone.

"No fair," she moaned as Christian's mouth latched on to her nipple.

Hawk followed Christian's lead. His lips trailed kisses up her spine then over to the place on her shoulder where he'd bitten her when he took her from behind. "Who are you calling?"

"Rafe. He can hack into the school system if he needs too. He can find out if Todd had a classmate named Hugh. Maybe Marta will be there, too."

Christian's hand went to her side, steadying her. Her nipple escaped his mouth with a soft pop. "Make the call," he said before reclaiming the tight bud and causing lust to coil in her belly.

Mystic made the call. She spoke quickly as Hawk and Christian did their best to make it nearly impossible for her to think.

Her breath was coming in and out in short pants by the time she finished talking to Rafael. "I'll get even with you both," she promised but her threat was ruined by the whimper that followed it as they eased her to her back and assaulted her with their lips.

Hawk's mouth found her ear. "I vote for a rematch. What about you Christian?"

Christian's fingers explored her wet slit. His cock was a hard ridge against her thigh. "I'm up for it."

Mystic snickered but willingly spread her legs. "Different stakes." She wasn't about to lose what she'd gained.

Hawk chuckled. She may have won last time, but she hadn't dented his confidence. "This time we'll just play for fun. Pick a number."

"Ten. You go first."

Hawk settled on top of her and sheathed himself in a single hard thrust. "One," he said, lingering until her channel was rippling along his cock, clinging to it before he thrust again. "Two."

She was almost sobbing in frustrated need, arching up to meet him by the time he got to ten and rolled off.

Christian's cock replaced Hawk's. Christian's mouth replaced Hawk's. His kiss was a tantalizing, sensuous glide of tongue against tongue as his penis slowly retreated from her slit then just as slowly reentered.

Masculine confidence crowded her through the bond. This time they planned to work together. This time their wolves wouldn't be allowed to interfere. This time they meant to win.

Mystic laughed silently and opened herself to them. She welcomed them into her body. She clung to them and came for them. She lost herself in the bliss of being with them.

It was late in the afternoon when the phone pulled Mystic from the warm cocoon of sleep. She reached for the receiver but Christian's hand got there first.

Rafe. The name had her crowding closer though she could only overhear Christian's side of the conversation. She waited for him to hang up instead of taking the information from his mind.

"We've got an address for a Hugh Campbell. He was a classmate of Todd's but as far as Rafe can tell, there's no death record for him. The address is for an apartment building near where Todd lived. Rafe's still working on finding a connection to someone named Marta."

Hawk rolled out of bed and stretched. Mystic admired his wonderful masculine lines before climbing out of bed, too. "We can hit a fast food place on the way to Hugh's place," she said and felt the room fill with masculine tension.

A muscle twitched in Hawk's cheek. She looked at Christian and saw the wolf glowering at her through his eyes.

"We can call Gabe and Gabby for backup," she said in a soft voice. "But it should be safe enough without them. We don't know if this Hugh is the one the Weres have been asking about. We don't know for sure he has any idea Todd was vampire. And even if he does and he's a vampire himself, he's too young to be anything but completely suspended during the daylight hours. My fathers were both reborn in the seventeen hundreds and they don't stir at this time of day."

Christian's wolf growled down the link. She nibbled on her bottom lip and refrained from reminding him about the "fucking game".

"You'll follow our lead?" Christian finally said.

She moved around the bed and wrapped her arms around his waist. She knew what it had cost him to give in without an argument. Everything in his nature demanded that he protect and serve.

"I'll follow your lead," she said before pressing her lips to his.

He didn't open for her immediately. The wolf's pride required a show of submission.

Mystic ran her tongue along the seam of his mouth and rubbed her naked body against his. The ease with which she offered the display surprised her. It came so naturally. They were turning her into a wolf, she thought in the instant before Christian's mouth opened and his kiss made everything else fade.

By the time their lips parted his cock was a hard line pressed to her belly and her inner thighs were slick with arousal. Mystic stroked her hand down his spine and asked, "What time do you have to go to work today?"

"I don't. I took care of my critical stuff so I could take a few days off."

"Good." She gave him a quick kiss before stepping out of the embrace. If they didn't leave soon, they'd end up back in bed.

Hugh's apartment building didn't look promising as a vampire's home. It was well lit and busy.

"What floor?" Mystic asked.

"Fifth," Christian answered.

They used the elevator to get there. There was no answer when Hawk knocked on Hugh's door.

Christian pulled a small black case from his pocket and opened it.

Hawk gave a soft whistle. "Nice set of picks. Police issue?"

Christian chuckled and along their bond Mystic could feel the camaraderie starting to form between her two alpha wolves. She wanted to pull them both into a hug and tell them how happy it made her. Instead she let them feel her contentment, what it meant to her to have them getting along instead of growling and snapping.

Hawk turned away from the door. He cupped her cheek with his hand and leaned in to nuzzle and press soft kisses against her mouth. Amusement and tenderness filled the link. *Some fighting is inevitable when wolves gather to form a pack. But we'll work things out. Neither of us wants to be banished to the doghouse by our Angelini mate.*

Mystic laughed. The longer she was around Hawk the more she realized she'd misjudged him at the Zevanti compound. She'd seen him as an ultraserious alpha whose only goal was to gain a pack of his own. Now she saw his humor and playfulness, his vulnerability and pride, his willingness to compromise when necessary.

The click of a lock yielding drew their attention back to apartment door. In an automatic maneuver Hawk positioned her behind him.

Christian said, "I'll go in first and make sure we're clear. You stay with her."

"Go," Hawk said.

It took only a minute for Christian to search the apartment and wave them in. Mystic went right over to a small desk. "We've got the right Hugh, here's a photo of him with Todd. There's a girl in it."

Hawk and Christian joined her. Hawk turned on the desktop computer while Mystic took the picture out of its frame. There were no names on the back. "Do either of you have a cell phone with a camera?" she asked, remembering how casually Skye had managed to record Todd Moore's driver's license.

Christian shook his head. Hawk said, "No."

Mystic looked down at the photo. If she could get it to Rafe he might be able to find out who the girl was and whether or not she went by the name of Marta.

The computer finished booting. Hawk made quick work of looking through the desktop files. Hugh was a gamer.

"Looks promising," Christian said. "Most of it's magical role-playing. A guy like that would be interested in vampires."

Hawk clicked on the browser option and went to the history file. Nothing. Either Hugh didn't surf the web or he was careful to clean out his cache before shutting down.

Mystic opened the desk drawers. Office supplies. Gaming manuals. Financial records. No research files on vampires.

Christian knelt down and pulled the most recent bank statement from a labeled folder. He scanned it before picking out another one.

Mystic felt his interest spike even before he reached for a third statement midway between where the first two had been. She knelt down next to him. "You've got something?"

"Maybe. Or it could be nothing." He showed her the first statement. "Here he's got two direct deposits going in, one in the middle of the month, one at the end. He's got a job. Now look at the number of withdrawals. Lots of checks, lots of debit card usage. Looks pretty much like the activity in most people's checking accounts."

Christian put the first statement down on the carpeted floor and showed her the most recent one. "Big change. Just enough money going in to cover the checks for rent, utilities and car payment, and all of the deposits were made using ATMs."

Mystic glanced at the third statement. It was dated four months ago and had very little activity.

Hawk leaned against the desk. "Looks like he's trying to ease himself out of having a paper trail, maybe so he can disappear without an official death certificate. Every human in Vegas is a walking ATM machine for a vampire, even a fledgling."

Christian pulled more statements from the file. He spread them out on the carpet by date. "Or he's involved in some criminal activity and doesn't want to leave anything behind for the IRS or the police to confiscate or use against him if he gets caught."

Mystic compared the statement. The change from lots of activity to minimal activity happened over a period of time starting five months earlier, two months after Todd Moore's human death and burial. She glanced around the apartment. Despite the furnishings, it had a rarely used feel to it.

Christian put the bank statements back in the drawer. Mystic hesitated before sliding the empty picture frame into a file folder.

"He might guess someone's been here and spook," Hawk said.

"If he knows Todd Moore is missing or the Weres have been asking about him, he might already be spooked," Mystic said.

Christian closed the drawer and looked around the apartment. "For all we know, the Weres already hunted him the same way they did Moore."

Mystic nodded. Hawk said, "Let's finish looking around and get out of here."

There was a cocktail napkin from Wolfsbane in a trashcan next to the bed. Mystic remembered Roman adding the name to the list of clubs and saying it was a place with a mixed crowd. "Maybe we should check this club out tonight," she said.

Her statement was met with stony outward silence and subvocal growls. She ducked her head to keep from smiling but couldn't resist saying, "If we go after dark, Roman can go with us. We should be safe enough then."

The bristling outrage of alpha wolves flooded the bond. She instantly regretted teasing them with her other mate. The last thing she wanted was disharmony.

Hawk pulled her to him. His mouth found the place he'd bitten each time he'd mounted and taken her from behind. His teeth clamped down, sending a pulse of need straight to her cunt. *You're asking for trouble. Do you want us to prove just how capable we are of seeing to all your needs, including your safety?*

She shivered at the sensual threat in his words. She closed her eyes and melted into him, appeasing his wolf with her submissive yielding. "I know I'm safe with you," she said to the man.

Hawk chuckled and her spirits lightened. He nuzzled her neck before releasing her.

A hasty glance at Christian and she relaxed completely. Apparently both her mates had taken her teasing in the spirit it was meant.

Christian picked up a pad of paper left on the nightstand. He turned on a table lamp and tilted the pad of paper underneath it.

Mystic could see the faint impression of numbers. "Find a pencil?"

She felt his surprise and lifted her eyebrows in response. "I do watch *CSI*."

He laughed. "Find a pencil."

There was one in Hugh's desk in the living room.

Christian rubbed the lead over the impression left on the paper. "Looks like a phone number."

"Call it from here?" Hawk asked.

Christian shook his head. "No landline. Hugh probably uses a cellular. Unfortunately he doesn't keep his phone bills so we don't have a number for him."

Mystic touched her finger to the edge of the tablet. "Rafe might be able to use his computer skills to find out more now that we know *this* Hugh is the one the Weres have been asking about."

Christian's eyes narrowed. Mystic couldn't resist the urge to lean in and press her mouth to his. *It's better this way. Let him do the hacking so you can keep a low profile. You're a policeman in this city.*

Cops aren't in the habit of using lock picks, Christian said, but she felt how much it meant to him that she wanted to protect his reputation.

They left the apartment and the building without incident. Her cell phone rang just as she was sliding into the front seat of Hawk's car. It was Gabby.

"You're okay?" Gabrielle asked.

Mystic grinned. At the risk of riling her wolves up again she said, "You can't beat vampire blood."

Gabby snickered. "Well, I can think of a lot more pleasurable ways of getting it besides being gutted."

"Me, too. Are you and Gabe at the hotel?"

"Just finished eating in one of the restaurants. Is Hawk with you?"

"Yes." Mystic took a minute to fill Gabby in on the visit to Hugh's apartment.

Gabby said, "Gabe and I came up with an idea." There was an uncharacteristic hesitation. "Maybe I should talk to Hawk."

Mystic was torn between smiling and frowning. It made her happy to think Gabe and Gabby viewed Hawk as their alpha and might be part of the pack he intended to form. But at the same time, she hated losing the easy camaraderie she'd always shared with her friends.

"Talk to me first," Mystic said, "in case he's inclined to veto your idea."

"Gabe and I want to go back to Bangers. We don't know for sure the rogue Weres left in a car last night. I'm not exactly terrifying in my fur. If I was wearing a collar and leash, I doubt many people would think wolf when they saw me. Maybe I can pick up a scent."

Mystic laughed as excitement charged through her. "That's a great idea! If I'm holding the leash even fewer people will notice." She checked the sky though she knew just by the feel of the day that it was approaching sunset. "We'll head to Bangers now."

Audible growls met her pronouncement. Mystic calmly closed her cell phone and met the wolf stares of her two mates.

Chapter Seventeen

ဢ

It was a good plan, one he should have come up with and implemented himself, Hawk thought as they parked behind Gabe's Jeep a couple of blocks away from Bangers. If Roman had been home, he and Christian could have left Mystic and taken care of this.

I don't think so, Mystic said.

Hawk's lip lifted in a silent snarl. She was still flush from her victory in the bedroom. Next time he wouldn't underestimate her when the stakes were so high.

Before mating with Mystic, he hadn't considered how different the mental link would be from that of a pack bond. With her, there was a seamless merging of minds instead of a limited channel for communication. It was going to take some getting used to.

They got out of the car and immediately Mystic was engulfed in a hug from Gabby and Gabe. When they parted, Gabe said, "We swung by a store and picked up a collar and leash." He rolled his eyes and grinned. "It took forever because we couldn't agree. I thought spikes were appropriate but Gabby wouldn't have it."

"It's my neck, my choice."

Mystic laughed. Happiness uncurled in her chest like a wolf waking up. It felt so good to be with her friends and her mates, it felt better than good, stronger, different. It felt like home and that gave her pause. It made her wonder if what she was feeling was a sense of pack.

Around them the dusk faded into night. "Shift in the car," Hawk said to Gabby.

Mystic got in the car with her friend. She snickered when she saw the matching collar and leash. They were sky-blue with a herd of tiny black and white cows down the middle of them. "No rhinestones?"

"I'm waiting until after we hit the casinos. As soon as I rake in the jackpots I can buy real stones, maybe even have tiny gems glued onto my toenails. You think they'd survive the change? The beads Hawk's got in his hair have been spelled so they're a part of him."

"Worth a try, but start with something cheap." The car's dome light went off.

There was a rustle of clothing being removed. Mystic pressed against the door, giving Gabby plenty of room. The air in the car hummed with gathering magic and energy.

Mystic's chest tightened. Her heart raced. She grew short of breath and felt an instant of panic at the unfamiliar fullness, as though her skin couldn't contain her. There was sharp burst of pain through her center, then Gabby's wet wolf nose was nudging her hand.

"Remind me never to be in a small space with you again when you change," Mystic said. "You pack a punch!"

She rubbed her chest to try to rid herself of the phantom pain still lingering there. Something had changed because of the bond she had with Christian and Hawk. It probably had to do with their wolves responding to Gabby's change and wanting to emerge, too. Whatever it was, Mystic didn't want to revisit it anytime soon. For a second she'd felt as though she was going to split open and the magic was going to pour out of her—only instead of reforming into a wolf, she'd just be a mess someone would have to clean up. It wasn't a pretty picture and it definitely wasn't the way she wanted to leave this world.

A soft bark reminded Mystic she was in the car for a reason. She shook off the effects of Gabby's change and turned her attention to fastening the dog collar around her friend's neck.

Shock ripped through Christian with a one-two punch that made him think of a double-barrel shotgun. Mystic had a wolf form and Hawk already knew about it.

"Don't say anything to her," Hawk said in a low voice, his shoulder touching Christian's. "Put your thoughts behind a barrier. She's not ready to accept the possibility yet."

Christian nodded, in agreement with Hawk. "You guessed. Or you knew?" There was a sudden rawness inside him he couldn't explain and didn't want to look too closely at.

Hawk stilled. "On some level you knew it too, but you couldn't be sure. You're an alpha but you grew up without a pack." He surprised Christian by leaning more heavily into him and relaxing against him.

Only their shoulders and upper arms touched and yet there was the flowing sensation of beast against beast. It wasn't a sexual overture but Christian's cock partially filled and his chest flooded with warmth.

He tensed and would have pulled away but Hawk stopped him with a hand on his arm. "It's normal. A pack bond is forming between us. Even if a female wasn't at the center of our relationship, the closeness sometimes mimics the afterglow of sex."

And the shocks just keep coming, Christian thought as he took a deep breath and tried to deal with this newest one— because now that Hawk had pointed it out, he could feel the link between the two of them. He could feel lighter traces of it going to Gabe and Gabby. It felt good, right, like a part of him he hadn't recognized as missing was suddenly being filled in.

The car door opened. Mystic emerged holding a leash. Gabby jumped to the asphalt. "We're ready," Mystic said.

Christian stepped forward and wrapped his hand around her arm. His mind shut down to everything but getting this done and keeping her safe while they were doing it.

"Let's make this quick," he said.

Nobody argued with him.

Most of the people hanging around Bangers were already high on something other than life. A few of them commented about Gabby, a couple even took imaginary aim and pulled the trigger. Christian ignored them though Hawk had to step in and keep Gabe from losing his cool.

Nobody had bothered to clean up the blood in the parking lot. It was dried, dead, but Christian's hackles rose as the wolf surveyed the place its mate had nearly been killed.

He glanced at Hawk. Their eyes met. Last night he'd wanted to rip into Mystic's other mate and tear him to shreds, tonight the anger was directed at the rogue Weres.

They followed as Gabby led them out of the parking lot and into an industrial section. Christian kept thinking she'd circle back, return to the place where a car had been parked. Instead she kept going, tugging at the leash and nearly dragging Mystic in her excitement to follow the Weres' human scent.

Loud rock music greeted them as they left one industrial section and skirted the fenced edge of a run-down self-storage facility. A couple of the units had their doors open to expose amplifiers and instruments. One band was already practicing, another was setting up.

"Did they know any of you were Weres?" Christian asked. So far there'd been no weaving, no detours, no splitting up.

"They were nervous. I thought they picked up on something when Gabe and I got to their table. It looked like they were going to bolt," Hawk said.

The fence surrounding the storage units ended. A seedy area of town began. A pit bull chained up in a front yard further down the street went into a frenzy.

The area was known for gang violence, low-end prostitutes and drug deals for the down-and-out. *It fit*, Christian thought. If someone was making Weres from scratch and the survival rate after a mauling wasn't very good, this was the perfect place. There were plenty of disposable people to choose from, junkies who'd dropped out of society and life a long time ago.

Gabby whined and slowed her pace. She lifted her face. Her footsteps slowed further. Gabe said, "The scent's stronger here. There's a lot of coming and going, old and new track."

Surprise spiked through Christian. "You can communicate with her mentally?"

Gabe nodded. "But the range is a lot shorter like this. When we're both wearing fur, the distance is longer, maybe twice what's normal for most Weres."

This time shock stopped Christian in his tracks. "Weres have a psychic connection when they're wolves?"

Both Hawk and Gabe gaped at him. Christian's spine stiffened but before his hackles rose in defensiveness, Mystic said, *How could you know the ins and outs of what it means to be a wolf with a pack? The werewolf culture is self-contained and exclusive and very hierarchical. They don't readily share information.*

She leaned in and nuzzled his ear. *All pack members are ultimately connected by the sharing of blood, either through birth or rite. They can link mentally but only over short distances, and typically only when they're in their fur.* He felt her smile. *It's harder for them than it is between vampires or the Angelini and the ones they share blood with. It's especially hard between mixed forms. It comes easily and naturally for Gabe and Gabby because they're twins as well as pack mates. Hawk is a known alpha to them, he might be able to communicate with Gabby if he was in his fur. He could probably call her wolf and make her shift, or send the wolf back, but without a blood link, I doubt even he's strong enough to hear Gabby's thoughts now.*

Christian turned his head. His mouth captured Mystic's for a brief, appreciative kiss. *Thanks.*

There were few porch lights and the majority of the street lights had been shot out. Three houses in from the industrial section Gabby stopped at the corner of a yard.

There'd been a white picket fence once. What remained of it stood or lay down in sections of chipped paint and grayed wood.

A footpath was worn around to the back of the house. Gabby put her nose on the ground. Her tail thumped against Mystic's leg.

Christian studied the run-down, single-story house. It was darkened but that didn't mean it was empty. The edgy sensation along his spine made him think something supernatural was inside. "Can you sense anything?"

"Were energy," Mystic said. "But not a lot of it."

Hawk nodded. "One in fur at least. If there are others, they're still human. But unless this is a trap, I think it's only the one, probably left to guard."

"We go in?" Christian asked, already pulling his gun from its harness.

Mystic could smell the silver. Gabby whined as the scent reached her.

"Do you have a silencer?" Hawk asked.

"Yes." Christian pulled one out of his pocket and screwed it onto the barrel of the gun.

Hawk held his hand out to Christian. "I don't have a problem with shooting whatever comes at us, human or Were. You're a cop. Give me the gun. I'll take the responsibility."

Christian's lip curled. The wolf flashed in his eyes.

Mystic could feel Hawk's wolf respond. Subvocal growls filled the link as her two alphas squared off.

She wanted to interfere, to smooth things over, to mediate. She bit her lip to keep from doing it. This was something they had to work out for themselves. Christian had to decide whether or not he was going to be part of a pack and if so, whether or not he was going to share responsibility or let Hawk run things.

"This isn't police business," Christian finally said. "This is our business."

Hawk's hand dropped away. "Gabe and I can take the sides and go around to the back. I'm guessing there's a door. If there's a safe place to do it, I'll shift. On a signal you go in through the front. Gabe and I'll go in through the back. We won't be able to stop a wolf going out through the window, but at least we'll have time to search the place, maybe find out who we're dealing with. If we can take the wolf down without killing him, all the better, but I'm not counting on it."

"What's the signal?" Christian asked.

"I'll have Gabe tell Gabby to paw at the door."

"Sounds good." Christian glanced at Mystic. "She goes in behind me. Turn the lights on when we're in?"

"Yeah, safer for all of us that way. Okay, let's do this."

They split up. Despite nearly being killed by her last encounter with the rogue Weres, Mystic felt more excited than scared this time as she trailed Christian and Gabby to the front door.

It probably had something to do with the odds being in their favor this time — or it could be the gun. Silver bullets were a great equalizer when it came to Weres. Maybe in addition to some hand-to-hand combat training, she should also go out to the firing range.

Once again Christian pulled out his lock pick set. She wasn't sure whether or not anyone would report a breaking-and-entering in this neighborhood, or whether they'd even notice the sound of a door being kicked open, but it was smarter not to advertise what they were doing.

Mystic leaned down and unhooked the leash from Gabby's collar. Adrenaline surged through her system a few minutes later when Gabby scratched at the front door.

"Stand back and to the side," Christian said, checking to make sure she was in position before he opened the door and went in.

A wolf darted out into the narrow hallway as soon as the back door crashed open. He was big, gray, moth-eaten against the black shine of Hawk's fur.

Hawk snarled a command and the wolf went to its side, pee erupting in a show of terrified submission. Mystic breathed a small sigh of relief. She hadn't expected it to go so well.

Slowly Hawk approached. The other male whimpered, he scooted and crawled, retreating from the black wolf and trailing more pee as he did it.

Gabby edged forward as the wolf neared where they were blocking the front door. She showed her teeth and growled in a warning not to come any closer. The wolf responded by rolling to his feet and lunging, all pretense of submitting gone in an instant.

Christian reacted immediately, instinctively. A single shot to the head dropped the wolf just as it was leaping for his gun hand.

In a shimmer of magic Hawk was human again. "Gabe, go get your rental car. You and Gabby are going to take the body out into the desert. Burn it, then bury it."

Gabe left. Hawk disappeared long enough to get dressed. Christian said, "Let's search the place."

They started with the wolf's carcass. There was no brand, though no one had expected to find one.

The kitchen was a pigsty of take-out containers, cheap dog food, and beer. The bedrooms weren't much better. Sex-stained sheets were covered in grime and dog hair. A collar attached to a leash tied to the headboard hinted at games Mystic wasn't interested in learning more about.

"Matchbook from Wolfsbane," Christian said, kneeling among the squalor of dirty, perspiration-soaked clothing.

Gabby was digging through a pile of dark pants and shirts. When she gave a soft yip, Mystic left her study of the socks and dust under the bed and went over to investigate Gabby's find.

By the smell and size of the jeans Gabby was pawing at, Mystic thought they belonged to the Were being prostituted. She wrinkled her nose and picked them up. There was a photograph in the pocket. "Not that we needed confirmation these are the Weres who killed the fledgling, but here's a picture of Todd Moore."

Hawk looked up from where he was rummaging through a mostly empty dresser. "Anything in the background?"

Mystic studied the image. "Nothing, just a wall. If there were numbers at the bottom I'd say it could be a mug shot."

"So maybe finding the vampires isn't personal for them," Christian said, "and hunting them is their reward."

"Did Brann and Roman learn anything from Juric?" Hawk asked.

Mystic sought Roman with her mind. He was at Brann's estate. As soon as she opened the link desire and a need to feed rushed down the path to swamp her in heat.

She was instantly aroused, her panties wet in a heartbeat, and Roman made no attempt to hide his satisfaction at what he was doing to her. *The wolves have had you to themselves long enough,* Roman purred. *And from your memories I can see you've been quite busy. I am anxious for my turn to play a bedroom game with you. Be warned, you won't defeat me as you did your other two mates.* His laugh was a silky threat that made her nipples tighten. He was so old, so powerful his thoughts were like a physical caress stroking over her, through her.

Mystic closed her eyes and fought to steady her breathing. It took all her willpower to keep from cupping her breasts, from sliding her fingers into her slit in order to gain some relief. He was feeding her hunger, sharing his own with her, using the intensity of their blood connection to make her burn and need the same way he did. He was punishing her for taking so long to reach for him, ensuring she desired him as much as she did her Were mates.

She moaned when Hawk's hot, masculine body pressed against her back and his arm draped over her hip so his hand could cup her mound through the jeans she was wearing. His low growl was audible, his words were a snarl along their bond. *In a minute Christian and I are going to start fucking you. Your scent is driving us crazy. Your heat makes it nearly impossible to think about anything else except getting our cocks inside you. We'll take you with Gabby here. We'll take you with a dead Were in the hallway and not even care that the others might show up. I'd suggest if Roman is anxious to be with you he should let us finish here and leave.*

Roman pulled back though Mystic's body still shivered with the need to come. All it would take was for Hawk or Christian to put their mouths on her, to lick or suck her clit, to penetrate her with their tongues or even their fingers and she'd come.

Wolves weren't shy about taking their mates with others around. She and Gabby had witnessed it plenty of times, but she couldn't bring herself to ask for release in front of her friend—at least not until Gabby had a mate to attend to her needs.

Mystic clenched her fists. She thought about the hunt they were on—the photograph she'd taken from Hugh's apartment, the picture here, the cocktail napkin from Wolfsbane they'd found there, the matchbook Christian found here. Slowly the desperate need faded into a hum of awareness, a barely tolerable containment.

Did you and Brann learn anything from Dusan Juric?

Juric banished a son barely weaned from his vein to California and lost him almost immediately. He hasn't been able to find out what happened to him. Given the taint of a dark sorcerer's magic on Todd Moore's blood, it's possible Juric's son was captured or he allowed himself to be used voluntarily in order to create additional vampires. He wasn't strong enough to do it on his own. I find it interesting we've got Weres who were created – not born – hunting vampires who also appear to have come into existence unnaturally. Maybe they were both experiments – one successful, one not.

There was a thoughtful pause from Roman. *We need to capture someone alive, either a Were or a vampire. I'll speak to Brann. There are others here who are part of his line through Gian. He can assign some of them to the task of watching the house you've found. I'll use your memories to give them directions. Hurry up and finish searching, then get out of there.*

Gabe returned with the Jeep. Hawk helped him get the dead wolf wrapped in blankets and out to the car while Christian and Mystic quickly finished going through the house. There was nothing to identify any of the people living there though Mystic found a picture of Hugh in the pocket of another pair of pants and Christian found one of the same woman who appeared in the photograph with Todd and Hugh that Mystic had taken from Hugh's apartment.

"I think it's safe to assume this is Marta and she's a vampire, too," Christian said, slipping the photograph into his pocket as Hawk came back into the room.

"Gabby and Gabe are on their way," Hawk said. "Are we finished in here?"

"Yeah," Christian said, but hesitated when he got to the spot where the dead wolf had fallen. There was no blood, Hawk and Gabe had cleaned it up, but the Weres would know what happened if they shifted into their wolf form.

Mystic felt the weight of the death settle on Christian. She put her arm around his waist. "You didn't have a choice."

Hawk stepped forward. He gripped Christian's forearm. He locked his eyes to Christian's. "He could have yielded and had a chance at survival. The wolf knew. The man rejected. This death was clean and quick. If his actions required us to turn him over to the vampires, they might have made him wish he were dead long before they finished with him."

Christian gave a terse nod. Mystic rubbed her cheek against his shoulder and let him feel how much he'd already come to mean to her. He turned into her and captured her mouth. He took his comfort from her lips and tongue, from the press of her body against his and the warm presence of Hawk at his back.

"Wolfsbane next?" she asked when the kiss ended.

Christian's phone rang before either of her mates got more than a growl out. As he took the call, Roman's thoughts found her. *The number found at Hugh's apartment belongs to a cell phone. It's just been turned on. Rafe is giving Christian the location. You'll insist on going and your wolves can't deny you. Do not enter the house without me. I'll meet you there. When we're finished with our business, you'll be done hunting for the night.*

Mystic's spine stiffened at his autocratic pronouncement. There was steel in his voice but she wasn't afraid of him. *We'll see.*

Yes, we'll see.

Chapter Eighteen

✆

The house was fitting for a vampire lair. Old, gloomy, isolated from its neighbors and shrouded by overgrown shrubbery. It looked like it might have been built during the days of the gold rush, or at least before Las Vegas blossomed into Sin City.

Roman was already there, leaning against his sports car with elegant ease. Heat rippled through Mystic's belly and cunt at the sight of him. Her nipples tightened and she ached to tilt her head back, to offer her neck and feel the ecstasy of his bite.

She allowed herself a moment to luxuriate in the feelings and sensations bombarding her, the satisfaction and happiness that came with having him as her mate. Then she pushed them aside with a scowl and a mental reminder that his smug confidence at being able to limit her activities grated on her nerves just as much as Christian's and Hawk's had.

Roman's husky chuckle along their link only served to deepen the frown. *You won't win if you challenge me to a bedroom game,* he reminded her. *And you will not be going to Wolfsbane with Christian and Hawk. The young wolf and her brother can join them there.*

Mystic got out of Hawk's car. She wasn't foolish enough to goad Roman by wrapping herself around one of her Were mates, but she was tempted. Had she really thought he was easygoing?

She made a point of not looking at him though she was aware of him shoving away from his sports car and walking toward them. His laugh had her clenching her teeth, but she was powerless to stop her body from melting against his when he pulled her back to his front and kissed along her neck. "No greeting for the mate who spent a long, lonely day waiting for the sun to set and the moon to rise so he could *come* for the one he's bound to?"

"You're not playing fair," Mystic said, moaning softly when his hands cupped her breasts.

"And you played fairly with Hawk and Christian?" Roman said, chuckling when his comment was met with irritated growls.

He grazed the tips of his fangs over her vein until she shivered. "Once the fledgling is taken care of, you and I will take our leave. I don't think Christian or Hawk will insist on having you accompany them to Wolfsbane."

He glanced up at the men in question and Mystic felt their relief though it didn't filter into their expression.

"We can handle Wolfsbane," Hawk said. "Let's get this taken care of."

Roman pressed one last kiss to Mystic's throat before reluctantly setting her aside. Playing with her was a two-edged sword, especially after the visit with Juric and the fantasies he'd entertained since then.

He was thankful her other mates had somewhere to be and would view his taking Mystic away as desirable. He didn't want to share, not tonight. The suite he favored at one of the larger casinos was waiting for them, the night beyond taking care of the fledgling already planned in exquisite detail.

"Rafe didn't know who the phone belonged to," Christian said. "It's a throwaway."

"There's a vampire in the house, a young, tainted one," Roman said. "Brallin's old magic recognizes me even if the fledgling doesn't."

"Can you control the fledgling?" Hawk asked.

"Of course." Roman laughed softly as Mystic's worry found him. *If I didn't know you fret because it's natural to do so over a mate, I would be insulted. True, the fledgling will react violently when the mage's dark magic senses what I gained from Syndelle, but he's no match for me. Neither is it likely he'll have a chance to attack one of your other mates.*

The rich purr of a car's engine reached them. Roman glanced at Hawk and Christian. He said, "Brann will be here in a few minutes. If it were up to me, I'd lock Mystic in the car and order her to wait until we secure the fledgling, but unfortunately that's not an option. So I would suggest you patrol outside the house. You'll be safe as wolves. Mystic will need to enter first and invite Brann inside. One of you can do the same for me. It should only take a few minutes to subdue the fledgling. But if he manages to escape the house you should be able to take him down. Go for his arms, as close to the wrists as you can get. Even the newly dead can produce talons sharp enough to gut a wolf."

Mystic was surprised at how quickly Hawk and Christian evaluated Roman's plan and agreed with it. As Brann's car drew near, they stripped out of their clothing and shifted into wolves.

Her breath caught at how beautifully matched they were. They were of equal size, their fur thick and luxurious, their eyes fierce and sharp.

Sadness uncurled inside her. She'd long ago accepted her inability to change forms. She'd cried her tears when puberty came and went and with it the last window of opportunity to be like most of the other Renaldi females. Now, looking at Hawk and Christian, she felt a deep sense of longing and a jagged pain of loss at being unable to run with them as a wolf.

She hid her feelings behind a hastily erected mental barrier. She tried to tell herself the downturn in her emotions was the natural aftereffect of a fading surge of adrenaline, but the truth was she felt completely useless at the moment. Roman said she needed to open the door for Brann and invite him into the house, but Christian or Hawk could do it and still change in time to provide an external guard.

All of them would just as soon have her wait in the car. She was the weak link here, the one who jeopardized the others because of her vulnerability.

For one split second she was tempted to throw in the towel. No one expected her to be a hunter, not her parents, not the Renaldis or the wolves they were allied with. Her mates would just as soon she never leave the bed. They'd be quite content with pleasure and in the future, children.

Mystic stiffened her spine and lifted her chin. She forced the old insecurities and hurts back into the box they'd escaped from. She was an Angelini. Until the magic responsible for her creation made it clear her path was different, then she would do what she was supposed to do. She would learn how to hunt so she could take her rightful place in the supernatural world she lived in.

Brann's sleek sports car pulled to a stop behind Roman's. The blood connection between them hummed with the strength of his power. No wonder Hawk and Christian had agreed to Roman's plan to let her go into the house without even a small snarl of dissent. The fledgling wouldn't get close to her, not while she was in the company of the council's executioner.

With the smooth grace of an ancient, Brann covered the distance between them. He glanced at the wolves and said, "Try not to kill him if he manages to escape the house. His continued existence has yet to be determined but his death isn't sanctioned."

Christian and Hawk trotted away. Roman followed the wolves, fading into the night as easily as they'd done.

Mystic ensured her mind was open, the links she held with all four men making it possible for them to communicate and know each other's positions as well as what was happening in each location. Brann studied the house, seemingly lost in thought. When the others were where they needed to be, he made a sweeping bow and ushered her forward.

The lock picks felt awkward and unfamiliar in her hand, strange tools that made her feel as though she had two thumbs. Without the link to Christian she would have been forced to break a window.

His warm assurances and guidance helped her through the process. A small burst of pride made her smile when the second and last lock yielded with a satisfying click.

The absence of wards or protections surprised her given the taint of the dark mage's magic. There were no symbols carved into the doorjamb, no spells woven around the perimeter of the house. Even the house itself was easily breached, the windows large and old-fashioned, though perhaps the remoteness of the location had lulled the fledgling into thinking he was safe.

Over the years she'd met a few of those sired by Falcone and Yorick, but they were centuries old, long past needing her fathers' blood or guidance. She'd spent no time around true fledglings, but she would have expected a fledgling to be paranoid, fanatical about ensuring his continued existence.

She thought of the elaborate security system her parents had. Wards and alarms, well-hidden rooms secured and built to withstand even a fire. Longing flared up in that instant, excitement over the prospect of her fathers no longer having to fear exposure to the sun.

Mystic stepped into the fledgling's house. To Brann, she said, "You may enter."

He stepped across the threshold. Through their link she knew Roman was already inside, at the back of the house and in the kitchen.

Your mates will never again trust me with your care if I allow you to precede me, Brann said, his voice rich with amusement.

Mystic smiled despite the seriousness of the situation. She stepped to the side so he could get in front of her.

The house was old, large, heavily tainted — though the last came to her through Brann and Roman's awareness. As she moved from room to room with Brann, absorbing his impressions as well as Roman's in the way a dry desert hungrily pulls the rainfall beneath its surface, some of her old doubts and insecurities leached away. In their place was a budding confidence. She could learn to be a hunter.

They found the door leading to the cellar just as Christian heard the sound of a ground level window being opened. An image flashed though her mind, a man bursting through the concealing shrubbery at the side of the house. A jolt of savage pleasure followed, wolves after prey.

Hawk rounded the corner just as the fledgling neared. Hugh veered, sprinted. He was fast but the wolves were faster. It was over even before Brann got close enough to the struggling vampire to be heard.

"Stop," Brann said, needing only his voice to freeze the fledgling in place.

The mage's dark magic writhed and fought inside Hugh, but his body remained perfectly still even as his muscles pressed against his skin in an agony of suspended motion. The struggle intensified as Roman drew near. Frustrated, terrified, confused tears of blood leaked from the corners of his eyes.

Brann knelt beside them and caught the droplets on the tips of his fingers. He used the moisture to draw elaborate symbols on Hugh's forehead. The fledgling's eyes went blank. The taut muscles relaxed though the connection with Brann and Roman allowed Mystic to feel the dark magic still seething deep inside Hugh.

"You can release him," Brann said.

Hawk and Christian released their grip on Hugh's forearms. Mystic's throat tightened when she saw the strands of fur caught on the tips of Hugh's deadly talons. With a thought she assured herself he had not managed to draw blood.

Both of her mates growled, but underneath their macho protest she felt their pleasure at knowing she worried and cared for them. They backed away, not stopping until they were crowded against Mystic's legs in a furry blockade.

Roman's chuckle sounded in her mind. It made Mystic smile. Another vampire might have taken offense, considered it an insult to have Weres position themselves in such a way as to make it obvious they were guarding the very person he was already guarding.

I am not just vampire, Roman said, leaning in to brush tantalizing kisses along her neck. *I understand the beast's need to protect its mate above all other considerations. I would think less of your wolves if your safety wasn't constantly on their minds.*

Mystic relaxed into him. It felt good to have all three of her mates with her. They'd been together such a short time and yet she thought they'd already adapted and adjusted amazingly well.

She shifted her attention to the fledgling vampire. Several drops of blood glistened on Brann's fingertips. As she watched he rubbed his thumb and fingers together, a contemplative expression on his face. When he looked up, he said, "If it weren't for the mage's old magic and the power inherent in Juric's line, this one would be dead. He's fed only on humans since he was reborn as vampire."

"A troubling development," Roman said.

Brann nodded.

"What happened to Juric's missing son?" Mystic asked.

Brann wiped the blood from his fingers onto Hugh's shirt. "A good question, one our captured fledgling will be receptive to answering in his current state." He removed a black-handled athame from a sheath hidden inside his shirt and casually sliced through the buttons holding Hugh's shirt closed. "Tell us how you came to be vampire, from the very beginning."

"We were in Laughlin—"

"We?" Brann said.

"Todd, Marta, and me."

"Go on."

"There was someone Marta was supposed to meet. She didn't tell us then. She just said she wanted to get out of Vegas and would we go with her. Later we learned why she wanted to go. She met—" Hugh's eyes closed. His back arched.

Brann nicked Hugh's neck with the athame. He gathered the droplets of blood and added more symbols to those he'd already written on Hugh's face.

The fledgling's back dropped to the ground with a soft thud. His eyelids fluttered open. "She met Egan Walsh. He calls himself The Dark Wizard." Hugh licked his lips. "We've played against him online. Only Todd and I didn't know it at first. We only knew it afterward. He always plays a wizard. Sometimes he has vampire servants, sometimes he has werewolf servants. But most of the time he plays solo. His usual strategy is to get the vampires fighting the wolves, and the black witches fighting the white ones so he can concentrate on destroying the other sorcerers.

"Marta slipped away from us. We looked everywhere but we couldn't find her. We hung around for days. When she didn't come back we told the police about her being missing then came home. A week later she calls Todd. She says the police are going to get in touch with us and we need to go along with what they say, not argue with them.

"The next day it happens. They tell us Marta was found dead, overdosed on drugs even though we knew she never did anything worse than smoking pot. They said her brother found her and her body had already been released for burial—only she doesn't have a brother.

"Todd went back to Laughlin. He disappeared too. Two weeks later he called to tell me to buy a suit for his funeral, same thing. When they found him it'd look like a drug overdose. No autopsy, no embalming, he knew his family wouldn't allow it. Just a quick ceremony and a hasty burial.

"Marta and Todd came to my place afterward. Stupid. It was stupid. They just about killed me. They thought they could turn me without Egan Walsh but then they lost their nerve. It took me days to recover. It took me weeks to get over being scared."

Hugh smiled. His fangs glistened. "But I couldn't forget what it felt like. I wanted it. I wanted the rush of being able to do it. To step inside the game. I wanted the game to be real for me too, not pretend. They took me to Egan.

"There was a vampire. Egan kept him naked, thin, like he was being starved to death. He looked barely legal. Totally feral. There were symbols painted all over him. There were symbols on the door leading into the room and painted in a circle around a mat on the floor. They left me in with him. I thought I'd have to screw up the courage, but as soon as I got close enough, I couldn't stop myself from going to him.

"It hurt. It was like being savaged. I lost consciousness and when I woke up I was in a room, starving, starving. They pushed someone in. A prostitute. I drank and drank and drank until there was nothing else. I didn't even care about killing her. I didn't care when another girl was pushed into the room. She screamed. She fought when she saw what I'd done to the first girl. But as soon as I bit her, she smiled. She died smiling and my heart started beating."

Christian and Hawk both growled deep in their throats. Mystic felt Christian's desire for justice on behalf of the dead. He wanted to lunge forward and rip Hugh to shreds.

She dug her fingers into the fur on the nape of their necks. She was sickened by Hugh's account but tried to remind herself he might be blameless under both Angelini and vampire law. A newly created vampire had little control. His deeds became the responsibility of the one who'd made him. It didn't mean Hugh was innocent, he'd have to be questioned further—especially about what he'd done since and what he'd known before agreeing to become vampire. At the moment the prostitutes' deaths weren't what was important.

"And after you found new life?" Brann said, his voice a smooth purr though he had not only the power, but the right to pass judgment and execute Hugh where he lay.

"Egan kept me in the room. After that he always kept one of us locked up. I didn't know it then, but Todd and Marta were getting stronger. They started going to a place called Wolfsbane. Sometime werewolves wandered in. They didn't know it at first. They thought they were humans, psychics maybe since they knew Todd and Marta were vampire. It was hard to hypnotize them, but sometimes when they were drunk, or when they dared one another, they'd offer a wrist or a neck.

"The blood made Todd and Marta more…independent. They were stealing for Egan, doing what he said. We all were. It seemed fair and we were coping okay until Toby.

"Toby's brother pimped him to Egan. That's what Egan liked — boys. Marta said she'd seen Toby before, and others, even younger. She said Egan couldn't get it up for an adult.

"Egan wanted to turn Toby. He had Todd bite Toby, drain him, give him his blood, only it didn't work. Toby didn't come back."

Nausea rose in Mystic's throat. She turned in Roman's arms so she could press her face to his neck and try to chase away the images with his clean scent. In that moment she was glad Todd Moore had screamed in the torturous rise of the sun even though he might well have been as much a victim as the young boy.

Hawk and Christian pushed against her legs. She ran her fingers in their fur, trying to soothe them as well as herself. This was why the Angelini had been created, to hunt, to protect the humans from becoming prey to the supernatural world. Beneath the horror Hugh's recitation brought, the fire to see this through until the bitter end burned hotter than ever in Mystic.

Roman's arms tightened around her waist. His cheek rubbed against hers. *We can't undo what has happened but we will see justice served.*

Behind her Brann said, "Go on."

Mystic forced herself to face Hugh.

"Todd and Marta tried to free the vampire who made us," Hugh said. "Egan caught them. He hurtled curses and froze them in place. Then he dragged me out of the room where I was kept. We watched while he slit the vampire's wrists and drained the blood. There wasn't much, less than a beaker full of it.

"I don't think the vampire had fed since I was thrown in with him. He was thin and gaunt, almost skeletal. At the very end Egan took the heart. He ate it. He laughed in between bites and said we wouldn't free ourselves from him. We were his until he decided we were more trouble than we were worth."

Moonlight glinted off the blade of Brann's athame. "And are you his now?"

"Only if I'm close enough for his spells to find me."

"The three of you escaped together?"

"Yes."

"How did you manage it?"

"Egan was preoccupied with the werewolf. He didn't realize Marta and Todd were strong enough to leave without his command. They'd slipped me notes, we had it planned."

"What werewolf?" Brann asked.

"A male. Egan told Marta and Todd to capture one. They took his blood, so much of it he passed out. He came to as they were carrying him into the house. He shifted. Somehow they got him in a cage. I heard it. They told me about it but I didn't see it."

"The werewolf had a brand?"

"I don't know."

"Have you been back?"

"Yes, but Egan's gone. We went back to kill him but someone else was living in the house. Even the realtor they'd rented it from didn't know where Egan was. We checked."

"You've killed others, besides the prostitutes you were given?"

"Yes. It's what I have to do to stay alive. Feeding isn't enough."

"Here in Las Vegas?"

"Sometimes. We spread it out, go other places. Find junkies and prostitutes mostly, people that won't be missed right away."

"Where's Todd?"

"I don't know. He was supposed to meet us last night but he didn't show."

Brann frowned. "He took blood from you?"

"Yes. The first time, when he and Marta nearly killed me."

"He can't reach you with his mind?"

"Only if we're near one another."

"What about Marta?"

"The same."

"Where was Todd going to hunt the last time you saw him?"

"Wolfsbane. He wanted to try for werewolf blood. I told him it was a bad idea. I reminded him that in the game The Dark Wizard set wolves against the vampires. I figured if Egan could make us from a captured vampire then he could make Weres from the one Todd and Marta delivered."

"And Marta? Where is she tonight?"

"Wyldfyres maybe. She's been trying to get up the courage to go there and be around other vampires."

Brann glanced at Mystic. "I can question him further in Rafe's presence. Perhaps my companion can find The Dark

Wizard through the online game, but for tonight I think it's more urgent to capture the remaining fledgling. Do you have anything else you wish to ask him?"

Mystic took a minute to think, to touch Hawk and Christian's minds as well as Roman's. All seemed to agree the council's executioner had done an excellent job in gathering the information they needed.

"You'll judge him later?" Mystic asked.

Brann shrugged. "Perhaps. Or I might turn him over to a tribunal composed of vampire, Were and Angelini and let them decide his fate. It's too soon to tell."

"I think we're finished with him for now," Mystic said.

With the ease of long practice Brann thrust the athame into the fledgling's heart. "There are cells underneath Fangs. I will take him there and arrange for Gian to keep him guarded." An elegant eyebrow lifted as his attention shifted to Roman. "You will accompany your mate to Wyldfyres?"

Roman would prefer she never step foot in Wyldfyres, never see the excessive, brutally carnal and depraved side of vampire existence, but it was unavoidable. "I will accompany her."

Brann gathered the fledgling in his arms then stood. Silence reigned as they walked back to their cars, each lost in thought.

Hawk and Christian shapeshifted and dressed then crowded Mystic in their human forms just as they'd done in their furred ones. She put her arms around their waists, hugged them to her and Roman found he didn't mind. The three of them standing with her, offering their protection and caring, felt right to him.

"We'll go to Wolfsbane," Christian said, brushing his thumb across Mystic's mouth before she could protest. "Gabe and Gabby will join us."

"Some of Brann's vampires will be there as well." Roman touched his mind to Brann's to make sure he spoke the truth.

Mystic said, "I take it the other Weres haven't shown up at their house."

"Not yet," Brann said. "At sunrise it would be best if the wolves took over." Along the blood link with Roman he added, *At the moment only a few of my line are able to walk underneath the sun. I won't risk Syndelle by letting others know the Masada lives among us and her blood will free us from the curse of eternal darkness. Perhaps it will become necessary once the Angelini finish with their meeting or if we learn the dark mage's magic has returned as well, but until then, her secret must be kept safe.*

Roman gave a subtle nod of acknowledgement. He owed a debt to Syndelle he could never repay.

"We'd better get going," Hawk said.

Roman thought again of the hotel room. "Mystic and I will return at nightfall tomorrow."

It was easier than it would have been in other circumstances. Though he had no direct mental link to Hawk and Christian, he could read their thoughts easily. Better she be with him, safe in bed or wherever else he intended to fuck her than to be with them either at the club or when they took over the surveillance of the rogue werewolves' house.

Hawk and Christian agreed without snarling, growling or raising their hackles. Roman chuckled silently. They were indeed making great progress in getting along well together.

Chapter Nineteen

🙵

I can't believe I'm going along with this, Mystic thought as Roman opened the door of an exclusive shop and she stepped outside. Cool night air glided over her bare legs before traveling upward to caress her exposed cunt and bare back. There was hardly enough material clinging to her to be considered a dress, much less one whose price tag had made her cringe. But Roman had insisted, in fact he'd picked the thing out and refused to let the clerk bring a selection of panties into the dressing room.

"They'll only get in the way at Wyldfyres," he'd said.

She shivered thinking about it. Her nipples were already tight points against the thin, clinging material of the dress. She didn't pretend it was only because of the temperature.

Roman's hand settled on her arm in a possessive, guarding gesture as he guided her to his sports car. She turned into his arms as he opened the door for her.

He was stunning in black. Elegant and deadly.

"If there was time, I'd insist on making you my companion before we go to Wyldfyres," he said, his voice one of purring menace.

Mystic's palms settled on his chest. Lust poured through their link and pooled in her cunt lips. "I'll be safe with you."

He cupped her breasts and rubbed his thumbs over her nipples until she was shivering, unable to keep her eyes open under the onslaught of need his touch evoked.

"Always," he whispered against her lips. "You will always be safe with me."

She opened her mouth for him, welcomed his tongue. He was gentle despite the fierce desire raging through him.

The kiss lasted forever and not long enough. Her lips clung to his when he tried to leave her. *Brann and Rafe are waiting for us*, he said, though she could feel how tempted he was to use their passion against her and avoid the trip to Wyldfyres. They both knew Brann could easily handle Marta by himself.

Mystic forced her hands away from Roman's chest. She ached for him, knew how much he wanted to be alone with her. She wanted the same thing, but she also wanted to see this hunt through.

With a sigh she slipped into the passenger seat. As he closed the door and walked around to the other side of the car, she could only shake her head at how quickly her life had changed, at how needy she'd become for the mates she'd been convinced she didn't want only days ago.

Roman chuckled. "You hadn't met me then."

Mystic bit her lip to keep from smiling. The last thing she intended to do was feed his ego.

He laughed again then started the car before taking her hand in his. "Promise you'll stay by my side at Wyldfyres."

"I will."

Rafe and Brann were waiting for them in front of the private vampire club. The entranceway wasn't visible from the street, which was probably for the best considering the outfits the fledglings guarding the door were wearing.

The female was bare-breasted, her nipples pierced and adorned with loops. The male's cock protruded from a slit in his leather pants, studs ran along the top of his penis and through the tip. When his eyes settled on Rafael, he began to harden despite the fear Brann's presence evoked.

"Open the door," Brann growled, making Rafe's smirk widen.

The relationship between the council's executioner and his companion fascinated Mystic, even as it stirred dark fantasies. She couldn't imagine her mates having sex with one another, she wasn't even sure she'd like them to, but watching Brann and Rafe together…

The doors parted to reveal an elegant, tiled foyer, its walls lined with erotic paintings and photographs. There was a choice of open doorways. From the right came the sound of leather striking flesh, of chains subtly clinking and voices commanding submission. Mystic couldn't resist the temptation to move toward the door and look through it.

A red-haired woman wearing a companion's necklace was bent over a vampire's knee and being spanked. A blonde companion was tethered to a narrow bed, at the mercy of the vampire who claimed her as he alternated between feeding from her femoral artery and sucking her clit.

Mystic's cunt clenched and Roman's hand tightened on her arm. *When we get to the hotel, I will show you what it's like to submit to a vampire master if you're still curious. But this place is not the place to explore that pleasure.*

Her cheeks heated at how easily he read her, at how a lifetime of *knowing* without actually *doing* had left her feeling like a sex maniac.

Roman laughed. *I take exception to that thought, as would Hawk and Christian. It's not lack of experience driving your lust, but the presence of mates who would happily fuck you night and day.*

His words served to increase the aching emptiness she felt between her thighs. "Can you sense Marta?" she asked, changing the topic before she started shaking with the need to have him inside her.

"No, not yet," Roman said. "But I doubt we will in this place. We'll have to rely on our eyes. Because of the sorcerer, some of the old mage magic has found its way into Marta. How much of a hold it has gained or will gain on the vessel containing it, how much awareness Marta has of it is unknown, but the magic itself will in all likelihood subside to levels that aren't easily detectable."

"Why?"

It was Brann who answered along their shared link. *It would mean death if the taint of Brallin's magic surfaced here. The youngest vampires might not recognize it, but the old ones would. A fledgling, especially one with no master and no understanding of our rules would have no chance of avoiding insult and ending up in a challenge that would result in death. Just as the magic Syndelle carries within her can cloak and hide itself when necessary, the mage's magic can do the same.*

He glanced at the blonde and red-haired companions then at the open doorway beyond them. "Rafe and I will take a moment to check the playrooms." His voice was a dangerous purr. "It has been a while since my companion was reminded of how lucky he is to have fallen into my hands."

Rafe's eyelids lowered to hide his thoughts. But he went willingly with Brann.

"Shall we?" Roman asked, nodding toward the door to their left.

Mystic looked down the wide hallway in front of them. It ended at a staircase guarded by vampires.

"Unless Marta is in the company of someone very old or very powerful, she will not be allowed in the rooms above us. They are held apart for those who prefer to share their pleasure only in the presence of peers," Roman said.

"Is that where you go when you come here?"

"I have been upstairs. What takes place there is not so different than what takes place down here. There are just fewer people to witness it." He urged her toward the door to their left and she suddenly found herself reluctant to go, to see for herself this part of his life.

I have warned you about that direction of thought, he said. *Do not force me to punish you here. There will be no other women for*

me. There can be no other, nor do I wish it. But if it will ease your
mind, I will tell you this has never been a favored haunt of mine.

She let him guide her through the door and into a room
where a human slave in a minuscule dress was stationed to
collect coats. The room beyond it contained a number couches,
loveseats and chairs, all wide, heavy pieces of furniture meant
to sustain a variety of abuse. Twosomes and threesomes were
scattered around the room, men and women in various
combinations, all feeding on humans wearing the bands of
slaves, all fucking as they did it.

"Who do they belong to?" Mystic asked, finding the sight
of so many blood slaves disturbing.

"The slaves?"

"Yes."

"Some are tied to Wyldfyres. Some are brought here to be
used at will—either as reward or punishment for service to
their masters."

Mystic shuddered. She'd spent time around vampire
companions and humans bound for their own protection or
because they were held in high regard, but she'd never spent
much time around slaves—those considered completely
disposable by the majority of the vampires who owned them.

Music throbbed from the next room, low and primitive,
its beat inviting the rub of flesh against flesh. Mystic laughed
as soon as they stepped through the doorway and she saw the
dance floor.

It was surreal, a mix of modern lighting and ancient
architecture. Color danced off rounded columns that made her
think of Greek and Roman temples. Dancers bumped and
ground and rubbed against each other on the open floor until
the primal beat drove them to the columns. And there they
fucked, men and women both with their back against the
smooth stone and their legs wrapped around their partner's
waists.

She saw no slave bands on the dancers, only rich jewelry and companion necklaces. Without conscious thought Mystic's hand went to her bare neck and she felt the absence of something she'd never had.

I can make you my companion tonight, Roman said, leading her to the dance floor and taking her into his arms.

The heat of his body and the persuasive purr of his voice tempted Mystic. She wanted to be his companion, to take what he offered, to join with him in a vampire's most sacred bond.

She ached to feel his fangs sliding into her neck, to feel his lips against her skin as he drank deeply. She longed to touch her mouth to him and take his essence in a covenant that could never be broken. But she had other mates, and feminine intuition whispered their names, insisted they be present when she became Roman's companion.

I want Christian and Hawk to be there, she said, closing her eyes and wrapping her arms around Roman, giving herself over to the music.

Roman rubbed his chin against the luxurious softness of Mystic's hair. He accepted her desire to include her other mates, understood it, but he wouldn't wait much longer. The need to bind her was too deeply ingrained, the compulsion to do everything in his power to keep her safe pervasive.

Vampire instinct and animal urges pounded through his veins, making his cock pulse in time to the primitive, heady beat filling the air along with the scent of sex. He wanted Mystic, here, now, always.

Her blood called to him. Her body wept for him.

She was aroused. Wet. Ready.

Roman could feel the interest in her, her presence noted by fledgling and ancient alike. He didn't intend to leave any doubt in their minds as to whom she belonged to.

Possessiveness filled him along with a savagery he'd rarely experienced in any form but the gryphon's. His fangs elongated. His cock throbbed.

With a growl he maneuvered her backward until they reached one of the columns. Her heart thundered against his chest and the scent of her arousal deepened. She knew what he intended. Her acceptance rippled through their bond like waves of shimmering heat.

He jerked her dress up and unzipped his trousers before plunging inside her, his movements fast and sure, commanding. Satisfaction buffered the rawness of his hungers when she wrapped her legs around his waist and offered him her neck.

Dominance radiated from him as his fangs pierced her, as he took what she freely offered and sent a message to any watching. She was his.

Pleasure poured into Mystic, so intense there was no room for embarrassment. Roman's bite was ecstasy, his cock an exquisite organ created for the sole purpose of filling her.

A moan escaped. Then another. She clung to him as his penis forged in and out of her sheath. Deep. Hard. Each thrust a claiming, a declaration.

There was no resistance in her. No thought other than to welcome him, love him, yield to him.

When his fangs retracted, she wanted to beg him to keep feeding. But then his neck was against her mouth, the mating mark she'd given him earlier throbbing against her lips in temptation. All restraint vanished when she bit him. Reality narrowed to sensation, to hungry flesh writhing and reaching, and finally gaining release.

If it weren't for Roman pinning her to the column, Mystic didn't think she'd be able to stand. Then again, if it weren't for the support of the column, she wasn't sure he'd be able to pin her.

The thought widened her satisfied smile. He might be really ancient, but —

Careful, he warned, the amusement in his voice making her think of warmed honey. His hands reached between them, tucking his penis back into his pants before zipping his trousers and smoothing her dress down.

He straightened and led her from the dance floor to where Brann was now waiting. Brann's eyes met hers. When one elegant eyebrow lifted, Mystic's cheeks heated. It was a human reaction, at odds in a place like Wyldfyres—but when it came to fucking, the Angelini were modest, preferring privacy or to share intimacy only in the presence of those they were emotionally close to.

She glanced away just as the throbbing, primitive beat segued into a strip show theme song. Couples moved off the dance floor. Brann and Roman both stiffened.

The music changed again, this time to a song with a sensuous, swaying beat. A big breasted human stepped through a door set in a wide column next to the disk jockey's booth. Her smile was enticing, her steps sure as she slowly peeled her clothing away.

It was obvious from the start that she wasn't dancing for the watching audience. Her attention was split between three male vampires.

Mystic's eyes narrowed when she noticed the faint imprint on the woman's wrists as if only moments earlier she'd been wearing slave bands. Her uneasiness grew when the music came to a stop and the woman's eyes flashed with a hint of panic as a thin, unattractive male vampire stepped forward and slipped a collar around her neck before leading her away.

Another song started. Another female stepped through the column doorway and began stripping, this time to a jazzy beat.

"What's going on?" Mystic asked, hating to ask, but unwilling to ignore her suspicions.

Roman fingers circled her wrist. His thumb stroked back and forth over her pulse. "There is no escape for a human who becomes a vampire's slave—except in insanity. They will always need a vampire's blood in order to survive."

"I know that."

"And you also know how badly it can end for the human involved. Some vampires simply kill their slaves when the novelty or usefulness wears off. Others give them away or trade them—but some prefer to avoid negotiation and bargaining and implied alliance altogether or it suits them to distance themselves from the fate of their slaves for other reasons. This woman and the last have been *freed* by their masters." Roman shrugged. "They might well belong to the club and have been replaced by fresh stock. But they won't survive unless they're claimed. They dance to entice interest and they come with no strings attached."

Mystic's stomach knotted. She'd guessed as much, but it still horrified and sickened her.

The song reached a crescendo and the dancer pulled her g-string off and went to her knees. Her back arched to display her breasts while her fingers plunged into her slit, pumping in and out to the rhythm of the beat.

Two vampires stepped forward as the last note faded. The crowd stirred with interest, perhaps hoping for a fight. But one of the vampires yielded his claim by retreating.

The woman was led away and the music began again, this time with a fast, primal, beat. Mystic's heart nearly stopped when Rafael stepped through the door. Her breath *did* freeze in her chest until the light glinted off his companion necklace.

Her glaze flew to Brann's face. His features were tight, his eyes burned with the promise of retribution—but there was no denying the lust. It was in every line of his body, including the rigid length of cock pressed against the front of his expensive trousers.

Rafe once did this for a living. I believe that's how he and Brann first met, Roman said, amusement and anticipation sliding down the link with his words.

Mystic couldn't take her eyes off Rafael. She'd instantly understood Syndelle's attraction to him. He was innately sensual and definitely lust-worthy with his long blond hair and tanned, lithe body.

She'd had to guess what the draw was for Brann. Attitude mostly. But now...as Mystic watched Rafe command the floor, defiant, alluring, taunting and enticing. Now she understood. If she weren't already mated... If he weren't already claimed...

Careful, Roman warned again, pulling her back against his front as the music ended with Rafe stopped in front of Brann in a provocative, challenging *take-me* pose.

Mystic saw the flash of purpose in Brann's eyes as he stepped forward and grasped Rafe's golden braid, forcing Rafe's head back to emphasize the companion necklace fitted like a tight collar around his neck. Brann traced the links of chain until he got to the coin-like medallion etched with protective script and a warning that Rafe was claimed. When he brushed his thumb across the surface of the metal in a sensual caress, Rafe's hips jerked, his face tightened and arousal beaded on the tip of his cock.

Mystic's cunt clenched. Earlier thoughts of seeing them together returned.

They were engaged in private conversation along their bond, but the conversation played out in their bodies. Brann's free hand cupped Rafe's balls, fondled and squeezed until Rafe moaned and closed his eyes.

"You are free to join us," Brann said, not taking his hand off Rafe's hair as he guided him away from the dance floor.

Mystic saw the row of doors along the far wall and guessed they led to bedrooms. Instead she found a smaller version of the feeding room.

Her breath caught when Brann stripped out of his clothing and forced Rafe to his knees. Her cunt spasmed as she watched Brann's fingers curl around his cock in the instant before Rafe's mouth found him.

Roman's hands tangled in her hair. She could feel his desire, his need.

Mystic knelt in front of him. Her hands went to the front of his pants, teasing him through the fabric before a command along their link had her freeing his erection.

She tasted herself on him and found it darkly erotic. Lust pulsed between them and beat against her tongue as she rubbed it over the heavy veins and smooth skin of his cock.

Thoughts of Rafe and Brann faded though the sound of their pleasure fed her hunger. Arousal slid from her slit, filling the air with her scent. She could feel what it did to Roman, how it made him quiver with the desire to put her on her hands and knees and mount her.

Do it, she whispered, cupping his testicles and holding his cock head between her lips, sucking him.

His fingers tightened on her hair in response. His hips jerked, shallow thrusts as he fucked into her mouth.

The heat in the room built. Mystic's moans joined Rafe's.

Her cunt lips were flushed and parted, her clit erect and throbbing. But when she put her hand between her legs to ease herself, Roman ordered her to stop.

"While we're here, your pleasure is mine to command," he said, making her whimper as he pulled from her mouth.

He guided her to her feet and turned her toward the back of a heavy leather chair, forced her to bend forward and grasp it. Mystic spread her legs without being told, lowered her upper body so he could see how ready she was for him, how much she needed him inside her.

Brann and Rafe had gotten on the couch in front of her, Rafe on the bottom, his legs spread, his hips jerking as Brann's cock rubbed against his. They were both so masculine, so beautiful that Mystic couldn't take her eyes off them as their lips met in a ravenous, hungry kiss.

She gasped when Roman's penis slid between her legs, gliding back and forth over her clit and belly, rubbing in the same rhythm as Brann was playing with Rafe. She endured it as long as she could before reaching through her legs and taking him in hand, guiding him to her entrance.

Please, don't make me wait.

Roman filled her with a single thrust, then held still. In front of them Rafe's hand found Brann's cock and guided it home.

His face was a mask of agonized pleasure. Brann's was fierce possessiveness. The image of them together burned into Mystic's mind before she closed her eyes and gave herself over to the ecstasy of Roman thrusting in and out of her.

Chapter Twenty

ജ

Wolfsbane was packed and only a small percentage of those crowding the club were human. All the tables were claimed, as were the booths, but Christian and Hawk were content to rest against the dark wood of the bar.

The male and female bartenders were both shifters, golden with thick manes of hair. Christian thought they might be cougars. Their movements had the smooth, fluid grace of a mountain lion. Mates, maybe. The male's vibes were protective, his focus on serving drinks but his awareness extending to what was going on around the female. When she turned, Christian's opinion changed. Siblings. They had the same startling light brown eyes.

The bartender brought the beers he and Hawk had ordered then moved away. Without Mystic's presence, they were reduced to verbal conversation. Given the crowd, it meant they couldn't openly discuss much of what was on their minds.

Christian took a swallow of beer. In the past he'd always avoided places like this, where pack wolves came to intermingle with vampires and other shifters. He didn't need the hassle, didn't need the conflict inherent in being a lone wolf and a cop.

On days when he was honest with himself, he also admitted he avoided places like Wolfsbane because he didn't need to stir up feelings of isolation and loneliness. He lived in a human world. He was *content* living in a human world. Or at least he had been.

He took another drink from the chilled mug and glanced at Hawk. He felt the beginnings of a pack bond forming between them. Hell, more than the beginnings. They shared a woman. They'd spent hours in bed with her, competing at first but then working in tandem to make her scream in orgasm. They'd hunted together and been linked mentally while they'd done it.

Christian shifted position to give his cock some relief. He couldn't think about Mystic and not get hard. It was taking all his willpower not to part the barrier between his mind and hers. He knew she was fine, safe, probably already at Wyldfyres. Knowing anything more would have him repeatedly jerking off in a bathroom stall.

Hawk's face told Christian he wasn't alone in his suffering. Without meaning to he said, "After this, I want to get away for a while, go on a long honeymoon."

The pronouncement was met with raised eyebrows and a flash of white teeth. "You'll invite Roman and me to the wedding I trust, and the honeymoon won't be a twosome." He cocked his head. "It's a romantic gesture. Very human. Mystic will be touched by it. I think she'll agree to a marriage and I doubt Roman will protest."

"You don't care?"

Hawk shrugged. "It's not the way of our kind. Some do it, usually those who are more visible in our businesses, more in the public eye. Most of the important assets are owned by the pack, not the individual. Inheritance isn't an issue, at least not when it comes to the outside world. If I'm successful in my bid to separate, a corporation will be formed by our council as a place to accumulate assets for the benefit of all of us."

Christian frowned. The thought of being completely dependent on some nameless corporation run by Weres he didn't know gave him the chills.

The tiny braids of Hawk's hair shook as he laughed. "It's not as bad as you're imagining. We have legitimate jobs and get paid for doing them. The money is ours to dispose of as we see fit. We have the freedom to buy our own houses if we want to, to live completely apart from each other if we want to, but why would we? There's comfort and companionship, security in knowing you're with people who will guard your back and come to your aid in an instant."

"So why leave? Why start something new?" Christian asked though he could guess the answer.

"I'm too strong an alpha to be satisfied living under the rule of others. My father, uncles, the majority of the elders. I respect them too much to challenge them and their leadership doesn't deserve one. They're good men, honorable men. The normal way would be to find a weak group, one where there's a void in authority, or where those in charge should be stripped of their power. The downside is you inherit a dynamic, situations and people you might not choose to deal with otherwise."

"Wouldn't be my first choice either," Christian said. "Hard to know who and what to trust."

"Exactly."

Christian contemplated the situation. He'd assumed there must be some kind of governing body, some kind of policing to keep werewolves from fighting with each other or becoming known to the human population. But until now he'd never had someone he could ask, someone who'd explain the intricacies to him. "You think you'll get what you want from the council?"

"With Mystic as a mate, yes. The Renaldis have a lot of allies. Their females are as valued as ours are. They're considered equal in status to an alpha bitch."

Christian grimaced. He knew Hawk's words were praise and not condemnation, but he didn't like hearing Mystic labeled a bitch.

Hawk laughed again, correctly interpreting Christian's thoughts. Christian hesitated, remembered the moment Gabby changed in the car and he'd truly, without any doubt, felt the wolf hidden deep inside Mystic. "How do we convince Mystic she has the same abilities as the other Renaldi females?"

"We don't."

Christian opened his mouth to protest then closed it. Hawk was right. It was a sensitive, painful subject for Mystic. Any attempt to convince her would only make her worry she was destined to disappoint them. For a brief instant he wondered if Roman could hypnotize her deeply enough to get her to embrace and accept the wolf, but he pushed it from his thoughts. It'd be a violation of her trust and regardless of the end result, it wasn't the right way, for any of them.

As if picking up on Christian's thoughts, Hawk said, "When the time is right, we'll help her through the change. We're both strong enough. Every time we connect with her, mate with her, the bond deepens and strengthens. Eventually she won't be able to resist the call."

Christian nodded. He felt the truth of what Hawk was saying. He was already so connected to Mystic he hated being away from her.

"You'll want to remain a cop?" Hawk asked.

"I don't know," Christian said, surprising them both.

Hawk signaled the bartender for another round of beers. Christian examined his own unexpected answer. A couple of hours ago he would have answered differently.

The weight of the dead Were hung on his conscience, not because the kill wasn't righteous but because he saw the conflict with his sworn oath to uphold *human* law. It was different for Rico, Skye Coronado's mate. He might be mated to an Angelini and share her with a vampire, but he was human. He stayed out of supernatural affairs unless they touched on one of his cases, and even then, he worked it from a human perspective and kept a buffer of deniability separating him from his mate's world.

Christian's lone wolf status and human upbringing had allowed him to skirt the edges, to venture into the supernatural world only when he had to and thankfully it'd only been peripheral to his cases. He was a hunter of serial killers and those willing to order multiple murders. There were plenty of humans who fit the category.

He was good at his job. Until Mystic had come into his life, it had defined who and what he was. Christian didn't think it did any longer. The scene at the rogue Weres' house played through his mind only instead of a wolf, a man attacked them.

His training would still have kicked in. Quick, deadly. A kill shot. There was no such thing as aiming to wound. But faced with the body of a man, his badge would have burned a hole in his honor and his soul. "Have you ever had to…eliminate a threat?" he asked.

Hawk passed Christian a second beer and laughed silently at the odd turns Fate and magic could take. He'd reconciled himself to sharing Mystic with another wolf. He'd thought it would be Jagger or someone from the Zevanti pack. Now he couldn't imagine a better fit than Christian and yet he would never have considered it possible with someone who'd been raised outside of a pack. "Yes. Overseas. On behalf of Uncle Sam."

Christian's surprise was easy to read. Hawk didn't often think about his days in the service. He didn't miss them. He'd done what he needed to do for longer than he'd originally signed on to do it. "You're not the only one of us to wear a uniform."

"Army?"

"Marines. First and last time without hair," he joked, shaking his head just enough to make the beads woven into his braids click together softly.

Christian lifted his mug in a silent salute. "I wouldn't have guessed."

"Not many of us can do it. You have to be able to control yourself at all times, under all circumstances."

"Yeah, I can see that."

"What would you do if you weren't a cop?"

"Don't know. Until today I never thought about not being one."

Hawk hesitated. He didn't want to rush Christian but he didn't see any point in pretending the question didn't need to be asked. "You'd wear a brand?"

Christian exhaled over the foam of his beer. "For Mystic, yeah, for her I would."

* * * * *

Rafe's clothing was in a neat pile outside the room. A human dressed in a risqué version of a maid's outfit stood to the side. She curtsied, holding the position until they'd all stepped through the doorway.

With a casualness Mystic didn't think she'd ever manage, Rafe dressed in full view of anyone who cared to watch. Then again, he'd already shown his magnificent, fantasy-worthy stuff.

She couldn't help herself, her attention flicked back and forth between Brann and Rafe. Images of them together played out on the screen of her mind. They were right for one another, right for Syndelle.

With a thought she checked up on Christian and Hawk. They were still at Wolfsbane, comfortable in each other's company, and with Gabe and Gabby who'd just arrived. Already she could sense the pack bond forming between the four wolves. It pleased her. Though the Zevantis would have preferred for Gabe and Gabby to migrate to separate packs for political reasons, they wouldn't prevent them from allying themselves with Hawk and her.

Mentally she rubbed against Christian and Hawk then laughed at herself for the wolflike gesture. Their heat found her, a sensation of warm fur that made her quiver inside and grow wet again despite having been completely satisfied by Roman several times already.

No sign of the rogue Weres?

No, Hawk said. *But there are traces of their scent here and they seem to favor a certain table. We've managed to secure a booth where they won't immediately see us.*

A ripple of awareness flowed into her from Roman and with it came the faintest taint of the dark mage's magic. *Marta just arrived,* she said, *or someone equally tainted.*

She read their thoughts, knew they accepted she was safe, but still they both said, *Let the vampires handle the fledgling.*

Mystic shook her head, amusement filling her along with the warmth of being cared for by such macho men. *As if I'd attack a vampire in a place like Wyldfyres where the majority of the humans are naked and wearing slave bands.*

Growls met her comeback. But underneath were humor and a touch of curiosity about a club where the only werewolves who could safely enter were those who had the unfortunate destiny, at least in Hawk and Christian's opinion, of being a vampire's companion.

Mystic let the link fade so she could concentrate on her surroundings. She spotted Marta a few minutes later. The fledgling was practically drooling over the naked humans who were available for blood, sex and perhaps more if their owners allowed it.

A blond waiter wearing nothing but slave bands stopped next to her. Her hands went to his chest then traveled downward to measure and weigh the abundance he'd been gifted with. Even soft, his cock was huge, and his testicles...

All three of your mates can serve you better, Roman said. His voice held the savage warning of a lion.

Mystic shivered. The desire to tease him rose up, a dark path leading to fantasies she'd never lingered on before he'd come into her life.

You have to admit, he's impressive, Mystic said, glancing up at Roman from beneath lowered eyelashes, licking her lips to add emphasis.

His nostrils flared. The cold flames of vampire fire burned in his pupils even as the part of him that was beast pressed against his skin with the need to dominate her completely.

Roman leaned in. He didn't touch her physically and yet she felt surrounded by him, held and enthralled. He radiated power, desire, menace—possessiveness. *Do it again,* he challenged.

Mystic's attention returned to Marta and the slave. She'd ordered him to spread his legs, or he'd done it on his own. Now she knelt in front of him, one finger stroking his inner thigh, tracing the flow of hot, rich blood through his femoral artery while the index finger of her other hand glided over the dark blue vein on the underside of his erect cock.

The fledgling seemed completely unaware of anything beyond the roar of blood, the heavy testicles and rigid penis of the man in front of her. Mystic imagined herself kneeling in front of Roman, not with Marta's predatory intensity but with the submissiveness of a vampire companion.

She felt Roman's anticipation, vampire lust and a lion's desire to pounce. She answered his challenge with the slow, slick glide of her tongue over her bottom lip.

His response was immediate, fierce. His fingers tangled in her hair and forced her head back. Fangs plunged into her exposed neck and sent a shock of pleasure straight to her clit. She whimpered, helpless against the heat and need burning her from the inside out.

Roman widened his stance. He positioned her so her throbbing clit pressed hard against his thigh. One hand remained tangled in the hair at her nape while the other glided down her spine. He yanked her skirt up, exposing the globes of her ass for anyone who cared to watch, demonstrating for all that he was the master.

The erotic feel of leather against her inner thighs made Mystic's cunt clench. As she'd done with Christian the first time, she sought relief. She ground against Roman's thigh, rubbed her engorged knob against hard muscle and the masculine promise of pleasure.

She wished it could be skin against skin but his pants weren't a barrier to sensation. The room around them faded as soft mews gave way to low moans, as the urgent press and retreat gave way to hips bucking followed by the keening of release. And through it all Roman fed greedily at her neck, feasted on both her blood and her orgasm, the vampire and the man satisfied they'd made an impression on their mate.

Mystic sagged against him. She would have melted into a puddle of delicious satisfaction at his feet if he hadn't held her upright.

Roman licked his tongue over the bite mark. His lips curved upward in a smile against her skin.

Despite everything she'd done and witnessed since stepping through the front door of Wyldfyres, Mystic still blushed when she eased away from Roman and was greeted by Brann's, "If you two are finished amusing yourselves, perhaps we could attend to the true business of the night."

Their focus shifted to Marta. Another slave had moved in, anxious for the ecstasy of a bite and perhaps sensing the fledgling was young and inexperienced, capable of draining him and forcing his owner to step forward and offer a wrist. Mystic thought it was a dangerous gamble.

The second slave was black-haired, more favored by nature than the first but Marta barely gave him a glance. "If she is like Hugh," Brann said, "ignorant and untutored in our ways and our laws, once she's satisfied herself with blood it'll be only a few minutes before she offends someone far more powerful than she is. Since the fledgling appears to favor blonds, Rafe can lure her away from her current quarry. I doubt she'll recognize him for what he is, but she'll be drawn by his beauty and the heady richness of his blood. To a fledgling, he'll be irresistible."

Rafe's eyes gleamed with challenge. He altered his stance so his cock was more pronounced, a hard thick ridge against the front of his pants. With the easy grace of a man well versed in seduction, he fondled his barbell studded nipple, circled and rubbed and tweaked as the ruby at the ends of the barbell glittered and winked. "Only to fledglings?"

"You try my patience," Brann purred. "But I'd prefer to wait until we get home to Syndelle before taking you in hand again."

Rafe snickered and stopped playing with his nipple. "Be right back," he said.

It was as easy as Brann said it would be. The slave, even naked, was no match for Rafael's allure.

Mystic knew Marta was tainted by Brallin's dark magic, but she was still surprised when the fledgling calmly approached, not fighting as Hugh had done once he recognized the ancient vampire creation magic flowing through Brann and Roman's veins.

Roman said, *It is as Brann said, just as the magic Brann and I have gained from Syndelle submerses itself deep inside us while we're among so many other vampires, the dark mage's magic does the same. Somewhere else, either alone or among humans, the magics would react to one another. She'd instinctively flee or try to kill us. But here she doesn't dare.*

We have much to learn still. Until Brann can question Hugh and Marta further, until we capture Egan Walsh, we don't know whether the dark magic fills him in the same way the creation magic of the vampire fills Syndelle, or if he is just a tool, a faulty vessel allowed to play and perhaps stir up trouble for vampire and werewolves alike.

As soon as Marta and Rafe joined them, Brann wrapped his hand around the fledgling's arm. "You will come with us now," he said, his voice barely audible but his power such that Marta's eyes immediately glazed.

They left without hurrying though Mystic was well aware of the surreptitious glances the other vampires were giving them. Speculation would follow, but only after the council's executioner was no longer in the club.

Chapter Twenty-One

ஐ

The hotel suite Roman ushered Mystic into was everything she'd anticipated. She wasn't a stranger to opulence and luxury, her parents would never be accused of slumming in their choice of family vacation accommodations, but the casino's high-roller suite, elaborately done in a Greco-Roman theme complete with naked statues screamed outrageous, expensive decadence.

"It suits you," Mystic said, laughing softly as she wrapped her arms around her *ancient*, vampire mate.

"Careful," he warned, "or I might throw you into the lion's den. It was once considered a fitting punishment for any number of crimes."

Mystic nibbled on his bottom lip. "I'd like to see the lion's den, and the lion. Will you show me?"

"Later," Roman promised, amused at how pointless it was to threaten her. He was beginning to think the terms *ancient* and *vampire* were forever melded together when it came to him.

They are, she said, easily skimming his thoughts. *But it's the same for my fathers so you're in good company.*

As long as you don't think of me as *your father.*

Her tongue slipped into his mouth, coaxed his fangs into elongating as her hand found his erection and caressed him through the material of his pants. *I don't think you have to worry about that.*

Roman's fingers speared through her hair. For long moments he gave himself to the moment, savored her eagerness to touch and kiss him despite how often she'd been taken by her other mates, despite what they'd already done at Wyldfyres.

Alone. At last. He almost didn't know where to start.

I can help, she said, her laughter filling his thoughts, carnal images goading him into action. With a chuckle he swept her up and carried her into a bathroom nearly as large as Christian's bedroom.

A quick glance told him his call ahead had netted the results he wanted. The sunken tub was full. A chilled bottle of champagne and bowl of chocolate-covered and deep red strawberries waited on an elegant, raised serving tray.

Mystic's gasp of surprised pleasure and the rush of tender feelings along their bond were his reward. He captured her mouth with his. The dress he'd bought for her came off with the ease it had been designed for as he placed her on her feet, his lips still on hers.

Her moan vibrated through Roman, added to the animal heat building inside him. He deepened the kiss, loved how quickly her fingers found the buttons of his shirt, the zipper of his pants, how anxiously she helped divest him of his clothing.

This was how he liked her best. Alone. Naked. Hungry for him and him alone, excited only by what they were doing to one another.

He could live with sharing her, had already come to accept it, even to enjoy it, but he needed this, too. Centuries of a sometimes unbearably lonely existence now seemed like a small price to pay to gain her as a mate.

Their tongues twined, rubbed as their bodies pressed together, heated skin against heated skin. His cock pulsed and leaked, urged him to forget about the bath, the strawberries and champagne, to carry her to bed instead.

Roman resisted, resisted even the urge to cup her breasts, to kneel and bury his face between her thighs. With a groan he picked her up again, carried her to the tub and slipped into the welcoming water of the bath.

Only when he was sitting with her settled across his lap did he let his hand drift to her chest so his fingers could capture a love-bruised nipple. Her hand quickly mimicked his, her fingers tweaking, tugging, sending a bolt of need straight to his cock.

He bucked when her other hand found his penis. His mouth lifted from hers in a panting gasp when her thumb rubbed over his cock head.

"Stop," he said, but his voice lacked compulsion.

She arched her neck, offered the pulse pounding there. "Bite me," she whispered, commanding with the squeeze of her fingers, with her touch.

"I want to feed you first," he said. But still he teased them both, tested his own restraint by putting his mouth on her throat and touching his fangs to her skin.

His hand left her breast to trail downward to her clit. She whimpered when he found it, moaned and shivered as he stroked and rubbed, drove her to a small shuddering release.

Mystic mellowed against him, like a cat settling in, content to be petted for a while. Scenes from Wyldfyres floated lazily through her mind. "Is it pretty much like that every night?" she asked.

"It changes depending on the patrons. But regardless of who is in attendance, it's always a dangerous place."

Roman's hand slid up to cup her neck. "Next time I take you there, you will wear the necklace of a companion." His tone was implacable.

Mystic smiled, a feline smile of contentment. "Okay," she said, letting him feel her willingness to accept what he offered when the time was right, when her other mates could be included.

He leaned in and brushed a kiss over her lips. "Even to make you my companion I wouldn't share you tonight, not when I finally have you alone again."

She laughed and wrapped her arms around his neck. Moved into the kiss. *Alone* and *at your mercy. Don't forget the second part.*

He chuckled, finding it hard to believe she'd been a virgin before meeting Christian, but he knew from her memories that she had been. She was a natural seductress, a siren he would willingly follow to his doom.

For long moments they kissed, hands exploring, tongues twining, rubbing, time slowing so they could savor each other, love each other. Hearts beat in unified rhythm, desire flowed along their bond, unrushed.

Roman was short of breath when he lifted his mouth from Mystic's. His attention was drawn to the platter of strawberries and chilled champagne for an instant, but he knew they would wait. He needed to feed a deeper hunger.

With the control only a truly ancient and powerful vampire could muster, Roman elongated a single fingernail, turned it into a sharp talon. His eyes didn't leave Mystic's as he scraped above his nipple and drew blood.

Her soft cry ratcheted up the ache in his cock to exquisitely painful levels. He moaned when she put her mouth on him, swirled her tongue over his nipple then suckled.

Trust, it was a supreme act of trust on her part to drink from him, to take what he offered, knowing it was part of the ritual making a companion, knowing how desperately he wanted her bound to him in that way. She drank deeply, the pull of her lips making his penis pulse. The sound of her pleasure joining his as she plastered herself to him, ensured their skin touched in as many places as possible.

"Mystic," he whispered, the need to come building though he couldn't force his hands away from where they tangled in her luxurious hair.

He grunted when she twisted on his lap, repositioned herself to straddle him without her mouth leaving his nipple.

His hips bucked when her hand guided his penis to the flushed, swollen lips of her cunt.

She was tempting fate, testing his control. But no power on earth could have stopped him from sliding into her slit.

They both shuddered when he was all the way in, held tight in a hot fist of welcoming heat. She gave a hard bite to his nipple before kissing upward, the wound on his chest closed by the time she got to his mouth.

Roman's hands left her hair, slid downward to grasp her hips. She tasted of magic and blood. Of him.

It was intoxicating, a binding of his senses as thorough as her Angelini claim to him. He craved her profoundly, more intensely than a newly risen vampire craved blood. She was essential to his existence.

Please, she said, rising off his lap the little distance he allowed.

Roman's hands tightened on her hips. He struggled to remain still inside her but her sheath rippled along his length, clenched and unclenched. He gave up the fight when she lured his tongue into her mouth and began sucking.

With the grace and strength of a vampire he rose to his knees in the deep tub. Her legs went around his waist, her arms around his neck. He held her easily as he began thrusting, driving hard and deep, the angle of their bodies sending erotic sensation through her clit.

Roman swallowed her cries. He fed on them in the same way she'd fed on his blood. He wanted to consume her, to swallow her down.

Lust and need weren't large enough words to contain what he felt as he fucked her. Pleasure was too tame a description for the riot of sensation and emotion he felt.

Mystic, he said. A prayer. A plea. Then all thought was banished as his hips jerked frantically, as her channel spasmed in orgasm and his body answered in a hot wash of seed.

He settled back into the water, his cock still lodged in Mystic's sheath. "That was nice," she murmured, a teasing glint in her eyes as she added, "There are advantages to having a mate who was alive during *ancient* times, when sex in the bath was an everyday occurrence. Practice makes perfect, and your technique is definitely perfect."

Roman chuckled, finally reaching for one of the strawberries he'd intended as a *preliminary* to their lovemaking. He selected a plump, red specimen and carried it to Mystic's lips.

Next you'll be bringing out the whipped cream, she said, taking his offering as she reached for a strawberry to feed him.

I don't need any enticement to explore every inch of your flesh with my lips and tongue.

Mystic gave herself over to feeding him strawberries and being fed in return. She was already drunk on his attention, on his blood, but she didn't turn away from the champagne when he opened the bottle and poured her a glass.

"To having ended up with a very satisfactory mate," she teased, touching her glass to his, loving the way he was quick to laugh.

She didn't doubt he was beautiful, elegant death. But then she'd grown up in a home with vampires, and she found it comforting to have a mate who was familiar to her, even if he was still a stranger in so many ways.

"I'm glad the magic chose you," she whispered, pressing her lips to his, the bond swelling with the depth of her feelings.

They lingered in the tub until the champagne and strawberries were gone. "Let me see you now," she said after they'd gotten out of the water and dried themselves off with plush, peach-colored towels.

He became an eagle first, golden in color, his sharp talons digging into the discarded towel. The lion followed, immense, its powerful presence making the bathroom suddenly seem small.

Mystic's heart danced erratically in her chest as she knelt down next to him. If he was elegant death in his vampire form, then he was savage death in this one.

She tangled her fingers in his mane as her other hand stroked the fur of his back. Werewolves were larger than ordinary wolves, heavier and stronger. But she thought Roman's lion was life-size—not that she'd ever been up close and personal with the animals she'd seen at the zoo. Still, she imagined he was four or five hundred pounds of raw muscle and feral menace.

The air in front of her shimmered. Beast became man.

"You're beautiful," she said.

"No more beautiful than my Angelini mate."

He pulled her into his arms then stood. His lips captured hers and held them captive as he carried her into the bedroom.

Mystic's cunt spasmed when he set her on her feet and she saw the silken strips of cloth on the bed. They were blood red, four slashes against the white bedspread.

"I promised you a taste of what you saw at Wyldfyres," he said, trailing a finger down her spine.

Erotic fear shivered through Mystic. Her heart rate tripled, its beat thundering in her ears. Instinct fought desire. She licked her lips, suddenly, inexplicably nervous.

Maybe she had some wolf in her after all, Mystic thought. She trusted Roman enough to take his blood and beg for him to take hers, but the thought of being physically bound, tied and helpless...

The need to fight or flee swelled, filled her like a stretching beast, made her short of breath. Muscles tensed, bunched. "Maybe we should ease into this," she said, shooting a quick glance at the bed. "I could tie you up first." Not that strips of cloth would hold him for even a second if he wanted to be free.

"Next time," Roman promised, his voice a rough purr over her naked skin.

Mystic shivered again. It took courage, more than she would have thought, more than she imagined she had to crawl up on the bed and stretch out, waiting for him to tie her.

She felt his satisfaction through the bond, saw it in the way the vampire flames flared and burned in his pupils. When he was finished tethering her wrists and ankles to the bed frame he straddled her.

She loved the feel of his heavy testicles against her stomach. Moisture gushed from her slit despite the wild hammer of her heart.

His heat swamped her. His desire hovered over her like a beast ready to pounce and she struggled against the silken ties.

"It won't do any good," Roman purred, his mouth close to her throat, his breath whispering across her pulse an instant before his fangs touched her flesh.

She gasped as a shard of white-hot lust shot through her breasts and settled in her nipples. "Please," she said, tilting her head, offering what she knew he craved.

Roman closed his eyes and fought for control. His cock throbbed, ached with nearly painful intensity.

Mystic's heartbeat was a siren call urging him to pierce her neck and feed. But if he yielded, he'd never be able to keep from fucking her.

No, he said, denying them both the intimacy they craved.

He forced his fangs to retract but the effort cost him. A shudder went through him. His testicles drew up hard and tight. He groaned and dropped his head, pressed his face to her skin and inhaled her.

She was pure magic. Angelini and vampire and wolf. She was pure woman. His, though traces of Christian and Hawk were there too, bound to Mystic as surely as his own scent was forever woven into hers.

With a low growl Roman kissed his way down to her breast. She cried when he claimed a nipple and began sucking.

"Bite me," she said, her heels digging into the bed, her back arching, trapping his erection against the heated flesh of her abdomen.

Arousal beaded on his cock head, wet her skin like an erotic lick. He moaned, remembering the ecstasy he'd experienced in the tub as he'd fed her. His fingers found her other nipple, tugged and squeezed in time to his suckling.

She writhed against him. Her hips canted so her soft, flushed folds burned his flesh, pressed against him in a wet, sultry kiss of invitation.

The roar of her blood left him straining, panting, fighting against the urge to sink his fangs into her skin. She was swollen, wet, parted for him, her clit stiff, throbbing, begging for his attention.

"Please," Mystic said, pleading for his bite, pleading for release. She felt as though her heart had split and left her chest. Now it beat in her cunt, in her nipples.

The muscles in her arms burned from straining against the silken bonds tethering her to the bed. She wanted to touch him, to use her hands to strip his control so he'd give her what she needed.

A sob escaped when his mouth left her nipple and kissed downward. She wanted him to hurry but he took his time. She was shaking by the time his mouth found her clit.

The bond between them held no hiding places. She could feel Roman's lust. His desire to fuck equaled his desire to feed but neither overrode his desire to give her a taste of what she'd seen at Wyldfyres, to demonstrate he was a mate who would give her whatever she desired regardless of what it cost him.

She cried out when he stroked her swollen knob with this tongue then sucked it into his mouth and kept sucking. Her hips jerked in time to the pull of his lips. The play left in the silken ties binding her ankles to the bed enabled her to lift her buttocks from the mattress, fight to drive her clit deeper into his mouth. White-fire pulsed through her as he drove everything from her mind but the feel of his lips and tongue.

He took her to the edge of orgasm repeatedly, backed off before she found release. By the time he lifted his mouth from her clit she was quivering, strung tight as if her body had become a bowstring connected to the tethers keeping her in place.

Tears flowed down her cheeks. Her nipples were tight buds. Through Roman's eyes she saw herself and understood completely the tortured look of pleasure she'd witnessed on the restrained companion's face at Wyldfyres.

Erotic fear returned in a rush when Roman knelt between her thighs and his hands gripped her buttocks, parting them so arousal slid down unimpeded over the pucker of her anus. His fingers followed and she fought instinctively, tried to evade the fingertips working moisture into her back entrance, stretching her.

Roman's face was a mask of fierce hunger, all humanity stripped from it. She felt his driving need to be the first to claim her ass now that he knew she'd never been taken there. Growls filled their mental link as his pupils expanded until only a tiny rim of blue remained. Vampire flame gave way to something ancient, something that existed only in his memory. Gryphon.

There was true fear for a single heartbeat, but Mystic forced it away. She tilted her head back, offered her throat in a show of submission.

Roman left his place between her thighs. He covered her body with his and she whimpered when his cock head pressed against the opening of her anus.

His lips found the pulse in her neck. His teeth gripped her skin, held her heartbeat in his mouth as he slowly forged inside her virgin back entrance.

Dangerous. This was a dangerous game to play with a powerful mate who'd been a beast before becoming a man. But it was too late. Much, much too late.

Mystic moaned as he pushed inside her. His thrusts shallow, his cock smooth hot steel.

Sweat covered their skin by the time he was all the way in. He hovered above her, taut muscles and harsh breathing a testament to the struggle going on inside him.

Mine. The word crashed into her with primitive intensity and a bestial urge to mate.

Yours, she said, giving what she could to the core of him, the part of him that would never manifest physically again.

Yours, she repeated, using what freedom the tethers allowed to move so his cock retreated a few inches, then reclaimed her dark entrance completely.

It was enough. The beast yielded to the vampire it had become with the death of the old mage. Mystic screamed when Roman's fangs pierced her neck, blending pain and pleasure as his hips thrust in and out of her in a darkly carnal taking.

Chapter Twenty-Two

☙

Warmth filled Mystic as soon as she stepped through the door of Christian's house and saw him. She went straight into his arms and felt as though she'd returned home. He was her first mate, the one who'd made the first inroads into her heart, though Roman and Hawk had found their way as well.

He was the mate most like herself, a supernatural being who'd existed without a true place in the world he was a part of. "Miss me?" she asked, rubbing her lips against his in greeting, soaking in his warmth and familiar scent.

"I don't like sleeping without you," he admitted, capturing her mouth, plundering it with his tongue as the ridge of his erection burned through their clothing and made her cunt spasm.

She clung to him. Welcomed him. The magic stretched inside her like a living thing, like a wolf whining and fawning as it reunited with its mate.

The heat of their need and the intensity of their emotions washed over Roman in waves. The lion and eagle deep inside him pressed for intervention, felt threatened by the depth of her feelings toward her wolf mate, but the man, the vampire understood the complexity of love and recognized Mystic's heart was big enough to hold each of the men in her life.

He allowed the sharp edges of their thoughts and feelings to blunt into smooth-flowing desire before he stepped into them, pressed his front to Mystic's back. His fingers brushed against Christian's abdomen as his hands slid up and down Mystic's side. "Let's go to bed," Roman murmured. "Hawk and I have shared you. Let Christian and I show you what it's like to have two men inside you at the same time."

Mystic's shiver was answer enough. Heat burned along their link, expanded to serve as a conduit allowing him to touch Christian's thoughts and emotions. The Were was willing, more than willing.

Roman smiled, thinking of the "fucking game" Mystic had played with Hawk and Christian. Apparently it had served several purposes. Where before there had been resistance in Christian, pain over having to share her with other men, now there was acceptance, enjoyment, a sense that what had been gained outweighed what was lost.

They moved to the bedroom and stripped. Roman's cock pulsed and ached at the sight of Mystic naked, her expression sultry, inviting as she lay down on the bed.

Christian joined her there, his skin the same dusky color as hers. They were beautiful together, but then she was no less beautiful when she was with Hawk or with him.

Roman crawled onto the bed. He was content to cede her mouth to Christian. At the moment the pulse beating on the inside of her thigh and the scent of her arousal drew him downward.

He paused to suckle at her breast, to lave his tongue back and forth over her love-abraded nipple as he smoothed his hand over her abdomen and cupped her mound. Her hips jerked subtly. Pleasure and pain blended and blurred, coursed down the link until both his cock and Christian's were straining, beaded with arousal.

Roman grazed her with his fangs, heard the way her heart raced in anticipation of his bite. He forced himself away from her breast, panted as his lips traveled over her belly. Regardless of how many times he'd had Mystic during the night, hunger roared to life inside him, insatiable in the need for her sex, her blood, her soul.

He licked over her pulse, tasted the honey of her arousal and shuddered. Despite the shower they'd taken together before leaving the casino hotel, he could still smell himself on her.

It satisfied him in a primal way. Filled the core of him with deep contentment.

Roman groaned as his mouth found her slick folds. He growled as he pressed his tongue inside her, automatically reaching down the bond so his thrusts were in sync with Christian's.

Need filled Christian, intense and consuming. Only Roman's presence between Mystic's thighs kept him from rolling on top of her and thrusting his cock into her slit.

He would never get enough of her. He didn't even care what having her in his life might ultimately cost him. Already what he was before, how he defined himself, had changed. It would keep changing until they'd found a balance, and it didn't matter, not as long as he had her.

A moan escaped when Mystic's hand found his erection. Christian's hips bucked as lust spasmed through his cock.

Don't!

He bucked again when her thumb rubbed over the tip of his penis. The wolf growled in a promise of retribution. It pressed against his skin. Its essence reached inside Mystic, looking for what it knew was hidden.

She writhed underneath him as his tongue fucked into her mouth, as the wolf rubbed against Angelini magic and warm, unrecognized beast. If only she'd believe... If only she'd become...

The wolf inside him quivered at the prospect of mounting Mystic in her furred form, of mating with her under the moon. The man struggled to keep his thoughts cloaked. But it was hard—it grew harder as he fucked through the tight fist of Mystic's fingers.

She eroded his control in a way that should shame him, might have shamed him if he didn't know Roman and Hawk were no better at resisting her. He couldn't stop the wild jerk of his hips. Didn't protest when the vampire took charge, urging him onto his back and telling Mystic to get on top of him.

Christian cried out when Mystic guided his cock to her parted, heated entrance. His guttural *please* was drowned in a hot sea of sensation as he slid all the way in.

Home. She was home and now he was, too.

His fingers tangled in her hair. His mouth ate hungrily at hers.

He didn't think it could get any better. But then she whimpered and along the bond he heard Roman whispering to her, coaxing her. He felt the jolt of ecstasy she experienced when Roman's fangs slid into her neck and almost whimpered too as Roman began working his way into her anus.

It was so darkly erotic that Christian's mind shied away from thinking, preferred to give itself over to unbearable pleasure. She was always tight, wet, hot, but now...

Christian moaned. He felt engulfed in liquid flames, consumed by fires that burned away all resistance, all barriers.

Christ. He wasn't bi-sexual. He had no desire to get up close and personal with Roman's cock if it was just the two of them. But this...

There was no defining it. No labeling it.

There was no resisting it.

They moved without conscious thought. Rubbed against each other as pleasure doubled, tripled, rebounded and expanded. As bodies strained, writhed, fought—only to fill the room with cries when orgasm came, leaving then shuddering, shaking, their hearts racing and lungs laboring.

Christian grunted as Roman rolled off. He growled when Mystic started to follow. Her soft laugh and dancing eyes were a balm to his soul, a buffer keeping his masculinity intact.

"I know you'd prefer to stay in bed," she teased, nibbling his bottom lip. "But it's nighttime and we've got a hunt to get back to."

"Let Hawk handle it. He's got Gabe and Gabby with him. They're heading to Wolfsbane right now."

Mystic was tempted. She couldn't help herself. Being in bed with her mates had a way of weakening her resolve, especially when those mates were getting along well.

Somehow she managed to roll off Christian and get to her feet. Reluctantly the men followed her example.

"Hawk called a few minutes before you got here," Christian said as he pulled on his clothes. "A couple of vampires are watching the Weres' house."

They left a few minutes later. Mystic wondered if it made sense for them all to be at the same place, but as soon as they got to Wolfsbane she was glad they were.

"I think we're going to get lucky tonight," Gabby said, greeting Mystic with a hug in the parking lot. "It's like they're holding *The Howl For The Barely Legal* and *Fledgling Night* in there. I've never seen anything like it. The blood's going to start flowing, one way or another."

Mystic grimaced when Christian's hand settled around her arm like a vise. "I want you to stay in the car. In fact, you, Gabby, Gabe and Hawk should all stay outside to watch the doors. There's a front entrance and two emergency exits. Roman and I can take the inside. The Weres won't recognize us even though we'll recognize them."

Hawk agreed without an argument and Mystic suspected the men had settled beforehand on this strategy. Suspicion caused her eyes to narrow. For a moment she was tempted to slide into their memories in case this was their way of keeping her safe, but she didn't. She trusted them to honor the agreement they'd come to when she won the "fucking game".

Mystic turned her thoughts back to what Gabby said about the mix inside the club. It was the perfect hunting ground.

Christian's thoughts ran the same road as hers. He said, "If the rogues are frustrated the sun got Todd Moore before they could run him to ground, they might look for another victim here tonight where the sight of a Were offering a vampire his neck wouldn't raise any suspicions."

Roman nodded. "Your point is well taken. Let the small wolf and her brother take the back while Hawk and Mystic guard the front." He glanced around at the number of cars already filling the parking lot. "If I remember correctly, the side exit can be monitored from the back."

"I should be with either Gabe or Gabby so we can all communicate with one another," Mystic said. She put her hand up to forestall the argument she saw forming on three of the five faces in front of her. "I know we can use cell phones," *but the mental link is instantaneous and provides more information than words can ever convey. If I'm with Gabby or Gabe then no one is left out of the loop.*

They didn't like it. She didn't need to hear the rumbled growls through the bond to know they hated the idea of her not being with one of them.

It took all the restraint she had not to go further, to press harder for independence. Hawk's features were taut. She knew he was remembering the last time they'd encountered the Weres.

Roman broke the tension by saying, "Keep the small wolf with you, Hawk. Let Mystic and Gabe take the back. There will be vampires inside I can command if necessary, or we can summon Gian and Brann. Our goal is capture, not slaughter. Once inside, the Weres will be trapped."

Reluctantly Hawk and Christian agreed, though Mystic could feel how much it cost them. "I won't do anything foolish," she said, kissing each of her mates before sliding into the Jeep with Gabe.

He snickered as he turned the key in the ignition. "Gentlemen, put your collars on. Prepare to be leashed and commanded by the sultry Mystic, a woman who requires *three* men in order to satisfy her needs."

A laugh escaped before Mystic could stop it. She knew from *years* of experience it was a *big* mistake to encourage Gabe.

"Stop," she said, backing it up with a slap to his thigh. "Or you're going to end up as a piece of fur decorating someone's wall."

He grinned, totally unrepentant and unafraid. "Just telling it like it is and thinking I'm going to steer clear of the Angelini when it comes time to mate. I'm going to find myself a nice little human and put a collar on her."

Mystic snorted. "One look at you and any sane human would start running."

Gabe's teeth flashed white. "Sounds good to me. Nothing like a chase to get warmed up for the main event."

They drove around to the back of the nightclub and parked at the rear of the lot. It wasn't dark enough to hide the fact there were people in the car, but neither the moonlight nor the lights on the building reached deep enough to reveal their faces.

"Not much on security," Mystic said, not surprised by the lack of cameras and the desolate, almost violence-inviting area in back of the club.

"It's not much of a place on the inside either," Gabe said. "Maybe a shade above Bangers, or below it if you get off on the bare-breasted waitresses they've got over there. Then again, whoever owns this place probably figures shapeshifters, vampires and humans mix it up, it's always going to lead to broken furniture and bloodstained upholstery, so why invest the capital to make it a classy joint."

Mystic nodded. She'd seen the inside of Wolfsbane through Hawk and Christian's thoughts. It looked like what it was, a place where young werewolves could go in order to break pack rules and taboos, to embrace the whole "what happens in Vegas, stays in Vegas" motto.

Compared to the clubs her parents favored, it was a dive. It was good for little more than hooking-up.

"I could do it better," she murmured, thinking about Fangs and Wyldfyres. Just because sex and blood were usually at the top of the menu when it came to vampires and werewolves didn't mean they were the *only* thing that could be served.

"You could do what better?" Gabe asked, manipulating his seat for a long stint of watching and waiting.

"Run a nightclub for supernaturals—and select humans."

Gabe's head whipped around. "Here?"

"I don't know." She laughed softly. "Our great adventure seems to have gone sideways. We haven't exactly done the town like we planned to."

"You can say that again." He cocked his head. "The Werewolf Council won't turn Hawk's petition for a pack down, not with you as a mate and Roman thrown into the equation. Hawk asked Gabby and me if we'd join."

Mystic reached over and took his hand, squeezed it. "The Zevantis will agree."

He nodded and squeezed her hand in return. "There's no sanctioned pack in Las Vegas. There'd be trouble since most alphas wouldn't be able to tolerate trespassers or loners on their turf and many couldn't be trusted to discipline outsiders. There'd be war when rules had to be enforced. But maybe there needs to be a pack here, to monitor what's going on. Maybe that's why we happened to stop when we did and discover not only the tainted fledgling but the rogue Weres. In a place like Vegas, it could have gone on for a long time before anyone figured it out. It could have led to even bigger problems.

"Think about it, Mystic. If any pack could settle here, it'd be Hawk's pack, your pack. The Renaldis have strong ties to the Weres. You've got strong ties to the vampires plus you *are* Angelini.

"Christian has ties to human law enforcement. And Roman...Roman is the Ace in the Hole. He's the trump card—vampire and shapeshifter legend. If we settled here, our pack could own bars or casinos or specialty clubs catering to supernaturals, anything we wanted and we could also work with the vampires to make sure things didn't get out of hand."

His enthusiasm was contagious. The picture he painted was so real Mystic could imagine herself stepping into it. "Did you talk to Hawk about this?"

Gabe grinned. "No. It didn't cross my mind, at least not my conscious mind, until you pointed out you could do a better job at running a club."

"I'll talk to him then. I'll talk to all of them. We haven't exactly had time to discuss the future."

Gabe's teeth flashed white again as he snickered. "You've been too busy fucking."

"*And* hunting," Mystic said, trying to sound offended but failing.

"Yeah, but that's just to stretch your legs so you can get back to spread—"

She slapped his thigh. "Finish that sentence and I will personally turn you into furry slippers and a matching robe."

Gabe laughed, then they both settled in to watch. With a thought Mystic checked in with her mates. They were relaxed, relatively speaking, but only because she was within reach and the bond allowed for immediate reassurance.

An hour passed. Then a second.

Inside the club the action was heating up. Mystic shared Christian and Roman's observations with Gabe as a way of passing the time. Occasionally a vampire and Were slipped through the back or side exit for a furtive bite or a quick fuck.

She and Gabe amused themselves by rating the performance as if they were judges at a carnal Olympic event. But overall, watching and waiting was still boring.

A lone female stepped through the back door. *Vampire*, Mystic thought, *not a fledgling, but young, and from an ancient, important line.* She could almost hear a family name but she knew the knowledge wasn't coming from Roman, it was coming from inside herself.

Mystic's eyebrows drew together. She concentrated on the female vampire, expected to see a Were emerge from the nightclub. Instead the vampire pulled a cell phone from her pocket and put it to her ear.

While the vampire talked, Mystic reached for the whispered name buried in her thoughts, tried to make sense of it. It evaded her, tested her, forced her to leave behind the limitations she'd always accepted about herself.

Finally she found the word she sought. *Licata*. It rang through her with such sureness a laugh of joy escaped. It had to be a sign she was being readied to bear the mark of a hunter, or maybe it was just something she'd gained from Roman's blood. She found she didn't care. It was a useful ability to have, one that would serve her well if Las Vegas became home.

Mystic turned to Gabe and said, "The vampire talking on the phone belongs to Sabatino Licata's line. And before you ask, no, I don't have a blood-tie to her."

Surprise lifted Gabe's eyebrows. "Cool," he said, then cursed as a dark cargo van pulled into the back lot and parked in a way that blocked their view of the side door.

"Could be here to meet the vampire," Mystic said, watching as the female closed her phone and put it back in her pocket.

The panel door of the van opened. A man stepped out. Were. There was a fleeting tension in the vampire, but then she smiled, fangs elongated.

There was a brief conversation, hardly more than an exchange of names. The Were waved his hand toward the van. The vampire shook her head.

Gabe grunted as the Were shrugged then unzipped his jacket and began unbuttoning his shirt. "Looks like a hookup instead of a pick-up."

"This performance might score a five," Mystic said, resuming their earlier game.

"Not even. Wham bam, thank-you ma'am for the bite. This guy just wants to be food. And look at her. She can barely stand to touch him. No way is she going to do the nasty."

Mystic snickered. Gabe had a point. The vampire was arched away from the Were. Her hands in his hair, positioning him for her strike, were the only places their bodies touched.

"Were blood must pack an awesome punch," she said. "It looks like she's fighting herself but the temptation to sink her fangs into him is winning over her revulsion."

"Maybe that's why she came outside. Couldn't stand being around so many Weres inside."

Mystic frowned. The longer she watched the scene play out the more it bothered her. She didn't know why but... "Maybe one of us should—" Hawk's voice cut her off. *The weak female and a male have arrived. They're on foot. They're just about to go inside the club.*

Mystic turned to Gabe. He gave a small nod, indicating he'd gotten the same message from Gabby. Through the link Mystic, Roman, Christian and Hawk communicated, tried to determine the best strategy. But before they'd settled on one, Mystic turned her attention to the female vampire and Were.

Shock made her gasp. Awareness and sudden understanding struck as a knife blade gleamed, flashed in the dull light before it plunged into the vampire's heart. "Rogue!"

Chapter Twenty-Three

❧

Her hand was on the Jeep's door handle instantly. Beside her Gabe mirrored her actions as the Were swung the vampire into his arms and hurried toward the black van with its open door.

Mystic's heart pounded in her ears along with the shouts of her mates for her to stop, to wait. She couldn't afford to. From inside the Jeep she hadn't heard the van's engine, but now she knew it'd been left running for a quick get-away.

The Were looked around as if suddenly aware he wasn't alone. He hesitated and the hesitation cost him. It allowed Gabe to get close enough so it'd be a race to the van.

There was panic, fear, the look of a cornered wolf in the rogue's eyes. Gabe had his knife out. Mystic cursed herself for not being armed.

Cunning slid into the Were's eyes. But there was no time to understand what it warned of before he pulled the knife from the vampire's heart and shoved her toward Gabe.

The female's fingernails turned into deadly talons. She slashed wildly, furiously, her focus on Gabe and the knife he held. Blood instantly stained the front of Gabe's shirt. The vampire's eyes flashed red. Her mouth widened to reveal her fangs.

The black van peeled away as Gabe stumbled. The vampire lunged at him but not before Mystic jumped on the her back and grabbed at the female's wrists—screamed when fangs slid into her forearm, ripping and opening a vein—not to feed but to kill.

Whether it was sudden awareness of Angelini magic and vampire blood or Roman's slamming through the back door and commanding, "Stop!" the female ceased fighting and immediately went to her knees, her head bowed.

Roman was there in an instant, peeling Mystic off, sealing the wound in her arm, his emotions bombarding her with the same intensity as Christian's. It took her an instant to realize Hawk's feelings weren't swamping her because he was busy stuffing a male Were's body into the trunk of his car as Gabby stood guard, blocking a clear view of what Hawk was doing.

With a thought Mystic saw what had happened while she and Gabe battled in back. The rogue male and female inside the bar had probably witnessed Roman and Christian's rush toward the exit and guessed their pack mate was in trouble. They'd fled and when Hawk and Gabby tried to intercept them, the male rogue pulled a gun but Hawk was quicker, the silver in his bullets more deadly. Now the weak rogue female wept and clung to Hawk, rubbed herself against him in a way that said, *I'm yours now.*

Mystic's lips pulled back in a snarl. For a split second she felt pure wolf, ready to stalk around the building and rip the other female to shreds. But then instinct gave way and the emotions crowding the link subsided as Hawk's activities and the female Were's presence took on significance.

She started to pull away from Roman's arms only to have them tighten on her. It brought her focus back to the mates who were touching her, to the vampire who was kneeling, shaking with uncharacteristic fear, to Gabe who was bleeding.

Fear rushed in. Mystic gasped and Roman's arms tightened again, this time in a hug before he released her and went to Gabe.

Gabe pulled his shirt up, winced in pain as his flesh gaped. "A few minutes of privacy and I'll be good as new," he said.

Roman bent over. From where Mystic and Christian were standing she couldn't see his tongue slide across Gabe's skin but she knew he was electing to heal the wound so Gabe wouldn't be forced to waste energy by shifting forms in order to do it.

Christian's arms closed around her, pulled her back to his front. She relaxed against him, trusted Roman to take care of Gabe while she took care of Christian.

She could feel Christian's need to hold her, to assure himself she was okay. His emotions were back under control, but his wolf was agitated.

I'm okay, she said. *Gabe and I couldn't let the rogue leave with the vampire.*

I know. His thoughts flashed to Hawk and the Were female. *It's almost over now. We'll question her. We'll hunt, but only after you've gone to the firing range and learned how to handle a gun. This is the second time things have gone bad. If we lose you —*

Fear and pain choked his words off. She covered his arms and hands with hers, wove her fingers through his.

I'm willing to learn, more than willing. I hate feeling incompetent, inadequate, unable to do what I'm supposed to be able to do because I've had no training. Even if we weren't hunting the Weres, I'd still like to know I can take care of myself. I want a long, happy life with you and Hawk and Roman, but I want to know I'm not helpless without you.

She felt the effort he was making to accept, to understand. He buried his face in her neck, rubbed his lips against her skin. A shudder went through him and it was like a damn opening, allowing the built up pressure behind it to flow away. *I'll start teaching you what you need to know as soon as we get home.*

Roman straightened away from Gabe. His face was a mask carved in stone, but even from a distance Mystic saw the deadly, blue flames of an angry vampire in his eyes.

She stepped out of Christian's arms and over to the kneeling vampire. Though she felt the protest in both her mates, she still put her hand on the female's shoulder. "We aren't going to hurt you."

The vampire looked up and at such close range, Mystic could only think *Stunning*.

Roman closed the distance between them and the vampire trembled violently.

I guess I know what my threat potential is, Mystic said. *So much for being a dreaded Angelini vampire hunter. She didn't flinch when I touched her but she may stake herself in your presence.*

Some of the tension flowed out of Roman, Mystic pushed to eliminate the rest of it. *You know what happened. She's not at fault here.*

Mystic's thoughts flicked to Hawk who was questioning the rogue Were. *We have other things to do besides further terrorize a young vampire from the Licata line.*

The cold flame in Roman's eyes dimmed to only a hint of death. His eyebrows lifted as he offered his hand to the female vampire and helped her to her feet. "What's your name?"

"Anissa Licata."

"You are free to go without fear of retribution for the injuries you caused. But the debt you owe for your life is not forgiven."

She whispered, "Thank you," before quickly disappearing into the club.

Christian cocked his head. There was a newfound respect in his eyes as he looked at Roman. "I've never seen a vampire tremble with fear or act timid."

Roman shrugged. "Not all humans should be turned. Sabatino Licata is old-fashioned when it comes to family. He turns very few who aren't related to him, but ultimately every child born of his mortal line becomes vampire, or dies in the process."

Christian's face hardened. "He makes them vampires whether they want it or not?"

"There are few choices to one born Licata." Roman glanced at Gabe, then Mystic. "Just as there are, in many ways, fewer choices for those born Were and Angelini. Now I would suggest we rejoin Hawk and Gabby so we can finish this hunt. And given what Hawk has in his trunk, it would be best if we left the immediate area in case the police decide to drop in for a raid."

* * * * *

Mystic climbed out of Roman's sports car and went around to where the others were waiting. They'd parked in a darkened, industrial area several miles away from Wolfsbane.

It make her think of a movie scene, a clandestine meeting of mob characters gathered for a hit. And if Anissa Licata had been timid on her knees, a near-perfect character in a dark plot, the Were female named Chelsea was an even better victim though a watching audience would wonder how someone who'd been beat down and left helpless by a lifetime of abuse could warrant a one-way trip to a desolate location.

As Chelsea cowered and shook, Mystic felt pity for her. She found it too easy to remember what she'd seen in Bangers, to re-experience the guilt she'd felt at doing nothing when Chelsea was led to the private booth and forced to service men for money. But even those thoughts and feelings didn't reduce the urge to rip the female to shreds every time she reached for Hawk and clung to him.

"Please," Chelsea babbled. "I'll do anything, just don't let them find me."

Hawk's wolf was repulsed by the Were female. Though his senses were limited by his form, she smelled unnatural to him. That combined with her cowering weakness made the beast want to attack. It didn't help that Mystic's unacknowledged wolf also wanted to lunge and savage.

He pulled Chelsea's hands off his arm and chest yet again. A low growl sounded as he did it. This time his lips pulled back in warning, the wolf saying, *Enough.*

"What have you learned?" Christian asked.

"Four rogues remain. Three males and the alpha female. According to Chelsea, the Were captured by Egan's fledgling vampires is also still alive and being held by the sorcerer." Hawk glanced at Roman. "We need Brann."

"You've got a location?" Roman asked.

"Yes." Hawk allowed the information to flow through the link held open by Mystic.

"They'll be gone by the time we can get there," Christian said. "The rogue who got away when Mystic and Gabe interrupted his hunt will warn the sorcerer and the others."

Chelsea slunk over to Christian. "No, they won't," she said, grabbing his hand and pressing her breasts against his arm in a bid to gain him as a protector.

Despite the seriousness of the situation, amusement rippled through Hawk when Christian jerked away like a pup evading a snake's strike. Anticipation followed with the distinctive growl of Mystic's wolf.

Its presence was growing stronger inside her, becoming more fully integrated. Slowly, without conscious awareness it was becoming an ingrained part of Mystic. Each time she accepted its voice, its thoughts, its instincts without adding a disclaimer, without laughingly labeling it as a *wolfie* manifestation she'd picked up from her mates, the wolf grew more real.

He'd be able to call it soon. He felt as though he could almost call it now, especially with Christian there, backing him up, adding his strength of conviction, both of them pulling on the ties binding them to Mystic.

She'd accept. She'd believe. Ultimately she'd *be* wolf, gloriously furred and running with them under the moon.

Hawk forced his attention back to the matter at hand. He hated the idea of parting with Mystic, of leaving her unprotected by one her mates, but the thought of taking her to the sorcerer's house was unacceptable. To Christian he said, "The captured Were is in wolf form, perhaps trapped in his fur from remaining in it too long. Chelsea is the last of the Weres created by being thrown into the cage and mauled. She's never seen the wolf in human form. We're both strong enough alphas we may be able to force a change. If not, then at least we might be able to calm and control him long enough to get him to safety."

"And Mystic?" Christian asked.

"She and Gabby and Gabe can take Chelsea to Fangs for safekeeping. They can take my car and have Gian arrange for the disposal of the body. I'm not crazy about driving around with it in the trunk."

Hawk's eyes bored into Christian's in a wordless exchange transmitted along a masculine bond, one demanding they keep Mystic away from whatever was waiting at the sorcerer's house. They felt her wolf bristle, saw her stiffen in protest. But before Mystic could object Roman reached over and stroked her cheek, as if he too could feel her beast and was petting it, soothing it.

"The best hunters are those who use their resources wisely. Brann and I are well suited to dealing with the sorcerer's magic, just as Hawk and Christian have the greatest chance of helping the captive wolf regain his humanity. But the task of securing Chelsea is no less important. The remaining rogues haven't yet been run to ground."

Relief settled over Hawk when Mystic nodded and said, "Okay. Let's go."

"Wait," Roman said. Despite what he'd told Mystic, he wasn't willing to let her leave with the rogue until he assured himself this wasn't a trap.

He took a step toward Chelsea. The ancient, mage's magic flared to life, corrupted and twisted in the Were.

She cowered away from him, tried to cling to Christian and when he wouldn't let her, sidled over to Gabe. Gabe grabbed her forearms and held her facing Roman.

Chelsea reeked of fear. Her eyes were wild, her heart thundered. Beast and vampire alike responded. She acted like prey, struggled in Gabe's grasp, driven by instinct rather than thought, her mind chaotic.

"Enough," Roman said, compulsion thick in his voice. His will, his power, paralyzed her.

Unnaturally altered. Diseased. The impression was so strong it swamped him, made lion and eagle stir with uneasiness. She was Were and yet not pure Were, not in the same way as Gabe or Gabby or Mystic's wolves.

"Has the sorcerer tried to create others using those mauled by the wolf?"

Her breath shortened. Images of Chelsea and her pack mates savaging those they were ordered to filled her thoughts as a forced "Yes" passed her lips.

For the benefit of the others, Roman asked, "Did any survive or become Were?" though he already knew the answer.

"No."

Low growls greeted her answer. Roman pressed on, felt in her the same taint he'd felt in both the vampire fledglings. Mage magic bound to creatures whose blood it was never meant to be found in.

"Will your pack mates warn the sorcerer?" Roman asked.

"No. All of us want to escape him."

Roman concentrated on Chelsea. "You will go peacefully to Fangs," he said, and felt no resistance in her, no desire other than to obey and to escape her pack mates.

The taint on her still bothered him, the hint of twisted magic. But as Roman stepped back he remembered the male fledgling recounting how the sorcerer had cut the heart from Dusan Juric's son and eaten it. Perhaps it was the subtle hint of vampire that left him uneasy.

Roman turned away. "Brann is waiting for us. Let's finish this hunt. Then perhaps we can show Mystic more of Las Vegas than its underbelly."

Hawk halted Mystic before she climbed into the car. He pressed the hilt of a knife into her hand, closed his fingers around hers, holding them to the smooth dark finish.

Roman's heart jerked at the sight of it in her hand, a vampire reaction to an Angelini holding a weapon capable of rendering true, final death.

"Don't put it down until you get into Fangs," Hawk said. "Promise me."

Moonlight glinted off the deadly, blade. "I promise."

* * * * *

Christian studied Egan Walsh's dilapidated house from the safety of a small strand of trees allowing them to watch both the front and back doors. "Must not have capitalized on having vampires as pets when he had the chance," he said, risking the comment despite Roman and Brann's presence nearby.

Hawk's teeth flashed white in the darkness. His gaze flicked to where Brann and Roman stood just beyond the wards guarding the sorcerer's house, one at the front, one at the back, the blood-link between the vampires allowing them to communicate.

"Either that or Walsh has watched too many horror flicks and thinks the setting is appropriate for an evil genius. With the emphasis on *evil*."

"You've got that right," Christian said, then tensed as Brann and Roman started walking, the wards apparently down. "Anything?"

The beads woven into Hawks beads clacked softly as he shook his head. "Probably a few more wards to get through before it'll be possible to sense whether anyone's inside."

Brann and Roman halted again, their movements synchronized despite not being able to see one another. This time they chanted, their voices soft, the words unrecognizable to Christian though goose bumps crawled over his naked flesh.

Next to him Hawk tensed, but neither of them spoke until the chant ended and the vampires stepped forward. "Old magic," Hawk murmured.

Brann gained the front porch. Roman gained the back. Gestures accompanied the chanting this time.

Christian's heart rate increased as seconds passed. Adrenaline surged when the ward fell and Brann signaled them. He and Hawk left the strand of trees, loped forward, him toward the back, Hawk toward the front, both of them naked so they could shift quickly, human so they could step over the thresholds and invite the vampires into the sorcerer's house.

Chapter Twenty-Four

ઐ

Gabe tried not to think about the body he was transporting. He wondered if he'd better get used to hauling corpses, if it'd come with the pack territory.

At least Mystic was with him. She'd be useful if they got pulled over by a cop. One look in her eyes and they'd be on their way, the reason for their stop fogged, if the cop remembered stopping them at all.

Damn! Despite the fact he'd yet to step foot in a casino, Sin City was turning out to be a hell of a lot of fun—a life-changing experience no less, and not just for him.

Mystic was different. More assured and self-confident, more... He wanted to say Angelini, but it wasn't only that. She seemed more...*wolf*. He could have sworn he'd seen pure wolf in her eyes when Chelsea was hanging on Christian, then making a play for Hawk.

Gabe shook his head. Probably he was imagining the wolf, buying into the fantasy atmosphere of Vegas, where everything seemed possible and anything could be bought. Or maybe Christian and Hawk were rubbing off on her, making her more wolflike.

It didn't matter. He loved Mystic like a sister, always had. It made him happy to see her coming into her own, no longer plagued by the insecurities and old hurts heaped on her by her grandparents and aunts. And it amused the hell out of him to imagine their expression when they learned she'd not only mated with two Weres but with Roman.

If Mystic became a kick-ass hunter aligned with the Coronado Angelini instead of the Renaldis... He was going to enjoy seeing her wolf relatives and judgmental grandmother and aunts whining and groveling. They'd have better luck going through their Zevanti allies if they wanted something from Mystic, an advantage he intended to point out when he and Gabby had to face the pack elders to explain why they shouldn't be punished for sneaking away with Mystic in the first place.

Gabe's amusement gave way to a laugh when Fangs came into sight and he saw the humans. He'd known what to expect, thanks to Gabby, but seeing it— Amazing. The vampires were amazing. Even if half the fun of dinner for a wolf was in the chase, he could still appreciate what he saw. "Nothing like room service, served à la carte," he said.

"Wait'll you get closer and see the fangs some of them have," Gabby said. In the rearview mirror he saw her glance at Mystic before she added, "Though maybe after Mystic tells us what it's like with Roman, we'll play pretend and let one of the humans bite us."

Gabe snorted. "No way."

He studied the parking lot and decided it would be better to leave Hawk's car at the curb, even if it meant they had to walk a block. The humans were spread out anywhere there was open space, standing around in groups or sitting. They had blankets and beach chairs. One of them was blowing up an oversized inflatable ball like he was at a concert while his companion sucked on a bong. Amazing.

Only vampires could get away with a set up like this. Gabe doubted Skye's cop mate and Gian's co-mate, Rico, had asked the police department not swing by and raid the establishment, which meant there were probably vampires positioned around the place, watching the sheep and keeping an eye out for cops.

Music blared from car radios, knocking out any sound from the club and filling the street with noise. Gabe frowned as he took in their surroundings. Industrial buildings, warehouses mainly. Not exactly Las Vegas glitz. Not a hell of a lot better than Wolfsbane or Bangers.

He understood the reason. It was a lot easier to contain a problem if it was isolated. There'd be big trouble if drunk shifters changed into fur coats and got into a brawl that spilled out on the Strip, or vampires went on a drinking binge and left a trail of drained corpses.

Still, if they formed a pack here in Vegas, he hoped Mystic would want something more upscale. Given Falcone, Yorick and Estelle for parents, he couldn't imagine her being happy in an isolated dive, not when she'd been in more classy clubs than a four-star entertainer.

"Mission accomplished," Gabe said cutting the car's engine. "We have officially arrived at Fangs. Now for the handoff."

He climbed out of the car but hung tight, waiting to flank Mystic and Gabby as they escorted Chelsea. As happy as he was not to be chauffeuring a corpse any longer, he'd be even more thrilled when the rogue female was passed off to Gian or one of the other vampires for safekeeping.

Chelsea smelled bad to him and it wasn't just the scent of someone who'd been used for sex by a lot of different men in a lot of different places. It was deeper, more primal, a revulsion springing from the wolf more than the man.

Gabby slid from the car, followed by Chelsea. Mystic came last, all three of them using the driver-side back door.

Mystic hesitated, her hand on the door, ready to close it. She glanced down at the knife in her other hand then at the crowd of humans in the parking lot of Gian's club.

They were here. They were safe. In a few minutes they'd be inside Fangs. Despite the black leather and studs, the filed teeth and body piercings, she doubted the humans were used to seeing people enter the club carrying knives. Still, she was reluctant to leave the knife in the car. She'd promised Hawk, and beyond that, she'd been vulnerable twice now, once at Bangers and once at Wolfsbane.

She shivered as she looked down at the knife and thought about Anissa Licata. If she'd had it at Wolfsbane, could she really have driven it into the vampire's back in order to stop the attack on Gabe?

Mystic's stomach lurched as she imagined it, as she felt the phantom slide of a blade through skin and muscle. She took a deep breath, pressed her insecurities into a cage and resolutely closed the car door.

When she looked up she caught Gabe watching her and saw the approval in his eyes. "Ready?" he asked.

"Ready."

Mystic put her free hand on Chelsea's arm. On the other side of the rogue, Gabby did the same.

The attention of the humans settled on them even though they were a block away. It prickled against Mystic's skin like a warning.

She studied the parking lot, then the darkened streets. Without conscious thought her senses flared outward, felt the vampires hidden in the night, standing guard over the club.

There were humans with some of them. Dinner or a snack perhaps. But they weren't the source of her uneasiness. Their hearts beat with the calmed rhythm of willing prey.

Mystic rubbed her knuckles against her pants. Her palms were sweaty around the hilt of the knife. *Almost there*, she told herself, measuring the distance to Fangs.

A second bouncer stepped outside. Gorgeous, human still though there was a vampire link. *Licata.*

Mystic blinked in surprise. She'd definitely gained from taking Roman's blood, and with it, Syndelle's.

Gabby's small sigh escaped on the other side of Chelsea. Unbidden one of Roman's memories slid into Mystic's mind, him meeting Gabby for the first time, teasing her over the man who'd just emerged from the club, Altaer, the scion of Sabatino Licata.

"I'd jump him, too," Mystic said, "if I didn't have mates of course."

Gabby snickered. "Maybe I'll bite him instead of waiting around for him to be turned and grow fangs."

Mystic laughed. She opened her mouth to say something but the words fled when Altaer tensed and started running, his attention on something behind them.

A flash of brown at the corner of her eye. A black van coming into sight, the cargo door open. They were quick impressions before a wolf was on Gabe, taking him to the ground, its teeth buried in his forearm, ripping, shaking.

Mystic didn't think. She lunged forward and drove the knife into the beast, hard and deep.

The wolf screamed in pain and fury, released Gabe's arm and turned to savage Mystic. She wrenched the knife free but before she could strike again, Chelsea screamed, "No," and hurtled herself on Mystic, biting and clawing like a feral creature.

Magic pulsed around them, Gabe shifting form, attacking the wolf who'd suddenly appeared.

Gabby joined Mystic in trying to subdue the rogue female. There was no time for thought, only action and reaction—instinct—prey and predator changing roles between one heartbeat and the next.

Then the van was next to them. A Were in human form jumped out, swinging a heavy chain, driving Gabe away from the wolf beneath him, connecting with Mystic's head and sending her tumbling, dazed, the knife slipping from her hand as she slammed against the van.

Blood. It poured over her, blinded her, added to her confusion though she fought against the hands pulling her into the van. "Vampire whore," a female voice said, "lover boy shouldn't have wasted his blood healing you after I gutted you the first time." And then there was a sweet, sick smell, followed by nothingness.

Gabby stared at the empty road, the pain and dread so intense they almost numbed her. She was coated in blood — hers, Mystic's, Gabe's. The rogues'.

A hand touched her shoulder, drawing her attention away from nothingness. "If any one of us is to blame, we're all to blame," Altaer said.

She blinked, saw the harsh lines etched on his face, the anger at himself for not getting to them soon enough to prevent Mystic being taken. "It happened so fast," Gabrielle said.

"Tragedy often does, but in this case, there's reason to believe she'll be recovered." He cupped her face and she shivered, remembering how easily those same hands had killed.

Chelsea's body lay only a foot away, her neck twisted, her eyes blank. The male Were who'd attacked lay near her, his throat ripped open. By Gabe maybe, or one of the vampires, she'd been too busy trying to prevent Chelsea from escaping.

The vampires were out in force now, Gian with them, moving among the humans, erasing their memories, stripping away their awareness of what had happened. The attack. Gabe's changing form. The corpses waiting, needing to be disposed of along with the one in Hawk's trunk.

Gabby's attention went back to the empty street. She reached for Mystic along the bond they'd formed as children, not hoping for a location, just for reassurance Mystic was still alive.

* * * * *

Even in wolf form and with a mental wall separating him from Mystic so he wouldn't be distracted in the sorcerer's house, Christian knew the instant something happened to her. The link became a dark abyss offering no reassurance other than the faint promise her heart still beat.

In front of him Roman's footsteps faltered. Along the beginnings of a wolf's pack bond with Hawk, Christian felt an answering agony, a compulsion to rush to their mate's side.

"Brann says the rogue Weres arrived at Fangs just after Mystic and the others left the car," Roman whispered. "Two of the rogues are dead but Mystic was pulled into the van. Gian's there, as is Skye. They're hunting for her. Leaving this unfinished won't undo what's already happened."

Christian's lips pulled back in a silent snarl. A part of him hoped the sorcerer eluded Brann and Roman so he could savage the man responsible for creating the rogues and the fledgling vampires before them.

He and Roman met Brann and Hawk at a staircase leading to a basement. Fury glowed in Hawk's eyes, the promise of death.

Brann's fingers danced over sigils carved into the wooden doorjamb, playing them like they were an instrument whose notes were silent.

Pressure built then fell away.

There was a werewolf below. His presence rubbed across Christian's senses like fur against fur.

Roman and Brann hurried down the staircase with Hawk and Christian at their heels. The sorcerer greeted them, chanting furiously, his voice full of gleeful confidence.

Symbols were scrawled on the floor and walls in dark, aged blood. A spell snapped into place at Christian's back, closing off the stairwell until Roman and Brann could unwind the ward.

From another room a wolf growled and yipped and howled in a confusion of noise as it threw itself against the bars of a cage. Christian fought the impulse to rush forward. He and Hawk stayed back, waited for a word or a hand signal from the vampires indicating what action they were to take.

This wasn't their fight though they could feel the press and swirl of ancient magic all around them. Slowly the sorcerer retreated behind first one circle and then another as his spells and curses were deflected by Brann and Roman and his wards failed to stop the vampires from drawing closer.

Sweat beaded and dripped from Egan Walsh's face. His hands shook and his lips began to tremble. Fear found its way into his eyes and into his scent until finally he was trapped in the last circle, in the smallest one.

It smelled of werewolf and vampire blood, of human and animal sacrifices made to ancient deities. It smelled of Brallin's banished magic, tainted by the ambitions of a sorcerer who didn't understand the power he played with.

Christian's lips pulled back. His growl was a constant rumble.

With subtle gestures Brann motioned for Christian and Hawk to take up positions along the circle. Roman started the chanting this time, the words a smooth blending of sound. Brann joined in moments later, the two of them speaking in different languages though their words interlocked in a powerful cadence.

The urge to howl built up inside Christian until he couldn't contain it any longer. He lifted his muzzle and added his song to the spell being woven by Brann and Roman. When Hawk did the same, the sorcerer began screaming and clawing at the air as the circle he'd withdrawn to became a deadly trap.

The sigils along the rim of the circle in front of Brann flared and burned with blue fire. It spread along the rim, turning into red flame when it neared where Hawk stood. Beyond Hawk, red gave way to blue mixed with orange, then turned pure red again as it reached Christian. When the hot flames of Were magic touched the ice blue of a vampire's in front of Brann, and closed the circle, the sorcerer burned. His shrieks filled the room for long moments and lingered in Christian's mind even past the point when nothing remained of Egan Walsh but a pile of ashes.

Hawk shifted into human form and went to the door leading to where the wolf was being held. Stench greeted him as soon as he entered the room. The Were's cage was strewn with human bones and the tattered remains of clothing, the corners piled with feces and slick with urine.

Christian trotted over and changed next to him. "Christ," he said. "Maybe Brann can reanimate Walsh and we can burn him all over again. He got off easy."

"Way too easy," Hawk agreed, looking at the gaunt wolf in front of them. There was nothing remotely human in its gaze, but at the same time its submissive, pleading body language didn't match what he read in its eyes.

Even if they could force a change, Hawk wasn't sure they could trust the Were. They had no pack bond with him. They knew nothing about who he was, what type of man he'd been before being captured and driven to the point where humans became his diet.

"What do you want to do about him?" Christian asked. There was impatience in his voice, frustration and anguish because the link to Mystic remained quiet and their responsibilities prevented them from leaving to hunt for her.

Hawk glanced at Brann. "Are Gabe and Gabby still at Fangs?"

"Yes. Gian and Skye and a couple of others are on their way to where the rogues hunted the fledgling, but others remain with Gabe and Gabby."

"Have Gabe and Gabby sent here."

"Done," Brann said.

Hawk turned his attention to the trapped Were. This time he noticed the symbols at the corners of the cage, melted silver poured into etched grooves. He pointed toward the written spell anchors. "Are we going to have to let him out before we can try to force a change?"

"No," Brann said. "There's no lingering magic."

"Good." Hawk studied the Were. "He's not an alpha, but he's not an omega either. We may end up resorting to a tranquilizer gun." He looked at Christian. "I've never done this before, but I feel the mechanics—if that makes sense. I feel like I could reach in and pull the wolf out of a pack mate wearing skin, or push the wolf back in if the pack mate was wearing fur. What about you?"

Christian's focus shifted inward. He slowly nodded. "Yeah. I think I know what you're talking about."

Hawk knelt in front of the cage. The wolf's hungry eyes followed him. "Might as well hit him with both barrels at once. Treat him like a weak pack mate. We'll try to push his wolf back by changing from wolf to human in its presence. Doing it that way, both of us evoking the magic at the same time will give whatever's left of his humanity a fighting chance to surface."

"You think he'll be able to hold the shape?"

"I think he won't have the juice to go furry."

"Let's get this done," Christian said, the air around him shimmering as he became wolf.

Hawk followed suit. They didn't need a signal. The emerging pack bond allowed them to feel the buildup of magic preceding a shift in form.

They tried to force the change three times, but succeeded only in sending the Were into unconsciousness on the third one. He lay on his side, panting heavily and shivering.

"I believe some restraints laced in silver might be in order," Brann said. "Something along the lines of these." He stepped forward, dangling four cuffs, each linked to a circle by a short length of chain. "Apparently our sorcerer friend didn't completely trust in his own power when it came to dealing with a Were."

Primal rage surged through Hawk. A growl escaped and was echoed by Christian. Brann's eyebrow lifted. "Shall I?"

There was no choice and Hawk knew it. He and Christian were both spent and Mystic was still missing.

"Yes," he said. They couldn't afford to waste any more time here.

They unlocked the Were's cage and stepped inside. Hawk knelt beside the wolf and searched for a brand. When he found one, he cursed.

"You know him?" Christian asked.

"Not him. His pack. The Calypso alpha is at the Howl as a guest of the Zevantis."

"Then we send him there with Gabe and Gabby," Christian said. "Let his alpha take care of him. And at the same time we head off a potential bloodbath if he comes out of this and tells the wolves he was taken by vampires in the first place."

Roman knelt next to them. "Your young wolves need to answer to their pack for bringing Mystic to Vegas," he said as he used a piece of discarded material to fashion a muzzle so the Calypso Were wouldn't be able to bite when he regained consciousness. "This is a good opportunity for them to return in better standing than when they slipped away."

Brann closed the last cuff. "There are others in place if the rogues return to the area they hunted the fledgling. Gian and Skye can join Gabe and Gabby when they pass on their way home. Given that two of the vampire fledglings are still alive and their blood is of Dusan Juric's line, it might be best to have one of mine and his Angelini mate present when the wolf is returned to his pack."

Hawk met Christian's eyes. "It's a sound plan. Agreed?"

Christian nodded. "Agreed."

They searched but didn't find anything that might lead them to Mystic. When they were done, and the Calypso wolf was handed off to Gabe and Gabby, Brann triggered a spell that burned hot and fast, leaving nothing but unidentifiable rubble in their rearview mirrors as they drove away.

Chapter Twenty-Five

🔊

Roman paced the length of Christian's living room. He cursed himself as he'd earlier cursed Hawk when Mystic was harmed in the fight at Bangers, as he'd cursed them all when she was injured at Wolfsbane. He should have taken the time to delve more deeply in Chelsea's mind. Should have questioned the vampire taint on her and wondered if she would gain some advantage from it. That could be the only explanation as to how her pack mates had known she was being taken to Fangs.

You will go peacefully to Fangs. His own words now mocked him. The compulsion he'd placed on the rogue Were was no better than a fledgling's attempt to control. He *knew* better, knew how easily literal meanings could both trap and allow for escape.

Chelsea's fear had been real, her willingness to obey absolute. But she'd been in *his* presence as well as that of two strong alpha wolves.

Gabe would one day be strong, as would the wolf Roman sensed in Mystic. But neither of them had the power of an alpha yet. And in the absence of a new alpha, Chelsea had sought her old alpha, or perhaps her old alphas had sought her and she hadn't been willing to hang on to the freedom she claimed to desire.

Roman felt no pity for her, no remorse that she was dead. Whether willing or not, her weakness had led to Mystic being taken.

He turned to Hawk and Christian, felt their rage, their agony, the heavy burden of self-inflicted guilt. It was a mirror to his own.

"She is still alive," Roman said, "and we will reclaim her. I think it's likely the rogues will hunt her as they did the fledgling."

"Or try to turn her," Christian said, his voice as grim as his expression.

A muscle spasmed in Roman's cheek with the thought of the Weres mauling her. Eventually she would shift form. The phantom wolf he'd gained from Syndelle's blood recognized the true wolf in Mystic. But he couldn't predict what would happen if she did, whether she'd be looked at by the rogues as a pack member or a threat.

"As soon as she regains consciousness we can use the bond to find her," Roman said, the muscles on his forearms standing out as he clenched his fists. If she were already his companion even that wouldn't be necessary. He could find her by using a vampire's ultimate ownership of any who was deeply bound by the sharing of blood. He could further protect and track her with magic woven into the companion's necklace.

The next time she was in his possession she *would* become his companion and her Were mates would welcome it. But in the meantime they could prepare themselves to hunt together, to work together without relying on the Angelini bond Mystic had forged between them. Roman said, "There is no way of knowing how this will unfold. I would suggest an exchange of blood so we can communicate regardless of location or form."

The wolf flashed in Hawk's eyes, feral and threatening, a natural response given vampires and Werewolves were once mortal enemies. The look faded quickly, yielded to acceptance, acknowledgement, a rare trust having less to do with Mystic and more to do with what Roman once was, gryphon, shapeshifter legend, vampire killer.

Hawk nodded and Roman turned his attention to Christian. There was reluctance, wariness, but it was offered by the man, not the beast.

Unbidden, images of their last interlude with Mystic came to mind. Since she rarely bothered to shield her thoughts from them, they both knew how erotic she found the sight of Brann and Rafe together. They also both knew how exquisite it felt to penetrate her at the same time.

Amusement found Roman despite the agony of Mystic's abduction. He chuckled and Christian's spine stiffened.

"I have lived in times when sex with women was done for pleasure and procreation, but what occurred between men was labeled the purest of love." His lips lifted to reveal his fangs. "Such love is not my inherent nature and not what I desire from either of you, though if Mystic wished it, I could take your ass and make you scream in ecstasy. But that's not the matter currently before us. The exchange of blood and what comes as a result of it can be enjoyable—or not. The choice is yours."

Christian's wolf growled, low and menacing. Hawk's joined it.

Roman turned his back with the confidence of an undefeatable predator, allowing them a moment to accept the inevitable. The bond needed to be closed completely. They needed to be able to communicate, both with and without Mystic holding a link open for them. Eventually it would have come to this anyway, only now the need was urgent.

Hawk was the first to reach Roman's side, though Christian was only a step behind. Without a word Hawk held his arm out, wrist up. Roman leaned over and bit.

* * * * *

Nausea greeted Mystic, a roiling she was helpless against. What little she had in her stomach escaped, spilling onto a floor that was subtly vibrating.

"She's awake," a female voice said and a kick landed in Mystic's gut with enough force to roll her onto her back.

A groan escaped before Mystic could stop it. Her shoulders burned and her hands were numb from the ropes binding her wrists together behind her back.

Her assailant's foot settled on Mystic's chest, but the darkness of the blindfold kept her from seeing a face. "You won't be as much fun to hunt as your vampire lover, at least not for me, but Eric and Reuben are dreaming about fucking you while they're wolves. They don't get to do that very often because I'm faster and usually there's nothing left to fuck by the time I'm finished. But this time, this time I'm going to run slow. You want to know why?"

Mystic's lungs burned as the weight on her chest grew heavier. She jerked as the female Were slapped her, the sound like the crack of gunfire. A second slap followed the first.

"Answer me. Do you want to know why I'm going to let Eric and Rueben have their fun?"

"Yes," Mystic croaked, fighting nausea and pain as she tried to filter what was happening in order to minimize the horror for her mates. She could feel their rage, could feel vampire magic combining with Angelini magic in an effort to guide them to her.

The foot on Mystic's chest lifted, then slammed down, making her cry out. "Because I remember you from Bangers. You got in my way and you made me look bad by living afterward." A knife blade slashed through Mystic's shirt and bra, scoured her skin without making her bleed. The tip of it stopped where the alpha bitch's blade had injured Mystic in the fight.

The knife point pressed harder. "Lover boy's not going to be able to save you this time. In fact he's going to sleep through all the fun." With a savage jerk the blindfold was ripped away, revealing sunlight streaming through the front windows of the van.

Sunrise. The awareness she'd gained from her vampire fathers told her the sun had only just come up. The stench in the van told her the two remaining males and the alpha female had been in it for some time, hiding out maybe as they repeatedly kept her knocked out.

They were still close to Vegas, or at least her mates had somehow managed to stay close. She felt their agony along the bond, their rage, their determination to get to her. Their love.

"Where are you taking me?" Mystic asked, locking onto the alpha female's eyes, hidden knowledge welling, whispering, *She's been fed blood from Dusan Juric's dead son*, in the split second before Mystic ears rang from another hard slap.

"Don't try that vampire shit on me," the alpha said, slashing furiously at Mystic's shirt and creating another blindfold from it.

Vision gave way to blindness with a savage application of cloth. A sharp kick followed, then a second.

"Stop it, Petra. She's not going to be much fun to chase if you keep that up," a male voice said with just a hint of strength.

Instinct and a lifetime dealing with wolves told Mystic the voice belonged to a beta male trying to step into the alpha position. The female growled but moved away, leaving pain and a sense of failure in Mystic.

If she bore the tattoo of an Angelini hunter then her own innate abilities along with whatever she gained from her mates would be amplified. If she'd insisted on being trained, then she would never have been taken in the first place. If she'd become Roman's companion sooner —

Mystic stopped the train wreck of her thoughts. She forced the feelings of failure away and silenced forever the criticizing voices of her Renaldi relatives. Along the bond she felt her mate's pride, their acceptance, their willingness to teach her whatever she needed to know. Now she had to do her part by staying alive long enough to learn it.

She willed herself to relax, to gather her strength, to prepare herself for what was to come. If they intended to hunt her then they'd give her a head start. She'd have no choice but to take it, to try to buy time.

Various scenarios and strategies played out in her mind. A variety of weapons presented themselves as she mentally raced through desert and woods, her thoughts expanded upon by Roman, Hawk and Christian.

They were gaining on the van, Hawk and Christian in one car, Roman in another, though at the moment both of their vehicles were in sight of one another. With a thought she knew others were heading toward the place where the rogues hunted the fledgling vampire while her mates had remained behind, guessing the Weres might choose to hunt closer to home since they didn't anticipate a lengthy chase.

The mountains near Las Vegas provided the perfect place. They were part of a national park spanning over six million acres. With so much land there was little risk of being discovered if the hunt began away from where the tourists camped. And anyone stumbling on the rogues or their prey would become a bonus kill.

Mystic skimmed Roman's mind to find out what happened at the sorcerer's house—and knew the hunt wouldn't be over, even when Petra and the two rogue males were dead or captured.

There will be others to finish this, Roman said. *The meeting of the Angelini will conclude soon and the Coronados will come to Vegas for a reunion with Skye and Syndelle. Sabin's sons are always up for a good hunt. I expect the same destiny that led you here at this particular time will play out in their lives as well. And if we are needed, we will offer our aid.*

The words rang with certainty and their truth flowed through her, bound in the Angelini magic responsible for her birth.

We're slowing, she said as the sound of tires on asphalt gave way to the crunch of gravel. She realized the air was cooler, scented with desert and forest.

The van stopped a while later. The back doors opened.

There was the sound of sliding metal. She noticed the smell of gasoline then and thought maybe it had been there all along.

One of the male Weres climbed in through the back door. He grunted. She smelled a hint of rubber. "Got it?" the one she'd identified as the beta male asked.

"Got it."

There was rolling, like wheels going down a ramp. An ATV, Mystic guessed a minute before its engine roared to life. Then more maneuvering, something else was removed from the van.

She was lifted roughly, an arm around her neck and another around her thighs. A couple of steps, a jolt, then she was dropped onto hard wood. A cart.

"Curl up unless you want to start with a broken leg," the male who'd been in the van said.

Mystic obeyed and a tarp was dropped over her. The same male said, "No fucking her, Eric. Just take her to the usual spot and let her go. Straight there, straight back. You understand?"

"I understand." The answer was sullen, petulant.

"Hurry up," Petra said. "We've already wasted enough time on this vampire slut. Any more of it and I'm going to forget about running slow so you can have your big thrill."

We need to ditch the cars and go overland, Hawk said as they passed another private road marked by a "No Trespassing" sign and barred by a chain.

They had a detailed map, compliments of Gian, and Christian's GPS unit. Both helped but without a tracking device on Mystic they couldn't readily determine which road would take them to her or lead them to the van.

I agree, Roman said. *I'm approaching a turnout. There's room enough for two cars here. I'll pull over and wait for you.*

A few minutes later they were standing next to the parked cars, hastily stripping as each of them mentally followed Mystic's progress.

Adrenaline poured into Hawk's system as the cart she was on stopped and she was dragged roughly to the ground. There was the rip of tape, a quick wrap around one ankle. Then her wrists were cut free.

Pain screamed through her arms and hands when blood rushed in. Renewed fury filled Hawk, merged with that of Christian and Roman.

"See you in a little while," the rogue Were said. "I'm looking forward to fucking you. It's going to be real good, the last thing you remember before Petra ends the fun."

With clumsy fingers Mystic tore the blindfold off. She captured the Were's face in her thoughts before he turned and got on the still-running ATV.

Pride roared through Hawk when she leaned over and bit into the duct tape tethering her to a tree. She was free and standing by the time the rogue disappeared from sight.

Magic shimmered. Where Roman had been, a golden eagle now launched itself into the air. Hawk shifted form as Christian closed his door then hid his keys on the undercarriage of the car. A heartbeat later he was standing next to Hawk as a wolf.

Ready? Roman asked and Hawk blinked against disorientation as his brain struggled to sort the images and input he was getting not only from Christian, but from Mystic and Roman.

Ready, he answered, his agreement blending smoothly with Christian's.

Mystic headed in the direction of her mates. In some places the undergrowth was thick. In others it gave way to dirt and rocks and scrub. She ran as fast as she could, found a natural rhythm and grace to it—and a moment of amusement when she realized all the nights spent dancing in clubs with her parents had left her more fit and agile than she would have imagined.

But then she heard the wolves howling and yipping behind her and knew terror again. They were closer than they should have been, and her mates still too far away.

Mystic stumbled in her panic, went down on her hands and knees. The magic welled up inside her, pressed against her skin like a beast trapped and trying to escape. Her breath froze in her chest, nearly caused her to black out and for an instant she was more afraid of her own body than the wolves behind her.

With a show of will she managed to get to her feet. The magic slid away and she started running again. Harder this time, until a stitch in her side forced her to slow her pace.

There was more open space now. She could cover it quickly, but the wolves would be quicker.

She wondered if she'd stand a better chance of surviving if she climbed a tree and waited. Roman was the closest. When she dared to view the world through the eagle's aerial view she saw how quickly he covered the ground. But she wasn't in Roman's sight yet.

Keep moving, he said and she obeyed, clutching her side, stumbling more often but continuing to move forward.

The sudden silence behind her added to her fear rather than reduce it. She entered another stand of pines and junipers. When she emerged she was on a fire road—but she was no longer alone.

Somehow the wolves had anticipated her, or at least one of them had. Petra. Mystic didn't know how she knew the brown-gray animal in front of her was the alpha female, but she did.

Lips pulled back in a snarl that seemed more like a savage smile. Yips of excitement filled the air again behind Mystic, the two males closing in quickly.

The magic rose in Mystic again with a force that nearly dropped her to her knees. This time it came with a howl, with the bristling sensation of a wolf determined to be free.

She wanted to lift her face and howl in frustration, in despair at not having the form her fear reached for in this moment of life and death. Instead she forced herself to look around for a weapon, a tree to climb, a way to escape or remain safe long enough for her mates to get to her.

The magic struck again, leaving her breathless. It burned through her in a spasm of pain.

Through sudden tears she saw the alpha female approaching. Along the bond Mystic's mates spoke with a single, fierce voice, the force of their will converging and joining with a surge of magic that altered her reality forever.

Change! they commanded as invisible hands seemed to rip her wolf from the dark place of denial where it had been caged for so many years. Muscle stretched and bones popped, body mass reshaped and reformed, the sensation more shocking than painful.

When it was over Mystic stood shaking, disoriented until she went down under Petra's attack. Instinct kicked in. Her world narrowed to the moment, to the fight for survival.

The wolf's form was too new, the transformation too unexpected and the fight too chaotic to allow Mystic to maintain a link with her mates. It dropped away, leaving Mystic completely focused on the alpha female.

Teeth snapped as growls filled the air. The will to live, to kill infused Mystic with energy and a ferociousness foreign to her nature. She fought with a savagery she'd never experienced, ripped at fur and muscle and reveled in the scent and taste of blood.

Mystic howled in a song of victory as Petra took a last shuddering breath then fell still, blood and internal organs spilled across the dirt. She howled in celebration of the wolf's form, but the sound of it was cut short by the presence of the rogue Weres.

Their scent reached her first, rank, unnatural, the magic at their core corrupted at their creation by a sorcerer's meddling. They were a perversion, an abomination to be repudiated, eliminated.

One of the males licked his lips as a penis extended and emerged from its sheath. He edged toward her as the second male circled.

Mystic crouched, bared her teeth, decided to fight rather than try to flee. She thought the circling wolf might be the beta and the more dangerous of the two so she turned slightly, trying to keep them both in sight as long as possible.

Her mates were near. She sensed it just as she sensed her bond with them. But she couldn't afford the distraction reaching for them would require.

The beta moved into her blind spot, forced her to choose, to commit. She shifted position and the wolf behind her darted in, ripped at her flanks before retreating.

Instinct drove her around and the beta attacked. His teeth sank into the fur on her neck as his hips thrust in an effort to find her vulva.

The weaker wolf yipped, darted in to bite in his excitement. His back arched and his penis slid from its protective sheath as he air-humped.

A scream filled the air, an eagle's cry. Mystic looked up in time to see golden feathers and extended talons give way to a lion's tawny fur and lethal claws.

The wolf was dead within seconds. His companion minutes later after Hawk and Christian knocked him off Mystic, killing him before he could regain his feet.

You did well, Roman said, padding over to rub against Mystic's wolf form. Hawk and Christian joined him, their pride and satisfaction making her heart swell and her muzzle lift.

Howls vibrated through the air along with a lion's roar. Victory was theirs and for the moment the hunt was done.

As the last note of celebration faded, magic shimmered, lion gave way to eagle. Roman launched himself into the air and said, *Run with your wolves now, Mystic. When we get back to Christian's house you'll become my companion.*

They took a moment to drag the carcasses into the woods and hide Mystic's ruined clothing until others could come and destroy all evidence of what had taken place. Then they ran, in joy this time instead of fear, two huge males and a smaller female.

Muscles slid smoothly under fur. Legs stretched and fur warmed in the sunshine. The scent of earth, of pine and juniper and scrub, of deer and fox—a thousand different things added to the exhilaration of being together, three wolves racing beneath a blue sky and an eagle's wings.

They didn't give her time to panic or worry. As soon as they got to the cars, a single word flared through the bond, this time offered as guidance rather than command.

Change. And Mystic found the way, let one type of magic yield to another, to the Angelini magic she'd known her entire life.

She was greeted by the press of naked bodies. By lips claiming hers and moving on to trail kisses along her neck and shoulders, her ears. By rigid cocks emphasizing how happy her mates were to have her back.

"I don't think I can wait to get home," she whispered, her cunt lips growing flushed and swollen with the need to have them inside her, to reconnect in physical intimacy.

They stopped at the first hotel they came to and when Mystic emerged from the bathroom after a hasty shower she found the mattresses pulled to the floor. A laugh escaped, amusement coupled with anticipation at the sight of the three men waiting for her, their flesh bared, their cocks hard. "I could definitely get used to this," she teased as she knelt at the foot of the joined mattresses then crawled toward them.

When she reached them Roman took her arm and urged her onto his knees. His pupils burned with blue fire. "Do you freely choose to become my companion?" he asked.

"Yes," she whispered.

He took off the necklace she'd seen only once before, a gryphon engraved with ancient, powerful sigils. Only now two wolves formed the clasp in a connection so smooth it looked as though they'd always been there.

Mystic's eyes teared. She knew he'd included the wolves as a symbol of how willing he was to share not only her body with Hawk and Christian, but this sacred joining between a vampire and his chosen. "How—" she started, intending to ask how he'd found a craftsman talented enough to alter a centuries-old necklace but Roman cut her off with a chuckle.

He stroked her cheek with his knuckles. "There are advantages to being *ancient*, and to being in Vegas, of course, where anything is possible, even finding a mate."

Roman leaned forward and pressed a kiss to her lips as he fastened the necklace around her neck. *Now and forever, with the taking of my blood and the acceptance of my medallion, you become mine to pleasure and protect in a covenant that will remain unbroken even in death.*

Now and forever, Mystic said, tangling her tongue with his in a sensual union that lasted for long moments and left her wet and ready.

When their mouths parted Roman leaned back and Christian's hand gripped her thigh, flipping her onto her back and making her accessible to all her mates.

She met his eyes and knew profound joy at what she saw there, what she felt along their bond. Acceptance. Loyalty. Love. A sense of belonging, of coming home. "Don't plan on leaving our bed anytime soon," Christian said before dipping his head and claiming her cunt with his mouth.

Lust streaked through her. She cried out as her back arched and her nipples tightened into aching points.

"Consider yourself warned," Hawk said, lying next to her, kissing her deeply before moving lower and capturing a nipple. *It'll be a long time and a lot of hours spent at the gun range and the gym before we let you out of our sight.*

Roman's mouth covered hers. His tongue slid against hers in the same rhythm as Christian's fucked into her slit and Hawk's rubbed against her nipple.

Mystic could feel the bond they had with each other, fed by their desire to keep her safe and held together by Roman's blood. It pleased her, deepened what she already felt for them. It humbled her to think three such dominant men could surrender parts of themselves because of her.

She hadn't wanted even a single mate, much less three. But now she couldn't imagine life without them.

You better not be able to imagine life without us, three voices said in unison, driving home their point with wicked tongues and decadent touches.

Mystic whimpered under their assault. Her fingers tangled in Christian's hair and Hawk's, holding them to her as she writhed against their mouths.

Roman's lips left hers. He positioned himself above her so she could take his nipple into her mouth as he took hers. *Finish it, Mystic. Bind your life to mine.*

A single fingernail elongated into a talon. As he'd done in the hotel tub, he opened his flesh so blood flowed over his nipple.

When he lowered his chest Mystic took what he offered. Dark, heated lust flowed into her and through the bond. Her cunt spasmed, clutched at Christian's tongue as her back arched, driving her nipples into Hawk's mouth and Roman's.

Their pleasure was her reward, their needs as important as her own. She gave to them as she took from Roman, as she accepted his blood into every cell and became his companion.

Ecstasy swamped her, lifted her to unexplored heights and took them with her. She cried out as orgasm slammed into her, felt their bodies react only to be reined in by the tight fist of masculine fingers as they gripped their cocks to keep from coming.

Roman pulled away from her, the wound on his chest closing as he rose to his knees. His eyes glittered with vampire fire and animal lust, with a man's need.

Hawk rolled to his back and urged her on top of him. She gladly covered his body with hers, welcomed his cock inside her with a moan.

His hands gripped her buttocks, spread her for Christian. Fingers coated with arousal found her back entrance, prepared her. And then Christian's penis was there, forging into her.

Mystic pushed herself up onto her elbows, her eyes meeting Roman's, commanding him to lean forward so she could take his cock as well. He groaned when she took him in her mouth, panted when she started sucking.

What should have been awkward, impossible, was made smooth by the bonds that held them together, by the lust that drove them. Though any one of them could have commanded the rhythm, it was her mouth that dictated, it was her desire they rode to completion. And afterward, as they lay panting, sated—at least for the moment—Mystic thought about her escape from the Zevanti compound. *Let the adventure begin,*

Gabe had said. But as Mystic stroked warm masculine flesh and cuddled with her mates, she whispered, "Let the adventure continue."

Also by Jory Strong

❧

Carnival Tarot 1: Sarael's Reading
Carnival Tarot 2: Kiziah's Reading
Carnival Tarot 3: Dakotah's Reading
Crime Tells 1: Lyric's Cop
Crime Tells 2: Cady's Cowboy
Crime Tells 3: Calista's Men
Crime Tells 4: Cole's Gamble
Death's Courtship
Ellora's Cavemen: Dreams of the Oasis I (*anthology*)
Ellora's Cavemen: Jewels of the Nile III (*anthology*)
Ellora's Cavemen: Seasons of Seduction I (*anthology*)
Ellora's Cavemen: Seasons of Seduction IV (*anthology*)
Elven Surrender
Fallon Mates 1: Binding Krista
Fallon Mates 2: Zeraac's Miracle
Fallon Mates 3: Roping Savannah
Familiar Pleasures
Spirit Flight
Spirits Shared
Supernatural Bonds 1: Trace's Psychic
Supernatural Bonds 2: Storm's Faeries
Supernatural Bonds 3: Sophie's Dragon
Supernatural Bonds 4: Drui Claiming
The Angelini 1: Skye's Trail
The Angelini 2: Syndelle's Possession
Two Spirits

About the Author

⍩

Jory has been writing since childhood and has never outgrown being a daydreamer. When she's not hunched over her computer, lost in the muse and conjuring up new heroes and heroines, she can usually be found reading, riding her horses, or hiking with her dogs.

Jory welcomes comments from readers. You can find her website and email address on her author bio page at www.ellorascave.com.

Tell Us What You Think

We appreciate hearing reader opinions about our books. You can email us at Comments@EllorasCave.com.

Why an electronic book?

We live in the Information Age—an exciting time in the history of human civilization, in which technology rules supreme and continues to progress in leaps and bounds every minute of every day. For a multitude of reasons, more and more avid literary fans are opting to purchase e-books instead of paper books. The question from those not yet initiated into the world of electronic reading is simply: *Why?*

1. *Price.* An electronic title at Ellora's Cave Publishing and Cerridwen Press runs anywhere from 40% to 75% less than the cover price of the exact same title in paperback format. Why? Basic mathematics and cost. It is less expensive to publish an e-book (no paper and printing, no warehousing and shipping) than it is to publish a paperback, so the savings are passed along to the consumer.

2. *Space.* Running out of room in your house for your books? That is one worry you will never have with electronic books. For a low one-time cost, you can purchase a handheld device specifically designed for e-reading. Many e-readers have large, convenient screens for viewing. Better yet, hundreds of titles can be stored within your new library—on a single microchip. There are a variety of e-readers from different manufacturers. You can also read e-books on your PC or laptop computer. (Please note that Ellora's Cave does not endorse any specific brands.

You can check our websites at www.ellorascave.com or www.cerridwenpress.com for information we make available to new consumers.)

3. *Mobility.* Because your new e-library consists of only a microchip within a small, easily transportable e-reader, your entire cache of books can be taken with you wherever you go.

4. *Personal Viewing Preferences.* Are the words you are currently reading too small? Too large? Too... ANNOYING? Paperback books cannot be modified according to personal preferences, but e-books can.

5. *Instant Gratification.* Is it the middle of the night and all the bookstores near you are closed? Are you tired of waiting days, sometimes weeks, for bookstores to ship the novels you bought? Ellora's Cave Publishing sells instantaneous downloads twenty-four hours a day, seven days a week, every day of the year. Our webstore is never closed. Our e-book delivery system is 100% automated, meaning your order is filled as soon as you pay for it.

Those are a few of the top reasons why electronic books are replacing paperbacks for many avid readers.

As always, Ellora's Cave and Cerridwen Press welcome your questions and comments. We invite you to email us at Comments@ellorascave.com or write to us directly at Ellora's Cave Publishing Inc., 1056 Home Avenue, Akron, OH 44310-3502.

COMING TO A BOOKSTORE NEAR YOU!

ELLORA'S CAVE

Bestselling Authors Tour

UPDATES AVAILABLE AT

WWW.ELLORASCAVE.COM

Cerridwen, the Celtic Goddess of wisdom, was the muse who brought inspiration to story-tellers and those in the creative arts. Cerridwen Press encompasses the best and most innovative stories in all genres of today's fiction. Visit our site and discover the newest titles by talented authors who still get inspired - much like the ancient storytellers did, once upon a time.

Discover for yourself why readers can't get enough
of the multiple award-winning publisher
Ellora's Cave.

Whether you prefer e-books or paperbacks,
be sure to visit EC on the web at
www.ellorascave.com

for an erotic reading experience that will leave you
breathless.

2645514